Praise for Heidi McLaughlin

The Beaumont Series

"If you want to read a book that is all heart—full of characters you will instantly connect with and love from the first page to the last—then *Forever My Girl* is the book for you."

—Jenny, *Totally Booked Blog*

"*Forever My Girl* is a sweet, loving, all-around adorable read. If you, like me, have a thing for musicians and reconnections, then this read is for you."

—*Jacqueline's Reads*

"This is an utterly moving story of second chances in life, of redemption, remorse, forgiveness, of loves lost and found again, of trust regained. Through alternating points of view, we feel both Liam's and Josie's emotions, fears, and sorrow. These are well-developed characters whose love for each other survives time and distance."

—*Natasha Is a Book Junkie* on *Forever My Girl*

"*My Unexpected Forever* completely outdid my expectations and blew *Forever My Girl* out of the water. *My Unexpected Forever* is without a doubt a book that I would recommend, and Harrison is officially my new book boyfriend!"

—*Holly's Hot Reads*

The Beaumont Series: Next Generation

"Heidi McLaughlin delivers a breathtaking addition to the Beaumont series. *Holding Onto Forever* is everything you want it to be and so much more. I fell in love all over again."

—*USA Today* bestselling author K. L. Grayson

"A roller coaster of emotions. McLaughlin takes you on a journey of two hearts that are destined to be together."

—*New York Times* bestselling author Kaylee Ryan

"Heidi McLaughlin delivers yet another heartfelt, emotional, engaging read! I loved every second of *Fighting for Our Forever*! You will too!"

—*USA Today* bestselling author M. Never

The Archer Brothers

"I *loved* everything about this book. It is an emotional story that will have you begging for more. Even after I finished reading, I can't stop thinking about it. A *must* read!"

—Jamie Rae, author of *Call Sign Karma*

"McLaughlin will have you frantically turning pages and make your heart beat faster because each page has something more surprising than the one before it. You'll be dying to see what happens next!"

—*New York Times* bestselling author Jay Crownover

"I needed this book. I didn't even realize how much until I read it!"

—*USA Today* bestselling author Adriana Locke

The Boys of Summer

"Heidi McLaughlin has done it again! Sexy, sweet, and full of heart, *Third Base* is a winner!"

—Melissa Brown, author of *Wife Number Seven*

"*Third Base* hits the reading sweet spot. A must read for any baseball and romance fans."

—Carey Heywood, author of *Him*

"*Third Base* is sexy and witty and pulls you in from the first page. You'll get lost in Ethan and Daisy and never want their story to end."

—S. Moose, author of *Offbeat*

"McLaughlin knocks it out of the park with her second sports contemporary . . . This novel goes above and beyond the typical sports romance with a hot, complex hero and a gutsy, multidimensional heroine. McLaughlin keeps the pace lively throughout, and just when readers think they have the finale figured out, she throws them a few curveballs. This novel will appeal to McLaughlin's fans and will win her many more."

—*Publishers Weekly* (starred review) on *Home Run*

"Heidi McLaughlin never fails to pull me in with her storytelling, and I assure you she'll do the same to you! *Home Run* is a home run, in my book."

—*New York Times* bestselling author Jen McLaughlin

"Top Pick! Four and a half stars! McLaughlin has hit the mark with her third Boys of Summer novel. There's more than one great story line to capture the imagination."

—RT Book Reviews

After All

OTHER BOOKS BY HEIDI McLAUGHLIN

THE BEAUMONT SERIES

Forever My Girl
My Everything
My Unexpected Forever
Finding My Forever
Finding My Way
12 Days of Forever
My Kind of Forever
Forever Our Boys
The Beaumont Boxed Set—#1

THE BEAUMONT SERIES: NEXT GENERATION

Holding Onto Forever
My Unexpected Love
Chasing My Forever
Peyton & Noah
Fighting For Our Forever

THE ARCHER BROTHERS

Here with Me
Choose Me
Save Me

LOST IN YOU SERIES

Lost in You
Lost in Us

THE BOYS OF SUMMER

Third Base
Home Run
Grand Slam
Hawk

THE REALITY DUET

Blind Reality
Twisted Reality

SOCIETY X

Dark Room
Viewing Room
Play Room

THE CLUTCH SERIES

Roman

STAND-ALONE NOVELS

Stripped Bare
Blow
Sexcation

HOLIDAY NOVELS

Santa's Secret
Christmas With You
It's a Wonderful Holiday

After All

HEIDI McLAUGHLIN

This is a work of fiction. Names, characters, organizations, places, events, and incidents are either products of the author's imagination or are used fictitiously.

Published by Montlake, Seattle
www.apub.com

Amazon, the Amazon logo, and Montlake are trademarks of Amazon.com, Inc., or its affiliates.

ISBN-13: 9781542020510
ISBN-10: 1542020514

Cover design by Caroline Teagle Johnson

Printed in the United States of America

Without you, these characters wouldn't exist.

PROLOGUE

Each morning, before the sun even rose, men and women walked the wide planks of the docks, preparing their boats for the day. The sounds of the marina echoed throughout the harbor: the scuffing of heavy boots, the whooshing of ropes coiling, the bubbling of water as the engines roared to life. They stocked their boats full of bait, loaded the ice machines to keep their catches cold, and stored groceries for those who were leaving for longer than a day. Those boats would dock days later; then the men would drop off their catches, restock their supplies, and call home to check in with their loved ones. At home, families were always on edge, watching the sky for an unexpected storm until that first call came in. They would listen to how the trip was going, happy to hear from their loved ones, but once they hung up, the worrying started again until the next call.

To some, this was their life, the way they made a living. For many, they had followed the path laid out for them by the generations before, and several worked with their families. To others, it was how they spent their summer, coming from as far north as Canada and as far south as California. Rarely would someone from the East Coast come here to earn some summer money, but it happened, and their accents made them stick out like sore thumbs in this tight-knit community.

Under the midnight-blue sky, the *Austin Woods* vessel floated through the channel and by the Driftwood Inn with its crew standing starboard, waving. They did this every time they went out, without fail, and would also do it when they returned, paying homage to their boat's namesake. No one seemed to care if anyone waved back; they knew she would be in her room that faced the water or in the inn's ballroom, alone. The way she had been for the last fifteen years.

The three-story manor looked like a mansion straight out of the *Luxury Home Magazine*, with its very own moat separating Cape Harbor from its neighboring town. The A-frame structure with its wall of windows was a sight to behold. Back in the day, the locals considered the Driftwood Inn the gateway into town—still to this day many tourists yearned to stay there just to see the purple-and-pink nightly sunsets through the massive floor-to-ceiling windows, to feel the sun's rays penetrate through the glass, and to stare at the majestic views of Mount Baker. There wasn't another hotel that could provide such a magnificent perspective. Others tried, but no one could replicate the essence of the inn, which made it utterly devastating for the community when the doors closed.

Standing in the attic window of her granddaughter's ocean-blue-and-white bedroom, Carly Woods held her mug of tea, guaranteeing that something occupied her hands when the fishing boat went by. She knew the boys meant well, but the pain she hid for most of the year crept back in. As much as it saddened her to watch, to see them wave, she never missed a morning nor evening. She always made sure she knew the schedule of the *Austin Woods* so she could keep track. Even if none of her family members were out to sea, she never gave up worrying about those who were. She glanced out to the rising sun and wondered what today would bring. They were due for a storm. The East Coast was already getting hammered, and it was only a matter of time before Mother Nature turned her attention toward the West. At this age, her heart couldn't take much more.

When the boat was out of sight, she rested her hand against the glass and dipped her head slightly. She recited the fisherman's prayer aloud, words she had learned from her grandfather and had recited when she stood with her mother in this very window when the men in her family set sail. Carly had sworn she would never marry a fisherman, and she had held fast until she had seen Skip Woods in a different light. They had grown up together, always hanging out in the same crowds. One day, everything changed. Their friendship quickly turned into love and marriage, and with the birth of their son, they became a family.

The warm honey concoction in her mug coated her throat as she sipped. A cough tickled her throat, and she did everything she could to push it away. The last thing she wanted was to have a coughing fit that would buckle her legs out from under her. She sat on the edge of the bed, placed her hands on her knees, closed her eyes, and focused on her breathing. She had learned the technique from the doctor she saw in Seattle to calm the spasms in her chest. She didn't want her friend and housekeeper to feel the need to rush to her aid, when she knew how to control her breathing—at least not yet. The meditation wouldn't always work—it was nothing more than a temporary fix—but for the moment the urge to cough seemed to subside.

She glanced around the room and smiled. In the corner sat her granddaughter's old dollhouse, which they had converted into a book-case one summer. They'd sat outside for days and had sanded and painted until they'd deemed it perfect. The same with her dresser. Together, they painted it a beautiful blue and added seashells for the knobs. Carly thought the beach theme was a bit odd considering where she lived, but her granddaughter wanted it, and whatever she wanted, Carly happily gave.

Her hand brushed over the mermaid quilt; the creature on it had blonde hair and a purple tail, with multiple tones of blue surrounding her. It had been a special request from her grandchild, who at the age of five had vowed she would become a mermaid and live outside her grandmother's house so they could see each other every day. That made her very happy. It would be her greatest joy to see her son's daughter every day, whether a mermaid or not.

Down the hall, she heard her best friend, caregiver, and live-in housekeeper moving in and out of the other bedrooms, humming loudly for Carly to hear. The song was unfamiliar, but she wasn't surprised that she felt calmness come over her. It was hard to put into words the kind of relationship she had with Simone. What had started out as an employee/employer arrangement had turned into a friendship. Simone had come to Carly after she had escaped an abusive relationship. Her own parents had passed at an early age, and she often thought of Simone as a sister or a daughter. At first, Simone had started as a maid before taking over the reception counter, and she had finally moved on to managing the entire inn. When Carly had closed the doors for the last time, Simone had stayed on and become everything to her. Simone was the one who'd helped her through her grieving period. And it was her friend who'd suggested the doors open again, even if it was only for the weekends.

Carly had scoffed at the idea, but Simone had refused to relent. "It would take too much to get the inn ready," Carly had said, but Simone reminded her that there was someone out there who could do the work; all she had to do was pick up the phone.

It had been years since she had opened the doors of her once-famed inn, letting strangers stay in what she considered her home, to enjoy views she loved so much, and eat the food she happily cooked for them. Losing the last piece of her life had been too much to handle. Many thought her mourning period would cease after a few months, a year tops, but when the mayor came to visit and found the door locked, even he knew Cape Harbor had changed forever. Even he couldn't change the mind of his lifelong friend.

She hated the deafening silence that her home now harbored, but the people who visited all held memories she longed to forget. For as long as she could remember, her house had been where her son's friends had stayed. Where they'd spent time together. Every day after school, the kids would bombard her kitchen, seeking fresh-baked cookies before doing their homework. She'd never minded that her home was full of children—whatever kept them safe while their parents were at work. Once they were older, they'd come after work, on the weekends, and at every holiday . . . until the day everything changed.

She stood and went back to the window. From here, she couldn't see the wharf but could hear the activity going on at the end of the channel. Despite everything, she loved knowing people were hard at work on the docks, helping the fishermen bring in their daily catch and making sure their boats were in the best shape to handle whatever nature would throw their way.

The sun rose. She felt the rays trying to burst through the window. It would be a warm day, one that would surely draw visitors out to the water. The laughter of others would carry through to her kitchen, making her smile until memories flooded her mind again.

Soon, the tourists would be here, clogging the streets and the waterway and having a good time. Still to this day, her phone rang with people asking if she was open and accepting reservations. When Simone answered, she wanted to say yes because the rooms were vacant and the inn needed life, but Carly remained steadfast. The answer was no and would always be no.

Her tea had cooled, and all the vessels were out in the ocean earning their keep. She took her leave, looking back at her granddaughter's room one last time. Years ago, it was dark green with trophies sitting on shelves and medals hanging from pegs stuck in the wall. Posters of hot rods and movies used to decorate the walls, but she and Simone had packed and stored the pictures neatly in the attic many years ago. There were days when she thought about bringing them down and poring over the memories, but she never found the courage to climb the ladder. There was so much of her life stored away in the room above her head that she often wondered what she had left.

The day was coming when she would need to clean out the attic, to finally part with the memories, but today was not that day, and tomorrow wasn't looking too promising either. Next week, she told herself. There was always next week.

Downstairs, she emptied her mug and turned on the kettle to heat more water. Her garden needed tending. Her rosebushes were struggling, as they often did with the soil on her property. Too much sand mixed with the dirt made it hard to grow anything but seagrass. She would ask Simone to go into town and buy a few bags of soil to help the roses thrive. Working on her flower bed would keep her thoughts off the inevitable.

Simone entered the kitchen, happily singing a different melody. Her blonde hair was up in a perfectly coifed bun, not a strand out of place. There used to be days when they would go to the salon together or take trips to the spa in Anacortes, but it had been years since Carly would even entertain such a thought. The idea of someone seeing her, let alone touching her, made her feel ill. Simone had done her nails, cut and dyed her hair for as long as she could remember. Usually in the summer when her granddaughter visited so they could play beauty shop.

Carly watched as she stored the cleaning supplies, washed her hands, and took a mug from the cupboard. Together, they waited for the kettle to whistle. Every so often, Simone would glance her way and smile. She refrained from asking her what she was thinking because deep down, she knew. Carly knew that Simone was right when she suggested she should reopen the inn, and at some point, she would have to consider doing that or selling—and selling the house *wasn't* an option. At least, not while Carly was alive.

The whistle blew, and Simone fixed their cups of tea. With it, she set out the pills Carly needed to take in the morning. She would also do the same at lunch- and dinnertime. Simone picked up her mug and walked to the back door. She paused and waited for Carly to follow.

They sat outside and basked in the rising sun. A few of the smaller yachts sailed by, with the people on board waving. Simone waved back, but Carly held her mug tightly in her hands. Not because she hadn't wanted to greet them, but because her hands were shaking, and she was afraid someone might notice.

"Summer will be here soon," Simone said.

She sipped her tea and closed her eyes as the tickle she had avoided earlier was back and much stronger. She coughed and felt her lungs tighten and seize, causing her to double over and gasp for air. She tried to set her mug down on the small table next to her, but it hit the edge and went tumbling down to the ground, shattering into tiny shards of ceramic as hot liquid spread across the patio.

Simone was in front of her, rubbing her back and coaxing her through the fit. Her words were soothing, but they wouldn't help the pain she felt in her chest. "It's time to make the call, Ms. Carly."

She nodded. It was all she could do, as she feared that if she opened her mouth, an anguished cry would escape. It was time for her to admit things she wasn't ready for.

ONE

Brooklyn thought she'd feel different as soon as the welcoming sign to Cape Harbor came into view. She anticipated a barrage of emotions to hit her as she neared the town line. She expected she'd have to stop, check her breathing, and remind herself why she was back. She had lost count of how many times she had tried to talk herself out of returning, unable to bring herself to get behind the wheel and drive north from her parents' Seattle home . . . until now. She would never turn her back on her family. It was the timing that bothered her the most, and that was what made her pull over. Even under the bright afternoon sun, the floodlight still illuminated the white-and-blue sign, and Brooklyn stood there, with a hood pulled over her head to hide herself from passing cars, looking at the name of the man who had changed her life. She was back for him, for his mother, and to face the past.

Instead of heading straight to the Driftwood Inn, Brooklyn detoured and drove down Third Street. This was the only town she had ever lived in or visited that hadn't had a Main Street. It was such a random thing she picked up on when she and her parents moved here years ago. She never understood why until she learned that when the town incorporated, the people counted the streets up from the harbor, numbering instead of naming, with First Street being the closest to the water.

Curiosity filled her. For years she had not asked questions about her favorite spots, mostly to avoid the feeling of being homesick, but also so she could forget. The less she knew, the better. The less she longed to return, the easier it would be to create a new life. That was what she needed to do: start over, put the past behind her, and move on.

At the red light, she closed her eyes. It only took her seconds to tell Carly she would come back, even though, deep down, it wasn't what she wanted to do. Yet, she owed the woman and could never tell her no. Brooklyn was content with the life she was living. She was one of the most sought-after home renovators, with homeowners paying her top dollar to come to them, to transform their visions into their dream homes. Her job afforded her many luxuries, except roots. She didn't rent a home, let alone own one. Each town became her stomping ground, until the next job came in. She traveled thousands of miles, back and forth across the country, leaving her mark everywhere she went.

The honking horn startled her. Her eyes flung open, and her foot automatically touched the gas before she slammed her foot back onto the brake, earning another long horn and probably a few choice words from the car behind her. She would never care about someone's overeagerness to punch the gas as soon as the light turned green. Her reasoning was asleep in the seat next to her, and she would never trust other drivers to stop at red lights. She watched the cross traffic before pulling into the intersection to continue down the road.

The slow pace she kept allowed her to take in the sights. The storefronts were all familiar and decorated red, white, and blue for the upcoming holiday. People lingered on the sidewalks, talking to friends; others wove through the foot traffic to get to their destinations. And then there were the tourists, stopping and taking pictures to capture their vacation memories: on benches, in front of the whiskey barrels holding various colors of tulips and the statues of Lewis and Clark and Sacagawea. Brooklyn saw a young couple go into Susie's Sweet Shoppe, the 1950s soda fountain, which served locally made ice cream, the best she had ever had until one of her jobs had taken her to Vermont, where she had tried Ben & Jerry's for the first time. Now they were her favorite with all their crazy flavors and different concoctions. Back when she lived here, she and her friends would meet at Susie's after school, on Friday nights, or after a game, whether football, wrestling, basketball, or baseball. Of course, the girls would become giddy when the guys showed up, especially in their baseball uniforms, stained with grass and dirt. Susie's always reminded her of the movie *Grease*, except with a black-and-white tiled floor and red vinyl booths. One year for Halloween, the owners hosted a sock hop, and everyone in town came out for the party. Next to the ice cream parlor was Ellie's, the local florist; Washington Savings Bank; and the family-owned deli, O'Maddi's. But it was the commotion across the street that got her attention. The open market on the corner displayed fresh fish, resting on packed ice, and the cafés had their wrought-iron tables and chairs outside, allowing patrons to enjoy the warm weather. People sat there, chatting happily among themselves, enjoying the fresh air and ambience of this small town.

At the next light, she stared at the fish market. It was busy; people waited in makeshift lines to place their orders while some had their cell phones held high, likely set to record the salmon being thrown over the stand and caught easily behind the counter, much like they'd see in Seattle at the Pike Place Fish Market. If things were still the same, it was the owner's sons—and now maybe his grandsons—who threw the ordered fish behind the counter to teens, who wrapped the product in paper and cashed out customers. This had been her first job. She had wanted to hate it, but the camaraderie had kept her coming back. She loved her coworkers, but the smell! Teenage girls did not like to smell bad in any way, let alone smell like fish. After each shift, she'd rush home to shower and change, and she washed her work clothes every night. Her mother begged her to quit, but Brooklyn loved the job. It gave her independence and money in her pocket.

She smiled at the scene and let her eyes rove over the people milling around. She did a double take at the woman standing on the street corner. Waiting to cross was her old friend Monroe Whitfield. Brooklyn recognized her instantly. Her friend hadn't changed one bit, with her strawberry-blonde hair pulled back into a ponytail. She couldn't recall a time when Monroe wore her hair down, unlike her sister, Mila, who never put hers up. The sisters were as opposite as night and day, from what Brooklyn remembered, yet best friends and inseparable. *What is Monroe up to these days? Is she married? Does she have any children?* If she were a better friend, she would've known these things. If she had kept in touch, if she had come back when expected, maybe her heart wouldn't feel as if it were about to escape the confines of her chest out of fear that Monroe might somehow figure out she was staring at her. The emotional part of her wanted to push the button to put her window down, stick her arm out, and call the name of the woman who used to be her friend. The logical part of her knew she shouldn't, and that saddened her. She knew the confrontations were coming; she expected them. She had no business going to look for them, though.

Once again, the car behind Brooklyn honked. This time, the driver laid on the horn for longer, making his impatience known. When she glanced in her rearview mirror, she could see the man flipping her off. She threw her hand up in the air, but he wouldn't be able to see her with the tinted windows of her SUV. She let off the brake pedal slowly, purposely. She had a problem with overly aggressive drivers and had encountered quite a few in her travels.

Thankfully, her car looked like any of the other tourist vehicles in town with her out-of-state Florida plates. Driving down the road, she saw plates from Oregon, California, Texas, and as far as North Carolina. The longer she drove, the more her head was on a swivel, taking everything in. Memories flooded her senses, making her smile. Many times throughout her life she had wished things were different and wondered what it would be like to go back in time and make different choices. She didn't care about altering her future, only changing one day. That was all she wanted to do. Make a better decision, say the right things, and not give up so easily.

When Cape Harbor High came into view, she pulled over. Very few students milled around, some sitting under the large oak trees, while others walked down the steps and turned in whatever direction they needed to go home. From here, her old house was approximately five blocks away. There wasn't a doubt in her mind she could still walk home with her eyes closed.

Sitting in the passenger seat, her daughter stirred. Brooklyn peered over and thought about waking her up but drove on. Carly was waiting for them to arrive and no doubt pacing the floor.

Back in the day, the Driftwood Inn was the hot spot of the town. Aside from the view that the guest rooms offered of the magnificent scenery, the ballroom alone was a sight to behold with the gold teardropped diamond chandelier that hung in the center of the room. Brooklyn always imagined she was Cinderella at the ball when she stood there. The ballroom itself held every type of party, weddings and receptions, school dances, and conference luncheons. In that room and under the beautiful light fixture, men had bent down on one knee to propose. It was where countless best men and maids of honor had stood, toasting their friends. It was where couples had fallen in love. And for Brooklyn, it was where she thought she'd have her wedding reception, dancing in the arms of the man she once loved.

Brooklyn pulled onto the crumbling driveway. Potholes, chunks of missing pavement, and weeds had taken over the half moon–shaped parking area. She put her SUV into park. Her finger hesitated on the push-start button, and she wondered if she had just entered the twilight zone. Nothing looked the same as she remembered. She finally pressed the button to shut off her vehicle and opened her car door, instantly stepping into a hole small enough that it could easily be ignored or missed if you were in a hurry but large enough to do some damage to an ankle if you were not paying attention. Brooklyn came around the back side of her car and stood there, staring at the darkened windows. In all her years coming here, she'd never seen the inn like this—drab, dreary, without life—and the carriage house attached to the inn wasn't faring much better. She scanned the area and noticed that the landscaping was fine but far from the pristine vista it once was. The effervescence of the inn was gone, and she had a good idea as to why.

Brystol opened the car door, having woken up, and slid out of the passenger seat with her arms stretching toward the sky. Mom and daughter glanced at each other for a second before Brooklyn turned her attention back to the inn, which seemed out of place for the oceanfront property. When Carly had called and asked her to come and renovate the inn, she had assumed she meant new paint, fixtures, and tapestries. She hadn't thought the inn would need a new life, but the cobwebs, overgrown shrubs, and chipped paint led Brooklyn to believe otherwise. The disarray she was witnessing was nothing like the prestige she had known the inn to have, and she was afraid of what the inside looked like.

"Did Nonnie close the inn?" she asked her daughter. When she spoke to Carly, it was always about Brystol and nothing more. It pained Brooklyn to ask too many questions about the people and life she once had in Cape Harbor, and she knew it hurt Carly as well.

Brystol shrugged and rubbed her eyes, clearly not fully awake.

"Do people stay here when you visit?" Brooklyn tried again.

Her daughter shook her head. "It's only Nonnie, Simi, and me."

No mention of the housekeepers, chefs, or waitstaff that worked around the clock to keep the inn a tourist destination. Carly had never said anything to her about closing the inn. Not that she would expect her to, and Brooklyn never asked, but she would expect her parents to say something at least. It had been years since she had been in Cape Harbor, but not Brystol. She spent her summers in Washington, split between here and Seattle, where her other grandparents lived.

"What about parties, luncheons? Does Nonnie have people in the ballroom?"

"No, why would they?" Brystol asked.

Because that's what the inn was for, Brooklyn wanted to tell her daughter. She kept her thought to herself. Her daughter knew nothing of what this inn could do, the joy it brought to the people of Cape Harbor and the many tourists who came through the beautiful town. When Brooklyn had left Cape Harbor, she had allowed guilt to consume her, shutting everyone out, including the one woman she shouldn't have.

To the left of the inn was a smaller dwelling where Carly lived. Brooklyn knew the inside well and loved the old charm of the carriage house. She had spent many days and nights inside those walls, doing homework, watching television, and falling in love. She had also spent a great deal of time worrying, right alongside Carly, who had always put on a brave face each time a storm rolled in and the guys weren't back in port. They had spent hours together, watching out the back window for the pink flag of the *Carly* to come into view. Without fail, whoever saw it first would point, and they would let out a sigh in relief. Their men were safe, for another day. There had been only one time when the pink flag wasn't blowing in the wind when the *Carly* returned to port—the day Skip Woods died. For the first time, Brooklyn had seen what life would be like if she were to marry Austin, a life full of worry and wonder, mixed with happiness.

The front door opened; Brooklyn's and Carly's eyes met. Neither woman smiled. It had been years since they'd seen each other, for no other reason than Brooklyn couldn't find her way back here. She stared at the once-regal woman, who was now frail and older than her years. She watched as Carly turned to Brystol, her face morphing into a wide smile. She held her arms open, and Brooklyn's daughter went running, yelling as she did, "Nonnie!"

After a long hug, Carly held Brystol's face between her hands. "Finally, my baby's home," she said, pulling the teen back into her arms. "You're getting so big."

"You say that every time I see you." Brystol laughed and stepped out of her grandmother's hold.

It took a moment for the two women to move toward each other. They met somewhat in the middle and embraced as if they hadn't seen each other in weeks, not years. The tension rolled off Carly in waves. Brooklyn could feel the animosity coming from Carly, and she knew there wasn't anything she could do about it. The decision to stay away had been her own, regardless of who it hurt.

Carly stepped away and crossed her arms over her torso. It was unseasonably warm, but it seemed like Carly was trying to keep a chill away from her or protecting her heart from breaking. Something Brooklyn knew too much about. Carly glanced at Brooklyn one more time before turning her back to her. They exchanged no words. None needed. Brooklyn knew Carly resented her for taking Brystol away. She resented her for a lot of things. That was another reason she never came back here—there were too many demons because of bad decisions.

Later, after the car had been emptied of their belongings and Brystol had filled Carly and Simone in on how homeschooling was going and where their latest adventures had been, Brooklyn found Carly sitting in the sunroom, rocking back and forth in her antique white chair. She took the seat next to her, sighed, and made the mistake of looking out the window. Boats filled the harbor, both commercial and recreational. But it was the vessel coming in, with its crew standing starboard and waving, that made her heart lurch, the ache she hadn't felt for years coming back tenfold, the knife that lived within her twisting its jagged edge. Her hand flew to her chest just as tears came rushing in. Fifteen years, that was how long it'd been. She wiped angrily at the hot, wet drops, wishing she could control her emotions better. This was one reason she'd stayed away. The memories were too painful, and she hated the way they made her feel.

With no words, Carly reached for her hand, causing Brooklyn to cry even harder. There was a time in her life when she thought of

Carly as a mother. In fact, most of the kids who walked through the doors felt the same. It was natural—this was the house everyone came to after school—but things changed. Death happened. She wanted to apologize, to tell Carly how sorry she was for staying away and how she thought Carly wouldn't have wanted to see her. She had sent Brystol every summer, thinking that would be good enough. She saw now it hadn't been. They held hands until Brooklyn's tears ran dry, but the pain still lingered, and she knew it was never going away.

TWO

Bowie Holmes slid his foot into his brown work boot and pulled the laces over and around the hooks, skipping a set about halfway up since a hook had broken. He pulled the worn-out piece of leather as tightly as possible. He repeated the same for his other foot before he stood and groaned. His hand went instantly to his lower back as he bent over, trying to stretch out his aching muscles. He desperately needed a new bed, and as he stood there, looking at his boots, he knew a new pair of those would do him some good as well.

Amicable or not, divorce was hard. When Bowie and his soon-to-be-ex-wife, Rachel, separated, they were anything but cordial, and both ended up with separate lawyers, which was something he'd wanted to avoid, but her parents insisted. His lawyer was sucking the life out of his checkbook, while Rachel's made sure he had to cover her fees too. He was getting royally screwed and couldn't even enjoy it. Nor could he do anything about it.

He went outside and whistled. Within seconds, his faithful companion, Luke, came running. Bowie held the door to his truck open as his dog jumped in. This was the one thing he wouldn't budge on with the divorce. He was keeping his dog, and he couldn't care less what Rachel's lawyer threw at him. Luke had adopted Bowie—at least that's how he told the story. When he was a pup, the black Lab had wandered onto a jobsite, climbed into Bowie's open-doored truck, and fallen asleep. He'd shooed, tried to chase the dog away, and told him to scram. The dog wouldn't leave.

Rachel was none too happy about having a dog in the house. She claimed she was allergic, but Bowie could tell that her sneezing fits were fake. The dog stayed, and mostly he ignored Rachel, following his master everywhere. The only time Rachel had given a rat's ass about Luke was when she'd told Bowie she was moving out and wanted to take the dog with her. There used to be a time when Bowie would have given Rachel any and everything she asked for, but there was no way he was letting her take his dog. Getting the message loud and clear, she'd packed her clothes, left his dog with him, and never looked back.

Luke hung his head out the window with his tongue dangling from his mouth. His ears flapped from the wind, causing Bowie to laugh. As he drove toward downtown, he mentally ticked off the phone calls he needed to return. Business was slow. The days of Seacoast Construction building multiple houses at the same time had gone by the wayside. Vacant or affordable land in Cape Harbor was scarce, and where Bowie failed, other companies succeeded. He was far too focused on keeping his company local, never branching out to the other towns. He held on to the belief that if he took care of the locals, they would take care of him, and it so happened that he was right. He was everyone's go-to for construction. The problem was, no one needed any repairs, or they couldn't afford them right now. For a while, he'd been able to make excuses; however, he was out of them now. He had no choice. He needed to expand the area he was willing to work, take jobs even when overnights were required, and he needed some advertising. Nothing hurt his pride more than when he saw a commercial for his competition. But those flashy ads on television cost money, which he didn't have, unless he laid people off. It had been months since he'd taken a salary, and even *he* was running out of money . . . mostly thanks to his ex-wife.

He pulled his truck up to the curb and shut off the ignition. He sat there with his arm resting on the door, waving at people as they walked by. A few stopped to say hi to Luke, who had become a local celebrity of sorts. Everyone in town knew who he was, and when they saw him sitting on the sidewalk or in the truck, they greeted him; some offered his dog a biscuit. Luke was the friendliest dog in town, and everyone loved him.

Bowie sighed and finally opened the door. "I'll be in the diner," he said to Luke, as if the dog knew which door led to the restaurant. As soon as he shut the door, his dog took his spot behind the steering wheel, watching as his master disappeared into the building.

Rachel waved. Bowie grimaced. He hoped she hadn't noticed, but she put her hand down, and her smile faded; he knew she had. Not that he was mad at her; he was just frustrated by the process of their divorce. They'd had a good life, until she'd wanted children and they could not conceive. She had wanted to try IVF, and he'd been willing until he saw the price tag. They simply couldn't afford it. Not without taking out a second mortgage on the house and a loan against his business. It wasn't like there was a guarantee either. If the process didn't work, they were out the money, in debt, and no baby to show for it. The risk was too much for him. Each step he took toward her now made him thankful he'd never caved. He never wanted to imagine what life would be like without a company to run, more debt than he had now, and a child to care for.

He slipped into the booth and smiled at Peggy, the waitress he'd known his whole life. She brought him coffee, asked Rachel if she was ready to order, and went on to the next table, writing nothing down and never asking what he wanted. She knew. He had the same meal every time he came in. The best part about eating there would come later, when Peggy brought the check. She would hand it to Rachel and walk away. Bowie was a town favorite. Everyone loved him. There was a time when they liked Rachel too. It took the people of Cape Harbor some time to accept her, though. Most of the grumblings through town had been about how Rachel thought she was too good for them. She was from a few towns over and had wanted Bowie to move, news that had spread like wildfire when his mother had mentioned it at her weekly book club years prior. The locals hadn't taken too kindly to the thought of Bowie leaving on account of his new girlfriend, at the time. She had moved here, and all was good, until she asked for a divorce and the townspeople shunned her again.

The former couple sat across from each other. Rachel rested her hands in her lap while Bowie played with the handle of his ceramic coffee mug, avoiding the large envelope on the table. He sighed heavily, a sign meant to convey to his ex he had other things he needed to take care of. He chanced a look at her. Her eyes were staring at the chipped Formica tabletop. "I'm here," he said gruffly.

She met his penetrating gaze. Her mouth opened to say something but closed quickly. Bowie cut eye contact and silently cursed his harsh tone. There was something she wanted; otherwise, why would she invite him to breakfast?

"Bad morning?" she asked. He wanted to reply sarcastically, reminding her that since she'd asked for a divorce, nothing had been easy for him. But he held his tongue and sat up straight in the booth.

"You could say that."

"Sorry," she mumbled and briefly stared at her lap before she placed her hands on the table and sighed. "You're probably wondering why I asked you here."

He shrugged. This was the last place he wanted to be. His company was failing, and he needed to focus all his energy there. The woman across from him had already quit on them—*on him*—and he was ready to move on.

Rachel cleared her throat and forced a smile that went unreturned by Bowie. "Should I cut to the chase?"

"You could say that."

She leaned forward and placed her hand in the middle of the table. He noticed immediately she was wearing a much larger diamond than the one he had put on her finger years before. His mouth ran dry, and his tongue thickened in his mouth, making it hard for him to swallow. He shouldn't be angry, but he was. He was livid and seeing red. They weren't even divorced yet, and she wore a ring from another man.

"Bowie—"

He held his hand up. He didn't want to hear what she had to say. For almost a year, he'd supported her, paid what his lawyer said had to be paid, done what his lawyer told him needed to be done. The counseling they went to, the blame he took because his wife couldn't get pregnant. The stigma of everyone knowing his marriage failed, all the while she was with someone else.

"How long?" he asked, knowing the question was open ended. He didn't care what she responded with; he wanted to know if she'd cheated on him.

"We met about seven months ago."

He sneered, shook his head, and fought the urge to slam his fist onto the old Formica tabletop. "Seven months?" His teeth clenched. "I've been supporting some other guy for seven months?"

"No." Rachel looked at him as if he were stupid for thinking such a thing. "He's employed."

"But not enough to support you?"

"I don't have a job, Bowie. What do you expect?"

He threw his hands up and scoffed at her ridiculous question. "I don't know, Rachel. Maybe you should apply for one. That's what most people do when they need money."

She rolled her eyes and slid the envelope toward him. He hesitated before his calloused hand grabbed ahold of the thick packet. Every time one of these showed up in his mailbox, he had to sign in triplicate and usually send a check to his lawyer. That thought alone sent his stomach into a fit of knots. "What's this?" he asked. It was a question he really didn't want to know the answer to, but he hoped the contents would be the end of his marriage.

Rachel cleared her throat but said nothing. His gaze intensified on her while his fingers worked the metal clasp on the back of the package. He wished she would blurt out what it was she wanted from him to make things easier. He'd much rather hear her demands than read them in black and white because the legal mumbo jumbo made his eyes cross and his brain hurt. He was a numbers guy—measurements and area calculations. He could look at a room, tell you the size and the exact number of gallons it would take to paint. But read a legal document? Not his idea of a good time. More so, he had to ask his mother for help, which to him was embarrassing. He hated airing his dirty laundry to her.

He pulled the stacks of papers out slowly, almost fearful of what they might entail. He took in everything he could on the page. *Dissolution of Marriage, Rachel Holmes—Petitioner. Bowie Holmes—Respondent.* The date and place of where they were married seemed to stand out over the other words on the paper. That was, until he came to line two: *Irreconcilable Differences.* That's how his marriage would end, because of differences.

"I've decided to forgo my request for alimony."

Bowie glanced at his soon-to-be-ex-wife. She had a smug look on her face, and he knew why. The next husband had money. He'd learned enough from his lawyer to know that alimony stopped once she remarried. "Is that so?"

"It's the right thing to do."

He knew better. Rachel never cared about what was right; she only cared about herself. She had shown him as much when she'd walked out. Still, he nodded and flipped to the next page, pretending to read.

"I also withdrew my request for my share of the house."

Bowie chuckled and set the stack of papers down on the table just in time for Peggy to bring their orders. Eggs over easy set on top of shredded hash browns with two sides of bacon and homemade wheat toast for him. Fruit and oatmeal for Rachel. She wrinkled her nose at the sight of his plate. She didn't like grease, fat, or anything else she deemed unhealthy. He was a meat-and-potatoes kind of guy, while she was a vegetarian. Not that he had anything against vegetarians—he just preferred lettuce on his burger and not by itself. Their different lifestyles meant they'd butted heads, often. When he was hot, she was freezing to death. When he was tired, she was wide awake and begging him to watch a sappy movie, something that would surely put him to sleep. When he wanted to relax and watch football, she pushed him into driving to Seattle for retail therapy, pulling him around from store to store and whining because he wasn't paying attention to her until he put his phone away. To most, their clashing personalities would've been a turnoff. Yet, despite their differences, he'd fallen in love with her, and when she'd left, it had broken him, and now he could call their differences irreconcilable.

"Thanks, Peggy. You've always known how to treat me." The comment was a jab toward Rachel, who preferred takeout over a home-cooked meal.

"My pleasure, sugar."

"You just need to sign the papers, and in ninety days we'll be divorced," Rachel mumbled. She dipped her spoon into the bowl of plain oatmeal but didn't take a bite.

He pushed his plate to the side, folded his hands and rested them on top of the table, and leaned forward. Rachel refused to make eye contact with him, something that irritated him to no end. "I want to make sure I understand what I'm reading or what you're telling me. I sign the papers today, and in three months, we're divorced?"

She nodded.

"And you take nothing from me? I keep my house, my business, and more importantly, my dog?"

She nodded again.

24

"Wow, he must have a great job if you're willingly walking away from everything." He was pissed. At her. At himself. At the whole situation. When she'd left, they'd both been angry, bitter—he more so than her because he couldn't give her what she wanted, a child. And now, after months of haggling and unnecessary payments to lawyers, she was walking away. He should feel relieved. A huge weight was being lifted off his shoulders, but his feelings were different. Sitting there, he saw another side of the woman he'd once loved. A side that made him ill and elated all at once.

He picked the papers up and looked at Rachel. "Do you have a pen?" As if she'd known the question was coming, she handed him one, and he scribbled his name on the pages marked by the yellow flags stating, "Sign here." When he was done, he gathered the documents, tapped them a few times on the table, and slid them back into the envelope. "Now what?"

"Now, I take them to the clerk's office for filing."

"When?"

"Well, I have to meet with my wedding planner—"

Again, he held his hand up to interrupt her. "I don't care about your future wedding plans. I'll file them today." He placed the envelope on the vinyl bench next to him, out of her reach. He wasn't going to wait for her to file the papers. He wanted the clock to start ticking down on their ninety-day sentence. He sat there and let the moment wash over him. He was free. His obligation to Rachel was over, and that made him smile.

He was also hungry, and his food was getting cold. He pulled his plate toward himself, picked up his knife and fork, and sliced through the eggs and hash browns, letting the yolk seep into the fried potatoes. He added ketchup and mixed everything together. This was his favorite part of breakfast. He intended to eat heartily, to fill the silence that lingered between him and Rachel and his thoughts with food. After two bites, Rachel had other ideas.

"Do you have anything to say?"

"About what?" he said, his words muffled by his mouth partially full. He signaled for Peggy, who strode over to their table.

"What do you need, sugar?" she asked, smiling at him with her back turned to Rachel.

"A Coke, please."

"And I'll take more coffee." Rachel held up her cup, but Peggy never acknowledged her.

"She doesn't like me much."

He shrugged and jabbed his fork into his pile of food. "The people of Cape Harbor take care of their own. You know that."

"I tried, Bowie. I really did. It's just that there were things missing from our marriage. Desires and needs that I have."

Her words pissed Bowie off. He slammed his fork down onto his plate, and Rachel jumped. He gritted his teeth and somehow got out, "You," before Peggy was back at the table with his Coke. He downed it, threw his napkin on the table, picked up the packet that contained his freedom, and stood. "I can't believe you. You didn't try—you quit." He threw a couple of dollars on the table and strode out of the restaurant.

He had fought for her, begged her. He'd cried when she'd told him she wanted a divorce, promised to change, be a better man, but none of his words had been good enough for her. She wanted more, and he couldn't give it to her. Even through his ire, he knew he was better off without her.

He shut his truck door with such vigor that Luke cowered in the far corner of the passenger seat. He had never laid a finger on his dog, other than to love him, and the sight of his faithful friend showing fear broke his heart. He had to pat his leg a few times to coax Luke over to him, but once the dog finally obliged, Bowie wrapped his arms around his scruff and buried his head in his fur. Luke brought him a sense of peace.

The shrill sound of his phone jolted Bowie away from Luke. He pulled his cell out of his pocket and checked the caller ID, thankful it

26

wasn't Rachel calling, but his secretary, Marcia. "Hello?" he answered gruffly as he tried to clear away his emotions.

"Bowie, have you heard the news?"

He shook his head and peered out the front window of his truck, hoping to see something that would answer her question. "Um . . . no. What's going on?" he asked, straining his neck to try to look down the road, eager to figure out why she had called.

"The inn." She paused. "They're reopening."

He went silent.

"Bowie?"

"I'm here."

"Mrs. Woods phoned. She would like for you to handle the construction for the renovation."

He gulped. A job of this stature could help him over the financial burden he was experiencing. Not to mention, it would give him some much-needed clout. "What did you tell her?"

"That you'd be right over to discuss the details."

He would. He would drop everything, assuming he had a full schedule, to work with Austin's mother. But something was amiss. The inn had closed when Austin passed away, and this month marked the fifteenth anniversary of his death. So why now?

Bowie hung up after telling Marcia he would head over to the Driftwood Inn. When he pulled into the circular driveway, the same one where he'd learned to ride a skateboard, broken his arm, and parked cars during many of the town's events, his heart fell into the pit of his stomach. He hadn't been here since his friend died—not that he'd intended to stay away. He'd thought about visiting often, especially when he and his friends had gathered on the beach to remember Austin. However, as time had passed, he'd felt he couldn't just show up on Carly's doorstep. He had a lot of groveling to do, but didn't know what he would say or how to even start because telling her he was sorry seemed like the wrong thing to say after being gone for so long.

THREE

Brooklyn stood on the front step of her new school, staring at the brick building, trying to psych herself up enough to walk the rest of the way. The bell had rung, and now she was late. Being as it was her first day, she wasn't too worried that the school would call her mom or bother her father while he was busy saving the people of Cape Harbor.

By comparison to her former school, Cape Harbor High was small. Tiny even. Over the weekend, she and her dad had driven over here and walked around the campus. The whole time she wondered where the rest of the school was. Surely they had football, baseball, and softball fields. And the building . . . it was only one story. Where were the classrooms? Where was the gymnasium? Did they even have a basketball team?

It had been her parents' intention to bring her here on Friday to meet with her teachers and to get a feel for the school, but with moving and the Labor Day holiday, time had slipped by them, and she faced the first day of school alone.

For the past year, her father had commuted between Seattle and his new office, not wanting to uproot Brooklyn from her life in Seattle. He had taken the job as the town's pediatrician, which had soon turned into him becoming a primary care doctor for everyone. The hospital was nearly fifty miles away, and the town needed someone close.

At first, her dad was home on the weekends, arriving late on Friday nights and leaving after dinner on Sundays. After a few months, every weekend became every other weekend, and then slowly became once a month, if that. Sometimes, he'd come home and leave the next day. He suggested that Brooklyn and her mom travel north for the weekends, but Brooklyn was busy with basketball, softball, and whatever else she had going on, so only her mother would go when Brooklyn didn't have a tournament or other obligations. It wasn't until she found her mother crying softly one evening that she realized she was the source of her mother's heartache. Her mom was lonely, and Brooklyn could change that. She hated the idea of moving away from her friends, from the life she was living in Seattle, but her heart hurt for her mom. She had given up everything to raise Brooklyn, tending to her every need, driving her to every event on their calendar. Her mother's life revolved around Brooklyn. Maybe it was time for her to give back.

One weekend when her father could finally come home, Brooklyn proposed they move, never fully expecting her parents to take her up on the idea. At first, she could see the confusion on her mother's face, but that confusion quickly turned into elation, and the following Monday, their house was on the market. She wasn't, however, prepared for things to move so quickly, but they did.

She spent her last summer in Seattle with her team and friends. None of them had cars yet, but all promised they would visit, especially since Brooklyn was moving so close to the water. A few even said they would sail up with their parents for the tulip festival the following spring. The friends made plans, and Brooklyn would make sure they stuck.

Now she wished she were back in Seattle, walking arm in arm with her best friend, Renee—who went by Rennie—as they entered their school. Their freshman year had been rough. The seniors loved to haze, and the girls had become the butt end of one too many jokes. Sophomore year was better, but it would be their junior year where they made their mark, where they showed everyone that their group ruled the school.

When Brooklyn told Rennie that she was moving, they cried together. Best friends since kindergarten, there hadn't been a first day of school they hadn't walked in together until now. Rennie had begged her parents to let Brooklyn live with them, and Brooklyn had done the same when she realized she didn't want to leave her friends behind. Neither set of parents would agree, leaving the girls no choice but to say goodbye.

Rennie would already be in class, moving on without Brooklyn by her side. She tried not to have those thoughts, but it was too hard to ignore. To make her mother happy, she had made herself miserable.

"Are you going to stand outside all day?"

She turned to her left to find a boy standing there with his hand clutching the shoulder strap of his backpack. The first thing she noticed about him was his height. He towered over her, making her five-foot-six frame seem small instead of average. He tilted his head to the side and smiled. Her eyes instantly caught the bright red line across his chin.

"What happened?" she asked him, pointing to the scar.

His hand rubbed against the spot, and he winced. Almost as if he forgot he had hurt himself. "Bad casting."

"Casting? Are you in a movie?" His comment confused her, and she was sure her face showed him as much. He laughed, and his hand went back to holding the strap of his bag.

"No, a fishing hook caught my chin."

She covered her mouth. Even though she had grown up near the ocean, she had never been fishing. It wasn't a hobby of her dad's, nor any of her friends'. Brooklyn reached out to touch the mark, her fingers coming close, until she dropped her hand. She had no right touching this boy, a complete stranger. She cleared her throat and asked, "Did it hurt?"

"Hell yeah, thirty stitches later and I'm good as new."

"Oh." She briefly wondered if her father had been the one to stitch up his chin. She leaned closer as if she were admiring the precision it took to put the boy's skin back together. His scar was healing nicely and probably wouldn't show if he grew a beard later in life.

"I'm Austin Woods, local fisherman, resident heartthrob, and late for his first day of junior year." He smiled and stuck his hand out to shake hers.

Brooklyn giggled and quickly covered her mouth. She hadn't meant to do that, but he'd made her laugh, and she thought he was cute with his russet-colored hair and rich brown eyes. She caught him staring and felt her body temperature rise. She took a step forward and placed her hand in his. "I'm Brooklyn Hewett, new girl and late for her first day as well."

Austin stepped toward her, holding on to her hand a bit longer than what would be deemed socially acceptable for two people who just met. Brooklyn didn't mind, though. She liked the way her hand felt in his. In Seattle, she'd had guy friends and had never given them a second thought. Yet, in a matter of minutes, she had developed a crush on this boy, the self-proclaimed resident heartthrob who liked to fish.

"What do you say I walk you in? I'd love to be your tour guide."

"What if we don't have the same classes?"

He chuckled, shook his head, and turned to stand in front of her. Her heart raced, the beats thundering in her chest as Austin stared down at her. "There's like eighteen kids per class. You'll be easy to find. Besides, now that I've found you, I'm never letting go."

Inside, he showed her where her locker was, which as luck would have it, was right next to his. This excited her. She told herself it was because he was a familiar face in a sea of peers looking at her, wondering who she was and where she came from. At her former school, when someone new came, you heard about it through the rumor mill, unless the new person was in your class. Here, you were front and center, like you were on display.

By lunch, she was frazzled. Peppered with questions throughout her first set of classes, she walked cautiously into the cafeteria, clutching the orange plastic tray that held some semblance of food. She decided she would ask her mom to make her lunch from here on out, especially since leaving campus wasn't allowed.

"Brooklyn!"

She looked around for the source calling her name. She had met a few other classmates earlier and was surprised when Austin wasn't at his locker when the lunch bell rang. She'd fully expected him to be there, waiting. At least, she had hoped he would be.

When she spotted him standing on a chair with his arms waving wildly in the air, she smiled. She hadn't meant to, but it was like her heart had taken over her senses. Love at first sight was what Rennie would say if she were here. Brooklyn wanted to agree.

She made her way through the small crowd, apologizing for bumping into people as she walked by them. The table where Austin sat was full, but that didn't stop him from giving up his chair for her.

"Where will you sit?" she asked after setting her tray down.

"Next to you."

Again, she felt her heart race, gallop, and skip. It was doing so many different palpitations she couldn't pinpoint just one.

"Brooklyn, these are my best friends, Bowie Holmes, Grady and Graham Chamberlain." He pointed to the two guys sitting across from her. "And that's Jason Randolph and Monroe and Mila Whitfield. Roe and Mila are sisters, and I'm pretty sure you figured out Grady and Graham are twins." Brooklyn glanced at Austin, who adjusted his baseball cap. She had, in fact, realized they were twins. It was really obvious, but she didn't want to call Austin out and embarrass him. Plus, she'd already met the girl he called Roe. The guys mumbled some sort of hello, and Roe pointed out that they had English together. Mila smiled, sort of, and offered a small wave.

"Where are you from?" Jason asked.

"Seattle."

"Why would you move here from Seattle?" Mila asked. There was a bit of snark in her voice, something that surprised Brooklyn. So far, everyone had been pleasant to her, but Mila seemed put off by her presence.

Brooklyn had been asked this question multiple times already and was wondering if there was something wrong with the town. She found the town to be cute, a little quiet, and completely opposite of what she was used to, which her mother loved.

"My dad is the town doctor," she said.

"I'm going to be a doctor," Jason added. "The University of Washington is where I'm headed."

"It's a really great school."

"Go, Huskies!" everyone except for Brooklyn and Mila said loudly. Brooklyn caught Mila staring. For the most part, she felt as if she fit in with everyone here, especially at this table, but Mila had a different vibe. She wondered if Mila had a crush on Austin and thought maybe she should find out before her own crush turned into something more. The last thing she wanted to do was come between a close-knit group of friends.

The rest of her day went as well as her morning. Each time she'd stop back at her locker to put her textbook away, Austin was there. They ended up having three classes together, one of them being physical education, where they partnered.

Once the final bell rang, Austin led Brooklyn through the parking lot and to his truck. He took her bag and set it into the cab and held out his hand for her to use as leverage to climb in. "It's okay," he said when she looked at him questioningly. "I'll never let go."

Brooklyn wiped the tears from her face as she sat at the top of the cliff overlooking the sound. She held her knees to her chest, rocking back and forth. Being back here brought on a barrage of emotions she wasn't ready to face. Everywhere she went, Austin was there, reminding her of the love they once shared. He had been her best friend, her constant companion, her first love. He had been her everything until they were both left brokenhearted.

"Did you let go, Austin?" she asked, directing her words toward the ocean. He was out there, somewhere, doing what he loved best.

Her phone rang, and she pulled it out of her pocket, smiling down at the screen. After sliding her finger over the screen, she rested the phone against her ear. "Hey," she said.

"Are you there?"

"I am."

"And? You know I'm dying for all the details."

Brooklyn sighed and dropped her head. "Carly closed the inn," she said, shaking her head. "I can't believe I've been so determined to stay away from here that I had no idea. I should've peppered Brystol with questions."

"What she does isn't your business, Brooklyn."

"I know, Rennie, but I can't help but think I had something to do with it. If I had stayed and raised Brystol here—"

"Stop," her best friend barked into the phone. "Just stop with the nonsense. You had to do what was best for you and your daughter. You couldn't stay there, not with everything that had happened. You would've never escaped the stigma of being Austin Woods's girlfriend."

"I know," Brooklyn said quietly.

"I can come up this weekend, if you want."

"Don't you have plans with Theo?"

"Meh, they can change. Besides, he'll be in Seattle midweek; we can take a weekend off."

Brooklyn stood and walked toward her car. Over the years she'd missed the Pacific Northwest, its beauty and everything it offered. She could ski in the morning and be at a beach by sunset, enjoying the best of both worlds.

"I may take you up on your offer, Rennie. I don't know how much longer I'll be able to keep everything bottled in."

"Don't worry, I'll be there. Before I hang up, have you seen him?"

Her question gave Brooklyn pause, and she almost stumbled over a protruding tree root. "No, and I don't plan to."

"Sure, ya don't." Rennie giggled. She said goodbye before hanging up, leaving Brooklyn with a scowl on her face. She glanced behind her, along the path that she and Austin had once walked, hand in hand, and tried to wipe her memories clean. She needed to move on, to bury the past and let it go.

Her phone chimed in her hand, a message from Rennie. She opened it, and her heart lurched. Staring back at her was a group photo from prom. One of her friends had asked Rennie to go with him, which had pleased Brooklyn. Brooklyn expanded the picture and studied herself, Austin, and the guy standing on the other side of her. Inseparable was what they used to be.

FOUR

Bowie went to knock on the wooden door, something he'd rarely done when he was growing up, and paused, his fist suspended in midair. He tried to come up with a valid excuse why he hadn't been around, why he hadn't stopped in to check on his best friend's mother, why he hadn't thought to bring his wife around and introduce her to the woman he used to consider a second mother. He came up with nothing.

He dropped his hand and contemplated returning to his truck. As much as he needed the job, he wasn't sure if he could face the person he had become after Austin's death. He was a shell of the man he used to be, but that was no defense for abandoning the woman who had taken care of him as if he were her own child.

He turned around and walked toward his truck. He had no business being here. As far as he was concerned, the job needed to go to someone that cared about the inn and the people who lived there. That wasn't him.

"Leaving so soon?"

Bowie stopped at the sound of Carly Woods's voice. He turned slowly to find her leaning against the doorjamb with her arms crossed over her chest. Aside from graying hair, she looked no different from what he remembered. He hung his head in shame and desperately searched for the words to tell her how sorry he was. It had taken him years to get over the passing of his friend, and most of the time, it still haunted him. His actions surrounding that day were never far from his mind.

"The answer is no, Bowie," she said, pushing away from the door-jamb. "Come in; we have business to discuss."

His steps were heavy as he made his way to the house. He shut the door quietly behind him and let the feeling of being in her home again settle in. Everything was exactly as he remembered. The flowered wall-paper still hung; he used to pick at the corners when he was little, and Carly used to call him an imp for it. He shifted his weight and smiled instantly at the familiar creak the floorboard made. No matter how many times he and Austin would try to sneak out, this piece of wood gave them away. He closed his eyes and with vivid clarity recalled slid-ing down the banister of the staircase. He could hear the laughter of his friends, the adults in the house telling them to knock it off even though that never stopped them. He could smell freshly baked cookies, could even taste the warm chocolate as it hit his tongue. There were many hours spent here while growing up. He fell in love here for the first time, with someone who never saw him for who he was until it was too late.

The sound of coughing pulled him from his daydream, and he fol-lowed the noise into the other room, where he found Carly bent over and her longtime housekeeper rubbing her back. Simone must've heard him come in because she met his gaze, offered a sad smile, and turned her attention back to Carly.

"Is there anything I can do?" he asked. Simone shook her head.

"This will pass in a moment. Why don't you have a seat in the din-ing room? We'll be there shortly."

Bowie continued into the other room. Instead of sitting down, he walked along the edge of the room, bouncing on his feet. He was feeling for weak spots in the foundation out of habit and taking mental notes of what would need replacing if he were to take the job. Oh, who was he fooling? He would take this job. Not because he needed the money, but because he owed it to Carly . . . and to Austin's memory. He decided then he would repair the carriage house for no additional profit. He'd do the work himself, bring the homestead up to code. It would be his way to make amends.

"Sorry for keeping you waiting, Bowie." Carly appeared in the archway. She forced a smile. The usual glint she had in her eyes, the one he remembered, wasn't there. She pointed toward the table, where he pulled the chair out for her and she sat. He walked around the table and took the seat directly across from her.

He cleared his throat. "I'm sor—" He stopped when Carly held her hand up.

"There is no need to apologize. Besides, if you do, I'll have to as well."

"For what?" he asked, shaking his head in confusion. What could the woman who'd nurtured every single one of her son's friends need to apologize for?

"For being vacant after Austin." She paused and drew in a deep, shuddering breath. "I should've been more welcoming to his friends. Not so shut off. Not so hidden. I could've easily reached out to you, and I didn't."

"It's understandable." And it was. Not only had she lost her son, but her husband as well, many years before. When Austin died, the town changed. Everyone suffered that loss. He was, and remained, such a beacon in the community.

"After being prodded for years, I've decided to reopen the inn. However, as you can imagine, the state of it is undesirable and in need of a more modern touch."

"It's historic," he told her. "I bet people will clamor to visit, to stay here."

She thanked him but shook her head. "The mattresses are lumpy; the fixtures leak. There's rust in the pipes. And it's dreary. This inn needs life; it needs love. I want people to come here and be happy, forge new memories which aren't marred by . . ." Carly didn't have to finish her sentence; he already knew what she would say . . . *death*. "I want the guests to come here and feel like they can escape reality, and maybe find something they love in the sunset they see outside their room—a safe, comfortable place where they can find the answers they're seeking in their life. I know new linens, paint, and furniture can't change everyone's outlook on life, but it could point them in the right direction."

Bowie focused on the woman across from him. The words she spoke used to be the adage of the inn. He wanted to ask her why she'd closed, but deep down he knew. Her son had died, taking away what life she had left. But still the question plagued him, why now? Not that he wanted to ask because right now meant he had a job, one that would pay him well and put him back on the map.

He cleared his throat, tapped his pen against his notebook, and said, "These are all easy fixes." That was his attempt at trying to steer the conversation back toward the repairs. "How many rooms again?"

"Forty. All in need of some care."

"Okay, and the timeline?"

There was a loud bang upstairs, and Carly turned herself toward it slightly, barely looking over her shoulder. Bowie saw Simone rush by and head up the stairs, her steps echoing loudly in the all-too-quiet house.

On instinct, he stood. He could hear muffled voices. "Does some . . . someone need help?" he stammered.

Carly shook her head. "I'd like the project done as soon as possible. I have a renovator you will work with. She knows my vision and what I want." She pushed a magazine across the table, leaving him no choice but to sit back down. Still, his eyes roamed. He surveyed the open expanse where the staircase was, and the area where footsteps now echoed. He hadn't heard of anyone living with Carly, aside from Simone, not that he would've paid attention. His divorce kept him in a fog lately, and anytime someone mentioned the inn or Carly, he ignored the comments out of guilt.

He opened the magazine to the flagged locations and saw what design ideas she had in mind. He would need to measure the rooms, order the lumber, paint, and new fixtures. "I see someone has spent some time watching HGTV?" He laughed as he continued to flip through the pages of room after room with shiplap covering the walls. The wood was easy to work with, even easier to paint.

"It seems popular."

"It is. What can you tell me about the renovator?" It wouldn't be the first time he'd had to work with someone. In fact, he liked it a bit better than following architecture plans. In his experience, renovators weren't sticklers for plans and would take suggestions when offered.

"I was thinking some of the rooms could be gray."

"Gray is very popular."

"And blue?"

Bowie scribbled her color suggestions down.

"And black?"

His pencil stopped moving across his notepad. He stared at his scribble, trying to comprehend what Carly was saying. She wanted a set of rooms painted black? An accent wall made sense, but full rooms? No, he couldn't.

When he finally glanced at her, she bore a sheepish grin. "It's bold, and the inn has always had this rustic feel. I want to liven it up."

"With *black*?"

"And I'd like to paint the paneling in the lobby white."

"White will make the wood beams pop."

"Or we could paint them," she suggested with a shrug.

Bowie leaned back in his chair as he recalled the vaulted ceiling in the lobby. Not unheard of, but cumbersome. He would need to bring in scaffolding to paint the ceiling and would need some extra manpower to get it done. Shouldn't be a problem. Worst-case scenario, he could hire day laborers from the next town over. What he couldn't put his finger on was why the drastic changes, and why so sudden? Especially after all these years.

He leaned forward, clasping his hands. "I know I haven't been around for—"

"Fifteen years," she interrupted somberly. "Time doesn't matter, Bowie. It's water under the bridge. Even if you had stopped by, I don't know if I would've welcomed your company. It's taken years for me to come to terms with the loss of my son, and now I have, I need to move on with my life."

"And reopening the inn is your idea of moving on? Why not just sell it?"

Carly spread her arms out. "This is my home. It was Austin's home. It's where . . ." She paused and seemed deep in thought. "Where would I go?"

"There are a few of those retirement places around. You could play cards all day."

"And give up my view? I'm not ready."

Bowie could respect that. Retirement homes weren't for everyone. He couldn't blame her, honestly. The view the inn had was spectacular. It was what drew people to stay here. He knew once she announced the inn was open again, the town would flourish with tourism. This was exactly what this sleepy little town needed, and maybe more opportunities would arise for him.

"Tell me about your wife."

"Um . . ." Her request caught him off guard. He was unprepared to discuss Rachel and truthfully didn't want to.

"Simone says she's lovely."

"Simone? But not you?" He already knew what her answer would be before she said it. Carly hadn't left the house since Austin's funeral, and if she had, he hadn't heard about it. Surely, people would talk. Years ago, he would look for her at the market or pier, hoping she would show up for the annual celebration Austin's friends held for him, but she never did.

"Do you have children?" she asked, ignoring his question completely.

He would not get the answers he sought. "Rachel and I are going through a divorce, and no, we don't have any children. I . . ." He paused and scanned his notes; the words were nothing more than a blur. If this had been fifteen years ago or if he had been a man and stayed connected with Carly, he'd have no issues telling her his problems. But this was now—he was embarrassed and didn't want to talk about life.

He couldn't take any more awkwardness; it was time to leave. He closed his notebook, placed it back onto his clipboard, and slipped his pencil into the front pocket of his shirt. "I have to go," he said, pushing away from the table. He showed himself out, slamming the door behind him in frustration.

"So stupid," he muttered to himself as he stalked toward his truck. He threw his clipboard onto the passenger seat and got a wet, sloppy kiss from Luke spread across his face. He nuzzled his dog, feeling somewhat calmer in his presence.

FIVE

Brooklyn felt so out of place in the grocery store; the trucker hat she was wearing was pulled down as far as possible, and dark sunglasses masked her blue eyes, likely making people assume she had a hangover. As she passed by the other customers, she couldn't help but stare, trying to figure out if she knew them or whether they recognized her. There was one time in her life when popularity had ruled, where she'd been the "it" girl because of who she'd dated. Everyone had known her, and everyone had wanted to be her friend. The truth was, she was hiding from the people around her and from herself. Ever since she'd woken up this morning in the strange yet familiar carriage house of the Woodses, she'd questioned why she was really here.

The obvious answer was for Carly, of course. Since the day she'd left, she'd vowed to never return. She wasn't from here, technically, and her parents had moved back to Seattle a year after she graduated high school. There wasn't a need or even a desire to stay connected with any of her friends. She had long shut the door on everything that had to do with Cape Harbor. Everything except for Carly—still, their relationship was mostly based on random phone calls that centered on Brystol and Brooklyn making sure her daughter spent time here each summer. Carly was the only reason Brooklyn would ever come back, even if she hadn't wanted to.

She pushed her cart up and down each aisle, marking off each item on Simone's list as she went along. Simone was going to feed the crew working on the inn. Carly had insisted upon it last night when the three of them finally sat down and started drawing up plans for the remodel. Brooklyn knew it was Simone's idea to reopen the inn. It hadn't taken her long to figure out that Carly had been living the life of a recluse, and she mentally kicked herself for not figuring it out sooner. Conversations she'd had with Brystol over the years played on repeat in her mind, as she searched for signs that Brooklyn should've picked up on indicating Carly needed help. Nothing stood out. And she'd never thought to ask her daughter if her vivacious grandmother had turned into an eccentric homebody. Brystol wouldn't have known the difference, and that made Brooklyn sad. Back in the day, Carly Woods was a sight to behold. A standout beauty among others, and the life of the party.

Brooklyn carried a tray of flutes filled with champagne around the crowded room. Everywhere she looked, women were dressed in glamorous ball gowns while the men were in tuxedos, chatting happily and looking more beautiful than Brooklyn could even imagine. After Carly had asked her and Monroe if they would fill in as servers for the annual Tulip Gala, a yearly fundraiser hosted by Carly and Skip Woods, Brooklyn found herself imagining what it would be like to attend the event as a guest. Her dress would be a full ball gown, in baby blue, with tiny diamonds sewn over the tulle covering. She would wear her hair up, in a braided bun, and a tiara, and when she would spin in a circle under the crystal chandelier, her dress would sparkle. Someday, she had thought to herself. Until her moment came, she would do what Carly asked.

She walked around the room, asking people if they would like a glass of champagne and taking their empty flutes if they had one. Monroe carried a tray of hors d'oeuvres, and each time Brooklyn passed by, her mouth watered. Bacon-wrapped scallops were her favorite and the only seafood she could stomach. She loved going out on Austin's boat, and she loved fishing, but couldn't bring herself to eat it. There was something about the smell that never sat right with her. Carly had tried numerous times, making the sea bass, salmon, and trout many ways, but Brooklyn could never find an acquired taste for seafood. She thought for sure, once Austin figured this out, that he would break up with her since his life revolved around fish, but he'd told her it didn't bother him if it didn't bother her.

"Mr. and Mrs. Woods, may I offer you a refill?" Brooklyn stopped at Austin's parents and held her tray out and smiled. Carly was dressed in a red gown with a massive diamond necklace resting at the top of her dress. She was beautiful. Skip was an older version of Austin, dressed in a tuxedo. While Brooklyn and Monroe worked the inside, Austin, Graham, Grady, and Bowie were outside parking cars as the valets, and later the teens would help clean up. They were always helping Carly.

"Oh, Brooklyn, let me introduce you to Mr. and Mrs. Long. Mrs. Long is on the committee with me. I shared some of your ideas for the tulip festival with her, and she loved them. Theresa, this lovely young woman is Brooklyn Hewett."

Brooklyn steadied her silver serving tray and shook Mrs. Long's hand. "It's a pleasure to meet you."

"You too. Carly speaks very highly of you."

Brooklyn blushed. She'd had no idea Carly was sharing her ideas with anyone but was happy to know that Carly thought highly of her. "It was nice meeting you." She was unsure what to say after a compliment like that.

Throughout the night, Brooklyn served food, brought fresh drinks, and cleaned empty plates away. When the auction started, she stood off to the side and watched as the roomful of people threw money at Carly. By the end, the fundraising total exceeded their expectations.

It wasn't long after the Tulip Gala that Skip passed away from a massive heart attack while at sea, and when he did, a little of Carly's spirit slipped away, but she was steadfast, making sure Austin and his friends only saw her smile. Austin was her light, her pride and joy, and when he died, it seemed that his mother went with him.

Carly had mere months to come out of her funk, especially if she wanted the inn to return to what it used to be: a staple of Cape Harbor and Skagit Valley. It was the awe-inspiring place where everyone loved to visit, even the locals. Once word got around that the inn was going to reopen, which in a small town like Cape Harbor wouldn't take long, Brooklyn expected companies to jump at the opportunity to host their holiday parties in the ballroom and to book their out-of-town guests to stay. She could see it now, the inn decorated for Christmas with thousands of white lights outlining the peaks and eaves of the building, and on the inside, trees of all sizes in the rooms guests would frequent, each styled differently. When she was a teen, she'd loved spending hours helping the staff give each tree its own identity. It was always the tree in the ballroom that would get the most attention. Hours upon hours, staff would spend decorating it with many strings of lights and bulbs. The topper was always a star to match the night sky. One time, Austin sneaked her into the ballroom to see the tree. On that night, the moon was low and beaming through the large windows. When he turned the lights on, everything sparkled. It was an image she would never forget. It had been years since she'd seen something so beautiful, and memories like that made her want to help bring back the prestige the inn's name once held. One thing Brooklyn wasn't sure of was whether the kitchen was going to open back up.

The real problem was she didn't know Carly's full plans. Last night, they only went over the remodel for the rooms and common areas, nothing more. It had been late by the time they finally sat down to discuss Carly's intentions for the inn. The new design was modern, and straight off one of those television makeover shows that Simone fussed about. She said the inn needed character, something special to make it stand out from the others because no one wanted to leave their home only to travel and stay in a place that was similar. The inn was supposed to be a getaway, a retreat from reality. Brooklyn agreed, but Carly held fast and strong to her concept. She loved the newer, fashionable look, and she was, as she reminded both women, the owner.

Brooklyn had yet to venture into the kitchen to see the state of the equipment, almost fearful of the ancient appliances and to see the repairs the galley would need. No doubt everything would need replacing, and she wasn't sure the funds were there, at least not until the inn started pulling in a steady income. The two went hand in hand. It was going to be hard to open the inn and not offer the full-service menu customers had grown accustomed to. Carly had long since let her staff go and shut everything down. Brooklyn wasn't even sure if she should broach the subject with Carly or ask Simone, who seemed to have a tighter grasp on what needed done around the inn.

"Brooklyn?"

She froze at the sound of her name. She was facing the cans of condensed soup and thought briefly about ignoring the person to her left. How could anyone recognize her? Her hair was longer than it was the last time she was here and back to its naturally dark color. Her hat sat so low she had to tilt her head back to look at items higher on the shelf, causing her neck to strain. She'd kept her head down since arriving and hadn't spoken to anyone. And no one outside of her family knew she was here, which was how she intended to keep things. In and out, like every other job she did.

"Brooklyn Hewett, is that you?"

The woman wasn't giving up, leaving Brooklyn two choices: ignore her and move on or confront the person blowing her cover. Unfortunately, she made the decision when she turned her head slightly to see who was blocking her cart. Monroe Whitfield stood there with her long strawberry-blonde hair styled impeccably in a ponytail, her floral dress fitting like a glove, and the most perfect smile she could muster. She'd seen her yesterday, standing on the street corner and looking radiant, just as she was now. Brooklyn averted her eyes, looking down at the yoga pants she had on. Her muddy shoes had likely left a trail behind her as she walked through the store, and her sweatshirt had holes and paint stains all over it. She was dressed like a slob. More so, she felt like one.

"It's me, Monroe."

There was a hint of desperation in her voice, forcing Brooklyn to react. She wanted to run, to leave her cart behind and go back to the sanctuary at the inn or at least in her SUV. But even she knew that slipping in and out of town was going to be a challenge despite her hopes otherwise; Rennie had told her as much. She set the can of soup she was holding back onto the shelf and turned fully to give Monroe, the woman she'd once considered to be one of her best friends, her full attention.

"Of course, I remember you," she said, pasting on a smile. "I'm sorry—I'm just caught off guard; I didn't expect anyone to recognize me." Brooklyn slipped her sunglasses off, then set them in her purse.

Roe, as Brooklyn used to call her, was the second person she'd met after starting at Cape Harbor High and they had most of their classes together. They became fast friends and confidantes. Roe's sister, Mila, had been an aspiring actress at one time, something that Monroe hated but still had encouraged her sister to fulfill her dreams. The Whitfield sisters were as thick as thieves, and at the time Brooklyn considered herself lucky to be in their fold. It took only days for Brooklyn and Monroe to become best friends. When she wasn't with Austin, Brooklyn was with Monroe, and sometimes Mila. They would spend hours gossiping about everyone. Monroe regularly complained about her parents and how they treated her and her sister differently, often feeling they favored Mila because she was "going places." Weekends were spent on the beach, at the lake, and dancing in the back of Austin's pickup truck to music from the '70s and '80s. Plans were made for after graduation. Mock weddings discussed, with Brooklyn marrying Austin and Roe marrying one of the Chamberlain twins. It hadn't mattered which one, as both were equally hot. It was Monroe who had known Brooklyn's deepest and darkest secrets, and likely the reason she had left town when she did.

"I love this song," Roe yelled as she turned the dial up on the portable radio. She reached for Brooklyn's hand and pulled her to her feet. They danced, swaying their hips back and forth, throwing their hands up in the air. The truck rocked wildly, causing the girls to laugh.

"You're going to bust my truck," Austin hollered through laughter. They were stopped at some pond, trying to beat the late-summer heat. All summer, the gang would explore the area, finding ponds, rivers, and campgrounds to hang out in. At night, they would converge on the beach for a bonfire. Those nights were Brooklyn's favorite. She loved sitting with her back pressed against Austin's chest, his legs holding her close. She was ridiculously in love with him.

"Dance with me," Brooklyn said, extending her hand to Austin. He shook his head and sipped on a bottle of beer.

"I'd rather watch." He winked.

"I will." Bowie stood and joined the girls, encouraging Austin to do the same. Brooklyn's lower lip jutted out as she stared at her boyfriend. Her hand remained suspended in the air as her hips moved to the music, but Austin wouldn't comply.

"You're such a jerk, Austin," Monroe yelled out. She took Brooklyn's hand and spun her in a circle. Still, Brooklyn wasn't giving up on Austin.

He never relented.

Monroe came toward Brooklyn with open arms. They hugged, even though Brooklyn felt completely out of place. She didn't deserve the fact that Monroe was being so nice to her after she had left all those years ago without warning or provocation. She'd deserted her friends in their time of need. They had lost their friend, the man they had all grown up with. When she should've consoled them, they were consoling her, and the guilt was too much to bear.

"What are you doing here?" Monroe asked.

"I'm here for the summer, visiting Carly." As soon as the words were out of her mouth, she wanted to take them back. She could've been passing through; she could've been doing anything other than what she said. But it was too late. She could tell by the expression on Monroe's face her words had done damage. Brooklyn, who'd cut ties after Austin died, hadn't, in fact, cut ties at all.

Still, Monroe feigned a smile. Something Brooklyn knew she could do all too well. Ironically, the years of accepting that her younger sister was the favorite, even among the community, had made Roe one of the best actresses the area had ever seen.

"That's right—with Austin's memorial service coming up, of course you'd come home." Monroe reached out and squeezed Brooklyn's hand . . . a sharp jab right to the heart. That one stung. She hadn't been a good grieving girlfriend, at least not to the local people or their friends.

Brooklyn inhaled deeply, finding some inner strength to let the comment roll off her. She deserved it. "I'm not sure if Carly is up for attending."

"But you'll be there, right? It's such a wonderful way to remember Austin. The town does a fireworks display, but you probably know that since Carly pays for it. There's a reading on the pier, and sometimes people get up there and tell stories about Austin. As time passes, though, more and more of our friends don't come back or they can't get the time off from work. We're all so spread out around the country now with our careers. But for those of us that do come back or are still here, we always meet on the beach for a bonfire. You should come—bring Mrs. Woods if she's up for it. I've tried a few times over the years to reach her, but she's never taken visitors. It's nice to know you've been speaking with her and that she's okay. I miss her as much as I miss you. I know everyone would love to see you."

She expected that to be a lie. She knew one person who could go their whole life without ever seeing her again, and she felt the same way. As nice as it sounded, she would have to memorialize Austin in her own way, with his mother, watching from afar. Too much time had passed, and Brooklyn's excuse for giving up on everyone was, at best, weak and selfish. She hadn't counted on needing to explain her absence, nor had she wanted to.

"How are you? How's Mila?" Brooklyn asked. Now that she'd seen someone familiar, her emotions were all over the place. Aside from Austin, she missed Roe the most. There were many times when Brooklyn picked up the phone to call Monroe, to beg her to come to Seattle—or wherever she was at the time—to see her. But she couldn't bring herself to do it.

"Mila's . . . Mila," Monroe said with a shrug and a long, exaggerated sigh.

Brooklyn felt like there was a story there, one that would take a few beers to coax out of her. Right then, it hit her like a ton of bricks that there was no way she could hide out until the renovation was complete.

"I'm teaching third grade at the school. What about you? Are you married? Kids?"

Brooklyn shook her head slowly. She wasn't going to answer either question. "I travel a lot with my job. I don't really have time to date."

"What do you do?"

"Design work, mostly. Home renovations."

"Oh, just like on TV. Maybe you'll get your own show someday."

Brooklyn loved Monroe's enthusiasm and her ability to look past the obvious elephant in the room.

"Look, here's my number. I have to get back to work. I'm helping proctor some exams at the high school today." Monroe handed her a slip of paper. "I'd love to see you before you leave."

Brooklyn smiled but offered no response. Monroe gave a little wave and grin before leaving her standing in the aisle where she had found her. She sighed and turned her attention toward the shopping list, trying to remember where she was before a small sliver of the past came back to haunt her. Unwilling to go through that again, she slipped her sunglasses back on and pulled her hat down even lower, hoping that she could get out of the store and back to the inn before she ran into anyone else.

SIX

Bowie thought about slamming his head against the side of his rig to knock some sense into his brain. Today had been one of those days where nothing was going right, but everything had seemed to fall in place, exactly where he needed his life to be. Putting his ex-wife issues aside, he needed the Driftwood Inn job. As much as he didn't want to tell himself it was about the money, it was. He needed it. His crew needed it. Reaching inside the cab of his truck, he picked up the clipboard and patted Luke on the head before tucking tail and walking back toward the carriage house. He knocked once before the door swung open and Carly smiled at him.

"I believe I forgot my manners, ma'am," he said. "And how to conduct business. If you still want my services, I'd be honored to complete the job for you."

"There isn't another contractor I would ever consider hiring, Bowie. You were Austin's best friend. He would want this." Her words cut him, and they cut deep. He wasn't going to argue with her about her son; there was no point. If Austin were here, he would likely disagree with his mother.

"If you don't mind, I'm going to take some measurements." Bowie pointed to the double doors that would lead to the lobby of the inn.

"Of course, come this way." Carly pushed the door wider, inviting him back into her home. She led him through the dining room, kitchen, and down the dark back hallway that still lacked electricity, where she unlocked a door. He stepped inside first, letting the cold, drab, dark inn settle upon him. Cobwebs were now a staple of the decor, and white sheets covered most of the furniture in the lobby. The space belonged in a horror film. Lights flickered overhead, one popping and fizzing out almost instantly. Behind him, Carly chuckled. "I'm not sure what I'm thinking with this project."

Me neither, but Bowie kept that thought to himself.

"The cleaners will start tomorrow. Simone will supervise. Once the walls and woodwork are cleaned, it shouldn't be a problem to paint, right?"

Bowie shook his head. "Do you only want to paint in here, or do you want a new counter?" he asked as he pulled on the top of the lobby desk, testing to see how sturdy it was. His father had built it, thirty or forty years before, but it still seemed to have held up over time.

"Yes, I believe so. Although I do reserve the right to change my mind."

Of course, he thought while he surveyed the room, mentally counting how many gallons of paint he would need. His hand ran along the woodwork as he tried to determine whether it would be easier to sand or use a deglosser. Both would be time consuming, considering the amount of wood they would need to cover. The woodwork was pine, a thinner wood known to show its knots. Most people loved this look. Others, like Bowie, found it hard to work with. The decision on how to handle the wood could be something he and the renovator decided. "What did you say the renovator's name was?"

"I didn't." Carly moved into the foyer, turning on more lights, most of which seemed to be dead. She found this comical for some reason, and Bowie made a note to have the electrical wiring checked out. He would also need to check out building codes on commercial property.

It had been some time since he had done any work on the commercial side, and he wanted to make sure inspectors weren't going to find any issues. He watched her for a minute, wondering why there was secrecy regarding the renovator. He had worked with his fair share from the Seattle area.

Bowie followed Carly as she moved through the main floor. When they came to the ballroom, he saw a lone rocking chair with an afghan sitting by the massive window. He knew instantly this was where she sat. He would, too, but for other reasons. He left her standing by the double doors as he went to the window. The view was indescribable. People along the harbor had tried to emulate what they'd seen from this ballroom, but no one had come close. He would know because he'd either built or renovated many homes along the cliff, and none of them compared to what he was seeing now.

"The windows stay," she said, as if she thought he was going to suggest they change. He wouldn't do anything different here and didn't bother to respond. In due time, he would see the sunset from this window, reminding him of a different time in life. A time when all he cared about was drinking with his buddies, sneaking stolen glances with the girl he was in love with, and thinking he was invincible.

Carly shut off the lights, an indication that she was ready to move on. She paused in front of the grand staircase, her hand resting on the end of the banister. It was almost as if she was deciding whether to go upstairs.

"Mrs. Woods?" Bowie tentatively asked. "Is there more on the first floor that you want to look at?"

It was a long minute until she acknowledged him. "I need to talk to . . . I don't know yet."

"Talk to Simone? Do you want me to get her?"

Carly shook her head. "Shall we?" she asked with a smile. She climbed the wide planked steps one at a time. Bowie stayed a step or two behind her, fearful that she might fall. He realized he'd been mistaken earlier when he'd assumed the color of her hair was all that had changed. The death of her son had aged her, more so than what he deemed normal. His mother was still full of life, running half marathons and working. She had pep in her step, whereas Carly could barely move around. He'd had no idea death could affect people like this, and the thought that he could've possibly prevented any of this by coming around and being present in her life weighed heavily on him.

At the top of the stairs, the second-floor hallway was laid out in front of them. He knew there would be another staircase halfway down, as well as an elevator. Whether the elevator worked was a whole other question. He wasn't going to test it out now; he'd wait until he had a crew member here.

She set off toward the first room. The inside was much like the downstairs, covered in cobwebs. He made a note to have the place fumigated, as well as to have the building checked for rodents and termites. This was turning out to be a much bigger job than he had thought. An idea came to him, one that would allow him to stay on as staff once the remodel finished. He could be the handyman, or his company could, making sure the inn was always functioning the way it should be. He'd talk to her about a permanent solution once the job he was there to do was completed.

Each room they entered as she led him through was like the previous, and he noticed that Carly made no bones about it. She told him her design ideas, what colors she wanted for each of the rooms, and he continued to argue with her that the lodge theme was their best bet, but she wasn't listening. His pleas for change fell on deaf ears.

They finally found their way downstairs, once again avoiding the kitchen. The temptation to walk in there was great, but he would wait until tomorrow, when he came back to measure for wood. He could do that now but wanted to give the cleaning crew she hired a chance to wipe the grime away. Maybe then, Carly would see that changing the decor wasn't necessary.

He left Carly in her house and went back outside. He walked the perimeter, making notes. The driveway needed to be dug up and repaved, and for the most part, the windows were sound. He moved brush away from the foundation and ran his fingers along the creases, looking for weak spots. Still, he decided that adding a layer of concrete to the exposed portions would be helpful. While out there, he stopped and admired the view. He hadn't had a chance to take his family's boat out yet this season—with the divorce and his company failing, he hadn't felt like it. But standing there, seeing the barrage of colorful sails of the sailboats, made him miss being out on the water. It had taken years after Austin died for Bowie to set sail again. It was something they had loved doing together. His best friend gone, his life changed forever.

After Austin passed, Bowie had found himself questioning life. What was the purpose of it? Why was he given the one he had? He spent most of his nights drunk, and during the day he longed for the person who shunned him, and his best friend. His life was in turmoil. He hated himself for what he had done, and he couldn't even atone for his actions. Water under the bridge—that's what Carly had said to him. Would she have said the same thing if she knew that while her son was dying, the unthinkable was going on? Probably not. In fact, Bowie was certain that if Carly knew the truth, she would've never called him to do this job.

Fifteen years ago, Bowie and Graham had put their lives on hold searching for Austin. Every morning they would take a boat out, trailing close to the shore, looking for his body. They went as far north as Canada, as west as they could before the temperatures dropped, and south until the water warmed, knowing there wouldn't be anything left if Austin had gone this way. The men wanted, more than anything, to bring Austin home, giving Carly closure. They weren't the only ones looking. Fishing crews put their jobs on hold to look for Austin. Every day, the townspeople would wait down by the docks as the boats came into port, hoping for an answer.

Bowie focused on his clipboard as he rounded the house. Out of the corner of his eye, he saw a black SUV barreling toward him. He jumped out of the way only to lose his footing after the vehicle almost sideswiped him. "Fucking out-of-towners," he grumbled as he brushed his dirty hands against his pants. Determined to give the driver a piece of his mind, he went toward the car. The driver's door was open, and a foot dangled out. He gripped the side of the door and peered into the cab. Bent over the console, the driver was rummaging through something, ignoring him and the fact that she could've killed him. "The inn's not open. You'll need to head back into town. You'll find a place on Colonial, three blocks up from Third."

The driver froze.

"Hey, are you okay?" Panic set in. Bowie wondered if the driver needed medical attention, maybe had suffered a heart attack, which could be why she hadn't seen him. Maybe she was slumped over and not ignoring him. He reached for her arm and pulled her upright. He moved closer, leaning in as far as he could to get a look at the woman. His heart stopped. His lungs ceased to inhale or exhale. He didn't know for how long, but he was sure every vital organ in his body shut down as he took in the woman. He knew her . . . *well*.

And he hated her.

She'd ruined his life.

He despised everything about the woman sitting in the driver's seat. He recoiled at the feel of her arm pressed into the palm of his hand, and he stepped away as she slowly slid out of the SUV. She shut the door and leaned against it. Bowie desperately wanted to see her ocean-blue eyes, yet the thought of looking into them made his stomach roll. "What are you doing back here?" he seethed.

She looked down at her shoes. He followed. In fact, he was looking her up and down and unable to stop himself. She had filled out over the years. Her once-slender body now had curves and muscle, and she was still as beautiful as she was the day he met her. Bowie closed his eyes and wished the images of a young Brooklyn away from his mind. He had shut the book on his past a long time ago, and yet, here she was, standing in front of him.

"I asked you a question."

Brooklyn let out a mechanical chuckle. "I could ask you the same thing. What are you doing sniffing around the Woodses' property?" She stepped toward him, ready to do battle. She pulled her sunglasses off and stared Bowie dead in the eyes. His knees buckled. For as much as he hated her, he loved her the same. But he would never tell her.

"Oh good, you're both here. We can go over the plans now that you're back, Brooklyn."

They both turned toward Carly, who was standing on the small porch with Simone by her side. Oddly, she appeared pleased, and Bowie couldn't understand why. Carly smiled, beckoned them in, and turned back toward the house.

Bowie took this opportunity to give Brooklyn another cursory glance. She was gorgeous. *But why is she here?* It couldn't be for Austin's memorial. She hadn't shown up the other fourteen years, so why start now?

That's when it hit him. She wasn't here to pay tribute to Austin. Brooklyn had returned to renovate the inn. If he wanted the job, he was going to have to work with the one woman who could bring him to his knees and drive him off a cliff at the same time—and as far as he was concerned, he was screwed.

SEVEN

The music was thumping. Loud bass echoed down the street, a sure sign that the cops would be out later to bust up the party. This alone made Brooklyn want to ditch, but Austin insisted they make an appearance. Always concerned with making appearances. In Seattle, Brooklyn had been popular. She'd had friends everywhere, from different high schools and even at the University of Washington. It had not been unusual for her to have an invite to the hottest frat party or to come sit in the student section during the Apple Cup. Things were different in Cape Harbor. Austin wasn't just popular; he was the most sought-after guy she had ever met. If the girls weren't chasing him for dates, the guys were chasing him to hang out. Everyone wanted to be Austin's friend, and sometimes Brooklyn couldn't understand why. To her, he was just Austin, the guy she fell in love with shortly after she moved here. But to everyone else, he was a god. The community worshiped him . . . it wasn't like he was a star athlete or anything—he was just Austin Woods, the guy who made everyone smile. He was charismatic, sweet, and loving, and he volunteered for everything. He was someone you could count on. People adored him. They wanted to be in his presence. But dating him had its challenges. They couldn't go out without someone bothering them. And everyone referred to her as "Austin's girl," as if she didn't have her own identity, or she was a piece of property he'd acquired in a trade deal. Still, Brooklyn was so head over heels in love with him she brushed most of her complaints under the rug or confided in the one other person who understood what it was like to be in Austin's shadow, Bowie.

The group of friends walked down the street, huddled together. Bowie and Austin led the pack, talking animatedly about their trucks and how they couldn't wait to have enough money saved so they could buy a lift kit. The girls were in the middle of the group. Brooklyn, Monroe, and Mila, all dressed up as if they were heading out for a night in the city. Behind them were Grady and Graham Chamberlain, twin brothers whose parents owned the local watering hole, the Whale Spout. Graham had big plans to leave town after graduation. He wanted to travel, explore the world until he decided on a place to live. Of course, he had yet to choose a career that would allow this and figured he'd pick up odd jobs in each city, state, and country he visited and hitchhike to save money. Grady, on the other hand, wanted to own a fleet of fishing vessels. That was Austin's intent as well. The two of them had created a business plan and even thought of a name: the Chamberwoods Fishing Company. Brooklyn had other ideas. She wanted to head back to Seattle, even Portland, and become a labor and delivery nurse. Her roots weren't in Cape Harbor, and she couldn't see herself staying here. That was something Austin couldn't understand.

After arriving at the house party, Austin walked right in, and the room parted as if he were Moses and this were the Red Sea. Everyone stopped what they were doing, just to say hello to him, and he ate up every bit of the attention. If the group thought they could follow Austin through the room, they were mistaken, as a mass of people closed in around their favorite person. Within seconds, there was a beer in his hand and introductions made to the people he didn't know . . . all while his girlfriend looked on.

She hated these parties. She hated everything they represented. She hated that they would fight later. She hated how insecure they made her feel. She hated how he flirted, how no one cared that she was in the room. Most of all, she hated that Austin ignored her. Even though she came with him, she wanted to be home. However, staying home meant a night of pacing and waiting for the phone to ring, even though he wouldn't leave the party to call her. One time she was late to a party, and when she walked in, Austin was in the corner with another girl. He said nothing happened. She believed him. It wasn't like she could prove otherwise, and no one would ever come forward to say anything ill against him. Her only choice for her peace of mind was to put herself through the agony of being at the party. It was the only way to know if he was faithful. This wasn't how she expected their relationship to be, though, because when it was just them, he was the perfect boyfriend.

Bowie wanted to shake Austin. More so, he wanted Austin to wake up and realize what he was doing to Brooklyn. Brooklyn was, without a doubt, the most beautiful girl in school. Strike that—she was the most beautiful girl he had ever seen, and he felt the only reason she was with Austin was because he happened to see her first. If the roles were reversed, Bowie wouldn't drag her to any parties. He'd take her out to a nice restaurant for dinner or on one of the boat cruises. They'd go whale watching or drive along the coast. He'd take her out on his boat and hold her while the sun set over the Pacific. He'd cherish her. But instead, he was forced to watch from afar. He watched as his best friend treated the woman of Bowie's dreams like a toy. It wasn't that Bowie wanted Austin to share. No, he wanted Brooklyn for himself.

He found her sitting on the back stoop, looking out over the fenced yard where couples lay together, making out under the stars. It wasn't the best place, but when you were a teenager, you took what you could get. Bowie handed her a beer, popping the top for her so she knew it was fresh. He loved that she held tight to her "I'll get my own drinks" rule, out of fear someone might slip her a mickey or something. Bowie would kill them if that ever happened.

"Do you want to go sit on the swing?" He nodded toward the large oak tree where a bench swing hung. If anything, sitting there would give them a bit of privacy, and she wouldn't have to listen to anyone from inside the *house going gaga over Austin. Brooklyn led the way, and Bowie waited until she sat before he took the spot next to her. The swing was old and worn out, but the chains were brand new. His father was a general contractor, and Bowie often accompanied him to jobs. The expectation was that Bowie would follow in his father's footsteps, take over the family business, but Bowie wasn't sure he wanted to. Bowie had ideas of grandeur. He wanted to go to school to be an architect. He wanted to build skyscrapers in cities like Los Angeles, New York, and Chicago. He wanted an apartment overlooking a metropolis and a home along the beach—neither of which he'd be able to afford working at his father's company. Mostly, he thought about following Brooklyn to college. He knew it was stupid to think about his best friend's girl like that, but he couldn't help it.*

Bowie's foot pushed the swing back and forth, keeping them at a slow pace. Brooklyn held her can of beer in her hands, never taking a sip. She wasn't much of a drinker, at least not at these parties. When it was just their group of friends, she'd let loose and drink. He hated it, though, because when she did, she and Austin were like these other couples, making out in front of everyone without a care in the world. As much as he hated to admit it, he liked these parties because they gave him private time with Brooklyn. Eventually, he hoped he would get over this crush. She was new in town, a rarity, and in time he expected his feelings to subside.

"Do you have plans for Christmas?" he asked her. She had only been in town for a few months. He knew she missed Seattle. She talked about it a lot. Her friends, the school she went to, and how their homecoming dance was at the convention center in one of the conference rooms, and how she had the ability to go to the mall without having to plan a day trip.

"My dad gave the staff the day before and day after off, so I'll probably have to work."

"Does he let you give shots or do stitches?"

Brooklyn laughed. He loved the way she sounded. He also loved her smile. It could change his outlook on a crappy day, anytime. "I've given a couple of flu shots, but I'm really nervous that I'm going to hurt someone. I'll learn a better technique once I'm in nursing school."

"You can always practice on me," he told her as he bumped his shoulder with hers.

"Thanks. I might take you up on that. What about your plans?"

Bowie shook his head. "My entire family lives within twenty miles of here. We all meet at my grandparents'. The women cook, the men do macho things like repair parts of the house that don't need it, and the grandkids play video games, get in the way, and play football outside, ruining our church clothes."

"Sounds like a lot of fun, actually."

"You should come. One more mouth to feed won't make a difference."

She looked back at the house and sighed. Was she wondering what her boyfriend was doing, who he was with? Did she know that the Woodses hosted big holiday feasts and that Austin would be busy? He wished she would break up with him. Bowie wanted a chance with her, and as bad as it sounded, he knew he was better for her than Austin was.

"You can bring your family. We have enough for everyone," Bowie said. He wanted her at his grandparents' house with him. He wanted to hear her laugh at his dad's dumb jokes.

Brooklyn stared at Bowie. "Why are you so nice to me?"

He shrugged. The answer was on the tip of his tongue. He could tell her right now it was because he was in love with her, but he could never say that aloud. "Because you're a cool chick," he said, instantly regretting his words. "What I mean is, you're fun to hang out with."

"But Austin's in there." She pointed toward the house. "Monroe, Mila, Grady, and Graham are all in the house with him. And you're always with me. Does he send you out to babysit or something?"

Bowie felt his stomach drop. He thought about storming into the house and punching his friend for putting these thoughts into her head, but he knew it wouldn't do any good. Austin would just charm his way out of the situation and make Bowie look like a fool.

"I'm not much of a partier," he told her. "I come because it's what we do."

"I come because I'm afraid he will cheat on me if I don't."

Bowie shook his head. "He wouldn't do that."

She peered sharply at him, her eyebrow raised. "How could you be so sure?"

"Just something I know, is all." Bowie sighed. He wanted to move closer to her, press his thigh against her. He desperately wanted to know what her skin felt like. Instead he stayed where he was, with one arm draped over the back of the swing and his hand holding the can of beer to his leg.

"You probably wonder why I stay with him or why I let him act this way. Sometimes I ask myself the same questions or imagine if I hadn't met him on my first day what I would be doing now. Maybe I'd be inside dancing with some other guy, or at home studying. But when I think like that, my heart hurts. It hurts so bad that I want to cry. I'm in love with that stupid boy in there, and he has no idea how much. Sometimes, I feel like he tells me he loves me because it's the safest thing to say. I just want him to see me."

In that moment, Austin stepped out onto the back steps. His eyes roamed the yard until they landed on Brooklyn. At the same time, a smile broke out on both of their faces. She got up, without saying goodbye to Bowie, and made her way to Austin. As soon as she was within arm's reach, Austin pulled her to him, kissing her deeply. The couple walked back into the party, leaving Bowie alone.

"I see you, Brooklyn," he mumbled into the darkness.

EIGHT

As far as standoffs went, the one happening between Brooklyn and Bowie could go down in history. Neither was willing to move, to even budge, and the only things lacking were witnesses, who had both deserted and sought cover inside the home. If Brooklyn hadn't known better, she would've thought this was a setup, a ploy to get two former friends back together. But Carly had no idea what she was doing, what kind of hell she was creating for Brooklyn. To someone like Carly, this was as innocent as donating money to a homeless person.

Brooklyn wished she hadn't taken off her sunglasses. Behind their darkened lenses she could hide, she could remain mysterious, but something had compelled her to remove them. She wanted—no, she needed—to see those radiant blue eyes of Bowie's that she remembered. Only, they held no life, no expression. They were icy, harsh, angry, and pinned on hers.

Over the years, she had dealt with confrontation of all kinds. Homeowners who were upset with her work or who changed their minds hours before the job would be complete. Contractors who added unnecessary beams or walls that would change her design completely. There were the men who wanted more from her even though she was clear from the beginning—she was married to her job. Brooklyn could handle her own quite easily; she had learned from the best. And until now, she'd thought she had seen it all. But the anger in Bowie's eyes, coupled with confusion, was uncharted territory for her. Her eyes diverted, and she stepped back. Bowie was close. Far too close for a friendly game of "nice to see you again." As much as she'd tried to forget, images of the last time she'd seen him replayed in her mind. His outstretched hand, the words he said to her—all came flooding back. She felt sick to her stomach. She shouldn't be here. She should've told Carly no, but deep down she felt like she owed the woman.

She focused every which way but on Bowie. Everything interested her right now: the torn-up driveway, the gutters that had accumulated fallen leaves that needed to be taken care of, and the cars that continuously drove up the road, bypassing the inn and essentially forgetting about the woman who lived there. Very few people lived on this road, so where were they going? And who were they? People who considered themselves friends of Austin's? The same friends that left his mother alone for years? She may have left after his funeral, but at least *she* had her reasons. What were theirs?

Her wandering eyes finally turned toward the carriage house, where her daughter was. She wasn't ready to explain Brystol to anyone, let alone Bowie. She'd figured out after her encounter with Monroe at the store earlier that no one knew she had a daughter. Yet another mystery when it came to Carly. She was starting to question what went on here during the summers, and whether Carly ever left the house. Brystol never complained when she would come back to wherever Brooklyn was working, always telling her mom that she'd had the best time with her grandparents. Brooklyn always assumed Carly was part of that statement. They were close, Brystol and Carly. "Thick as thieves" was what Simone called them. And yet, while she stood there, she mentally kicked her own ass for not prodding her daughter for more information. She should've been adult enough to deal with the pain. If Brystol had told her that her grandmother lived the life of a recluse, Brooklyn would've done something sooner. What she really needed to do was talk to her parents. How come they never mentioned anything when they came to pick Brystol up for the summer?

She chanced a look at Bowie. That was a mistake. His penetrating gaze made her already upset stomach twist into knots. He tilted his head, appraising her.

"I asked you a question," he repeated for the third time.

"I'm fairly certain we both know what we're doing here, Bowie. The question is why?" In her field of business, renovators were a dime a dozen. Carly could've easily called someone from Seattle or Portland to do the job. The reason Bowie was here was simple. She knew he was in construction. Right out of high school he had followed in his father's footsteps, something he always swore he would never do. Brooklyn had declared she would leave after she graduated high school. She had wanted to move back to Seattle with her parents and attend the University of Washington to become a nurse. She hadn't. She'd waited for Austin. Austin, who'd promised her they would move once his business took off. The business had thrived, and yet the move was pushed off for one reason or the other until both Austin and Brooklyn had had enough.

Moving from a metropolis to a small town had a way of changing your path as well as your life. The hopes and dreams she had when she arrived in Cape Harbor were quickly set aside. Her new friends weren't dreamers. Not in the sense that she was. Mila was already practicing her acting skills in local productions, and Monroe had already started tutoring. Bowie worked for his father, even though he hated it. Austin and Grady were fishing every chance they got and talking about heading to Alaska for summer break, where they could make enough money to start their own business after they graduated. Brooklyn, Jason Randolph, and Graham Chamberlain were the only ones destined to leave. Jason and Graham had left, as planned, but Brooklyn had stayed.

She'd fallen hard for Austin Woods, which in her eyes had meant his dreams became hers. Her mother had been the same way when she'd met Brooklyn's father. Love at first sight, drop everything for the man you were in love with, and follow him to the ends of the earth. Brooklyn was following the example her mother had laid out for her, despite her parents encouraging her to do what she wanted; that love would still be there if it were meant to be. When Brooklyn would bring up the career path she wanted to follow, Austin would always tell her there would be time for her to do her thing once his business took off. *There would always be time.* The problem was that it didn't matter to Austin if it was five minutes, six hours, forty days, or three years. It just simply meant not right now. Thinking back, Brooklyn should've seen the signs early, but that first love was all-consuming. Being in love meant something to her. It meant she had a purpose, a reason for being, that moving away from her life and friends in Seattle had been a good thing. She was head over heels for this boy, and she put her dreams aside to help him fulfill his.

Regret lived inside of Brooklyn now. She had battled with it for years. Guilt over leaving after Austin's funeral. The blame she put on herself when he died. The remorse she felt for staying away. Shame for her actions in general. Years of therapy hadn't been able to cure her; of course it may have helped had she stuck it out with one therapist, but her job wouldn't allow for that. Moving from place to place was how she operated. She chose to live out of hotels because they were easy, no commitment, and her permanent residence was a post office box in Jacksonville, Florida. Yet deep down, she knew Brystol wanted friends—she wanted to feel like a normal teenager—and giving her daughter a stable homelife would be the right thing to do. She often thought of sending her to her parents, letting her daughter grow up in Seattle. Go to a real school and make real friends. But the thought of not being with Brystol every day literally made Brooklyn ill. She was her reason for breathing, for waking up every morning. Brystol was the only reason she was back in town and staring down the man who had been the catalyst for everything disintegrating before her eyes all those years ago.

Brooklyn sighed heavily. The loud, exaggerated sound was meant to get Bowie's attention. His eyebrow popped, almost as if he knew what she was doing. No, he definitely knew. He knew Brooklyn better than she knew herself. At least, he used to.

"What happened to you becoming a nurse?" he asked. She couldn't tell if his tone was snarky or just curious. There was a time when he'd known her hopes and dreams and she'd known his, but those days had long passed.

"What happened to you not becoming your father?" Answering a question with a question was the easiest way to avoid giving an uncomfortable answer. As soon as she'd found out she was going to be a mother, her dreams of being a nurse had been put aside, and she'd started doing what she knew how to do best, answering phones and setting schedules for a construction company in Montana, which had turned into painting the interior of homes after she'd had Brystol. Bowie had taught her how to use a paintbrush, and she had always found the job therapeutic, taking her anger out on the walls of unsuspecting homes by jabbing the brush a little too hard in the corners or pressing the roller irately into the walls, until a general contractor who'd liked her a little too much had handed her a hammer and told her to imagine whoever had hurt her was on the wall that he needed torn down. Brooklyn had done just that. Beating the old plaster until it was dust. She'd worked with that contractor for about three years, taking home-improvement classes at the hardware store until she'd set out on her own. Remodeling had become her therapy, and still to this day, the person she imagined each time she hit the wall hadn't changed.

"Things are different since you left," he told her. She found his statement both odd and accusatory. She gathered he wanted her to ask what changed or who, for that matter. While she was tempted, she didn't want him asking about her and her life, so she didn't take the bait.

Just then, the door to the carriage house where Carly lived opened, and she stood in the doorway, looking at Brooklyn and Bowie expectantly. She wanted to get down to business—that much Brooklyn knew. There was something about this whole situation that felt off to Brooklyn. The phone call, asking that she come back to complete the renovation, and now Bowie being there. She couldn't quite put her finger on it, but her gut was telling her something was amiss.

Bowie fell in step behind Brooklyn, following her into the dining room, where they sat across from each other. On the table, the renderings Brooklyn had drawn for the project were spread out, covering every inch of wood. They weren't as detailed as she would have preferred but better than nothing. She could show Bowie the full scope of her ideas if he wanted or needed to see them, but, in her experience, the contractors did as they were told.

She watched as Bowie picked up each sheet, studying her hand-drawn work. It had taken her years of night school to master the art of fine lines, arches, and framing, but she had. She sketched her ideas first before she put them into her computer. Most of her clients still loved the idea of paper; they loved holding the concept in their hands. With most of her custom jobs, she would frame the drawings and hang them on the wall for her clients, as it was their vision that helped Brooklyn. It was a small gift from her to them.

"These are amazing," Bowie said aloud.

"Thank you." His eyes shot directly to hers. She smiled, even though she hadn't meant to. She hadn't even intended to acknowledge his compliment either.

"Let's get down to business, shall we?" Carly suggested as she entered the room with a tray of iced tea and small sandwiches, reminding Brooklyn that she still had a car full of groceries.

"I'm afraid I need to unpack the car first." She got up immediately and went back to her car. From the rear of her SUV, no one could see her. She used this to her advantage, finally letting her tears flow. They were hot, angry, and full of longing. There had been a time in her life when she'd told Bowie everything. It wasn't long after they met that he had become her best guy friend. The one she could talk to about everything, including Austin. He encouraged her to go to college, to do what she wanted, but she never listened. If she had . . .

No, she refused to think about what her life would be like without Brystol. Her daughter kept her sane and focused and gave her purpose.

Being a single mother never bothered her; she never thought about what it would be like to have a partner to help or someone else to depend on. Mostly because there was no point in wishing for someone to come along. Even if she wanted, Brooklyn hadn't had time to date. Brystol was her priority. Her daughter was also at the age where it would be nice for them to have roots, a stable home. Homeschooling was great, easy, but her daughter needed friends. Maybe that's why Carly had summoned her back, to give Brystol a chance to grow up in her father's hometown surrounded by family.

"Hey, are you okay?" Brooklyn felt his hand on her back before she registered that Bowie was speaking to her. She shied away and tried to wipe her cheeks dry without him seeing. Of course, he knew something was wrong; he always could sense when she was feeling down.

"Fine." Her tone was sharp despite needing to clear her throat. She started gathering the tote bags from the grocery store, determined to carry them all so Bowie couldn't hold it over her head later.

"Are you sure?"

"Yep." She wasn't, but that wasn't the point. Brooklyn wanted Bowie as far away from her as possible, and yet he couldn't take a hint. He brushed up against her as he reached into the back of her SUV. Goose bumps sprang to life on her arms and legs, and excitement coursed through her body. How long had it been since a man made her feel this way? She knew the exact date and time when she'd had desire pooling in her belly. For as wide as the trunk of her car was, there was nowhere for her to escape.

"What are you doing?" She stopped and tried to step back, but the heavy bags kept her in place. "I can do this."

"No one is saying you can't."

"Then leave," she huffed.

Bowie stared, and under his penetrating gaze she felt two feet tall and completely admired all in one. How was that possible? They'd had a history, but their friendship had ended, just like the others she'd had.

"God, you're beautiful when you're angry."

She opened her mouth to respond.

She waited for the words to come.

Nothing.

Instead, Brooklyn took as many of the bags as she could muster and walked toward the house with Bowie hot on her heels. Simone met them at the door, smiled coyly, and reached for a tote.

"I don't know what you and Carly are up to, but it won't work."

"I have no idea what you're talking about, dear." Simone whistled her way into the kitchen as if nothing were amiss.

When all the bags were deposited safely in the kitchen, Carly beckoned them back to the table. "Now, about the inn. When do you think it could open?"

Bowie cleared his throat. "I'm thinking three to five months."

Brooklyn laughed. "What, do you plan to do the work yourself?"

He tilted his head slightly. "No, I have a full crew."

"So, with mine and yours, that gives us a team of ten, plus us is twelve. Do you think it's going to take twelve people five months to do a renovation with minimal construction? It should take six, maybe eight weeks." Even as she said this, she wasn't comfortable with the timeline, but Carly had insisted they move fast on the renovations.

He opened his mouth and closed it quickly. He reached for the drawings, perusing the designs. "We need to make sure the foundation, electrical, and the roof are up to code. Building permits must be obtained, and those take time. We have to order enough lumber to add forty accent walls of shiplap because Kenyon's Lumber won't have that much in stock. The paint, fixtures—it all takes time. I'm being realistic here, Brooklyn."

Every fiber of her wanted to argue with him, but he was right, and she had no intention of telling him so. She looked at Carly, who looked very pleased with herself, even though the night before she'd told Brooklyn that she wanted life back in the inn and had suggested that five rooms open as soon as possible. Maybe now Carly would listen to Bowie because she certainly hadn't listened to Brooklyn.

NINE

The Whale Spout was Cape Harbor's only watering hole, apart from a few restaurants that served alcohol. The front door was made up of only planks, and the wide plank floors creaked when walked on. The walls were covered with old fishing nets, a couple of lobster and crab traps, a broken oar, images of the lost fishermen from town, anchors, and really anything a local donated. The bar top happened to be an old deck from a shipwreck that supposedly dated back to the early 1900s, according to the old-timers who sat in the same corner, day after day, telling tall tales meant to entice visitors to stay. Tourists flocked here to hang out with the locals and to hear fishing stories that were so ancient no one really knew if they were true or not, and each time Bowie happened to sit in on one, the tale grew taller. Not that he cared. Those stories were part of the charm of the small coastal town, and what kept people coming back. The hospitality, the sights, and the amazing sunsets made his hometown a favorite place for people to visit.

The Chamberlains owned the bar, and had for as long as anyone could remember. It had been passed down from previous generations, and it only made sense that Graham would run it when he returned from California after Austin's funeral. What he and his parents hadn't counted on was Grady becoming the town drunk.

Bowie walked toward the end of the bar and took the last stool available, resting his arms on top of the bar and slouching down, clearly defeated. He was so lost in his head that he hadn't even bothered to look at the other patrons to see if any of his friends were there. Truth was, he wanted to drink. He wanted to celebrate the fact that his divorce would be final . . . a thought that gave him pause. He'd gotten so caught up in the inn he had forgotten to stop by the office and ask Marcia to file the divorce papers. Tomorrow, he told himself. First thing in the morning he'd drive over and file them. And while he wanted to rejoice, he also wanted to get so shit-faced drunk that the day would be nothing but a blur. He wanted to drown his sorrows and memories, erase everything from his mind. At this point, he'd really like to forget about the last twenty years of his life or so—go back to the moment when he met Brooklyn Hewett and look the other way.

"Surprised to see you here, Holmes. We have a dart competition going—want to join?" Deep in his funk, he hadn't turned around to acknowledge the voice he recognized as one of his employees, knowing that it was Chris Johnson standing behind him with his hand on Bowie's shoulder. Chris was the newest member of the work crew and would have been the first one Bowie laid off if he hadn't taken the reno job at the inn. He felt stupid for even having considered passing up the work. At first, it was his feelings for being an inadequate friend to the Woodses, but then Carly went and dropped a bomb—not just any bomb, but the bomb of all bombs that would undoubtedly destroy Bowie . . . *Brooklyn.*

"Uh, not tonight, but thanks," Bowie mumbled to Chris. Chances were, he couldn't hear what his boss had said over the loud music and voices that filled the bar. Nonetheless, Chris stepped away, leaving Bowie to wallow in his self-pity. He was going to hell. In a handbasket or whatever the saying was. It honestly didn't matter because Bowie had a one-way ticket, and there wasn't anything that could be done to stop him.

As if by magic, a pint appeared in front of Bowie. He glanced up and saw his good friend Graham behind the bar, tending to another patron. Bowie sipped the cold beer slowly. As much as he wanted to drink until he passed out, he also wanted to keep his wits intact. Any minute, he expected Brooklyn to walk in and continue ruining his night. After she'd questioned him in front of Carly, he'd felt emasculated, worse than Rachel ever made him feel. He couldn't deny that she knew her stuff, but to be showed up in front of others—that was a hard pill to swallow.

He had so many questions; mostly he wanted to know what was going on and why Brooklyn was back. Was she purely there to do the renovation and go back to wherever she came from? Or did Carly know something? Had she suspected all those years when she'd helped nurture Austin's friends that he'd felt something for Brooklyn? No, he was sure there was no way Carly knew anything then, nor was she playing matchmaker now. Aside from him and Brooklyn, the only people who knew were Graham and Rachel. Actually, Rachel had found out by accident. That particular year, Bowie was struggling. He was missing his friend and told Rachel everything and then said he never wanted to speak about it again. A weight had been lifted off his shoulders, but it was short lived. Once the anniversary of Austin's death rolled around, Bowie was back on edge, wondering if Brooklyn was going to storm into town, wrecking him. And she finally had.

Graham placed another beer in front of Bowie. He looked up and tried to smile. Graham set his hands on the edge of the bar and bent over until he was eye level with him. "Want to tell me what's going on?" Graham asked. The man was a vault and would never share the stories people told him while sitting at his bar. Plus, since they had grown up together, there wasn't much they didn't know about each other.

Bowie shook his head slowly and picked up the next pint to take a drink, finishing it off without a pause and setting the glass down with a thud. It was going to be a long night, and he suspected Graham would supply him with plenty of booze to get him talking.

"I haven't seen you like this in years. Not even when Rachel asked for a divorce. Is Luke okay?"

Luke? He turned cold at the mention of his dog's name. Where was he? Bowie tried to recollect whether he drove him home or left him in the truck. There was no way he'd leave his faithful companion in the cab while he sat in the bar. He had never been that careless before and if Brooklyn's return meant he was . . . well, that was unacceptable. Luke was his best friend, and he would never do anything to hurt him.

Bowie got up from the bar and went outside. There was a chill in the air, and he shivered, crossing his arms for comfort. He jogged down the block until he came to his truck. The cab was empty. His head rested against the window as he cursed before pushing himself away from his truck. He *knew* Luke was at home. He had dropped him off after he left Carly's. After he'd fed Luke, they'd gone for a long walk along the beach, a place where Bowie always found a bit of calm amid the madness that was in his life. It hadn't worked tonight, which was how he had ended up at the bar.

He was losing his mind, and for what? A woman? A former friend who had walked out on the people who loved and cared about her the most? Not worth it. "She's not worth it," he mumbled into the night sky.

"Who isn't?"

Bowie jerked in shock and found Monroe Whitfield standing in front of him. She smiled softly and pushed her hands deeper into the pockets of her jacket. Along with the Chamberlain twins, she had grown up with Bowie. While Monroe was beautiful, he wasn't attracted to her. Sometimes, he wished he was, though, because his mother loved her. He did as well, but only as a friend. He looked around and realized he was back at the bar. Was he really that deep in thought that he was losing time, or was he drunker than he realized? Either that or Graham was spiking his beer.

"Hey, Roe. You snuck up on me."

"Really?" She tilted her head and smiled. "Pretty sure if I hadn't said something, you would've plowed me over."

Bowie ran his hand over the back of his head and sighed. "Sorry. I'm in a fog."

"Rachel?" she asked.

He shook his head slowly and motioned toward the door. "You going in?"

"Yeah, do you know if Grady's in there?"

Bowie wasn't sure what Roe saw in him other than a charity case. Everyone in town knew Monroe tried to help Grady. Late at night, she would be seen driving around, looking for him, trying to get him to go home. The accident that had taken Austin also had taken Grady, but in a different way. Everyone had been affected, lost someone they loved, but Grady had taken the death of Austin the worst.

Again, Bowie shook his head. "Sorry," he said, pointing to his head. "Foggy." Bowie held the door open for Monroe and followed behind her. Graham yelled her name, and she waved. Monroe chose to sit at a table, likely expecting her sister to join her later. Bowie was torn. Go back to sit at the bar or go converse with one of his oldest friends. Graham made the decision for him when he sat two beers down on the table along with a bowl of popcorn and two menus. The Whale Spout served some of the best finger foods this side of the Sound.

Bowie sat and studied the menu even though he knew what was offered. All around, others filled the silence with clapping, hollering, and cheering when someone hit a bull's-eye or sank the eight ball in the designated pocket.

"You're not playing?" Monroe motioned toward the dartboards.

"I'm not really feeling myself tonight." He tossed the menu down on the table and picked up his pint, chugging half of it. "I thought I left Luke in my truck. So stupid," he said after wiping his mouth with the back of his hand.

"Did you hit your head or something?"

"No . . . I don't know."

Monroe leaned forward and rested her hand on top of his. He regarded her, wondering what she was thinking. "Brooklyn Hewett is back in town, Bo. I saw her at the grocery store today. Our encounter was weird—it was like she was hiding or something. She wore dark glasses and a hat. I don't know. She didn't act like she was happy to see me, though. I wonder what she's doing here."

That makes two of us.

Bowie sighed. "She's renovating the inn."

"What? Why?"

"The inn is going to reopen."

"No, I figured that much." Monroe waved him off. "I heard some rumblings around town earlier today. But why her?"

Bowie pulled out his phone. He tapped the screen a few times and finally slid it over to Monroe. After he'd left Carly's, he'd done what he'd always vowed he would never do—he'd searched for Brooklyn on the internet. He only had to type her name and the first letter of her last name before her website and hundreds of links and images popped up. She wasn't just someone who painted interiors but one of the most sought-after decorators and renovators in the country. Her client list was a who's who of celebrities. Anyone from actors to singers to professional athletes. Not to mention clients who paid top dollar to have Brooklyn redo a room in their house. Brooklyn had made a name for herself. That's why she was here. Carly wanted the best, and the best just happened to be her son's former girlfriend.

Bowie cut the lights of his truck as he pulled into the driveway where Brooklyn lived. Her downstairs neighbor found a reason to complain about everything, so he was doing his part to keep things civil. He was half hoping

Brooklyn would be waiting for him so they could be on their way. When she wasn't, he let out a sigh of relief and leaned his head against the back window and closed his eyes. He had a few seconds to gather his thoughts before he was going to spend all day with the woman of his dreams, working alongside of her, in close capacity, with paint fumes overriding his senses. If he were to make a move or say something about his undying affection, he couldn't be held responsible—at least that's what his subconscious told him as he pictured Brooklyn in the paint-splattered coveralls his father was insistent that she wear. They were far from sexy, but it was Brooklyn, and she could wear a burlap bag and be the most beautiful woman ever. For as long as he'd known her, he'd never thought of her as anything but gorgeous. Thinking of her like that was dangerous. She was his best friend's girl and had been since the day he met her.

Of course, he wasn't foolish enough to think that Austin wouldn't show up later or that Brooklyn wouldn't take far too many breaks to talk to her boyfriend. It was the weekend, after all, and Austin and Brooklyn normally spent it together. Bowie also wasn't foolish enough to think that Brooklyn asking for a ride was anything more than her not wanting to drive herself. Still, he'd had the presence of mind to stop at the café to pick up two extra-large coffees and Peggy's freshly made cinnamon rolls, which made his truck smell more like a bakery than a stinky work truck.

The motion-sensor light flicked on, startling Bowie. He rubbed the sleep from his eyes, looked at his dashboard to see the time, and barely caught a glimpse of Brooklyn as she passed by the front of his truck. The dome light came on when she opened the door, and she smiled at him. "Morning," she mumbled. Clearly her smile was not an indication of how alert she was. He couldn't blame her. His father wanted them on the jobsite by six a.m. to get the rooms painted and the trim work up. They were behind schedule, which was the reason they were working on Sunday.

"Here, I thought you would need this." Bowie handed her the foam cup, which she immediately brought to her nose and inhaled.

"Thank you. I smell cinnamon as well."

He turned his head away from her and smiled. Bowie had scored big-time bonus points with her by buying those rolls. "Peggy had just pulled them out of the oven when I arrived."

"Mm-hmm," she hummed as she took a sip of her coffee.

"Are you sure you want to do this?" He hated asking her because he absolutely wanted to spend the day with her, but she didn't need to work the weekends. As the secretary to Seacoast Construction, her job was Monday through Friday. She was in charge of booking jobs, making sure the bills were paid, writing paychecks, and helping the company with their branding. Painting houses was not a job requirement.

Brooklyn nodded. "I need the extra money."

"For what?" He shouldn't pry, but he wanted to know.

"I'm trying to save for nursing school."

"Does Austin know?" It had been years since he'd heard her talk about nursing; he thought she had given up on her dream of becoming a nurse because she rarely mentioned it. He tried to recall the last time she brought it up, and it must've been shortly before they graduated high school, when everyone talked about going off to college.

She dropped her head and sighed. Bowie left it at that and pulled out of the driveway. On the way to the jobsite, he kept the radio on and only turned it up when the weather report came on, knowing full well it would grab Brooklyn's attention. Everyone in town watched the weather, but it was the fishermen's wives and significant others who were really in tune with it. Most of them could tell by the clouds or the quick shift in air pressure what the day was going to be like. He left his question alone, not prodding her for an answer. He knew his friend well enough to know he was never leaving Cape Harbor. The only problem was, Brooklyn had yet to realize it.

Bowie pulled up to the jobsite and shut his truck off. He opened his mouth to say something, but Brooklyn had already slipped outside, leaving him no choice but to follow. He unlocked the door to the house and turned on as many work lights as he could. Inside, he handed Brooklyn the gray coveralls. "They're not fashionable, but they'll save your clothes from paint splatter." She thanked him and stepped inside the work clothes. He never minded wearing them but loathed seeing them cover her perfectly toned body. He would much rather work alongside of her in her shorts and tank top. After she was fully covered in the most hideous outfit known to man, Brooklyn began to braid her long dark hair. An act that turned Bowie on. He swallowed hard and fiddled with some tool in order to distract himself from staring. Only, he couldn't keep his eyes off her for long. They were alone, and it was getting harder and harder for him to keep denying his feelings for her.

"Do you want to eat or get started?"

"We can start," she said.

Perfect, *he thought. Bowie loaded the navy-colored paint into the cup, secured the nozzle, and handed it to Brooklyn.*

"What am I supposed to do with this?"

He chuckled. "You're going to paint the wall. It'll be simple. I'll show you." It was like he had a light bulb moment. Over the years, he'd always looked for excuses to touch her, to caress her skin, to press his thigh to hers—all harmless flirting was what he told himself when it was pure torture for him. He didn't need an excuse now. It was his professional duty to show her how to operate the paint gun.

Bowie directed her to the largest wall and with his hands on her hips, which was completely unnecessary, he stood behind her. His heart thumped loudly, and he feared she would feel it tapping against her back when he leaned in. She tilted her head toward him and, if he wasn't mistaken, stepped back so they were pressed tightly together.

No, he definitely wasn't mistaken. There wasn't space between their bodies, and he was going to relish the moment as long as possible.

"Why didn't you go to college and become an architect?"

Her words hit a sore spot deep within his chest. That had been his dream, to design skyscrapers in cities, but he couldn't leave Brooklyn behind. He was in love with her, and as long as she stayed in Cape Harbor, he would too. He knew his feelings would come back to bite him someday, that he would regret giving up his dream because of a woman who belonged to another man, but to him, it was worth it. He'd rather live on the sidelines in her life than not see her every day.

"Dad needed help." The lie fell easily, although it was partly true. His father could always use the help, but Bowie stayed because of Brooklyn. He'd tell her . . . someday. "Why didn't you go to college?" he countered. "I remember your first day of school, you sat at the table and told everyone you're going to be a nurse."

She shrugged and turned slightly to look at him. "I fell in love." Her voice was barely above a whisper. He wanted to ask her if she felt the same way about him as he did her but couldn't bear the rejection.

So many things could've been said in that moment, but words failed him. He studied her hard, looking for any sign that she was referring to him but hadn't a clue what to look for. He could've easily leaned in and pressed his lips to hers, but he held back, not willing to tempt fate. Sure, he had dated over the years, but not a single woman held a candle to Brooklyn. Bowie was going to have to shit or get off the pot where she was concerned because he dreaded his future. He didn't know if he could stand up next to Austin as Brooklyn walked down the aisle. Unfortunately, he would have no choice.

"We should start." Bowie motioned toward the wall. He placed his hand on top of hers and pushed her finger against the trigger. "Slow and steady wins the race," he told her as they moved the spray gun back and forth. Brooklyn was a natural and picked up the task easily, leaving him no choice but to start working on the trim. Even though they were on a deadline to finish the house, he spent his day watching her and making excuses to be next to her. To him, she was his sun, and he was going to bask in her warmth until he had to return her to his best friend.

Bowie shook his head. He would have to call and thank his father for hiring Brooklyn after they finished high school. In a way, it was all his fault. If he hadn't offered her overtime on the weekends, she would've never learned how to paint, which she managed to make a very successful career from. Yep, Brooklyn's return was his father's fault.

After Monroe had scrolled through, clicking links and gasping at some of the images, she finally sat back with a stunned look on her face. "It seems that Brooklyn has made quite a name for herself," Bowie said as he locked the screen on his phone and slipped it back into his pocket.

"She probably brought a television crew with her. She's going to turn Cape Harbor into a spectacle."

"Not that I saw."

Monroe's eyes went wide. "You saw her? Where? Why didn't you tell me?"

Bowie wanted to chuckle, but it was hard finding the silver lining in the situation, at least for him. "I saw her at the inn."

"What were you doing there?"

He leaned back and tried to smile. "Speaking with Carly. She's hired me to do the construction."

"Shut the front door." Her hand clamped down on his wrist. "Bowie, this is amazing. It's just what you need to expand your business, and after Rachel . . . well, you could use the distraction."

It was something, but not the distraction he was looking for, and he wasn't sure *amazing* was the word he would use. For his crew, this was a good thing. For his mental health, probably not. As far as anyone knew, the only animosity he held against Brooklyn was due to the fact that she had ditched out on everyone after the funeral. No one knew that she had broken his heart and ruined their friendship at the same time.

He wasn't exactly thrilled to work with Brooklyn, despite her impressive résumé. He should be honored—at least that's what all the other contractors said in their blurbs on her website. Everyone she worked with loved her, which meant his job should be easy, yet he felt like he was about to go into a gun battle with a knife—a butter knife at that. Knowing he would have to see her and hear her voice every day for months left him feeling like what little hold he had on his life was slipping through his fingers. He wasn't emotionally strong enough to deal with all of that . . . *with her.*

As the night wore on, more and more of his friends meandered into the bar. The table he and Monroe sat at now overflowed with people laughing and telling jokes. The mood was light, regardless of how Bowie was feeling.

Toward the end of the night, Graham finally joined them. He brought another round of beers, and everyone clanked their glasses together. "Jason called earlier. He'll be here for Austin's celebration," he said, causing the table to go silent.

"And Brooklyn's back. It's like the whole gang is back together for the anniversary," Roe added solemnly. Graham's and Bowie's eyes met across the table. They shared a look. Bowie sensed that Graham knew why he was in such a funk tonight.

"Fifteen years," someone said with a sigh. The mood quickly turned somber. No one spoke. No one drank. Bowie was too focused on the cheery tabletop to look for the owner of the voice. But whoever said it was right. This year was a milestone. Every five years the celebration would get bigger. Until when? Bowie wanted to know when they'd stop mourning their friend and start living again, because he felt like he was going through the motions, day in and day out. Everything had changed for them that night fifteen years ago. Dreams and flourishing careers had been put on hold, relationships ended, and people left.

"Hey, did anyone see Brooklyn Hewett? Man, time has been very good to her. She's hotter now than she was in high school. What I wouldn't give to hook up with her."

Bowie scanned for the person speaking. Once he spotted him, he tried to recall his name but couldn't. The guy was a year or two younger than Bowie and not someone who ran with his crowd. Still, the words pissed him off. The last thing he wanted was to hear people go on and on about Brooklyn, particularly in that manner. Especially when everyone was coming home to honor Austin.

TEN

Brooklyn sat with her toes in the sand and a blanket wrapped around her shoulders. The tide was still out, and she could barely hear the waves crashing against the shore. Seagulls chirped overhead, squawking louder when they found a morsel of food or an enemy came too close. She loved everything about the ocean, minus the gulls. When she was twelve or thirteen, she had been down on the docks in Seattle, and not one, but a whole group of birds had flown above and done their business at the same time, each plop landing on her head, shoulders, and arms. *Mortified* hadn't even begun to explain how she had felt. She had cried for days and sworn to always wear a hat when she was near the water from that day forward.

The memory had her touching the brim of her cap. Yesterday, when she had run into Bowie, she had thought for sure he would say something about it, comment on how it used to be Austin's. But he hadn't. Maybe he hadn't noticed because he'd been far too busy throwing daggers at her, trying to emotionally maim her in the driveway for even stepping foot in Cape Harbor again, and sending her into an emotional whiplash. She didn't blame him. She couldn't. Things between them could've been different if she had called, written a letter, or even told him she was leaving, or stayed. She hadn't. She had chosen to run. She had chosen to deal with her actions privately because she had known any relationship she and Bowie had had was over, and seeing him every day would've destroyed her even more. Knowing he was there, within arm's reach, would've been torture. The relationship they had known, the one that had been cemented in her life from the time she had arrived, was over. Leaving had been her only option.

Boats began to leave port, setting out for the day. Even in the early dawn, she could see the crew waving as they motored by the inn. In her heart, she knew who it was. She didn't wave back, knowing they weren't acknowledging her but the woman who lived in the home behind her. They were paying respect in their own way—a way that didn't make sense to Brooklyn. What Carly needed was people to surround her, to help her. And yet, she only had Simone, and Brystol when she was here. She wanted to shake each one of Austin's friends, including those fishermen who likely never even knew him, and ask how they could forget about his mother. *Their* mother. The woman who had taken every one of them in without question or reservation. She had opened her door, her life, and her heart to them, and they all had ditched out on her. Brooklyn wasn't much better, but at least she had given her Brystol.

There were a few joggers running up and down the coastline, and by the middle of summer, there would be more. She and Simone were going to sit down today, once painting started, and figure out a marketing strategy. They planned to reach out to the former guests, inquire if they were interested in a return stay, and offer them a discount for a future booking. As much as Carly wanted to rush the project, Brooklyn was going to follow Bowie's timeline, even though with their combined crews they could easily open five rooms at a time. Waiting made more sense. It gave her more time to make sure everything was perfect. The only thing that had bothered her after the meeting with Bowie was how long it would take him to get supplies. One call and she had a delivery scheduled to arrive this morning.

She would plan a grand reopening party, a gala of sorts. Something that would encourage Carly to don a beautiful gown, get her hair done,

and show her granddaughter what the inn used to be like. Even thinking about organizing an event like this put a smile on Brooklyn's face.
She had spent countless nights dancing in the ballroom, with the moon
shining through the window, and she wanted to do it again.

She hadn't been back in town more than twenty-four hours, and
she already wanted Brystol to experience everything she had growing
up here, the majesty that seemed to surround the inn when people
from all over filled the rooms. The sunsets, bonfires on the beaches,
the close friendships she'd made in the short time she lived here. These
were important parts of life that she was denying her daughter. Brystol
needed to make lasting memories that didn't revolve around her mother's job. Mostly, though, Brooklyn wanted Brystol to be happy. Carly
as well.

The sun rose, beating down on Brooklyn's back. She closed her eyes
and basked in its warmth. She hoped for a warm day with a breeze.
She intended to open windows so she could hear the ocean while she
worked and smell the sea's salt air as it wafted through the inn. She
wanted to hang wind chimes because it reminded her how life used to
be here. Of all the jobs she had done in the past, she preferred the ones
on the coast. The ocean was her place; it was where she belonged. To
her, working inland was boring, and there wasn't an escape. Sure, some
towns had amazing vibes, great festivals, and beautiful parks, but there
wasn't anything like a pier where you would run into a sea lion waiting
for his fisherman friends to return with a snack, or sitting on a dock
with your feet in the water, watching as the sailboats came in and out
of port. Life was always different by the water. It was hard to explain
to people who hadn't lived along the coast. It was a feeling, a sense of
being, and Brooklyn missed it . . . she missed belonging somewhere.

It had taken Brooklyn a few years until she was ready to face the
water. For the longest time, she wouldn't go in, afraid she'd swim out
too far in her quest to find Austin. As far as she knew, his body was
still out there. And if it wasn't, Carly hadn't said anything. Nor had

Brooklyn asked. The story of what had happened that fateful day only needed telling once by Grady. No one would ever forget his story.

Brooklyn looked up and down the beach. Not a long way from where she was sitting was a bonfire pit. Back in Seattle, her friends hadn't really done this. They were into shopping, sailing, and spending time on yachts. But here, this was what she and her friends had done on the weekends.

"Daddy, may I go to a bonfire this evening?"

"With who? You just started school."

Brooklyn swallowed. "Austin Woods. He's a local boy, a fisherman, and in my class. He invited me. There's a group going, so it's not just the two of us." She purposely left out the part about Austin being the resident heart-throb, the cutest boy she had ever laid her eyes on, and how when he smiled, her heart raced so fast she swore she was having a heart attack.

"His parents own the inn that we stayed in, David. The one right on the water. The view from our room is what sold me on living here," Brooklyn's mother, Bonnie, chimed in. "What time will you be home?"

Brooklyn perked up. "Oh, I don't know. Um . . ."

"Midnight and not a second later," David bellowed. He tried to act gruff, but Brooklyn saw through the act. She smiled and kissed her father on the cheek.

"Thank you, Daddy."

From her house, Brooklyn walked two blocks until she came to the large seawall. She all but galloped down the wooden steps, slipping her shoes off as soon as she touched the sand, and walked hurriedly toward the inn. You could see it from anywhere in town—it was the tallest structure and set partially on a cliff.

The closer Brooklyn came, the louder she could hear everyone. They were laughing, and their giggles were contagious. She stood there, watching the group of friends. They seemed in tune with each other, much like she had been with Rennie, who she couldn't wait to tell about Austin.

"Brooke, you made it!" Monroe stood and rushed over to her, then slipped her arm in hers.

She didn't bother correcting her on the shortened version of her name. Usually she would have, but that was before she had moved. Here, she wanted to be a different person.

Monroe brought her into the circle and introduced her to a few new faces, but her eyes were set on Austin, who was walking toward the group with his arms full of wood. As much as she wanted to go help him, she knew showing her cards too soon would not bode well for her. She waited for him to see her, and when he did, he winked.

Brooklyn had no idea a wink could do so much to her insides, but they were spinning. She was having heart palpitations, her palms were sweating—which meant sand was sticking to her—and her mouth was parched. In all her life, she had never felt this way.

As soon as the sun set, the ambience shifted. Boys and girls coupled together, sharing blankets, and some even wandered off toward the surf or the shacks. Brooklyn felt out of place, even though Monroe was still sitting next to her, but she was canoodling with Grady Chamberlain.

Still, Brooklyn sat there, watching the blue and red flames of the fire dance around, determined to have a good time. Her head bobbed to the music, she laughed at jokes she heard, and she smiled when people asked her questions. It wasn't until she shivered and a blanket was draped over her shoulders that her night turned around. Austin sat next to her, his shoulder touching hers, and while sharing the same blanket, she realized she had been faking having a good time . . . her good time started as soon as she stared into Austin's brown eyes.

Brooklyn wiped at the tears that had started to fall. It had been years since she thought about Austin and that first bonfire. That night, she'd thought for sure he would kiss her, especially when he walked her home, but he hadn't. The kiss came the next day, and it was explosive. It was a game changer for her. They had almost gone all the way, but Austin had stopped them, saying their first time needed to be special, not in his truck or on the beach where people could see them.

Unfortunately, their first time was anything but special. Not because Austin hadn't put in every effort but because she had cried, which made Austin think she regretted losing her virginity. She hadn't felt that way at all. She was just in pain. The days following were awkward for them. Brooklyn thought for sure they were going to break up, that she had given away her virginity too soon, but Austin was giving her space. It turned out that they both needed time to sort out their feelings after what they had done, and once they did, they became inseparable.

The sound of someone trudging through the sand brought Brooklyn's attention back to reality. She turned and saw her daughter coming toward her with two mugs in her hand. The smile that broke out over her face was automatic. Brystol sat down next to her and handed her a piping hot cup of coffee.

"How did you know I was out here?" she asked, inhaling the sweet aroma.

"Nonnie told me." Brystol motioned toward the inn. Brooklyn turned and saw Carly standing in the window of the ballroom, likely looking out over the sea.

"You know I was just a year older than you are when I moved here."

"I like it here. I like being on the beach."

"How much of it have you seen? Because I'm under the impression that Nonnie doesn't leave the house."

Brystol shrugged. "Simone and I go out a lot, but Nonnie . . .. sometimes she's really bad, Mom. Like, she cries or is sick with a cold. Simone and I do a lot of things like go bowling or to the movies. She takes me digging for clams and out crabbing. And sometimes Nonnie comes with us if we go to Seattle or Port Orchard."

"Why didn't you tell me?"

Brystol sipped from her mug. "Nonnie said telling you would make you worry, that your job was stressful."

Brooklyn wanted to chide her daughter for keeping secrets, but she couldn't. She could've asked better questions; she could've showed Brystol that she cared about what happened here. Moreover, she could've been a better friend to Carly.

"Is Nonnie sick a lot?" Brooklyn hated pumping her daughter for answers, but until she could get Simone alone, this was the only way to find out what was really going on here.

"Simi tells me not to worry, that Nonnie will be fine, but last summer I got really scared when I found Nonnie in the bathroom. She had blood around her lips."

Brooklyn pulled Brystol under the blanket and held her. The lifestyle Brooklyn had chosen wasn't conducive to raising a child, but she made it work. However, Brooklyn knew that having friends was something Brystol was missing, even though her daughter never complained. When Brooklyn wasn't working, they explored the cities and towns they were staying in, visiting museums, libraries, parks, and whatever else they could find to satisfy the homeschool requirements. Brystol spent a lot of time on jobsites, helping the crew do their math calculations, which helped her master geometry. They were best friends, but she knew her daughter needed more.

"I'm thinking of taking some time off or at least booking jobs that are local after the inn is finished."

"Where?"

"Here or maybe Seattle," she said, smiling at her daughter. Staying in Washington would give Brystol full access to her grandparents and would afford Brooklyn peace of mind if she had to travel or work late. "You'd have to enroll in school."

Brystol's eyes went wide with excitement. "I could go to homecoming and prom. I've always wanted to get all dressed up. I see the pictures of you and Dad all over Nonnie's bedroom and wish I could be a princess for one night."

An ache shot through Brooklyn's heart. She tried to wish it away, but it lingered. Carly kept photos of her and Austin, still to this day. Somewhere in a recess of her parents' basement, there was a tote full of mementos. The last thing she remembered putting in there was Austin's obituary. That was all that was left of their life together, aside from Brystol.

"It would be funny if I went to the same school as you and Dad."

Brooklyn wanted to laugh and cry at the same time. Nothing about it would be funny at all, but she understood why her daughter wanted to go there.

"You think so?"

"Yeah, it would. I bet there are teachers there that you and Dad had. They probably know all your secrets." Brystol bumped her shoulder into her mom's and winked.

Brooklyn blushed. The last thing she wanted was for her daughter to hear stories of how teachers had caught her and Austin in one too many compromising situations.

"Who was the better student?" Brystol asked, saving her mother from any potential humiliation.

"Your dad was a good student, but I was better. Your dad's focus was on fishing. He just wanted to be out on the boat or in the middle of the stream fly-fishing. He came to school every day, though, but soon as the bell rang, it was time to go. I remember when the sun would shine, he'd beg me to skip school so we could go out on his boat or go hiking. We never did, though. Your grandparents would've been so mad."

Brystol stood, reached for her mother's hand, and helped pull her to her feet. Together, they walked a few feet toward the water. Brooklyn shivered as a wave washed over her bare feet but didn't care once she saw her daughter bend to pick up a shell. Within seconds, Brystol's hand had a sandy pile stacked up.

"Nonnie will love these," she said.

"She does love her shells," Brooklyn added as she searched for her own.

"Where did Dad take you on dates?"

Brooklyn sighed. "Cape Harbor is small, but we made the most of it. Louie's pizza parlor is downtown—most of the time we went there. Sometimes, when our parents would allow it, we'd drive to Anacortes, or we'd go to Skagit Valley. One spring we went to the tulip festival with Nonnie—it was so beautiful—and before Grandpa Skip passed away, we sailed out to the islands. Nonnie and I ran in the lavender fields while your dad and grandpa fished."

"Yeah, but what would you do? Did Dad, like, buy you flowers?"

A crouched-down Brooklyn smiled. She pulled a dead starfish from the sand and brushed it off before standing upright and handing it to Brystol. "He did. And he paid for dinner, the movies, all the normal stuff. I paid too because it's important to be equal. We hung out with our friends. Bowie, Jason, Graham and Grady, Monroe and sometimes her sister Mila, and your aunt Rennie. When we were older than you are now, we'd go bowling, to the movies, or we'd just go hang out at the river and jump off rocks. A lot of the time we would hang out on the beach out in front of Nonnie's."

They continued to walk down the beach, scouring for shells. When their pockets were full, and they finally noticed their surroundings, they had wandered quite a way from the inn.

"Hey, Mom."

"What's up?" Brooklyn asked.

Brystol pointed toward the house they were in front of. "It doesn't look like it has beach access, but it's for sale."

Brooklyn stared at the house they were standing in front of. The seawall seemed to limit the owner's access to the beach, which wasn't a big issue, but could be when it came time to sell it. That thought gave her pause. Was she really considering buying a house to flip it? She was, and she loved the idea. From what she could see, it needed work, but nothing she couldn't tackle—of course, the inside could be a different story. "Is this some kind of hint?"

Her daughter giggled.

"We have a few months before school starts; we'll figure it out together."

"Do you know what I find funny about you and Dad?"

"Nope, tell me."

"That he fished all the time, and you worked for the fish market. Fish really smells, so you guys must've been . . ." Brystol pinched her nose and waved her hand in front of her face.

Brooklyn laughed. "Grandma hated that I worked there, but it was fun. If we stay, maybe you should get a job down there."

"Nope." She shook her head. "I'll work for you or Nonnie. I think it would be fun to work at the inn."

"Yeah, I'm pretty sure it would be, and Nonnie would love having you there. Come on." She motioned toward the direction they needed to head. "Work waits."

"Or we play hooky?"

Brooklyn leaned down and kissed her daughter on her forehead. Playing hooky sounded amazing. The idea of spending the rest of the day on the beach with her daughter was more enticing than painting. Normally, she loved work. It kept her mind busy, and that was something she needed to do right now.

"Let me get this project started, and then we'll take a day to explore the area."

"Deal!"

They trudged through the sand and found Carly waiting for them on the deck. Brystol ran up the stairs that led to the shared backyard of the main house and inn. By the time Brooklyn reached her daughter and Carly, they had the shells spread out on the picnic table.

"You ladies were busy this morning," Carly commented on the collection.

"I believe you're the one who told me that morning is the best time to gather shells." Brooklyn brushed her hand over Brystol's long dark hair. "Why don't you run in and take a shower. I need to get to work, but I need an hour of reading from you before you start bugging Simone, okay? And don't forget your book report."

"Okay, Mom." Brystol kissed her grandmother and disappeared into the house while both women watched her.

"She's happy here."

"She loves you, Carly. Of course, she's happy."

"Can you do me a favor?"

Brooklyn glanced at Carly and smiled. "You know I'd do anything for you."

Carly stared at her with a guarded look. "Stay."

"What do you mean?" Deep down she knew what Carly wanted, but something inside told her she needed to hear the words.

"Make a life here. Give Brystol a home. Let her grow up with her father's friends. With me."

She sat across from Carly and prepared to ask her a barrage of questions. "Why don't they know her? Why haven't they come around? Why haven't you left this house?" She hadn't meant to ask so many at once, but they just wouldn't stop coming.

"Losing Skip was hard, but Austin's death crippled me. If it weren't for Brystol . . ." She paused, and Brooklyn knew what she was going to say. "Simone tried to bring life back to me, but to face everyone, to see the look of pity and sorrow on their faces—I wasn't ready."

"But you are now?"

Her mouth curved into a smile. "You're here. My granddaughter is here. You both give me purpose."

Brooklyn reached across the table and held Carly's hand. "I'll think about it. Truth is, I have so many thoughts about moving back here, mostly for Brystol. She seems to think it'd be funny to go to school where Austin and I had." Carly's brow shot up, causing Brooklyn to laugh. She had been on the receiving end of one too many calls about Brooklyn's and Austin's schoolyard antics.

"Brystol needs roots."

"It would be nice to come home to a home. The thoughts are there, Carly. I promise you."

Brooklyn left Carly sitting at the table. She went into the house, to her room, and changed into her work clothes. As soon as she heard the backing-up beeps from the delivery truck, she ran down the stairs and out to the front. She saw Bowie's crew, but not him, and a few of the guys sent up from Seattle by a friend of hers. "Where the hell is he?" she mumbled as she walked out the door and prepared to start her day.

ELEVEN

Bowie woke to Luke licking his face. He tried to push his dog away, but to no avail. His head hurt, pounding like a jackhammer was right next to him. He groaned aloud, earning another round of wet, slobbery kisses from his best friend. He had drunk too much, laughed too hard, and mourned a lost friend right along with his lifelong friends. They had stayed at the Whale Spout long past closing, talking about nothing yet seemingly everything. The elephant in the room was Brooklyn's return. Her close friends were pissed, at least those who used to be close to her. Monroe seemed to be the only one who understood why Brooklyn had left, while others did not, and a few kept going on about how well she had aged and how they would like to take her out. Those comments had pissed Bowie off, and the only way to shut out the voices had been to drink more.

He reached for his phone, thinking it was past the time Luke normally ate. When his clouded eyes finally registered the numbers, he sat up too quickly and felt sick. He barely made it to the bathroom before the appetizers he and Monroe shared the night before, and the copious amounts of beer he drank, came back full force and without pause. Once his stomach was empty, his throat parched, and his ribs aching, he lay there on the cold tile floor, contemplating life. He hadn't been this hungover in years . . . not since Austin died and he found out that

Brooklyn had left. For weeks after, he had drunk himself into a stupor to numb the pain from the realization that in a matter of days, he had lost both of his best friends.

His phone rang. The shrill tone made his ears bleed. By the time he made it back to his bedroom, the ringing had stopped, only to start again. He pressed the accept button and brought the offending electronic to his ear. "Hello?" His voice was raspy, and not in the sexy sort of way. It hurt to speak, think, and move. The only thing Bowie was planning to do today was sleep.

"Boss, you're late. This chick is screaming her head off about some demo that needs to be done, and me and the guys are waiting for ya."

Bowie let the words sink in as reality slapped him in the face. Brooklyn was back to do a job, nothing more. She hadn't come back to make amends or make up for lost time. She was here to work. "Fuck," he grumbled. If Bowie wanted the job at the inn, he had to get his sorry ass out of bed and get moving. There wasn't a doubt in his mind that Brooklyn would pull the plug on his company where this project was concerned. "I'm on my way."

It took Bowie twenty minutes to dress, feed Luke, and toss a few aspirin down his throat. He needed more sleep, gallons of coffee, and for the ringing in his head to stop. He wasn't prepared to deal with Brooklyn, not today. He could barely function, let alone move enough to lift a hammer or think quickly. The ton of bricks pushing against his temple reminded him that he was old—much too old to get drunk.

For a moment, he wished Luke were human so he could drive him over to the inn and maybe do his job or make important decisions for him. Or at least a pack mule so he could carry things for him. Luke was neither. What he was, was eager and proudly sitting next to Bowie as they made their way through town.

Cars lined the road leading to the inn, more than Bowie expected to be there. He tried to recall his meeting yesterday, wondering if he had missed something important, like a change in plans. He was sure he hadn't. He tried to pull into the driveway, but a bulldozer dumping old concrete into a dumpster blocked him. He would have to walk, which wasn't a problem for him but was for Luke. He didn't want his dog to get hurt. There was no way Luke would stay in the truck, leaving him no option but to put him on a leash.

At the front of the inn, his crew lingered in the driveway—or what used to be the driveway. There were piles of lumber, drywall, and piping and spools of wire lined up along the side. He hadn't ordered any of this and instantly felt his blood start to boil. Brooklyn had overstepped, and he would have to put her in her place. Before he could even move to find her, she yelled out his name.

"Bowie, you're late. Not just a few minutes late, but hours late, and that's not acceptable."

"I'm—"

"Don't tell me you're sorry. I don't like excuses. What I do like is progress, and right now your crew is behind. We have a timeline to keep, and if I have to, I'll set a deadline. I've never missed one, and I'm not about to start because you can't get your shit together and be at work on time!" She was in his face, looking up at him. He could see how she could be menacing to someone who didn't know her so well. To some, she was probably a bitch, but her reviews said otherwise. Everyone loved working with her; however, at this point in time, all he wanted to do was pick her up and toss her into the ocean to cool her fiery temper. "And you stink. I can't believe you showed up hungover. What is wrong with you? Carly needs this. It's the least we can do for her." Her voice was quiet. He thought for a moment that she was trying to spare him some embarrassment.

"Rough night," he muttered.

She scoffed. "Get your shit together or you're fired."

"You can't fire me. Carly hired me, not you."

This made her laugh, which pissed him off even more. She didn't bother with a response. She wouldn't need to. Deep down he knew she was right. It wouldn't matter who hired him; she was Brooklyn Hewett, and she got whatever she wanted. If that meant he had to grovel to make sure he wasn't out of a job, so be it—he knew he couldn't lose this opportunity, no matter how difficult it was going to be. He watched her walk back into the house, flipping him the bird as she did, and then glanced at his crew, who were looking everywhere but directly at him. She hadn't needed to embarrass him. He was doing fine with that all on his own. He hated her more now than he had yesterday, when his life was just complicated. Now it was downright messy. There was no other way to spin it: Brooklyn was back, she was in charge, and he had to be at her beck and call . . . something he wasn't looking forward to.

After what seemed like hours, Bowie and his crew were finally tearing down walls, replacing pipes, and sanding down the dark wood that would eventually become white. Everywhere Bowie went, Brooklyn was there, either supervising or working. He watched her from afar, taking her in. She was dressed in shorts and a tank top and wore tan work boots. But it was her hat that really caught his attention. For as long as he'd known her, she'd always worn one. He didn't find this odd, but soothing, as if *his* Brooklyn—the one he remembered—had come back. After high school, her hair was shorter than it was now and braided, like it had been yesterday when he'd seen her. The darker color truly highlighted her skin tone.

"She's beautiful."

Bowie cleared his thoughts at the sound of Carly's voice. He didn't know what to say to her and whether he should agree with her. He shouldn't—that's what he told himself. After the run-in this morning, he wanted to forget she existed, which was proving to be difficult. Still, he was determined to finish the job and walk away just like she had.

"I've asked her to stay."

"Why?" He hadn't meant for the question to sound rude, but it had.

"She needs to put down roots, and this is her home." Carly was nonchalant about her statement. She left Bowie there to wonder if Brooklyn had given her an answer or not. He didn't want her to stay, to clog up his mind with the past, and he would tell her as much when the opportunity presented itself. She needed to finish the job, get the hell out of town, and never come back, as far as he was concerned. Except, he wanted her here and was unwilling to admit that to himself.

By the time Simone yelled for lunch, Bowie had finished sanding the entryway. He went outside, dusted off, and followed his crew to the picnic tables. Simone stood there, dishing up plates with sandwiches, chips, and fruit and cans of pop. "Thank you," he said as he took a plate from her. "You and Mrs. Woods didn't need to do this."

"Well now, you're just being silly if you think she wasn't going to feed you. She's always fed the people who came to her home." She had. There wasn't a kid who went hungry around here, thanks to Carly.

Bowie sat down and whistled for Luke. He had felt confident that his dog wouldn't take off or go anywhere near the construction happening outside once he had shown Luke the backyard. At best, he figured Luke was down on the beach chasing the seagulls and swimming in the ocean. He shouted his name, and moments later the pooch appeared at the top of the stairs that led down to the beach. He appeared ragged and ready for a nap. Bowie patted his own leg, beckoning his dog, but he didn't come. Luke ignored his master and kept his attention on the stairs behind him. His tongue hung from his mouth, and his tail wagged excessively. Bowie watched as a young girl ascended. His breath caught, and the bite he had just taken felt like a lump lodged in his throat. He knew her, but from where? She crouched down and ruffled Luke's mane before giving him a kiss on his nose.

He watched her every move, unable to take his eyes off her. Her presence mesmerized him. Luke, too, seemed to be enamored by her because he was following her toward the house instead of coming to see what his master was eating. When she was out of sight, Bowie sat there, staring at his food. He couldn't eat, his appetite lost, and he couldn't understand why. Clearly, she was a visitor or a neighbor, and it would make sense for her and Luke to bond. His dog was friendly; he loved people. So then why did she seem so familiar to him? The imaginary lunch bell sounded by way of his crew getting up and thanking Simone for the meal. Still, he sat there wondering what had just happened.

"Your dog is really sweet," Simone said as she came to brush away the crumbs. "He's made himself at home here."

"Who was the girl?" he asked, ignoring the positive comments about his dog.

Simone continued cleaning and smiled. "That's Brystol."

"Does she live around here? I've never seen her around town, but I feel like she's familiar."

She shook her head.

"Simi, may I go into town with you?"

Simone glanced up just as Bowie turned toward her voice. "Of course, sweetie."

The young woman was a few feet away, smiling. She had the same smile as . . . *her mother.* Bowie swallowed hard, but the lump blocking his airway stayed put. He was having trouble breathing. The miniature version of Brooklyn was standing there talking to Simone as if they'd known each other for longer than a day or two.

"Is the black dog yours, sir?"

"His name's Luke," Bowie barely whispered as he tried to decipher all the thoughts running through his mind. If this girl was comfortable here, did that mean she was Austin's? There was no way Carly Woods would hide her son's daughter from his friends.

"He's very nice. I asked my nonnie if he could stay in the house with me while you worked."

"Nonnie?"

The younger version of Brooklyn smiled. "My grandma. She owns the inn."

Bowie stood. He wasn't sure where he was going, but he needed to get the hell out of there. Austin had a child, and no one knew. Not even one of his friends had been invited to be a part of her life. They hid her away like a dirty secret or an abomination. He wasn't sure which, but neither made sense to him. Why wouldn't Carly have told him that Austin's blood still flowed?

Because he hadn't been a good friend—that's why. He didn't deserve to know anything about the Woods family, let alone be present in the life of a daughter his best friend never had an opportunity to raise. However, he couldn't help but think that he could've been there for Brooklyn, helped her out, been her support system, been there when she gave birth. Austin's friends would've made sure the girl was loved by all, cherished, and knew the best parts of her dad, but instead, no one had said anything. No one had bothered to share the news. He had so many questions surrounding Brystol, Brooklyn, Carly, and their actions. He was hurt. He wanted answers that he knew he wasn't due, but he planned to ask the questions anyway.

TWELVE

Brooklyn perched herself on the top of the ladder and scrutinized the scene below her. Four of Bowie's men were in the lobby with her. One was deglossing the trim, one taping plastic to the floor—which, in her opinion, should've happened right after they'd removed the furniture. The third man was on his cell phone, and the fourth was standing off to the side with his hands on his hips, staring at the pile of scaffolding that should already have been up and ready for use. If it had been, Brooklyn wouldn't be on the ladder trying to tape off sections of trim.

She was already frustrated by Bowie's efforts. The way he conducted business was not to her level, nor was it the level she had learned from his father. It was Bowie's dad who gave her a job with Seacoast Construction after high school as his personal assistant. The job wasn't much, but it paid her rent and put food on her table.

She returned to the task at hand, stretching as far as she could without tipping the ladder or falling off. She was trying to give Bowie some leeway. He had sworn his team was efficient and worked fast. None of which she was witnessing. She pulled at the tape, ripping off a chunk. She was about to slap it to the wall when Bowie's booming voice interrupted her. He was screaming loud enough that he could be heard throughout the house, but his words were unclear. She scanned the room, watching as his employees scrambled to look busy.

The brushstrokes of the man who was working with the liquid sander suddenly became faster. The pieces to the scaffolding started to clank together. The gent on the phone now had a bucket and rag in his hand, and the plastic floor covering seemed to unroll much faster.

Brooklyn was laughing when Bowie entered the room. If his employees thought he was mad at them, they didn't show it. Bowie slowly turned toward Brooklyn and huffed. She conjured up an image of a bull turning red with steam coming out of his nose, making her giggle even louder.

She had started to climb down when Bowie's words stopped her. "How long did you think you'd get away with it?"

"You'll have to be a little more specific."

"Do you think this is all a joke?" he asked. "You act like we meant nothing to you."

Brooklyn was confused. What the hell was he going on about? She finished her descent, and once her feet were firmly on the ground, she handed Bowie the tape. "Look, I don't know what you're talking about, but your crew in here is really slow and needs to pick up the pace. They stand around, waiting until you come in before getting to work. It's unacceptable." She used their lack of efforts as a buffer between her and Bowie. It was the only way she could cope with him around right now.

Bowie's mouth dropped open. She had no intentions of going tit for tat with him and left him standing there. He could deal with his crew, or she would. It didn't really matter to her; she just wanted the job done efficiently and effectively.

Upstairs, she went from room to room, checking the progress. Walls were open, exposing pipes that needed to be replaced. Lights from the ceilings were sitting on the floors, with gaping holes overhead. She found one man standing on a ladder, only she couldn't see his head because he was in the ceiling, likely working on the wiring. Spools of wiring cluttered the hallway, and men walked by her with their tool belts clanking.

Tape measures had a distinct sound to them when being pulled from their cases. Brooklyn watched as a two-man team measured the exposed wall and jotted notes down. If she listened carefully, she'd hear the buzz saw that was outside, slicking through the wood. This excited her. Creating something out of someone's vision always brought her joy. Once the shiplap went up, she'd bring Carly up here so she could see the progress. Everything she wanted out of the magazines would be exactly as she liked. Brooklyn would make sure of it.

Down the hall, she came across Bowie's men. She walked in, expecting to find them sitting down. Much to her surprise, this room was further along than the others she had inspected. This pleased her, but there was no way she'd give Bowie the satisfaction of knowing. But she would give his guys a compliment because they deserved it. "Looks great in here."

"Thanks, boss lady," one replied.

Brooklyn walked to the end of the hall and used her master key to unlock the room. It had been years since she had been in here. She flipped the switch, and the light dimly lit the room. Before looking at anything, she went to the window and pulled open the blinds, letting the sun beam through. This room aside, Brooklyn decided she was going to make sure the windows were open in all the rooms. The inn needed the sun; it needed to have life brought back into it. She left the room, avoiding even a glance at the bed. Her life had changed in this room. It was where she had become a woman. But recalling those memories right now was too painful. One thing was certain: she wanted the furniture gone, sooner rather than later.

Downstairs, she saw progress in the lobby. The scaffolding was finally up, and work was being done. She went back to the house, needing a break. In the living room, Brystol was on the floor with the remote in her hand. Nothing odd except for the fact that she was using a dog as a headrest. "What are you doing?"

"Waiting for Simi so I can go with her."

"Where's she going?"

"Into town. Wants to stock up on food because Nonnie insists on feeding everyone."

Brooklyn gave her daughter an odd look. "How do you know this?"

Brystol sat up and shrugged. "Nonnie talks really loudly sometimes."

"Did you finish your reading?"

"Yes, and I wrote my book report. I emailed it to you."

"Thank you for doing it without me asking." Sometimes home-schooling was a struggle. It was hard to find a happy medium, which was another reason she should do the right thing and enroll her daughter in school. A constant schedule and structure could do her some good. "Whose dog is this?"

Brystol turned and started petting the black dog. She leaned down and kissed him before burying her face in his coat. If this wasn't a sign that she needed to put some roots down for her daughter, she didn't know what was. Living on the road, going from hotel to hotel, wasn't the right life for a teenager.

"One of the workers'. I don't know; I talked to him out back at lunch. His dog is really nice."

"Seems it. Does Nonnie know you brought him in?"

Brystol nodded and resumed her position. The dog didn't seem to care that she was using him as a pillow; in fact, he seemed rather content. Brooklyn went into the kitchen, now hungry and a bit angry with herself for missing lunch earlier. She rummaged through the refrigerator, pulling out the makings for a sandwich. With her arms full, she closed the door and jumped. "Don't you have people to supervise?"

"I wanted to talk to you," Bowie said.

"It can wait until after I eat." She wasn't suggesting or even asking; she was telling him. She expected Bowie to leave, but instead he pulled out the barstool and sat down. She eyed him warily, wondering what he was up to, but she was serious—he had people to manage and should be there.

"Excuse me, sir."

Brooklyn glanced up at the sound of her daughter's voice. She was standing next to Bowie, and he was looking at her like she was a long-lost relative.

"What's your name?"

"Brystol," she said sweetly.

Bowie glanced at Brooklyn, who diverted her eyes back to her sandwich. She tried to spread some mayonnaise, but her hand was frozen. She supposed she should introduce them but couldn't bring herself to open her mouth. She had a hard time understanding Carly's logic and wished she would've known before she came back to town. She preferred being prepared for any situation, not that you could really prepare for something like this.

"I'm Bowie, an old friend of your mom's."

"And my dad's," Brystol said proudly. "Nonnie talks about you all the time. She's even shown me some of the houses you've built, and she's told me stories about how you and my dad would do crazy things that would more often than not end up in one of you going to the hospital. Like the time my dad convinced you to jump off the garage into the swimming pool and you broke your arm." Brystol laughed. "Nonnie tells me all the time that I should be like her boys. Anyway, I was wondering if I can take Luke for a walk after I come back from the store. We'll only go to the beach." Brystol spoke a mile a minute while Brooklyn kept her eyes on Bowie.

"He would like that, but if he starts bugging you, let me know."

Brystol laughed. It was a genuine laugh and tugged at Brooklyn's heart. She needed to make a change, and fast. Brystol deserved better.

"Thanks, I will. Bye, Mom."

"Bye, be good and don't buy a ton of sugary crap." The words likely fell on deaf ears. Not that Simone would allow it, but Brooklyn felt better giving some motherly structure.

"It's pretty shitty finding out that Austin has a daughter this way."

Brooklyn sighed. This was a conversation that she hadn't wanted to have, but Carly had put her in this position. She'd thought, with the girl being here every summer, people would've figured it out, and Brooklyn wouldn't look like she was hiding her daughter. She wasn't. She was just hiding herself.

"That wasn't my intent."

"What was? To hide her the entire time you're here? To make sure none of his friends know her?" Bowie began to stand but gripped the side of the counter to steady himself. She tried not to pay attention to him, but his presence made her think about how life had turned out in Cape Harbor for Carly and made her feel even worse because she had left. Bowie opened his mouth to say something but closed it again and quickly retook his seat. He was angry; that much she could see by his expression. For as long as she could remember, Bowie had worn his heart on his sleeve. He'd always been there when she needed a shoulder to cry on, offering advice and comfort. She somewhat understood why he was upset, but honestly, it wasn't like she was going to broadcast that she'd gotten knocked up. It was her issue to deal with, not anyone else's. Besides, she hadn't wanted to feel guilted into staying in Cape Harbor.

She stared at him, unwilling to answer. He was making something out of nothing. If he and the rest of Austin's friends hadn't visited Carly on their own, would they really have come around if they'd known Austin's daughter was here? "I think you're looking for a fight, Bowie, and I'm not going to play into it."

He shook his head before tapping his fist on the countertop. "What happened to you?"

Brooklyn put the knife down on the countertop and took a step back. "I think you should go back to work."

"No, I think we should talk."

"We have nothing to talk about."

"We have everything to talk about. You walked out on me, on us."

"It wasn't like that, and you know it."

"No, I don't. In fact, I don't know anything." Bowie stood between the wall and counter, cutting off an easy escape route. In this moment, she hated this kitchen and wished it were open concept so she could escape and run to her room.

"You used to tell me everything, confide in me, and now you can't even stomach being in the same room with me."

"I think you know why," she said quietly.

"Talk to me, Brooklyn."

She shook her head and looked him square in the eyes. "I don't have anything to say."

"You may not have anything to say, but I do. You may have chosen to shut everyone out and disappear, but we didn't deserve it. We took you in when you were new. We made you one of us, and you bailed when shit got tough."

"There was nothing left for me here. He told me that he didn't love me and then went and died. How do you think that made me feel, especially after we . . ." Brooklyn stopped speaking. She closed her eyes and pulled the brim of her hat down farther. "Just go."

"Just tell me why you left. You at least owe me that."

She shook her head. "I did—there was nothing left for me here. Austin was dead. My parents were back in Seattle. There was nothing."

Bowie stood and came toward her until she backed up against the counter. They were face to face; rather, she stared at his chest. Her head rose slowly, until their eyes met. She looked at him, really took him in. With age, fine lines showed in his creased forehead. His eyes glistened, but also his nostrils flared. Was he sad or angry? Did he feel like she did? Hurt, upset, tormented, and confused?

She swallowed hard, and his name fell quietly from her lips: "Bowie."

"*I* was here," Bowie said. He let his words linger in the air before he turned and left. The last thing she heard was him calling for his dog and the front door slamming shut. She jumped, and without her consent, tears started flowing.

THIRTEEN

Bowie pulled into his parents' driveway and turned his key to shut off his truck. He opened the door and waited for Luke to jump out. Together, they trotted up the walkway. He knocked once before opening the door and saying, "Hello."

"Kitchen," his mom said back.

The Holmes house wasn't much bigger than where he lived. The three-bedroom ranch-style house sat on a corner lot, not far from where Brooklyn and her parents used to live. As he walked through the living room, toward the kitchen, he gave a slight chuckle at the decor. Knowing what he knew about Brooklyn now, she'd have a field day in his parents' house. He had never really considered it before, but the home's interior was outdated and in need of a face-lift.

He found his mom at the counter, cutting up vegetables. When he came in, she paused and pushed her cheek forward, expecting a kiss. He obliged, like he always did.

"Here for dinner?"

"Wasn't my plan, but if you're offering." Linda Holmes always had a hot meal for her son.

"What brings you by?"

"Dad around?"

"He's out back." She stopped cutting, picked up the dish towel that rested on the counter, and wiped her hands. "What's going on?"

"There's something I need to tell the both of you," he said.

Linda went to the sliding glass door, opened it, and yelled for her husband to come into the house. Her voice carried a hint of worry. Bowie wasn't trying to alarm her but could easily see why she would be. It wasn't every day he showed up needing to talk to both his parents.

Gary Holmes walked in, covered in grass clippings. "Where's the fire?"

"No fire—Bowie needs to speak with us." Even his father gave him an odd look. The three of them sat down at the table, his parents sitting across from him. His mother looked worried, and the reassuring smile he tried to give her wasn't doing its job.

He cleared his throat. "First thing I want to say is that Rachel and I have signed our divorce papers. As soon as I file them, we'll be officially divorced after ninety days." Carly asking for his services and Brooklyn's return had completely derailed his stop at the courthouse. After he left his parents, he planned to stop by his office and leave them for Marcia to file in the morning.

Bowie adjusted in his seat and glanced at his parents. "Second thing I need to tell you is that the Driftwood Inn is going to reopen."

His mother's mouth dropped open, and a tiny gasp escaped. "Did Carly sell it?"

He shook his head slowly. "She's reopening it and asked me to do the construction, which brings me to my third and fourth points of our impromptu family meeting. Brooklyn Hewett is back as well. She's some big-time renovator now." His eyes cut to his father. In a way, he blamed him for giving her odd jobs when she worked for him. "And she brought along her fourteen-year-old daughter." He sat back and let those final words sink in. He could see that his mother was going to hit him with a bombardment of questions, some of which he wouldn't be able to answer.

"Congratulations on the job." His father reached and shook his hand. The emotional stuff, Gary wasn't the best at, but his father meant well.

"I'm not sure what to say—I mean . . . a divorce. We knew that was coming, but Carly, the inn, and Brooklyn. She has a daughter?"

"Brystol. Luke's pretty infatuated with her."

"How? I mean, I know how, but . . ."

Bowie put his mother out of her misery and told her what he knew or at least what he could piece together. He, himself, still had a ton of questions but felt Brooklyn wasn't going to sit down and give him a dossier on her life anytime soon.

"And Brystol's been here before?"

He nodded. "From what I gathered, every year."

Linda shook her head. "I just don't understand how we didn't know."

Bowie shrugged. "No one knew, except Simone, and you and I both know she would never betray Carly's confidence."

His mother seemed to mull this over a bit before sighing. "Maybe I'll take some muffins over to Carly. I have a lot of groveling to do." She stood and went right back into the kitchen and started rummaging through the cupboards.

"I don't think you need to grovel, Mom. But I'm sure the muffins will be a big hit."

Bowie followed his father outside, where Gary showed his son his large almost-ripened tomatoes. Since retirement, Gary had developed a green thumb and grew most of their vegetables in the garden.

After dinner, Bowie went home, showered, and found himself too antsy to sit still. The walk on the beach he and Luke took did nothing to quell the energy stirring within. The walls of his house were closing in on him, and he needed to get away. Although the last place Bowie expected to find himself in again was the Whale Spout, nursing a beer. His hangover from the night before still lingered, but it was the silence of his empty house that made things worse for him. Even the normal solace he found in his dog wasn't enough to keep the demons from his mind. He hurt, and it wasn't the sort of ache he had after a long day's work. He felt stabbing pain in his heart, his head pounded, and he felt that at any moment he was going to cry. He wanted to slide down the wall and bury his head in his hands and sob. After Austin died, his mother told him crying was therapeutic. Back then, the tears came when he would least expect them: He'd be on the couch, and a fishing show would come on, or he'd drive by the place they'd meet for dinner. Mostly, though, he'd break down when he was alone on a jobsite because his partner, coworker, and the woman who had become his best friend had disappeared as well.

And now she was back and had brought the unimaginable with her . . . a child. Austin's daughter. A teenager who was a perfect likeness of her mother. When Bowie had seen the girl, he had been taken back to the day he saw Brooklyn, the first day of their junior year, with her long dark hair swaying back and forth as she walked down the hall. From the first time he met her, he was smitten. It was the way her eyes crinkled when she would laugh, how her hair would fall over her shoulder when she was deep in thought, and how she would look at him in class and blush because she caught him staring.

Bowie jerked the pint glass so hard that beer sloshed to the side and spilled onto his hand. Thinking about Brooklyn was not how he wanted to spend the evening. He downed the beer and signaled to the bartender that he wanted a refill.

"Rough night, cowboy?"

Bowie scoffed at the question and reached for the beer. The bartender laughed and wiped the spilled beer off the countertop.

"Where's Graham?"

"Night off."

"You're new," he said.

"Here, yes, but not to Cape Harbor. We went to school together. I'm Krista Rich. I was a couple of years behind you."

"Oh," Bowie said, feeling a bit ashamed for not recognizing her. He studied her for a few seconds before deciding to give up trying to remember. He couldn't focus on anyone or anything other than Brooklyn right now. He was letting her return consume his thoughts and emotions and couldn't see that ending anytime soon now that he knew Austin had a daughter. That's what hurt him more—not that Brooklyn had disappeared for fifteen years but that she had kept Austin's daughter away from everyone. His friends were never given a chance to be a part of her life, and to him that was unacceptable. When he saw her again, he was going to tell her, give her a piece of his mind.

Bowie picked up and downed his beer, determined to muddle his thoughts. There wasn't anything he could do about the selfish person Brooklyn had become, and even if there was, he wouldn't know where to start. He held his empty pint high in the air, waving it around a bit before slamming it down.

"Easy there," Krista said as she walked by him to tend to someone else. He knew, deep down, he was being unreasonable, but he was angry for so many reasons, and she and this bar were in his warpath. What made matters worse was each time Graham's newest employee walked by, she was laughing, and he could only assume it was at him.

When she finally set another beer down in front of him, he held it tightly, almost as if it were going to slip away and leave him like Brooklyn had all those years ago . . . like he wanted her to do now. His life would be easier if she wasn't here. His thoughts were starting to become muddled with the memories they had shared. These were moments he refused to remember, and to do that he needed alcohol to numb his thoughts.

From behind him the door swung open, and a familiar voice rang out. Bowie's spine tingled. He turned around slowly until he was faced with a blast from the past. Rennie Wallace stood in the Whale Spout with her arms held high in the air, as if she owned the place. Just like with Brooklyn, he hadn't seen Rennie since Austin's funeral. Another friend who had disappeared out of his life, not that she would've stayed. Their only connection was Brooklyn. She had introduced Rennie to everyone during Christmas break their junior year of high school. She fit in instantly and became a constant part of their group during vacations. Bowie always liked her because she was different from Brooklyn. Where she was quiet and shy, Rennie was loud and wild. She brought a different side of Brooklyn out, one that made Bowie fall more in love with her.

Graham had a thing for Rennie from the first time she came to visit. They were at his house for a holiday party, and he suggested they play spin the bottle. Bowie had protested, mostly because the temptation to kiss Brooklyn would be too great, and the last thing he wanted was to put her in an awkward situation, even though he suspected Austin wouldn't have cared. Still, everyone wanted to play, and as they sat in a circle on the floor with an empty Pepsi bottle in the center, he prayed each time Brooklyn spun that it wouldn't land on him. The last thing he wanted was to spend seven minutes in the closet talking with the girl he loved. Graham, on the other hand, found a way to make sure the bottle landed on Rennie, and there was no mistaking her swollen lips or Graham's cool demeanor and devilish smile when they came out of the closet.

At each visit, Graham and Rennie would sneak off, disappearing for hours at a time. It hadn't mattered where they were—in the woods, at the lake, down on the beach, or at a party—they had always found a way to be with each other. It only made sense that Graham would take Rennie to their prom, both junior and senior year. After graduation, the two headed off to California. Graham to San Jose State to study computer science while Rennie went to Santa Clara to study law. She was the debater of the group, the one with an opinion about everything, even if she hadn't always believed her own arguments. She'd argue the opposite just to piss off whomever challenged her, and she was damn good at it. Bowie had never thought to ask Graham if he kept in touch with Rennie because he was consumed with his own thoughts about Brooklyn, but now that he was staring at her, he wanted to know why his friend had never ended up with Rennie.

His jaw tightened when Brooklyn appeared behind Rennie. She had a smile on her face, something Bowie thought shouldn't be there after their encounter earlier. He felt like she owed him an explanation, an apology for what she had done . . . and not only to him, but all Austin's friends and the community. Yes, telling the town that you were sorry for hiding Austin's child was stretching things, considering it wasn't really anyone else's business. But the town pined for Austin— they felt his death over and over, year after year—and having his daughter here would've given them some closure. As he had those thoughts, he knew he was full of shit.

Seeing Rennie and Brooklyn together brought back a flood of happy memories, and he found himself smiling, despite the anger boiling within. Days when they were all together were simpler times. As teens, they worried about homework, curfews, and whose party to attend on the weekends. After high school, their biggest issue was adulthood. The things they loved never changed as they grew older. The bonfires, the weekends at the lake, and taking his family's boat out first thing in the morning so they had a coveted spot on the sandbar. He missed everything about the way their lives had been and had tried to do these things with Rachel, but they had never felt right. His actions had been forced, and he had run on autopilot.

He tried to look away before Rennie caught him staring. She grinned and took a few steps toward him. "Well, well, well, if it isn't Bowie Holmes." Brooklyn set her hand on Rennie's shoulder and whispered something into her ear before beelining it toward a table.

Great, he thought. He was either going to have to leave or stay and torture himself. He knew he would stay because being in the same room as Brooklyn was far better than knowing she was in the bar and he wasn't.

"Renee Wallace, long time no see." Only he wasn't looking at Rennie when he spoke to her; he was watching Brooklyn. When he finally turned his attention toward Rennie, he gave her a cursory glance. Slim, blonde hair mixed with browns and other shades of blonde. Eye makeup—which he hadn't seen Brooklyn wear yet—highlighted her brown eyes, and she was wearing a suit. If he had to guess, Renee was working for corporate America. He should know what her career choice was, but for the life of him couldn't remember.

Rennie sat on the stool beside him, leaving him no choice but to pay attention to her. Never in his life had he wished for eyes in the back of his head until now. He wanted to know what Brooklyn was doing, who she was speaking with, and whether she had her eyes pinned on his back, because he could swear daggers were piercing his skin. Against his better judgment, he peered over his shoulder to get one last look at Brooklyn. She was on her phone, typing away. Jealousy soared through him. It wasn't that he wanted to know who she was chatting with; he wanted to share the bench she sat on. He wanted to be next to her. To have her on the other side of him now so they could accidently brush their arms against each other. When he had cornered her in the kitchen earlier, he hadn't expected a flood of emotions to come back. Anger was what he wanted to feel, not longing. He was tempted to go to her, to grab her hand and pull her outside, where they could talk. Where he could say the things that were on his mind. Where he could kiss . . . no, he wasn't going there.

"She's single, ya know."

"Who?" He knew who Rennie was referring to but acted dumb anyway.

All she did was laugh and signal for the bartender. "You're like an open book. Your hard-on is poking the wall in front of you."

He adjusted himself on the stool, coyly glanced at his lap, and cleared his throat. He remembered now why Rennie had sometimes gotten on his nerves—she said what was exactly on her mind and never held back.

"You can't be mad at her."

"I can do whatever I want." As he said the words, he felt childish and saw himself as a five-year-old trying to torment Monroe into chasing him around the playground.

Rennie set her hand on his forearm and squeezed. "Trust me, Bowie. There's a lot that you don't know. You need to give her some time."

"She's had fifteen years to figure her shit out, Rennie." He lifted his pint and took a long drink, emptying half the glass. Rennie had no idea what she was talking about, none whatsoever. He was certain she knew Brooklyn's daughter and probably spent a good amount of time with her.

"Look, it doesn't matter. She's here to do a job, and then she'll be gone." He finished his beer and slammed the glass down on the counter. He pulled his wallet from his back pocket and opened it without thinking. His eyes caught the corner of a familiar picture he had carried with him for years. He withdrew it slowly, taking in every square inch of the faded photo of him, Brooklyn, and Austin.

"Yeah, keep thinking that." Rennie took her beer from the bartender and stood. Bowie had resigned himself to going home to wallow in his own pity party when he heard Rennie screech and yell out Graham's name. Bowie's heart sank. There was no way he was leaving the Whale Spout now.

FOURTEEN

Against her wishes, the woman she called her best friend took the empty stool next to Bowie Holmes. Brooklyn reached for the hem of Rennie's shirt to pull her toward the empty table, but her friend had a sudden burst of energy that propelled her toward Brooklyn's foe. Reluctantly, she sat and pulled her phone out of her pocket. She read Brystol's book report while she waited for her friend to come to her senses. She sent a text to her daughter, telling her she loved her, thanking her for the report, and asking her to let her know if she needed her to come home. As soon as she sent the message, she hoped Brystol would text back and request she return immediately.

She set her phone down on the table and pulled up a home design app to work on an idea she had for the carriage house. As much as she didn't want to look at Bowie and Rennie, she did. Every few seconds she found herself distracted, whether from a noise in the back of the bar, where people were throwing darts or shooting pool; a chair scraping on the wooden floor when someone stood; the waitress walking by; or the door opening. Each time she would look up from her app only to have her eyes land on Bowie. She studied the way he sat on the stool, rigid and put off by the fact that Rennie was talking his ear off. What she hadn't expected was the slight lift in the corner of his mouth when he turned and saw Brooklyn staring at him. She focused her attention back on her phone, determined to ignore what was going on not too far from her.

Rennie had showed up days earlier than anticipated. When she and Brooklyn had spoken on the phone, Rennie had said she'd visit on the weekend, not midweek. Not that Brooklyn minded. She needed to have her friend there, mostly to give her comfort. Brooklyn's rocky relationship with her former friends and town teetered on disaster, and Rennie would be the interference she needed to avoid everything else around her.

After Rennie had doted on Brystol for a bit, she had pulled Brooklyn out of the house, telling her that they needed adult time. Brooklyn preferred they walk along the beach, take a drive, or go down to the docks and watch the ships come in, anything that would allow her to hide behind her ball cap. The moment Rennie made a beeline for her car, Brooklyn knew they were headed for the bar. She thought about begging her friend—the idea of throwing a fit even crossed her mind—but she knew Rennie would call her out on her bullshit and give her one hell of a guilt trip.

Over the years, Brooklyn had thought about everything she would say when she saw her old friends again, how she would apologize and tell them she hadn't meant to stay away. Those practiced words had failed her when she had seen Monroe at the grocery store. The only person who could possibly understand her reasoning would be Bowie, yet words had failed her when she had almost run him over outside the inn. He was so angry: first when he thought she was trying to kill him with her vehicle and again when he realized she was the one driving said vehicle. Years of pent-up anger and longing for the man she used to call her best friend kept her tongue tied, and instead of jumping into his arms and telling him how much she had missed him or dragging him into the house to see Brystol, she let his anger dictate how their encounter would be. He hated her, and she was going to let him.

They hadn't discussed what they would do or say when they ran into their friends. There wasn't a doubt in Brooklyn's mind that Rennie would play it off as if they hadn't seen each other in months, not years. She had the knack for not caring what others thought, something Brooklyn wished she could master, and in true Rennie Wallace fashion, she had walked into the Whale Spout like she owned the place.

Brooklyn glanced toward the bar once more and let out a sigh as Rennie stood and started toward their table. They were going to have a decent evening with appetizers, beer, and conversation. She was certain no one would bother them. Sure, they would stare, point, and whisper among themselves, but they would stay away until the right time presented itself. That was, until the door swung open and Graham Chamberlain walked in.

"Graham Cracker!" Rennie yelled as she launched herself into his arms. The act looked effortless until her beer sloshed over the rim of the glass and landed down Graham's back and on the floor. Still, he held on to her. The scene made Brooklyn turn away. What she wouldn't give to have a welcoming party like that. If she had found the courage to pick up the phone a time or two over the last fifteen years, her homecoming would've been the same.

Graham let Rennie down and held on to her hand. They walked together to the table, and when Brooklyn looked up, Graham smiled. "Are you just going to sit there, or are you going to stand up so I can give you a hug?"

Tears formed as she stood, and Graham held his arms out wide for her. He held her tightly while she tried not to cry into his shirt. "I've missed you," he whispered into her ear. Words escaped her. She wanted to tell him that she had missed him as well, that she had thought about him often, but couldn't get her mouth to cooperate. Graham was the kind of man who didn't hold a grudge, and it showed.

The three of them sat down, with Brooklyn across from Rennie and Graham, who put his arm around the back of her chair. They had a history. One Brooklyn knew every detail of. They were never a couple unless Rennie happened to be in Cape Harbor visiting or when they both ended up in California for college, and then they were inseparable. Each time they would hook up, Rennie would give Brooklyn the run-down. As far as Brooklyn knew, the last time they had seen each other was Austin's funeral.

"Rennie Wallace, I have to say, you're a sight for sore eyes."

Rennie fanned herself, and Brooklyn rolled her eyes at the antics. "Why, Graham Chamberlain, are you hitting on me?"

The Chamberlain twins had all the charisma in the world. They were sweet, well-mannered boys who always opened doors and pulled out chairs, but it was their looks that had women turning their heads. Tall, with dirty-blond hair and green eyes, but it was Graham's crooked smile that could make any woman weak in the knees, and he knew it.

"Do I need to?" he asked her. Years ago, the answer would've been no, but Rennie was off the market and in love.

Rennie tilted her head to the side, chuckled, and shook her head. "Lots of things have changed over the years, Graham. Tell me, how have you been? Are you still in California?"

Brooklyn perked up. This was why she needed Rennie. She wasn't afraid to ask the questions Brooklyn needed answered. She was dying to know what everyone was up to these days but felt she had no right asking.

"I live here and run the bar for my parents."

"What happened to your tech job?" Brooklyn asked.

His lips went into a fine line. "Sold my shares and came home. Grady . . ." Graham stopped talking and shook his head, a clear signal he was done with this part of the conversation. He glanced over his shoulder and hollered for Bowie, who seemed reluctant to join them. Bowie sauntered over and hesitated before sitting next to Brooklyn.

"How nice of you to join us," Rennie snarked.

"How nice of you to visit us after all these years." His retort hurt. He had every right to be angry, but not at Rennie. She had no reason to visit. Brooklyn had left, and the last either of them had known, Graham lived in California.

Bowie sat back and put his arm behind Brooklyn, something he had done too many times to count when they were growing up. Whether the act was intentional or not, it made Brooklyn feel closer to Bowie. Their thighs pressed together, another thing that was entirely involuntary. Surely, the last thing either of them meant to do was touch.

Rennie leaned forward and focused on Bowie, moving her eyes up and down. Brooklyn felt a twinge of jealousy, but she knew better. "The years have been kind to you, Holmes. You've got this ruggedly handsome thing going for yourself. You're muscular in all the right places but still look like a teddy bear. You remind me of my cousin. He's a lumberjack, and all the women fawn over him."

"How very Paul Bunyan of him." Bowie's reply didn't make much sense to her, and by the look on Rennie's face, it confused her as well.

When the waitress walked by, Graham got her attention and ordered a round of drinks and one of everything from the menu.

"There's only four of us," Brooklyn pointed out.

"I'm sure others will join us," Graham stated. He and Bowie started talking, but Brooklyn tuned them out. She watched the door instead, wondering who would be next to walk in. Grady, Jason, Mila? Other classmates who she wasn't as close to but had been friendly with until she moved away? As she thought about it, seeing Monroe wouldn't be so bad. They could catch up, and Brooklyn could apologize for her erratic behavior at the grocery store the other day.

She continued to zone out while Bowie, Graham, and Rennie chatted away. Rennie had told her she was excited to catch up with Graham but also that Brooklyn needed to make peace with Bowie. He was once her best friend, and they both were still hurting over Austin's death. Over the years, Brooklyn had thought about Bowie, curious as to what he was up to. Was he married, and did he have children? She had missed their friendship, being able to talk to him about life, and wished she could have gone back in time and picked up the phone when she went back to her parents' house. She'd tell him about her pregnancy and ask him to go away with her. Their lives could've been different if she had just reached out to him.

The door opened, and in walked Monroe. Her eyes drifted over the patrons at the bar, almost as if she was looking for someone. Brooklyn stood and went to her. Monroe gasped and smiled softly.

"I want to apologize for my behavior in the store the other day. I was out of sorts and wasn't expecting anyone to notice me. I was unkind to you, when you've been nothing but a dear friend to me."

Monroe pulled Brooklyn into a hug. The women squeezed each other tightly, and when they parted, both had tears in their eyes. Brooklyn motioned toward the table. "Rennie's here, if you'd like to join us."

"I'd love that."

"It's almost as if the gang's back together," Monroe stated as she sat and looked around the table. "Jason will be here for the memorial, and I'm sure Mila will find her way back into town."

"And Grady?" Brooklyn asked. She hadn't meant to contribute to the conversation since she felt like she had nothing useful to add or say. "I haven't seen him yet. Does he still operate Chamberwoods?"

"Wow, Carly doesn't tell you much, does she?" Bowie smirked. He shook his head and brought his pint up to his mouth, only to pull it away before taking a sip. "Let me guess—you don't talk about Cape Harbor." He acted hostile toward Brooklyn but kept his thigh pressed to hers and angled his body toward her when he was speaking. If he hated her so much, why touch her? Why flirt? Why sit next to her? There was plenty of space where either of them could move, but he had chosen to be next to her, and it was starting to feel like torture. Even with his pent-up anger coming in spurts, she didn't want him to move. She liked having him next to her, and that bothered her greatly.

"We don't," Brooklyn said sharply. "And before you or any of the rest of you go throwing stones, you should remind yourself of how many times you visited Austin's mom. I, at least, spoke with her." Although their communication was strictly mundane or regarding Brystol and nothing more, and for that, Brooklyn hated herself. She had let Austin down, even when it wasn't her responsibility. He had made that perfectly clear.

She shook her head. "I'm sorry for my outburst. Since I came back, a lot of things have been brought to light."

Graham reached across the table and squeezed her hand. "Grady's around. He's not in the best of shape, and he pretty much lives in the past."

"I'm so sorry." Brooklyn gave him a sad smile as her heart broke. That day, the day Austin took his boat out when he shouldn't have, had changed the lives of everyone around him.

The waitress finally brought out the appetizers they had ordered and a stack of plates. She returned quickly with a round of shots and beer chasers. Brooklyn's stomach growled and filled with dread at the same time. She was starving and had always loved the pub food from the Whale Spout. Drinking, not so much. Drinking led to loose lips, and loose lips led to revelations that needed to be kept locked away . . . locked tightly away and buried at the bottom of the ocean.

FIFTEEN

Monroe stood behind Brooklyn mumbling something about the summer and how their plans were still going to happen. How they were going to have their bonfires on the beach; go rock jumping into the river; pack their tents and spend weekends deep in the forest, under the lush green trees, drinking beer and talking about their futures. Their plans. Plans that they made as a group. A group that existed with one less person. The person who everyone followed around because he was the leader of the pack, their mayor of sorts. Monroe pulled the hairbrush through Brooklyn's thick mane of chocolate-colored hair, gathering pieces to pin into place. The sun added natural highlights, a mixture of brown, red, and gold strands, making Brooklyn a natural beauty. Over the years, many of her friends and even strangers asked her who colored her hair and which salon her stylist worked at, hoping to achieve the same look. When she would tell them that she was born this way, or that the sun did all the work, many wouldn't believe her. Half the time Brooklyn didn't believe it herself.

Brooklyn felt the barrette snap into place but couldn't give it much thought after the initial push into her scalp. It didn't hurt, at least not as much as she wanted it to. She was numb and in desperate need to feel pain. To feel something stronger than the constant ache she felt in her chest. Her heart didn't exist as she remembered. She barely felt it beat, couldn't hear the thumping it made when she lay in bed at night. Her chest ached, burning whenever she would lay her hand there.

Two words were said over the roar of rain, and everything changed for Brooklyn. She had never known what it was like to lose everything, to know your dreams were disappearing and there wasn't a single thing that could be done to change it. With those two words, her whole life vanished, and all she was left with was regret.

Monroe fluttered around her like a busy bee, taking care of mundane things like making sure Brooklyn's shoes were on, that the buttons on the back of her dress latched tightly, and that the hat that Monroe had purchased for her fit perfectly. Another jab to the scalp hadn't brought enough pain to register in Brooklyn's mind.

"There, all set."

Brooklyn barely noticed Monroe standing behind her with her hands on her shoulders. She didn't know what day it was, where they were going, or how they planned to get there. She knew nothing, but somehow Monroe understood and had been by Brooklyn's side since the night everything happened.

Outside, the sun was bright and caused Brooklyn to squint. Seconds later, a pair of sunglasses covered her eyes, and she sighed. She lifted her face toward the sun and let the warmth wash over her until Monroe started tugging her arm toward the waiting car.

The black limo wove through town, making unnecessary turns. The funeral was for show. There wasn't a body to bury. Not a limb, a piece of clothing, or a lock of hair to put six feet underground, but people needed closure, and this was the way to get it. People lined the streets, as if a limousine driving to a funeral warranted some sort of parade. They waved, not knowing who was hiding behind the dark tinted glass. And there were signs. Signs everywhere with Austin's name.

"Everyone loved him," she muttered.

"They did."

"Don't you find it odd that people only profess their love for someone after they die? I'm surprised people don't test loyalty by faking their own deaths just to see how their friends will react. Who will show up at their funeral? Who will cry tears? Who will mourn a man they didn't truly know?"

That was Brooklyn's thought when she had received the phone call that Austin was missing. That he was faking his own death to see if she would leave like she had threatened after he had told her he didn't love her anymore. If he didn't love her, there was no reason to stay. She hadn't wanted to believe Graham when he had phoned. She had thought it was a joke, that if something had happened, his mother would call. She received her answer as soon as she showed up at the Woodses' house. Police were everywhere, and the chatter on the radio—the one Austin kept in his room—proved to be true. Her boyfriend, the man she had planned to spend the rest of her life with, was missing.

The car pulled into the parking lot of the church. It was filled with cars parked tightly together, and there was a yellow school bus dropping off a group of mourners. Austin's family would be the last to enter. They would walk down the red, worn-out carpet of the aisle, on display for everyone to look at, to feel sorry for. Brooklyn stared out the window, wondering what the hell she was doing. She was a mere shell of herself, weak and unable to function. In a few moments she would have to put on a brave face and be strong for Austin's mother. She was the girlfriend, and if Carly could function normally, so could she.

She didn't deserve to be there, at least not as family, but she couldn't exactly tell Carly why. The secret she kept weighed heavily on her, pushing down on her already-broken heart. It was her burden to bear and one she would take to the grave if she had to.

The car door swung open, and Brooklyn caught the eyes of Bowie staring down at her. All her mind saw was Austin standing behind him. They had been inseparable, best friends almost until the end. She knew Bowie's secrets, and he knew hers. His outstretched hand waited. It would make sense for him to escort her into the church, to sit by her, to be her shoulder to cry on. She had spent years doing that, confiding in him. But that was weeks ago. Life was different now. She ignored him and mustered up her own strength to climb out of the limo. Standing on her own two feet, she saw Graham up ahead and walked toward him, calling out his name softly. It was his arm that she reached for, and if he was confused, he didn't show it.

Inside the vestibule, Austin's family gathered. His aunts, uncles, and cousins surrounded Carly as if they were protecting her from more sorrow. She had lost everything. Both loves of her life taken by the sea. Yet, she was strong, an example to all the women out there. As soon as she and Brooklyn made eye contact, the crowd parted. They hugged tightly, like mother and daughter. "You'll sit next to me," Carly told her.

"I shouldn't. It should be your family." Truth was, Brooklyn wanted to sit in the back. She wanted to be the first one to leave.

"You are family."

Brooklyn wanted to argue with her, to tell her the truth. She nodded and squeezed Carly's hand. There was no way Brooklyn was saying anything. Not today, and not anytime soon. Aside from Bowie, no one knew about the last words Austin had spoken to her, and she was going to keep it that way.

"Brooklyn!"

She turned at the sound of her name and scanned the parking lot. Running toward her, in high heels, was her best friend. Brooklyn broke off from the group and rushed toward Rennie. The two friends collided and held each other tightly. "I'm so sorry," Rennie said.

The women parted and stared into each other's eyes. "He's gone, Rennie. I don't know what I'm going to do."

"You're going to come back to Seattle and stay with me until you figure it out."

Before Brooklyn could respond, her father touched her on her arm lightly and led her toward the church. Her family, her support system, surrounded her. She needed this. She needed their comfort, their warmth, and their love.

The large picture of Austin that sat at the altar was one that Brooklyn had taken of him a few months back. They had taken Bowie's boat out for the day and planned to spend the night on the water. The sun was setting, and Austin was glowing. He was leaning against the bow and just happened to smile when she pressed down to snap a photo. Once they were back on land, she rushed to the drugstore to have the film developed. The three days it took to get her roll of film back were pure agony. However, the picture had proved to be worth it. She smiled at the memory. One of their happiest . . . and one of their last.

The reverend took to the pulpit, opened his book, and started speaking. The words washed over Brooklyn as she stared at Austin's photo. She missed him. She hated him. She loved him. Every emotion she could possibly have was taking over her body and senses. She wanted to scream, to punch him, to dive deep into the ocean to look for him. She thought about swimming out until she couldn't swim anymore to wait for him. He would come for her. That much she believed. He wouldn't leave her there alone. Not like he already had. He wouldn't make the same mistake twice.

The voice behind the podium changed. It was one she knew well. She watched Bowie, standing there with a black suit and matching tie on. The only other time she had seen him dressed up like this was at prom. He had worn a suit their junior year and a tuxedo their senior year. Every other occasion, it was nice slacks with a sweater or button-down shirt. Same with Austin, although getting Austin out of shorts or hip waders was a hard task, and one he wasn't keen on doing much. She tuned Bowie out, not wanting to hear what he had to say about Austin. She knew the truth of how he felt about him and wanted to stand and ask him why he was up there. But she held it in. All of it.

The funeral procession was practically a parade. The five police cars the town used were putting on a display of red and blue. The two lead cars blasted their sirens, letting everyone know they were leading the empty hearse through town, giving Austin's imaginary body one last ride. Brooklyn stared out the window, looking at the harbor. It was empty. There wasn't a single boat out there. Every fisherman was somewhere in this line behind her, paying their respects to their lost friend.

The limo was full for this ride. All of Austin's friends crammed in, suffocating Brooklyn. She needed space to breathe, and right now Mila's mindless chatter about auditions, directors, and movie roles filled the close space, while Jason jockeyed for a spot to interject about school. He was following his dreams of becoming a doctor, something Brooklyn wished she had done. Graham sat across from her, his long legs stretched out, his ankle touching hers. He, too, stared out the window. Beside him, his brother, Grady, was passed out cold. This had become his life, drinking until he could no longer function, no matter the time of day. Brooklyn wondered when someone was going to say something to him. Was it going to be before or after Graham returned to California? Even though they were twins, they were vastly different. Graham was successful, working in Silicon Valley, while Grady stayed behind to open a business with Austin. The Chamberwoods Fishing Company had brought in decent money since its inception. But the future of the company was in limbo, as far as Brooklyn could tell. Grady wasn't in any shape to tie his own shoes, let alone run a business.

As soon as the car pulled to a stop, the doors opened. Ushers from the funeral home helped Brooklyn, Monroe, and Mila out of the car. Jason and Graham followed, leaving Grady in the back seat to sleep off his intoxication. Before Brooklyn could take a step, Bowie was in front of her. It hadn't even occurred to her that he wasn't in the car with them. He should've been, but then she thought that maybe he was with Carly, playing the dutiful best friend.

Bowie told the others that they would be right behind them, and when Brooklyn sidestepped to get around him, he shuffled as well. "You've been ignoring me for weeks."

Brooklyn said nothing.

"We need to talk about what happened."

She studied the ground and sighed. "Austin died. There isn't anything to talk about."

Bowie stepped closer and placed his hand on her hip. *The touch electrified her, and even if she wanted to, she couldn't bring herself to push his hand away.* "I'm not talking about Austin. I'm talking about us and what happened."

"Nothing happened." *Those were the words she had been telling herself repeatedly. She figured she would start to believe them sooner or later.*

"You know that's not true, Brooklyn. We can't let the guilt eat us up. We didn't do anything wrong."

Didn't they? It sure felt wrong.

"I have to go," *she said, stepping away from him. She didn't walk to Austin's gravesite or go sit by his mother. She walked down the road toward town, and never looked back.*

SIXTEEN

Over the next few days, Bowie did everything he could to avoid Brooklyn. When he needed to ask her questions about her designs, he sent his assistant foreman, Jarrett, to get the answers. When lunch rolled around, he scanned the area for any sign of her before he sat down. The person he couldn't avoid was her daughter. She was everywhere, and Luke was with her from the second Bowie put his truck into park. Brystol waited for them to arrive each morning, always with a large piece of driftwood in her hand, and every time, Bowie relinquished all rights to his dog. He reached down, almost absentmindedly, to pet Luke, only to remind himself that he was likely on the beach or snuggled up on the floor of Carly's home watching television with Brystol. A few nights ago, he had attempted to rest his head against Luke, much like he had seen Brystol do, only to have Luke growl and move away from him. "Traitor," Bowie had mumbled. His dog had fallen in love with Brystol, much like Bowie had fallen in love with Brooklyn. The Hewett women were going to be the demise of the Holmes men.

Despite knowing Luke was safe, Bowie peered over the fence. There were quite a few people on the beach, most likely tourists. The renovation project was on track, something he prided himself on, especially with Brooklyn nitpicking how slow things started off. His crew had completed the lobby earlier this morning, and Simone was already behind the desk, typing away on the computer. It was only a matter of time before life returned to the Driftwood Inn.

People marked their spots in the sand with blankets and coolers, most too close to the surf and not paying attention to the tide. Colorful umbrellas spread out along the beach, giving the khaki-colored space a rainbow-like feel. Kites flew in the air, kids screamed in delight, and dogs chased after toys and birds.

Bowie scanned the area for Brystol and Luke. He should've known they'd be in the area in front of the inn. From his vantage point, it seemed like Brystol stayed in view of the massive windows. He peered over his shoulder and thought he could see the outline of Carly, but he wasn't sure. It was clear to him that Carly had always been fully aware of Brystol's existence. But what he couldn't understand was why the rest of them weren't.

Luke sat in the sand staring into a space shielded by a white-and-blue umbrella with the name of the inn written on it. It was one of the guest umbrellas, a luxury offered to those staying here. There had been many summers when Bowie and Austin would wake early and make sure the beach chaises were set out and poles of the umbrellas pushed deep into the sand. Summers used to be different here until Austin died. He took a bit of the town and everyone living in it with him the night he drowned.

Luke's tail wagged back and forth, creating his own version of a sand angel. The sight brought a smile to Bowie's face. His dog was happy. His dog had a companion who could pay her undivided attention to him. Maybe he needed a friend, another pup to chase around. The idea of getting another dog wasn't high on Bowie's priority list, though. His divorce, however, was, and he was thankful that he had finally remembered to drop the papers off this morning. Also, it seemed like a good thing to avoid Brooklyn, who happened to be climbing the stairs.

With one last look, he surmised that Luke was in the best possible hands and went back to the picnic table to eat lunch. Simone had prepared spaghetti and salad for the workers, and each of the guys helped himself heartily.

All around him, the guys chatted about everything except work. Bowie picked up bits and pieces, mostly that they were excited for the weekend. One was heading to Anacortes to see a woman he'd started dating. Another had his kids this weekend, so they were going to chill at home. A few mentioned they were going fishing, while others reminded everyone at the table that the Austin Woods Memorial was coming up. Bowie hadn't forgotten, even though he tried every year. The town refused to let it go, and people who hadn't even known Austin came out to celebrate him. The weekend was nothing more than an excuse to have a street party. Only his true friends honored him the way he would've wanted, on the beach with a bonfire and a case of beer.

At first, the mayor had used Austin's death as a teaching tool. He had updated out-of-date laws and mandated that even if there was a blip of a storm on the radar, the port and docks closed to ships planning on leaving. There hadn't been an accident since, and the mayor was proud of himself. He used that little statistic every time he ran for reelection. The truth of the matter was, no one was stupid enough to take their boats out when it was raining after what had happened.

Bowie dreaded the anniversary of Austin's death. It would be him, Monroe, and Graham, sitting around and telling each other the same old stories. Mila would show if her schedule wasn't too busy, and Grady . . . he'd be around. Last year, he came but sat at the edge of the surf, letting the waves wash over him. He hadn't been right in the head since Austin's accident, despite the many attempts by his friends to help him.

Every town had a drunk, and Grady was theirs. Most people ignored him, crossed the street when they saw him coming, and acted like they didn't know him. Graham took care of his brother, while Monroe tried to help him get into a program—which had been a lost cause. Grady didn't want help—he wanted to forget, and he was drinking his way to salvation. Honestly, Bowie was surprised he was still around. He had long thought Grady would've passed away by now, and there were times when he'd go a few days, even a week, without seeing him downtown or sitting along the beach and assume that prophecy had been fulfilled. But Grady always showed up when friends started looking, never with an answer that could satisfy their curiosity of where he disappeared to.

Only the people of Cape Harbor knew about Grady's problem. He wasn't a bum. He didn't panhandle on the street corner. His parents made sure he had a roof over his head. His mother still did his laundry, his brother made sure he always had a place to drink, and he kept to himself. Some say the Chamberlains enabled Grady's problem, but those close to the family saw it otherwise. Only they knew what Grady had been through. They were simply taking care of their own, which was more than Bowie could say he had done for Austin's mom.

At the end of the day, Bowie didn't have to whistle for his dog because Brystol brought Luke to him. His dog was dead tired, barely able to drag himself to the truck. Brystol laughed as Bowie heaved his black Labrador into the cab.

"I'm going to miss him this weekend. He'll come back on Monday, right?"

Bowie leaned against the side of his truck, leaving the door open so Brystol could continue to visit Luke. "He goes everywhere with me."

"Really?"

"Yeah, it's a small town; everyone knows him. He usually stays in my truck or comes in with me while I'm running my errands."

"That's so cool. Most of my mom's clients have little dogs. They are the pampered kind that are carried everywhere and eat off plates at the dining room table. Luke's awesome, though. He loves to play." *And will never be pampered,* Bowie wanted to say but held back.

"Where do you and your mom live?" Bowie knew the question was out of order, but he didn't care. He wanted to know and knew Brooklyn would never tell him. He banked on Brooklyn not being forthcoming about life where he was concerned, and he was certain that if she had said anything about Bowie, Brystol wouldn't be standing here with him right now.

The girl shrugged. "Nowhere really. During the summer I stay with my grandparents in Seattle or with Nonnie here."

If he had been the friend he was supposed to be, maybe he would've been a part of the girl's life. He could've been a father figure to her, unless Brooklyn had someone filling that void. Bowie hadn't given much thought to what Brooklyn had been up to or where she had been until this moment. He found himself wanting to know everything about her, much like he had fifteen years ago. "And your mom?" he asked, letting curiosity take over. "Does she come stay here as well?"

Brystol shook her head. "My mom works a lot, different places."

"In Seattle?"

"No, we came from Arizona the other day. Before that we were in Tennessee."

He was thoroughly confused by her answer. Surely, Brooklyn had a home where she raised her daughter, and where her daughter went to school. But from the sounds of it, that wasn't the case.

"I know your mom travels for work, but where do you live? Where's your house?"

"Oh, we don't have one. We just move from job to job."

The kid was kidding, right? There was no way Brooklyn was raising her daughter like they were in a traveling circus. Bowie was at a loss for words. He wanted to pump her for more information but didn't know where to start. If she suspected anything, she wasn't saying, choosing to focus on Luke and not his idiotic questions.

"Brystol, come get cleaned up so we can go downtown." Simone's voice rang out, causing the girl to jump.

"I'll see you on Monday," Bowie heard her say to his dog. "Bye," she said to him, giving him a little wave as she ran toward the house. From where he was standing, he could see Simone holding the door open for Brystol. By chance, he looked toward the second floor of the house, just in time to see the curtains sway and a shadow move out of view. Was it Brooklyn? Was she watching him with her daughter?

He decided to snoop more and went over to her car. "Florida?" He looked back at the house, tempted to go knock on the door and beg her to just talk to him, but he couldn't. The less he knew, the better off he'd be when she left.

Bowie hopped into his truck and banged his hands against the steering wheel. For the life of him, he couldn't understand his frustration. Brooklyn had left him. She had left all of them. He shouldn't care why she was back or what she had been doing the last fifteen years.

But he did, and he hated himself for it.

He had long forgotten her, given up on trying to find her, and yet, here she was. He had thought things would be different when they came face to face, that she would apologize for leaving, beg him to forgive her, but she had simply brushed him off as if he were a stranger.

Bowie drove home in a daze, his cell phone vibrating on and off in his pocket during the entire journey. He had to carry Luke from the truck because the dog was dead tired and refused to budge. He couldn't even lift his head when Bowie told him they were home. As soon as he stepped onto his porch, he set his dog down so he could open the door. There was a slight movement off to his side. The fine hairs on the back of his neck rose in warning. If someone or something were to attack him, Luke wouldn't be able to defend him. In fact, his dog wasn't even growling. "Some guard dog you are," he mumbled into the open air.

He looked to his side and saw Monroe standing there, holding a six-pack. "What are you doing here?"

Monroe held up the pack of beer, tilted her head, and smiled. "I thought you could use someone to talk to."

Bowie hung his head. Monroe never came out and asked if he had feelings for Brooklyn, but he never hid them either. When they were teens, he had done everything he could to be near her, even if it had meant being a third wheel with her and Austin. Bowie held the door for Monroe and followed her into the house. He took the bottles of beer from her and motioned for her to go out onto his deck.

"I can't believe she's back. Part of me is elated because I've missed her. The other part is pissed off."

He nodded and took a long pull off the bottle. "Yep."

"She's the talk of the town."

"Small-town gossip is all."

"People seem to think the world of her. They're not even mad at her or anything." He took another drink while Monroe continued to talk. "I heard she has a kid."

"Daughter, named Brystol."

"I'm trying not to be mad, but it hurts. She just left us. I get taking a vacation, but to just outright abandon us like we hadn't lost someone important too is just rude."

"You seemed chummy at the Spout the other night."

"I try not to hold a grudge. Plus, she apologized for our earlier encounter."

"At least she's speaking to you. She doesn't talk to me, although I don't really give her a chance."

"Why not?"

That was an open-ended question that Bowie wasn't willing to answer. There wasn't a need to rehash an old crush, especially when it couldn't go anywhere.

"Don't have anything to discuss, I guess."

"What's it like working with her?"

Against his will, his lips turned up into a smile. He could tell Monroe that watching Brooklyn work was easily becoming his favorite hobby and that he thought about purposely skipping parts of his job so he could watch her take care of it. If it were Graham sitting next to him and not Monroe, he'd probably come clean about his lurking. As it was, Monroe only had suspicions about his crush and not actual facts.

"She's good at what she does, that's for sure. Hard worker."

"You sound like you're recommending her for a job."

He shook his head and brought the brown bottle to his lips. "Thanks for the beer."

"Uh-huh. How long is she here for?"

Bowie cleared his throat. "Until the job's done, I imagine. Carly hired her to redesign the inn. I do know Carly asked her to stay. Wants Brooklyn to put down roots for Brystol."

"Have you met her?"

He nodded. "She's a spitting image of Brooklyn. Walks like her, talks like her, even flips her hair like her. When I first saw her, this sense of déjà vu washed over me, and I thought I was back in school, seeing her for the first time."

"I can't believe she kept her a secret all this time."

Bowie glanced at his friend. "She didn't. According to Brystol, she visits every summer. Carly kept her hidden from everyone."

"Why?"

Absentmindedly, he started to pick the label off the beer bottle, only to remember he was drinking one of those fancy IPAs everyone loved these days. "I don't know, Roe. I'm tempted to ask her, but I'm not sure I'd like the answer."

He finished his beer and took another one out of the cardboard case. He wanted to blame his increased drinking on Brooklyn's return. It was only part of it. He was trying to numb his past from creeping up on him. Sadly, his attempts failed.

SEVENTEEN

As luck would have it, the coast was experiencing a heat wave with temperatures threatening to reach the high nineties. It was rare for this area to get above seventy-five. The days were mostly beautiful, even when it rained, and the nights cool. Except for this week. By the time Brooklyn woke up, she was in a full sweat. It was going to be a long day of labor under the scorching heat, which meant some unpleasant people.

She was the first one to arrive at the inn. Not uncommon, but as of late she and Bowie had an unspoken competition going on. She had no idea where he lived or how far he had to drive to get there, but there were mornings when he was already working by the time she got out of bed. Since her return to Cape Harbor, her sleep pattern had been off. There were nights when she stared out the window, looking out over the dark water and listening to the distant sound of the waves, waiting for her mind to shut. Other times, she was up before the sun and ready to start the day.

On this particular morning, she was the victor in beating Bowie to work, and she almost wished she wasn't. Over the years, Brooklyn had mastered a lot of crafts. She could use a power saw with no problem. She could replace a light and even a light socket. Sledgehammer, nail gun, and paint machine were no match for her. What she couldn't figure out was the old heating and cooling system. She pressed the button and waited for cool air to start flowing.

Nothing happened.

She pressed it again and waited. The inn was quiet, so she should've been able to hear the machine come to life, yet it sounded like the system wasn't even on. She pushed the small button harder.

Nothing.

Sweat dripped down her face, and she wiped it away with the back of her hand. She looked around the utility room—for what, she wasn't sure. The only thing she was sure about was that the unit wasn't working. She would have to talk to Bowie or his assistant to figure out why, or she could just order a new one. Nope, she couldn't. She had promised Carly that she would confer with Bowie on everything, even though that was never her style.

She gave up and went back into the main part of the inn. She'd act like an adult, and when Bowie arrived, she'd ask him to look at it, which she hoped would be soon because it was hot outside and inside, and she was starting to get cranky.

Brooklyn wasn't watching where she was going when she came around the corner. "Oof," her body exhaled, and she started tumbling backward. Strong hands caught her and pulled her safely into their arms, cocooning her. Her nose hit the man's chest, and as she caught her breath, she inhaled deeply. Her savior smelled of Irish Spring and clean linen. There was only one person she knew who used that brand of soap. She stepped back and slowly lifted her head to see if she was right.

"Are you okay?" Bowie asked, his voice husky; his hands remained where they were, touching her arms. Their eyes locked, blue upon blue, staring into each other's souls.

She felt the back of his fingers brush against her cheek. Her head tilted, pushing into his touch. Bowie smiled. She started to grin as well until she remembered where they were and what they meant to each other. It took her a moment to regain her composure. They were close, too close for her liking, and she needed space. She stepped back, far enough away that he couldn't touch her.

"B?" He used her nickname, one that only her parents usually called her.

"The air conditioner isn't working." She changed the subject as fast as she could. She was good at avoidance. Ignoring the elephant in the room was her specialty.

"Let's go take a look." Bowie motioned for her to lead the way. She felt self-conscious with him following behind her even though he had done it a million times before.

She led him through the utility door. "Don't let it shut; it tends to stick," she said from over her shoulder.

"I remember."

She should've remembered that Bowie knew. For years, she had blocked everything about Cape Harbor out, and now that she was back, she wanted to remember everything. All the good, while leaving the bad locked away. Bowie was part of it all.

She pressed the button and waited for the unit to come to life; this time it did. A look of irritation spread across her face until the machine started shaking, as if it were coming alive. Bowie stepped in front of her, shielding her from whatever that contraption was doing. The unit popped, and she shrieked.

"What the hell?"

"My guess, it's old and hasn't been on in fifteen years."

Brooklyn sidestepped Bowie, waving her hand in front of her face to push the smoke away. "Perfect. Definitely an item we didn't budget for."

"I think the newer systems are more energy efficient. I'll make some calls and see what we can get."

She sighed. "Thanks."

An awkward silence fell upon them. They would look at each other and then away, only to turn back. They were playing a cat-and-mouse game, and she had no idea which part she was supposed to be. She closed her eyes, and as she did, she felt him behind her. It had taken her years to forget him, to get over the way he had always been by her side, to not yearn for the way he had always known just what she needed. And now he was standing behind her, and she was desperate for him to hold her like he used to. Yet, she wanted to keep him at arm's length because she didn't want to hurt him.

Her pulse quickened, and in the silent, smoke-filled room, she was sure he could hear her heart beating rapidly. His hand touched her hip, and his other one rested on her shoulder. He moved closer. She could feel his chest against her back. What she wouldn't give to fall into his arms, to feel him hold her, kiss her, love her.

She stepped away from him and went to the door, tugging on the knob, only the door didn't budge. She could have sworn she had told Bowie to make sure it didn't close. She twisted the knob, only for it to spin in her hands. "Are you freaking kidding me?" she said through gritted teeth.

"What's wrong?"

His voice made her blood boil. Was he seriously asking her what was wrong? Could he not see that he had caused this?

She turned to him. *"You! Shut! The! Door!"* There wasn't a doubt in her mind that her cheeks where red. She was sweating, hot, and now angry . . . at him.

Bowie went to the door and tried to open it. She wanted to laugh when it wouldn't open but held back. Instead she kicked a box that was in front of her, except it wouldn't move, either, which only increased the frustration she felt.

"I'll just take the door off the hinges."

"Yep, whatever."

"What is your problem?" Bowie fired back.

Brooklyn huffed and crossed her arms over her chest. "You."

"Why? I didn't do anything," he pointed out as he came toward her.

"Ha, you've done everything."

"Name one thing, Brooklyn."

She couldn't. He was too close, invading her personal bubble.

"Why Florida?" he asked, thankfully changing the subject. Not that she wanted to talk about any part of her life with him. The less he knew, the easier it would be to leave.

"Excuse me?"

"What's in Florida?"

"A PO box."

He looked confused, and part of her was satisfied that she had made him this way. The other part of her felt stupid for being snobby. She sighed. "Self-employment laws are very favorable in Florida, so I keep a 'residence' there."

"Do you have a boyfriend? Partner?" he asked, moving closer. "Is there someone there or any other place you've been?"

"No," she whispered.

"Do you want to know what I'm at fault for?"

She couldn't look at him, nod, or even find the strength to say yes because her senses were going haywire. He was in her personal bubble again, and this time she wanted to grip his T-shirt and pull him toward her. Her hands shook and her heart pounded as he lifted her chin gently and studied her. "My only fault in all of this is that I loved you and never got a chance to show you how much." Bowie leaned forward. Their lips parted. She heard him inhale as they grew closer.

Suddenly the door opened, startling them. They stepped away from each other and looked to see who had come to save them. Simone stood there, smiling like a Cheshire cat. "Sorry, I didn't mean to interrupt."

"You're not," Brooklyn said as she walked toward her. "Just the opposite, really. The handle was stuck, and Bowie and I were just talking about replacing the door."

Simone rested the broom she held in her hand in the corner, never once taking her eyes off Brooklyn or Bowie. Brooklyn grinned, although she was certain it came out like a grimace. "Guess I better get to work," she said, leaving Simone and Bowie in the room.

Brooklyn hurried down the hall, desperate to get away from Bowie, and thankful that Simone had caught them before anything could happen. She still hadn't made a final decision on whether she and Brystol would stay in Cape Harbor, and kissing Bowie would only complicate matters. As it was, whenever he was around, her knees weakened, at times she felt dizzy, and her heart thumped so fast she thought she was going to faint. The last time she'd felt like this, she had just met Austin. The only difference now, aside from a lifetime of growing up, was that she was certain that if she acted on her feelings, Bowie would reciprocate.

The doors to the inn burst open, and men carrying every box size known to man came through and headed right for the stairs. The palpitations she had increased, but for a different reason. Bedroom furniture had arrived, and it was time to start putting the complete rooms together. She clapped her hands and followed. Putting beds together, decorating, and styling a room were passions of hers.

"Let's stack everything in one room," she told the crew. "This way we can work easily in the others without the boxes getting in the way."

"Sounds good, boss lady."

She opened the first box, examined its contents, and started taking the pieces across the hall. She pushed the window up, even though it was blazing hot outside, needing to hear the ocean and the laughter that wafted its way upstairs. She stood there, admiring the room. The shiplap wall was exactly what Carly had asked for. The new black light fixtures followed a nautical theme. The furniture for this room would be black, in a matte finish.

Simone and a couple of men appeared in the room, ready to help.

"I think I want to get this room done and show Carly."

"Oh, Brooklyn, I think that will be a wonderful idea. Tell me what to do."

And she did. She instructed the team on what had to be done and what items were going where. She assisted when needed, but she and Simone focused mostly on the bedding, table lamps, and artwork. Every time she unpackaged a new linen, Simone declared that it was the most beautiful or softest piece of fabric she had seen or felt.

When the bed, armoire, nightstands, and the small table and chairs were finally in place, it was Brooklyn's turn. Together, she and Simone made the bed, hung the artwork in the appropriate places, plugged the lamps in, and watched the curtains sway in the breeze.

"This was your idea, wasn't it?"

Simone finished straightening out the pillow on the bed. "For years, I've been asking her to do this. She needs it. She missed it. People have missed her."

"But she shut herself off from them."

Simone nodded. "And over time, they stopped asking about her. I think if they hadn't or if people had come to the door, she might have changed her mind. As it was, Brystol coming each summer was the only thing she looked forward to."

"You should've told me, Simone."

"And you would've what? Visited? Stayed? Nothing says she would have changed her mind then either."

As much as Brooklyn didn't want to agree, Simone had a point. Simone excused herself and said she was going to tell Carly she had something to show her, leaving Brooklyn to put the final touches on the room. After one more brush of her hand on the comforter, Brooklyn stood in the doorway and admired the work she, Simone, Bowie, and the crew had done. The slightest of breezes blew through the window. Brooklyn closed her eyes to clear her thoughts, and when she reopened them, she took the room in, as if this were the first time she saw it. What once used to be old, drab, and mundane now had a sense of calmness. She could easily see herself sitting on the chair in the corner by the window, curled up with a book. The view from here showed enough of the ocean that whoever rented this room could watch the sunset easily. For the first time since the project had started, Brooklyn thought about the inn reopening and how she wanted to be here for it.

Downstairs, more and more boxes were coming through, and there was a computer tech setting up the new reservation equipment. Brystol stood by, watching the man work and peppering him with questions. The fact that her daughter wanted to work here brought a smile to Brooklyn's face and an ache to her heart. Their lifestyle would have to change, which wasn't necessarily a bad thing, only different. They'd both have a home, something neither had had in quite some time.

The sound of high-heeled shoes caught Brooklyn's attention. She looked for the source of the sound, and when she saw Carly enter, she gasped. Since Brooklyn and Brystol's arrival, Carly had worn polyester pants and long sweaters around the house, a far cry from the classically dressed woman Brooklyn remembered, and the few times she had come to check on the progress of the inn, she had worn a sweat suit, one that surely smelled of mothballs.

Before her eyes stood the woman Carly once was. Her hair was curled and pinned away from her face, her lips were painted a soft pink, and her makeup was flawless. She had dressed in a white-and-navy pant-suit and was rocking a pair of red three-inch heels. Brooklyn wasn't sure if she should catcall the woman or offer her a chair before she fell over.

Carly waved her off. "Stop with the looks. It feels good to dress up for once."

Both Simone and Brooklyn looked at what they were wearing. Brooklyn was in her normal getup: shorts, T-shirt, and work boots. Simone matched her, minus the work boots.

"Would you like to see one of the rooms? Simone and I finished it before she came to get you."

"Of course." She turned to head up the massive staircase that would take her to the second floor, but Brooklyn stopped her and motioned toward the elevator. "Oh, I don't know. That thing hasn't been used in ages. I would hate for us to get stuck, unless you intend to send me up by myself." Carly's eyebrow rose, which made Brooklyn giggle.

"Bowie had it fixed. He also had the interior redone, so it matches more of the theme you're going for. He also tested it extensively, and while we may only have three floors of rooms, he had that thing moving up and down for hours, trying to confuse it."

"And did he . . . confuse the contraption?"

Brooklyn sighed. "Unfortunately, Bowie survived any misfortune." Carly eyed her again, and Brooklyn shook her head. "I'm joking. Come on," she said, taking her by the arm. Brooklyn wasn't really joking, though. Brooklyn had been working on one of the floors, painting the lobby area, when the elevator doors had opened. She had happened to glance over her shoulder to find a shirtless Bowie standing there. The way he had looked at her had made her already-warm body flush. Her heart had pounded, the speed increasing the longer they'd stared at each other. She had watched his Adam's apple bob as he swallowed, wondering if he was feeling the same as her. He had stepped forward, and she had followed, closing the gap between them. She had been within inches of his body and could see pebbles of sweat dripping down the planes of his abdomen. For weeks they had danced around each other, avoiding the elephant in the room when they were alone. They had a history, one filled with lust, longing, and pain. She had missed him over the years and had often thought about a life different from what she had now, one where he played a major part as her companion. Brooklyn had licked her lips, tasting her own sweat, and reached for him. He had grimaced and called out in pain as the elevator doors tried to squeeze the life out of him. Bowie had let out a string of curse words that would have rivaled a sailor's as the doors had continued to open and close, smashing against his arms. The doors had closed instantly, cutting them off and ending whatever fantasy she'd had playing out in her head.

Brooklyn suggested Carly do the honors by pressing the button. Within seconds, the doors opened, and Carly inhaled. Stylish gray paneling and a wooden rail had replaced the old cracked mirrors and gold railing. Brooklyn had hated the old elevator, and when she used to come to the inn would opt for the stairs. Even to this day, mirrors in elevators gave her an eerie feeling, like someone was watching her.

Carly pressed the number two on the keypad and giggled as it lit up. Brooklyn wasn't sure what was funny but played along. Anything she could do to make Carly feel good about reopening the inn. The old elevator used to creak, wobble, and sometimes miss its stop. Not now, thanks to Bowie. The smooth ride took only a few seconds, with the doors opening effortlessly. Together, the two of them stepped out into the second-floor lobby. Brooklyn moved to the side to give Carly some time to come to terms with what she saw. On the wall, for everyone to see when they came out of the elevator, was a painting of Austin's boat. Brooklyn had found the picture and sent it off to one of her colleagues, asking them to print it on wallpaper for her. She wasn't always a fan of wallpaper unless the occasion called for it, like now.

Carly went to the wall and ran her fingers around the trawler. She traced the fine lines of the picture until she had gone from one end to the other. "He was so proud when he bought this ship."

"I remember," Brooklyn said.

"He could've done anything with his inheritance but chose to follow in his father's footsteps. Reckless boy."

"Fishing was in his blood, Carly. I don't think there was a soul alive who could've steered him in another direction." Brooklyn had tried often.

"No, I suppose you're right—although I tried, many, many times. Do you ever wonder what your life would be like now if things had been different?"

Brooklyn didn't want to answer that question but did anyway. "I always imagine it a couple different ways. All of them end up with Austin and I married, with a couple of children. It's hard sometimes, watching Brystol grow up with only the memories we tell her."

"She reminds me so much of Austin, especially at this age. I am so very thankful for her." Carly turned toward Brooklyn. "You could've made a different decision."

She nodded. "If I had, I wouldn't be standing here right now." Brooklyn wanted to add that Austin could've made a different decision as well, but she kept that to herself because his mother didn't need to hear something like that. Not now. "Come, let me show you the room."

Carly followed Brooklyn the short way down the hall. There were new light fixtures, making the hallway brighter. The walls were now a creamy yellow, and the flooring was hardwood. "Where did the carpet go?"

"Tore it up and had Bowie install bamboo flooring. It'll be easier to clean, and the guests won't struggle with their already-heavy suitcases." There was nothing worse than the push-and-pull game down a carpeted floor.

"Huh, I liked that carpet."

"It was threadbare and had to go."

"If you say so."

Brooklyn fought the urge to roll her eyes. She swiped the master key card against the new door, which only led to another round of questions from Carly. She was so out of touch with modern technology; Brooklyn made a mental note to have Brystol sit down with her grandmother and teach her a few things.

Carly stepped into the room and had her head on swivel, taking it all in. "The wall is my favorite, and I love the artwork."

"Thanks, but Brystol gets the credit there. I let her pick something for each room."

Carly smiled. "You know, I love having her here. You could stay and run the inn."

She shook her head slightly and pressed her lips together. "I've been asked to do a job. It would start in October. I can't stay."

"Can't or won't?"

She wanted to stay and do the right thing for her daughter. She also wanted to leave and put everything behind her. It was easier living on the road. There wasn't anyone or anything to get attached to. "Carly . . . ," she sighed.

"Brystol can. She could start school, make some friends."

She started to respond, but the sound of her phone cut her off. "Hello?" she answered. "Okay, I'll be right down," she said before hanging up. "My parents are here. Do you want to come down with me or stay up here?"

"I'll stay up here a little while longer."

Brooklyn figured Carly would want to look at Austin's boat a little longer. As far as she knew, it was still shipwrecked at the bottom of the ocean, although its coordinates weren't exactly known. Teams of divers had looked, scoured the area for Austin and the boat, but each trip out had yielded nothing in return. Down at the Whale Spout, the old-timers who sat and chatted happily in the corner had woven their own tales—that Austin was still out there, sailing the seas. Brooklyn wished it were true, at least for his mother's and daughter's sakes.

"I'll be downstairs, probably at the house."

"Tell your parents I'll be there shortly."

She left Carly standing in the room and took the flight of stairs down to the main floor. As soon as she saw her mom and dad, she collapsed in their arms. "You have no idea how good it is to have you here."

EIGHTEEN

The idea of being awake before the sun was up was never high on Brooklyn's priority list. She preferred to sleep in, especially on the weekends. Austin had other plans, though, and wanted to take her fishing, so she was up, albeit slightly cranky, and waiting outside for him. When his truck rambled down the road, she hurried to the end of her driveway to save him from flashing his headlights into her parents' bedroom. He pulled up next to her and leaned across his bench seat to open the door for her.

"Good morning, beautiful," he said as she climbed in. She scooted to the middle and met his lips with hers.

"It's morning, but I reserve the right to say whether it's good or not."

"Ah, don't be that way. We're going to have fun today."

"If you say so." She sighed. Fishing was important to him, and he was important to her, which was why she was up so early. She rested her head on his shoulder while he drove down the road. Every so often, she would yawn and close her eyes, until he hit a pothole or took a corner sharply. She accepted the fact that she wouldn't be able to sleep and paid attention to where they were going, although she was slightly confused, as they were driving away from the water.

"Where are we going?"

"To pick Bowie up."

"Oh, he's coming with us?"

Austin hummed in agreement as he took another corner haphaz-
ardly. The boy thought he was a race car driver, only he had a truck
that didn't corner very well. He had also failed to mention that Bowie
was tagging along. It seemed that anytime she and Austin tried to be
alone, Bowie was there, lurking in the shadows. Sometimes she didn't
mind, like when they went to the stupid parties Austin always brought
them to or when Austin drank a few too many. Bowie always made
sure Brooklyn made it home safely. Truth was, she didn't much care for
her feelings toward Bowie because they muddled the way she felt about
Austin. Teenage hormones confused her greatly, and these boys were mak-
ing things harder for her.

They pulled into the Holmeses' driveway, and Bowie opened the door,
blinding Brooklyn with the dome light. She cried out and buried her face
in Austin's shoulder, garnering a kiss from him. In fact, he continued to kiss
her until she lifted her head and he could finally plant one on her lips. She
deepened the kiss, letting it go longer after the door was pulled shut, in an
effort to prove to herself that the other boy sitting next to her meant nothing.
The jury was still out on whether it worked.

"My mom made us breakfast and lunch." Bowie held a basket on his lap.

"That's awesome. I forgot about food."

Brooklyn didn't know if the pain she felt in her stomach was because of
the aroma coming from the basket or because Austin hadn't cared enough
to make sure they ate while out at sea today. She played it off as a simple
mistake because surely her boyfriend cared about her well-being.

When they arrived at the pier, the only sounds to be heard were the
subtle splashes of the water lapping at the surface and the other boats get-
ting ready to go out for the day, but other than that, the docks were quiet.

Brooklyn stood at the end of the dock and watched the light from the
lighthouse spin. She counted the seconds between intervals and followed the
beam of light as it hit shore. She had no idea how anyone could use that
light as a guide back to land but trusted that Austin and Bowie knew, and
honestly was too afraid to ask.

"*Brooklyn, what are you doing out here? Don't you know about Wally?*"

She looked over her shoulder at Bowie and turned farther to look for Austin. He was somewhere on his father's boat, and Bowie was out here with her. He was always where she was.

"*Who is Wally?*"

"*The walrus. Haven't you met him?*"

"*Are you pulling my leg or something?*"

Bowie shook his head. "*Not at all. Wally usually sleeps on the docks here. For the most part, he's harmless, but if you scare him, he may try and bite you.*"

"*You tell lies, Bowie Holmes. It's too warm for a walrus in Washington. They live in Alaska.*"

He held up his hand and displayed three fingers. "*Scout's honor.*"

"*Ha, are you even a Boy Scout?*"

"*No, but I'd never lie to you, Brooklyn.*"

For whatever reason, she knew this to be true. There was something about Bowie that told her he'd always be honest with her. From behind, she heard a large splash and leaped toward Bowie, who wrapped her in his arms.

"*What was that?*" she asked.

"*My guess, Wally. He's either awake and coming over to see what all the ruckus is, or he's looking for food.*"

Brooklyn shivered in his arms. "*I'm scared.*"

"*Don't be; I've got you.*"

The dock rocked, and a loud guttural growl came from the dark water. Brooklyn was tempted to lean over and look, but Bowie was pulling her away from the edge. She feared for her life but couldn't be bothered to run. She had to see for herself what was making that noise.

Two large flippers somehow grabbed ahold of the dock and heaved the rest of its body forward. Brooklyn squealed and jumped back as a black blob wiggled out of the water. It let out another growl, this time louder, but stayed toward the edge.

"Meet Wally." Bowie laughed.

Brooklyn slapped him in the chest. "You moron. That's not a walrus; it's a seal."

"Is there a difference?"

"Ugh," she groaned in frustration. "Don't you pay attention in science class?"

Bowie looked away sheepishly. The answer, she was sure, was no. Austin did, though, and he would prove that she was right. She marched off toward the boat and stood on the dock, calling for him. He came around in a rush, asking her what was wrong.

"Nothing. I need you to come tell Bowie he's wrong about Wally."

Austin jumped onto the dock and walked toward Bowie and Wally. "What's going on?"

Brooklyn crossed her arms and huffed. "Bowie seems to think Wally is a walrus. I said he's a seal. Who is right?"

Austin ran his hand over his hat and adjusted it a few times. He let out a sigh and finally looked at Bowie. "Sorry, man. She's right."

"What?"

Austin shrugged. "I figured you knew."

"Old man Potts said he brought one back with him, that it snuck on board."

"Old man Potts is like eighty, and he's been telling that story since he was twenty. If it were true, the walrus would've died a long time ago. Come on—we gotta go."

Brooklyn smirked at Bowie and followed Austin to the boat. He helped her come aboard and held her in his arms for a bit. "I love that beautiful brain of yours."

She blushed. He teased her often about how smart she was, but he was just as smart, if not smarter. They shared most of their classes together, and both excelled in science. As much as she wanted to be a nurse, she wasn't ruling out going into marine biology or something of the like so they could work together. Silly dreams, she knew, but couldn't help it.

Once Bowie boarded, he and Austin worked as a team to get the boat ready to go. As soon as Austin started the motor, he suggested Brooklyn put on a life vest and asked if she wanted to sit with him while he steered the boat. She thought she would stand next to him when she saw that there was only one chair, but he told her to sit. She did, and he stood behind her with his chest pressed to her back. He placed her hands on the steering wheel and told her to relax. Brooklyn loved being in his arms, and it was moments like this that made all the other stupid ones seem trivial.

They were sailing out toward the ends of the earth—at least that was the only way to describe it. It seemed that the farther they went out, the darker it was. The sun rose behind them, casting a beautiful orange, pink, and red glow over their town. Every so often Brooklyn would look over her shoulder and sigh.

"This is why we get up so early, so we're reminded of how stunning our home is."

"Like Bowie, you tell lies. You get up this early so you get the best fishing spots. It's a sport, and like every sport it has advantages and disadvantages. I know enough to know fish bite better in the morning."

"And where would you have heard such a thing?"

Brooklyn tilted her head toward Austin, and he smiled down at her. "This guy I met a few months back. He introduced himself as the resident heartthrob and local fisherman. He's told me a few things about fishing."

Austin chuckled. "What about the heartthrob part?"

"Meh," she said, giggling. "The jury's still out on that one."

He let go of the wheel so he could tickle her. Brooklyn yelped and jerked the boat to the left. Bowie let out a string of curse words, to which Austin yelled, "Sorry, man." Was he really sorry, though? Brooklyn wondered because he was hiding his laughter in her shoulder. Austin helped her get the boat back on course and instructed her to head straight. While she did, he held her and kissed her neck every chance he got.

They cruised for about thirty to forty-five minutes, out to what Brooklyn would call the middle of nowhere. There was land on both sides of them, but she wasn't sure if it was inhabitable or not. She wasn't going to ask, either, mostly out of fear that Austin would want to find out, and the last thing she wanted was to put herself in a Lord of the Flies *situation. She appreciated the lush scenery, though, and enjoyed the beaming sun. Even though she was supposed to fish, she hoped that Austin would suggest she read one of the books she had brought along and bask in the sun.*

Bowie watched some radar device that apparently told them if there were fish in the area. Austin finally dropped the anchor and told her to look over her shoulder. Behind her was their town, and if she squinted, she could see the faint outline of Cape Harbor. It was glowing, thanks to the rising sun.

"Wow."

"Pretty spectacular, isn't it?"

"Yeah, it really is. I guess this is why you wake up so early."

Austin kissed her on her nose. "That, and so I can get home to you." She reveled in his adoration. He simply was the best part of living in Cape Harbor.

"I love you," she said as she rose up on her tippy toes to give him a kiss.

"I love you, Brooklyn. Now it's time to fish. Bowie and I will bait your hook, but if you get a bite, you need to reel that baby in. Do you remember how I showed you when we were at the pond?"

Regrettably, she did. All hope was fading that she'd be able to sit by while the guys did all the work. Fishing was important to Austin, so this needed to be important to her. He had asked her to come out with him for the day, and she should be grateful. She did wonder, though, when Austin was going to take an interest in her hobbies. She'd love to take him to a baseball game, the batting cages, or even to the mall so she could put a fashion show on for him. Each time she'd asked, he'd been busy. There was always something to occupy his time, although he made sure to include Brooklyn in everything he had going on.

After they caught their max, they sailed back into port. Austin taught Brooklyn how to tie a proper knot and how to prepare the buoys. At the dock, Austin showed Brooklyn how to secure the boat, and then he helped her onto the wooden walkway and handed her his keys.

"Can you pull my truck up so we can load the fish into the back?"

She nodded and ran up the dock and to his truck. They had only been dating a few weeks when he had let her drive. At first, her nerves made her so jumpy she could barely turn the wheel, but after weeks of practice, she had no problems driving his truck.

The guys were waiting for her when she pulled up. She stayed in the cab until Austin came around to the driver's door. She scooted to the middle as he climbed in. "Where now?"

"The homeless shelter."

Brooklyn looked at the three coolers in the back, filled with fish. "Aren't you going to sell any?"

Austin shook his head. "Not today."

"Wow" was all she could muster.

"What?" he asked, looking over at her. His grin was wide, pulling his cheeks up, adding to his boyish charm.

She shook her head. "Nothing. I'm just in awe."

He turned and quickly gave her a kiss. "Maybe tomorrow you'll volunteer with me after church."

"I'd like that a lot."

The next day, she went with him to volunteer at the homeless shelter, and every Sunday after that, and even though the food donation was kept private, everyone there seemed to know Austin was the one who brought in all the fish.

NINETEEN

Carly stood in the doorway of Brooklyn's room. The two women stared at each other. Carly's expression was unreadable. Brooklyn's, however, questioned what Carly was doing. She was dressed in jeans, probably Gloria Vanderbilts or some other older-era fashion line, with a red polo and white sweater cuffed and draped over her shoulders. Every day since she had showed Carly the finished room, she had made an effort to dress better, which secretly made Brooklyn happy. She saw her daughter's expression each time Carly came down for breakfast. At first, shock, which turned into the biggest, cheesiest grin she had seen on Brystol's face. While Brooklyn and Carly hadn't always been the best of friends, they were cordial and respected one another. Carly had expectations of Brooklyn, who failed to meet many of them. Mostly on a daily basis. And Brooklyn . . . well, the only thing she expected from Carly was for her to be present in her daughter's life.

"What are you doing?" Brooklyn finally asked after Carly let out multiple audible sighs. She set aside the rendering she was working on and watched as Carly strode into her room. She stopped at the window and peered out. That was one of the best things about the house and the inn, so many rooms had a view of the ocean, and Carly had had the keen sense to decorate the rooms to reflect the beauty of the outside. The bedrooms were white with wrought iron beds. Small touches of navy blue created enough pop to make the room feel homey, beachy. Shells that Brystol had collected over the years added to the decorations. But it was the battery-operated candles in the windows that really set these rooms apart from the others. Brooklyn knew Carly did this so the seamen had a guiding light back home. Surprisingly, she felt at home here, despite the tension between the two of them.

"We should go out."

Brooklyn was confused. This was a woman who not only refused to leave the house but who also hid her granddaughter from the town, and now she wanted to go out? Although Brooklyn knew she wasn't much better. Last night she had a chance to go downtown with Simone and Brystol, but she chose to stay home, complaining of a headache when she was fine. Truth be told, she didn't want to run into Bowie. Rumors had spread that he was married, which made Brooklyn feel like a total fool for thinking he was flirting with her. "Where exactly would you like to go?"

Carly turned. She smiled at Brooklyn before turning to gaze out the window. "Do you know what today is?"

Unfortunately, she did. She knew the date all too well despite many attempts over the years to forget it. "I do."

"Tonight, your friends will gather on the beach . . . my beach . . . and celebrate the life of my son, their friend. They've done this every year, and tonight marks the fifteenth anniversary. Austin's been gone fifteen years, Brooklyn."

There were two things she wanted to say. One, they weren't her friends anymore—at least she wasn't sure she could call them that—and two, she was fully aware of how long Austin had been gone. She had a daughter to remind her of that every day. Instead, she sat there silently, watching Carly.

"Why would they do this? Sit on my beach where I can see them?"

In that moment, Brooklyn wanted to hug Carly, but she couldn't move from her seat. All she could do was answer her honestly. "I think it's because this was where we always hung out with Austin. This was *our* place, *our* beach. This was our home away from home. You made us all feel like we were your children. I don't think they're doing it to hurt you; more so, they're probably trying to show you they still care and trying to hang on to a little bit of the lives they had back then." Brooklyn couldn't be certain of this, especially since no one had come around to check on Austin's mom. If they had put in as much effort to remember Carly as they had her son, then maybe she wouldn't have turned into a recluse or closed the doors on the inn. Brooklyn's efforts weren't much better, but at least she spoke to Carly.

Carly breathed in deeply. Her hand clutched the windowsill as she started to cough. Brooklyn was by her side instantly, guiding her to the bed. She rubbed her back, like she had seen Simone do numerous times since her arrival, and tried to soothe her. When Carly pulled her hand away from her mouth, there was blood. Brooklyn didn't say anything. She had suspected something was wrong when Carly had phoned her, Brystol had shared her suspicions of the same with her, and now this. She ran to the bathroom and came back with a handful of tissues and a wet washcloth. Carly cleaned herself and returned to the window as if nothing were amiss.

"Downtown, people gather at Memorial Point and . . . well, I guess the word I'm looking for is *celebrate*. They're going to honor all the fishermen who have died at sea. Why they chose my son's date is beyond me, but regardless, they did, and I would like to go. I would like for us to go as a family."

Brooklyn gave in. Attending was the last thing she wanted to do, but Carly was sick, and if this was what she wanted, she would give it to her. She could deal with going downtown, mingling among people she really didn't remember. But going down to the beach tonight was out of the question. That was the last place she wanted to be. Once the remodel was finished on the inn, Brooklyn was out of there. Cape

Harbor held memories she'd buried long ago, and that's where she wanted to keep them.

Brooklyn drove Brystol, Carly, and Simone downtown. She parked as close as she could to First Street. There were barricades in place to keep traffic away from the street fair, which Brystol excitedly detailed for her mother, telling her which stop had the best fried dough, freshly squeezed lemonade, homemade ice cream, and the most beautiful jewelry. Brystol, of course, had bought a mermaid ring the night before when she came down with Simone.

As they walked along the street, memories came back tenfold for Brooklyn. She stopped in front of Hershel's Candy Store and watched the taffy puller stretch the taffy into figure eights. Next to the machine, a man dressed in all white set out a tray of freshly dipped caramel apples, some candied and others rolled in nuts. Her stomach growled, and she set her hand over it, as if to calm it down. It had been years since she tasted any of Hershel's candy, and she wondered if he still owned the place.

"Mom, did you come here when you lived here?"

She nodded at her daughter's question but kept her eyes on the displays. "All the time. I would buy your grandma her Mother's Day and birthday presents here, knowing full well that she didn't have a sweet tooth because I knew she'd share with me. Monroe and I used to come here after school and buy the taffy just as they were pulling it off the spindle. That's when it's best, when it's a little warm."

"Hershel passed away about four years ago," Simone said from beside her. "His sons run the business now and have expanded it down the coast."

"That's sort of sad; it was a staple of Cape Harbor."

Judging by Simone's sigh, she must've agreed. Everyone but Brooklyn moved. She stayed, mesmerized by the taffy and remembering how she used to love watching it when she was younger. Someone knocked on the window, startling her. She looked up and found a familiar face waving at her. She knew she couldn't run anymore and decided to step into the store.

"Brooklyn Hewett, I heard you were back in town."

"Hey, Clint, it's good to see you." She leaned in and gave her former classmate a hug. "I am back in town, for a little bit at least." Growing up, Clint would occasionally hang out with her group of friends. At one point, he had a crush on Mila, but that never went anywhere.

"Is it true the inn is reopening?"

She nodded and added a genuine smile. "Bowie and I have been renovating like crazy."

He shook his head. "I remember how heartbroken everyone was when Mrs. Woods shut the door. My dad tried to buy it, but she wouldn't even entertain an offer."

Brooklyn wasn't sure what to say. She didn't have any excuses for Carly's behavior, so she steered the conversation toward him. "I'm sorry to hear about your dad. I didn't know until now."

"He lived a long, happy life—that's for sure."

"He made a lot of us happy and kept the dentists in town in business. It's good to see you're doing your part and helping the economy."

"What can I say; it's in my blood. I hadn't heard you and Bowie were an item; is this recent?"

Brooklyn blushed. "We're not. Carly hired us separately to renovate the inn. Once it's done, I'll be back to work and living the dream." She threw up jazz hands and did a little dip to the side. She had no idea what spurred her to do this, but she felt like a complete boob. "I should probably go. It was good seeing you, Clint."

"I'm about to head out—gotta get provisions for the bonfire. I'll see you there?"

She smiled and nodded as she headed out the door. There was no use in telling him she wouldn't be there. By the time she caught up with her family, Brystol was deep into a bag of cotton candy, had a balloon tied around her wrist, and was wearing some light-up headband with tinsel hanging off in every direction.

Carly linked arms with Brooklyn and strolled down the street as if she owned it, proudly showing off her family and expertly dodging every question about where Brooklyn and Brystol had been by simply stating that Brystol spent every summer here, leaving people to ponder where the hell Carly had been. If the people of Cape Harbor were surprised to see Carly out and about, no one said anything. Most acted like they hadn't seen her in days, not years, and to Brooklyn this was concerning. During the few years she'd spent here when she was younger, everyone was up in everyone else's business. No one could do anything without a rumor starting or word spreading faster than wildfire. There was a reason gossip was called tea; it was because every nosy neighbor used the drink as an excuse to gossip.

The four of them continued through the street fair; each stop at a vendor turned into a twenty-minute gab session for people to fawn over Carly. After the fourth or fifth table, Brooklyn had had her fill. It was enough for her to become a recluse, and she could now completely understand why Carly shut herself off. Everyone was talking about Austin as if it were yesterday or last year when he passed, not fifteen years ago. She had loved Austin more than anyone aside from his mother, so she understood a little bit but felt like the town using his passing to come together every year since was a bit too much.

Austin was, by all accounts, the perfect person, according to the people they ran into. If there was an elderly person needing to cross the street, he not only stopped traffic but would get out of his truck to help them. He held doors and carried groceries, he would stop and help someone weed their garden, and he told his mother he loved her every day.

Aside from the kindness, he had the good looks. From the moment Brooklyn had met him, she was smitten, lost in his rich brown eyes. She saw her soul mate when she gazed into his eyes and knew that he was her future. Others thought the same. Some hadn't cared that he had a girlfriend and had tried their best to grab his attention. At times, it worked. At times, Austin paid too much attention to someone who wasn't Brooklyn, and those times resulted in them fighting. And as with most couples, hurtful words ensued. Through it all, Brooklyn wanted to be with Austin. She never had any doubt in her mind, even when he told her those dreams were hers and not his. Even when he said the most hurtful words possible. And even when she opened her heart again on that fateful night.

"Brooklyn."

The sound of her name and the tugging on her hand brought her attention back to the street fair. They were on the sidewalk with people passing by. She couldn't remember how she got here, too lost in her thoughts about Austin to pay attention. But Simone was standing beside her, facing the wall, shielding Carly.

On instinct, Brooklyn put her arm around Carly. "What's wrong?"

"She's tired. It's too hot out here," Simone answered for her.

"Let's go home, then." She contemplated her words as she waited for Carly's approval. Carly looked around, almost as if she were checking to see if people were staring. Brooklyn knew what she was doing and acted. "Just hold my arm. No one will be any the wiser because you've been holding it for the past hour and a half. Simone will be on your other side, and Brystol will clear a path for us."

Carly patted Brooklyn's hand and said, "Thank you." They did exactly as Brooklyn laid out. With Brystol leading the way, looking like an angry teenager, very few people tried to stop them. Many said hi, and Carly returned the sentiment but kept walking. Inside Brooklyn's SUV, she blasted the air conditioner and pointed it directly at Carly.

"That was fun," Carly said jovially. Simone laughed, but Brooklyn gawked at her like she had three heads. The woman had almost passed out, had spent far too much time in the sun talking to people she hadn't seen in years, and had had to leave due to exhaustion. That was fun for her? In some sense, Brooklyn thought it probably was, since Carly never left the inn.

Later that evening, they could smell the bonfire and hear the laughter. Brooklyn planned to go work at the inn to occupy her time, while Simone said she would start dinner. Brystol wanted to read, but Carly had other plans.

"I think we should go."

Brooklyn wasn't having it. "No."

"It would be awkward if I went by myself. Everyone knows you're here."

Thanks to you, the gossip mill, and the field trip you made us take. "You barely made it through the street fair."

Carly brushed off the statement. "I just needed a little water."

"I don't think it's a good idea."

Carly walked over to Brooklyn and took her face between her hands. The two focused on each other, and Brooklyn felt tears start to prick her eyes. "I've made many mistakes in the years since Austin died. I closed myself off, changed my whole life because of heartbreak. I know you've done the same." Carly paused as she worked through a coughing fit. This concerned Brooklyn. She wanted to tell Simone what happened earlier and talk to her about getting Carly in to see a doctor—if not in town, then one in Seattle.

"Are you okay?"

"I'm fine, dear. I'm tired of watching the world go by. Since you and Brystol arrived, I've realized how much I've missed. I'm reenergized. Simone was right—I needed the inn to reopen so I could find my purpose."

"Sometimes there are things worth missing, like what's going on outside. It'll make you sad."

"How do you know? Have you been before?"

Brooklyn shook her head. "No, but I imagine they talk about Austin."

"Maybe that's what I need. It's what she needs." She turned toward the staircase and yelled for Brystol.

"Yes, Nonnie?"

"Sweetie, some of your father's friends are having a little party outside—would you like to go with me?"

Brystol stared from her grandmother to her mother. Brooklyn sighed, feeling defeated. "We'll go for a little bit."

Carly clapped her hands together before she hugged Brooklyn. Without thinking, she smiled. Maybe Carly was right, and they needed this. It could be the closure the family needed.

Before they ventured to the beach, Brooklyn made sure she had a couple of bottles of water for Carly. With Simone in tow, they walked through the backyard and started down the wooden staircase leading to the beach. In a matter of seconds, Brystol was on the beach with her knees in the sand and Luke licking her to death. Brooklyn felt her heart drop to her stomach. She didn't want to do this. She didn't want to see the people she'd abandoned.

However, it was too late to turn back now. Her eyes slowly found the bonfire, and with it, the faces of those she had left behind all staring at her. She swallowed hard, and she stood there, taking in each and every glare. Everyone looked the same to her. She hadn't forgotten a single one of them.

She had turned to go back to the stairs when someone grabbed her hand. She glanced down at the manicured hand and followed the arm up until she met the soft eyes of Monroe. "Don't leave," she said, motioning toward the bonfire.

"I shouldn't be here," Brooklyn mumbled, and Monroe let go of her. "It's one thing to see everyone at the bar, but here . . ."

Carly came toward her and slipped her hand into Brooklyn's, tugging her along as she walked toward the group. Brooklyn thought about fighting her but shuffled her feet forward reluctantly.

"Mrs. Woods, here, have my seat." Jason Randolph stood and held out his hand, helping Carly to a spot on the log. He then turned to Brooklyn and pulled her into a strong, welcoming hug. "It's so good to see you," he said to her.

"You too." They pulled away and studied each other. "What are you up to these days?"

He smiled so widely Brooklyn couldn't help but do the same. "I'm a doctor. Just finished my residency at Mass General."

"That's awesome, Jason."

"Bowie told me what you do. I looked at your website; it's incredible. My fiancée is always watching those home makeover shows and taking notes."

"Thanks. I like it."

"And you have a daughter?"

She glanced toward Brystol and Luke.

"Stop hogging her," Monroe said, pulling Brooklyn away from Jason. "We have lots of catching up to do."

Brooklyn followed Monroe over to the bonfire. She sat, keeping her eyes on Bowie. He stared at her intently, and she couldn't decipher if he was angry that she was there or if something else was going on in his mind.

TWENTY

Every year since Austin had passed, Bowie and his friends had gotten together as if they hadn't seen each other almost every day. Sometimes all their friends returned, and other times, it was only Monroe, Graham, Grady, and him. This year, though, it was everyone. He was surprised to see Jason trudging through the sand earlier with a case of beer under his arm. He was quickly followed by Mila, who said fifteen was a milestone and that everyone needed to be together. Truthfully, Bowie wanted this gathering to stop. The reminiscing was painful. Grady was evidence of that. And Bowie wanted one year where they, as a group, didn't sit around and talk about Austin. Even their high school reunions, which, oddly enough, happened every summer as well, were geared toward remembering Austin. Sure, to the town he was a saint, but to Bowie, his best friend was a spoiled, self-centered asshole who didn't know how good he had it. Still, he had loved Austin, and hated himself for thinking harshly of him.

As Jason hugged Brooklyn, Bowie watched her. He desperately wanted to have his arms around her, to feel her body pressed against his. He missed the days when she would confide in him, when she would come running to him because of something Austin had done. He wished for the days when they were younger, holding hands as they jumped off the rocks and into the river together. He would keep his hands on her waist as they treaded water, acting chivalrous even though Brooklyn was more than capable of staying afloat without his help. It was his excuse to touch her without looking suspicious. Not that Austin was paying attention. There was always a girl or two at the beach with them, flirting any chance they could. It bothered Bowie that Austin would encourage it, that he would act like what he was doing wasn't a big deal. Bowie knew otherwise. He had spent countless hours consoling Brooklyn, being her confidant, hoping she would leave him. Only she never did.

Of all the places for Brooklyn to sit, she sat across from Bowie. He thought about going to Monroe to thank her for thinking of him but knew it was all happenstance. Their bonfire area wasn't big, by any means, but still from where he sat, he had a full view of Brooklyn. For years, he had buried his feelings. Did everything he could to forget, and now they were back, and there was no stopping them. The floodgates had opened the second he had figured out she was driving the SUV that almost ran him over. As much as he wanted to hate her, he couldn't. His heart, body, and mind wouldn't allow it, and as much as he wanted to stay away from her, to protect himself from being hurt, he found himself in her proximity, always trying to be near her. He tried to fight the connection he felt, tried to ignore it, but he couldn't. Watching her now, speaking with Monroe, he couldn't help but long for her. He wanted to lie out under the stars with her by his side, listening to her life. He yearned to hear the details of where her job had taken her, how she had managed to build such a successful business and raise a smart daughter.

He took stock of the differences from when she was twenty-two until now. The years had been good to her. He loved that she wore her hair longer, that she had filled out with curves he longed to touch. She was reserved, careful with what she said around people, almost as if the outgoing girl he once knew had changed into a shy, quiet woman. When they were alone, she closed herself off, even though he could see in her eyes she wanted to be there with him, to kiss him, feel his hands pressed against her. Yet, she held back, and he was fairly confident that Brooklyn planned to leave once the job at the inn was finished. Bowie wasn't going to let her go, not without a fight.

And now, here she was, looking directly at him instead of paying attention to whatever Monroe was saying to her. Their eyes locked, and even though a small distance separated them, Bowie could see her staring at him. He didn't dare look away. He wanted her to know he was doing the same thing, watching her.

He stepped toward her with intentions of taking her down to the surf so they could talk, but Monroe finally grabbed her attention, forcing Brooklyn to look away. He sat and focused on the red flames and embers from the bonfire, trying his hardest to sit there and pretend to mingle with his classmates. It was hot out and the fire was unnecessary, but it was their thing. They always had one. Back when they were teens, one of them—he couldn't recall who because they all suggested something stupid at least once a day—had the bright idea of burning a pile of driftwood. The blue and lavender flames were a sight to see and attracted beachgoers from all along the shoreline. What the boys hadn't counted on was becoming sick from the dioxins released by the burning logs. After a trip to the emergency room, they had learned their lesson. Shortly after the incident, the town banned all driftwood fires. Now that Bowie thought about it, they likely did so because Austin was involved, and nothing bad could happen to their precious Austin.

Bowie hated himself right now for thinking ill of his friend. The animosity he thought he had long buried was alive and kicking, and for no good reason. Austin wasn't there to defend himself, and Brooklyn . . . he could never find the right moment after Austin passed away to tell her how he felt, until it was too late. Carrying about the bitterness wasn't good for him or anyone around him. He studied their group. Brooklyn was deep in conversation with Monroe, while Carly spoke to Graham. He had no idea where Grady had run off to, probably back to the bar, but he saw Luke frolicking with Brystol and decided he'd rather be with them. He dug through the cooler and pulled out a fresh beer and bottle of water and made his way toward her.

"Mind if I sit?" he asked her. She glanced up at him, her eyes shining like a bright blue sky. Brooklyn's daughter was beautiful, a spitting image of her mother mixed with the best of her father. She pushed her glasses up the bridge of her freckled nose and smiled. He had hated wearing his glasses and was so thankful that his parents had allowed him to get contacts in middle school. Even now, he'd rather go to bed blind than put his specs on.

"Nonnie says you do this every year." She pointed toward the bonfire. "I've never been to one before."

Bowie handed her the bottle of water before he sat down in the sand. He pulled his knees toward his chest and rested his arms there. "You're not really there now, are you?"

She shrugged. "I like hanging out with Luke." Brystol nuzzled the dog, who pushed himself into her embrace.

"He loves you. I used to think he was my best friend until you came along. You know, I tried to use him as a pillow, like I had seen you do before, and he growled at me."

Brystol giggled, and it was the best sound he had heard in a long time. "Maybe I can visit him after you're done working on my nonnie's house?"

"Are you staying here?" he asked, knowing full well he was pumping the teenager for information about her mother. He wanted a little tidbit of information, something to tide him over until he came to his senses about Brooklyn.

"I told you earlier that I'm here every summer."

"How come we haven't seen you around then?" he fired back.

"Maybe you weren't looking in the right places."

"Touché, kid." He brought his bottle of beer to his lips and took a long drink. The amber liquid wasn't satisfying. "How old are you?"

"Fourteen. I'll be a freshman in the fall."

"Do you even go to school?" The question came out wrong, and before he could take it back or apologize, Brystol gave him a chiding look. He had seen it before. He had been on the receiving end of the same glare from her mother, many, many times. He chuckled and decided the beer tasted just fine and took another drink. "Sorry," he muttered.

"I'm homeschooled."

All he could do was nod. He wasn't a parent by any means but knew growing up this way was not what Austin would've wanted for his daughter. Of course, Austin would've had the girl fishing by now and probably spitting tobacco and wrestling gators or something.

"I know you don't like my mom," she blurted out.

He glanced at her but quickly turned away. Her eyes were sharp and accusing. It wasn't that he didn't like her mother. But not in the sense that he couldn't be cordial. Bowie couldn't explain his feelings for Brooklyn. He hated her and loved her at the same time.

"I . . . uh . . ."

"I know it's a complicated adult matter. That's what my mom says every time she wants to avoid talking about 'adult' things." The use of air quotes caused Bowie to laugh, which made Brystol chuckle.

"I'd like to get to know you, Brystol. Maybe teach you some of the things your dad would've done if he were here."

"Like how to fish?"

He smiled so wide he felt his cheeks stretch. "And how to sail. We could go hiking. Rock jumping. As much as your dad loved being on the water, he loved nature, and you're in one of the most beautiful states there is to explore."

"I'd like that, as long as my mom says it's okay."

Bowie peered over his shoulder and caught Brooklyn staring at them. Had she been watching them the whole time, wondering what he could possibly be telling her daughter? He held her gaze until she tore her eyes away. He watched her look down at the sand and wrap her arms around her torso. Was she cold? Not possible. So, what was she hiding herself from?

He longed to hold her, to ask her where she'd been and why she hadn't told him she was leaving. Hell, he wanted to know why she didn't ask him to go with her. They could've been great together, and Brystol would have a father because he knew, without a doubt and any hesitation, he would've stepped in to raise Austin's child as his own. They could've built a family, either here or someplace else. All he wanted was to be with her. Even now he had thoughts of what it would be like to start over, to move on. Thing was, he wasn't sure if he would ever be able to forgive her.

"Do you have any questions about your dad that I can answer for you?"

Brystol adjusted the way she sat by bringing her legs up. Luke moved as well and sat so he could lean up against his new best friend. "Why do you come out here every year on the anniversary of his death?"

"How do you know we do this every year?"

"Nonnie told me."

"Are you here when we do this?" Curiosity ran rampant through his mind.

She straightened her legs and pushed her feet into the sand. "No, Simi takes us to Seattle for dinner with my grandparents, except for this year. Nonnie wanted to go to the street fair."

"And did you go?" His mother was working a booth down there, and he wondered if they had crossed paths.

She nodded. "Twice. I went with Simi last night. It was a lot of fun. Everyone loved seeing Nonnie."

Anger moved through his veins. Everyone in town had dismissed Carly Woods. He and everyone around him had a lot of things to make up for now that she had opened the door back into her life.

"Do you know why you're named Brystol?" he asked her. He knew the answer without even conferring with Brooklyn but wanted to make sure Brystol knew.

She shook her head. "I don't think I ever thought of my name having a meaning other than my mom and grandma's names starting with a *B*."

Bowie smiled. He set his bottle down in the sand, pulled his legs up so he could rest his arms on his knees, and told her. "After we graduated high school, your dad and I, along with Jason and Graham, who are over there, and Graham's brother, Grady, piled into my mom's small sedan and drove from here to Bristol, Tennessee, to go to a NASCAR race. This was your dad's favorite track. It was one of the worst and best things we ever did as friends because the car didn't have a working air conditioner, and driving across country in August was miserable, but we had a blast. We each took turns driving so others could sleep, we ate off dollar menus from various fast-food places, used truck stops to shower, and would stop and visit tourist traps just so we could say we've been somewhere. The race, though, I remember it like it was yesterday—hot, humid, and under the lights. The roar of the engines, the smell of burning gas and rubber, and the feel of forty-three cars rumbling toward the first turn was something I've never forgotten. Nor does one forget that Dale Earnhardt won the race after starting twenty-sixth, making history, the way only the man known as the Intimidator could do."

"I don't know him."

"That doesn't surprise me. Your mom was never a fan of racing, even though we made her come to the track with us all the time."

"So I'm named after a racetrack?" She sounded skeptical.

Bowie nodded and then started second-guessing himself. "That's my best guess. Only your mom can confirm."

"My mom says that you and my dad were best friends."

"Every memory I have from growing up has your dad in it."

"That's pretty cool. I told my mom I think it would be funny if I went to the same high school as her and my dad. I don't know, though."

"About what?"

She glanced over to where her mom was. "If we're staying."

"Do you want to?"

"Yeah." She went back to petting Luke. "I like here better than Seattle. It's so quiet, and I can be on the beach whenever I want."

Bowie wanted her to stay. He wanted Brooklyn to stay as well and wondered if he could do anything to encourage her to make the decision to call Cape Harbor their home. He focused on his group of friends again and noticed not only that Rennie was here but also that Grady was approaching. He stumbled and almost fell into the firepit; however, Graham was there to catch his brother before he face-planted into the fire.

"You!" Grady screamed and pointed toward Brooklyn. "You," he said again, but this time the hairs on Bowie's arms rose to attention. "Stay here," he said to Brystol as he stood and ran toward his friends.

"Come on, Grady—you're drunk. Let's go home." Graham was trying to defuse the situation.

"When isn't he drunk?" Bowie heard Mila yell out.

Bowie stood on one side of Grady, while Graham tried to keep him in place, but the man was using his might to push through. "I fucking hate you," he screamed toward Brooklyn. Bowie looked toward her, but she was staring at the ground. Brystol, however, was right behind her, having disobeyed him. Her eyes were wide, and he felt the need to go to her, to shelter her from what was happening. Bowie didn't want Brystol to witness Grady's outburst and tried to push him away, but he held strong. "It's you who should've died. Not him. You don't deserve to live after what you did to him. You stupid bitch. Austin loved you, and you . . ." Grady stopped talking. He fell to the sand with the help of Graham. "She hurt him," he mumbled.

Brooklyn's head popped up, and her mouth dropped open. She glared directly at Bowie, who felt his heart fall into the pit of his stomach. Why would Grady say such a thing? And why was he so angry with Brooklyn? There was only one answer, but he couldn't ask the question that was on the tip of his tongue, and now wasn't the time to ask Graham. With that, Brooklyn stood, wiped angrily at her cheek while scowling at Bowie, and started toward the house with Rennie hot on her heels.

TWENTY-ONE

Brooklyn stormed through the house, slamming doors, stomping up the stairs to her room, and yelling about how stupid Bowie Holmes was. Rennie followed her and agreed with everything she said. That's what friends did. When it dawned on her that Rennie was echoing her sentiments, she stopped ranting and worked to control her breathing. She pointed toward the window, in the direction where the bonfire took place, and grunted. Rennie laughed.

"How can you laugh at a time like this?"

"Easy, you're being a bit overdramatic. So what if the town drunk says he hates you?"

"Rennie, he said I should be the one who died . . . in front of my daughter." Brooklyn held her hand to her chest. "I just . . . I shouldn't be here. It was a mistake coming back, and now Carly . . ." She let her words trail off. She never wanted Carly to think poorly of her, but the things that Grady had insinuated were enough to put a rift between her and Austin's mother.

"Who cares?"

"I do."

Rennie came to her and placed her hands on her forearms. "Carly's a smart woman. Hell, I bet everyone out there thinks that Grady Chamberlain is nothing more than a loose cannon. Of course he's going to blame you—you took off while everyone else dealt with the aftermath. You're an easy target. Let it go."

"What if Bowie told him?"

"Do you honestly think he would've done that, especially under the circumstances?"

She shook her head slowly, and as her body temperature started to regulate, she began to feel overdramatic, as Rennie had said. She covered her face with her hands and mumbled how there was no possible way she could go back out there, not after she'd stormed off.

"I'm fairly certain you're entitled to have a moment or two. What Grady said, those were hurtful words. I don't think you'll find one person out there who wouldn't have done what you did."

Brooklyn went to the window. More people had shown up, and she spotted Carly right in the mix of everything. She was thankful Jason was nearby because she would need someone to tend to her if she started coughing again. Who she didn't see was Grady, Graham, and Bowie.

"I think he's married."

"And you care, why?"

She shrugged. "I shouldn't care, but I feel like we're dancing around each other, flirting. I almost kissed him, and if he's married . . . I don't play that game, Ren. You know that."

"Ask him."

She shook her head and sighed. "It's just old feelings creeping back in."

Rennie joined her at the window, and they leaned against each other. "The people down there, they mean well."

"Carly hates that they do this every year, and she's not a fan of the town having the street fair during this time either."

"It started after he died, right?"

Brooklyn nodded.

"I'm sure whoever started the fair meant it to be a celebration and not so much a mourning. Which makes it hard for them to move on. Give the lost fisherman a statue, but leave it at that."

Brooklyn laughed. Earlier, when they were downtown, she had come across a statue of a fisherman. She had stood there, looking at the bronze man, wondering if it was Austin. That would make the entire town of Cape Harbor officially certifiable, but thankfully it was the first man to be lost at sea from town. They were honoring him as well, along with many others; they had just chosen to do it all on the day Austin had set sail and never returned.

"I don't get it," Brooklyn said as she continued to watch the people gather. "They've done this every year, and not a one of them knocked on the door to see if Carly was okay. If it weren't for Simone, she probably would've died."

Rennie clasped her hand with Brooklyn's. "I think you and Brystol saved her. Simone was just doing your job until you could return."

She shook her head and let the tears she had been holding back fall. "I don't want to stay here and give up my job, but I also don't want to leave, because I see what stability is doing for Brystol. She's happy here. She socializes with everyone. Normally when I'm on a job, she barely speaks to my crew, and now she's on a first-name basis with everyone. Bowie's crew dotes on her. And that damn dog." She paused and sought her daughter out. She was sitting off to the side with Luke right next to her, almost as if he was guarding her. "She wants a home, and if I stay here, I can give that to her."

"What are you afraid of?" Rennie asked.

"Giving up the life I've built. Being Brooklyn Hewett and not Austin Woods's girlfriend. You know how long it took me to come out of my funk, to realize that for years I allowed him to push his identity on me. I worked hard to get where I am, to make a name for myself."

"No one is saying you have to give that up, B. You can still be Brooklyn Hewett Designs; you'll just have a home base. Maybe you don't travel as much, or maybe you live with Carly, and she takes care of Brystol while you work."

Rennie was sounding more and more like Carly every day, and Brooklyn hated it because they were right. Roots were the foundation for growth, and Brystol needed some.

"I think we should go outside."

"I'm embarrassed," Brooklyn told her friend.

"In all the years I've known you, I've never known you to be embarrassed. Play it off, call it a teenage temper tantrum, spurred by Grady. Ha ha, he's so funny. Don't let his drunk ass ruin things for you."

Brooklyn knew Rennie was right, even if she hadn't wanted to admit it. In hindsight, Brooklyn should've given Grady a dose of his own medicine. Not that it would've done anyone any good.

Rennie pulled Brooklyn out of the house, down the wooden steps, and back into the fold. Graham was there first, hugging Brooklyn and telling her how sorry he was for Grady's outburst. She thanked him, spoke to a few of the people who had showed, and finally made her way over to where Brystol sat with Luke. She knew the town was about to light off fireworks and would rather be with her daughter, honoring her father, than with her friends remembering the man she had lost.

"Get him the hell out of here," Bowie yelled at Graham, who was desperately trying to push his drunken brother toward the stairs. Bowie turned, almost in circles, looking for Brystol. As much as he wanted to run to Brooklyn and apologize, his concern for Brystol was greater. He found her, standing on the outside of the group with Luke by her side. He was incredibly thankful for his dog and his affection for Brystol. He went to her, expecting to ask if she was okay, but she fell into his arms and buried her face in his chest. Bowie held her and placed a kiss on the top of her head, hoping to provide a bit of comfort until her mother came back.

"I'm sorry you had to see that," he said to her.

Brystol stepped back. "Who was that?"

He sighed. How could he explain Grady to her? Sure, he was still Bowie's friend, but not like they had been when they were growing up. Since Austin's accident, they had drifted apart, mostly due to what Grady had witnessed. The Chamberlains should've sought help for Grady after the disaster, but like most, had felt their son was okay. That couldn't have been further from the truth.

"Grady . . ." He paused and thought about how he wanted to approach the conversation. He looked at Brystol and saw her mom in every aspect of her features. He remembered Brooklyn, young and full of wonderment when she had first moved to Cape Harbor, and he saw the same in Brystol now and felt like she would understand what he was about to say. "Grady was with your dad when the accident happened, and he just hasn't recovered very well. He struggles with his demons sometimes."

"Why's he so angry with my mom?"

He shrugged because he was confused as well. "I'm not sure. His outburst caught me off guard. I've never seen him act like that. I think—"

"He has a drinking problem." Brystol threw the issue right in Bowie's face, leaving him no choice but to nod. "It's okay. My grandpa says that sometimes people can't help themselves."

"He's right."

"Maybe your friend will get the help he needs before it's too late."

Maybe. Maybe if everyone around town stopped enabling him. "I think he would probably appreciate it. Come on—let's go check on your grandma."

They made their way over to where Carly sat, along with Jason. The two were chatting away as if nothing was amiss. Brystol sat next to her grandmother, who pulled her into an embrace.

"My sweet B," Bowie heard the older woman say. Even though Brooklyn had left Cape Harbor, he was thankful she'd had the presence of mind to make sure Carly was a part of Brystol's life. He could see the love and admiration they had for each other. Brystol kissed her grandmother on the cheek, then called for Luke and separated herself from the group. He kept an eye on her, waiting to see where she was going and whether he should follow her. She took a spot on the sand, far enough away that she wouldn't have to listen to the adults talk. He wished she had a friend here to keep her company and mentally went through his employees, trying to remember who had children her age.

When Brooklyn and Rennie came down the wooden stairs to rejoin the group, Rennie came toward where he sat while he watched Brooklyn. She went right toward Brystol and sat beside her in the sand.

Without a second thought, he went to them. As he approached, Brooklyn smiled softly at him while he mouthed that he was sorry. They would have to speak about what happened later, when Brystol wasn't around, and he hoped by then he'd have a few answers from Graham.

Bowie took the spot next to Brystol, looked at his watch, and pointed to the sky. "Your father loved fireworks," he said to her. "Watch."

And as if on cue, the sky lit up with red and blue sparks. Everyone oohed and aahed. Bowie wasn't interested in the fireworks, though; he was studying the women next to him as they watched the display. He knew that they were going to change his life; he just couldn't figure out how.

When the fireworks ended, Carly called for Brystol. She told her mom and Bowie good night, gave Luke one last pat on his head, and ran toward her grandma.

"I think we're being set up," Brooklyn said to Bowie as she watched Simone, Carly, and Brystol disappear into the darkness.

"Want to go for a walk?"

She did but didn't want to come off as eager, so she pretended to think about it for a moment. Bowie, it seemed, had other ideas. He stood and reached for her hand. "What about Luke?" she asked.

He held up his other hand, showing her Luke's red leash. "He's hooked up. It's too dark for him to run around without supervision."

Brooklyn took his hand but let go as soon as she stood, then wiped the sand off the back of her shorts and fell in step next to him. They walked until the dry sand turned wet and then turned toward town.

"A setup, huh?"

She shrugged, but there was a good chance he couldn't see her. The moon wasn't overly bright, and there were very few bonfires on the beach at the moment. "I think this whole thing is a setup. She wants me to stay, mostly for Brystol, and I think Carly feels that if I'm back with all my friends, the decision will be a no-brainer."

"Is it?"

"No, it's not. I'm confused, especially when it comes to you."

"Why is that?"

She stopped in front of him and searched for his eyes. "Are you married?"

She expected him to take a step back, to put some distance between them, because she was sure she'd called him out on this little tidbit. Not that he had to tell her, but she felt like it was something he should've said to her by now, but he surprised her by stepping forward and placing his hand on her hip, just above the waistband of her shorts. His fingertips pressed into her skin, causing her to shiver.

"I'm not married, but I was. Our divorce will be final in a few months. They day I saw you, my world spun on its axis. I met my ex at the diner only to find out she was giving up her claim to alimony because she was getting remarried. We haven't been separated nine months, and she's already engaged to another man. At first, I was pissed because she's been taking my money, all while she's with this other guy, and then I realized I was going to be a free man in three months, so all was okay.

The day became gradually better when I got the call about the inn, and as much as I wanted to be angry that you came back, I couldn't be."

"Okay," she said quietly. Divorced, she could handle.

"Okay, what?" His hand moved from her hip to her hair, where he gently pushed the loose strands behind her ear.

She shook her head, unable to come up with a proper response. She couldn't make a commitment, not to him, and not to living in Cape Harbor, and she didn't want to waste Bowie's time with the back-and-forth going on in her head. However, denying her feelings for him was becoming harder and harder.

"You've been flirting with me."

"And you have with me."

She couldn't argue with him there. "You're easy to be around. Our relationship—the one we had before." She paused and gathered her thoughts. "Sometimes it feels like we could have it again if we tried."

"Is that what you want?"

"I don't know. I don't want to rush into anything and then leave, and I don't want the opportunity to pass by either."

"You're not staying?"

Brooklyn held her head high and said, "I don't know yet."

They stared at each other, both lost in the darkness with the waves pushing toward the surf. They were at a standstill, neither of them moving until Bowie cupped the back of her head and pulled her toward his lips. She placed her hands on his chest and pushed him away.

"Don't. Don't do that."

"Why not? What the hell are you so afraid of?"

She sighed. "You. I'm afraid of what you represent."

"What's that supposed to mean?"

"The past. Austin. This place. What we did."

"Get over it."

She threw her hands up in the air and scoffed. "Easier said than done. You aren't reminded of the damn past every time you look at your daughter. You aren't living in a house that is a shrine to the man that died on the night we . . ." She paused and took a deep breath. "I live with this guilt."

"And you think I don't?"

"I don't know what you live with, Bowie. I'm not here."

"You're right," he said, stepping toward her. "You're not here. You bailed when shit got bad. You left us all to pick up the pieces as if they were only ours to pick up."

"And what? You think I should stay and live with everyone hating me? Like Grady?" She shook her head. "No thanks." She turned away from him, but he wasn't having it. "Stop," she said when he stood in front of her.

"I'm not the enemy, Brooklyn. Your thoughts and memories of the past are, and yet you treat me like I've done something to hurt you when all I've ever done was be by your side and love you from afar. What happened between us had nothing to do with Austin's decision to be reckless that night."

"If we hadn't fought—" She looked away.

"If you hadn't fought that night, it would've been the next night or the one after that. The two of you were heading in different directions; you were from the start. Neither of you were willing to admit it because you were comfortable. Believe me—I get that. But to blame yourself, to blame me, it's not right."

"I know," she said quietly.

"If you know, then give me a chance. Give us a chance." He pulled her hand up to his chest, and she could feel his heart pounding for her. "As much as I hate to admit this, but seeing you, after all these years—my feelings are back. In fact, I'm certain they never went away, just dormant, held down by regret, guilt, and anger. Can you honestly tell me that you don't feel anything for me?"

She shook her head, which confused him greatly.

"Help me out, B. I'm a simple guy and need words."

Brooklyn laughed, although it sounded more like she tried to hold back a sob. "My feelings for you haven't changed in all these years. I've thought about you every day since I left. There were so many times when I picked up the phone to call you but could never press the last number. I didn't know what to say or how to apologize because telling you that I'm sorry didn't seem like enough. I made a mistake the day I left you, and I'm sorry."

His cheeks pulled so wide they started to hurt. "I'd like to take you out or at least have you over to my place for dinner. I'm not asking for much, B. Just a chance to see if what we were going to build together is still there."

"It's still there," she told him. "At least for me."

"Me too."

"Okay." She covered her face. "You must think I'm a moron. Yes, dinner at your place or wherever sounds great."

He chuckled. "And I'd like to take Brystol fishing."

"I think she'd like that."

"What about you? Do you want to come?"

She had a feeling he already knew the answer, but she gave it to him anyway. "That's a giant nope on my part."

"Yeah," he said with a sigh. "I figured as much."

They walked back toward the bonfire where everyone still sat. She excused herself and went back to the house. If she'd stayed, she would've had a beer or two, and she didn't want to be responsible for what she did or what words came out of her mouth. It was better for everyone involved if she wasn't there.

TWENTY-TWO

For the first time in years, Carly felt alive. She sat in front of her vanity, brushing her hair as she listened to the laughter down below. Austin's friends had come out to honor him once again, and she was thankful to have been a part of the celebration this time. Many people she didn't know or couldn't remember had come out, but his core group of friends was there, right along with his daughter. It hadn't escaped her notice either that Bowie had chosen to sit with her girls. She had watched them through the night, and if she hadn't known better, she would've called them a family. Every so often, Bowie would point at the sky, and Brystol would pay attention to whatever he was saying to her. When Carly wasn't focused on them, she stared out over the ocean, trying to pinpoint the spot where her son had perished as the embers from the fireworks disappeared into the water. As much as she hated the continual merriment, she loved that everyone came together for her son.

She looked at her aging skin and felt sad. Since Brooklyn and Brystol had returned, she'd noticed how old she'd gotten over the years. Carly pulled her skin, trying to erase the wrinkles that had taken over her life in the last fifteen years and for a brief moment saw the woman she used to be.

And she missed her.

She missed the person she used to be. The one who took care of everyone, who opened her heart and welcomed strangers into her home, the one who loved fully and subsequently lost everything. She missed the old days when her days were filled with laughter and her nights occupied by the sound of the ocean crashing on the shore and the taste of a nice chardonnay. After her husband and son had passed, she couldn't remember what it was like to feel arms wrapped around her, not until Brystol had understood what a hug was and could hold her grandmother in her tiny arms, and now she wanted one every day. From her granddaughter, the woman her son had loved, and his friends.

The inn was coming back alive, thanks to Brooklyn and Bowie, and Carly felt it was time to really give it her all. She would invite Austin's friends for dinner. She wanted them gathered around her table again, and she would make it a weekly event. Maybe on Sunday, after church services. And yes, she would go back to church to reconnect with the people she had long shut out, with her friends from the community. Seeing a few of them downtown earlier had shown her just how much had passed her by. She would host a card game, maybe start a book club and invite the new winery in Skagit Valley to host a wine tasting in the ballroom.

Yes, life was looking up for Carly.

She stood and went to the window and pushed the pane up. She closed her eyes as the voices from outside washed over her. The light breeze pushed against her white nightgown, and she smiled. She knew it was Skip and Austin greeting her, telling her how much they loved her. The only solace she took in the death of her husband and son was knowing that they were together.

Carly left her curtains open as she retired to bed. She fluffed her pillows and rested her tired, aching body against them. She stared out the window at the moon; it was moving slowly toward the horizon but was still high enough to cast a glow into her room. The familiar tickle was back, and she cleared her throat, hoping to get rid of it. She was going to have to tell Brooklyn before too much more time passed. There were things she needed to know. Unfortunately, it was a conversation she wasn't looking forward to.

Her eyes closed, and she thought of Skip and Austin, out on their boat, reeling in their catch for the day. She had always been so proud of her men, more so of Austin for starting a successful fishing company at such a young age. Not that she had expected anything less from him. He had always known what he wanted and had never had any qualms about going after his dreams. Brooklyn even being one of them.

He had confided in his mother about his relationship with Brooklyn. He had worried about Bowie and wondered if he was a better man for Brooklyn. Austin trusted that Bowie knew he'd never do anything to jeopardize their friendship. Brooklyn and Bowie were close, best friends, and that sometimes bothered Austin. Carly always reassured her son that Brooklyn loved him. She could see it in her eyes, and Bowie's too. Austin wasn't so sure. Brooklyn had dreams. She wanted to move, to head south and go to school, something Austin had promised her. He wanted to stay but couldn't find the words to tell her, mostly because he thought she'd leave him. Leave him for her best friend, because as sure as he was of their love for him, Austin told her that Bowie likely loved Brooklyn more.

After witnessing the closeness of Bowie and Brooklyn, Carly would agree with her son. Austin had tried hard to be a good man to Brooklyn but had had trouble prioritizing his life. When she should've come first, fishing did. He was no different than his father. They both had hooked the woman of their dreams and then set them aside while they continued their chosen paths.

She thought more of Skip and the last time she saw him. She had been busy in the kitchen, the inn was full of guests, the dining room had tables full of people, and her cook had called out sick. Skip was leaving, heading out to sea. He had told her the night before it would take them a while to get where they were going. She remembered telling him to pack his warmer clothes because it was cold up north and she didn't want him catching a cold. A cold would turn into pneumonia, and they were far too busy to deal with something like that.

Before he left, he had wanted to speak to her, but she couldn't leave the kitchen, or maybe it was that she hadn't wanted to. Her business, much like Skip's, was important to her. Her reputation in the community was stellar, and she didn't want a mishap to tarnish that.

He begged, and she brushed him off, offering him her cheek for a quick peck and asking him what day he was due back. "After the catch," he told her. That meant once their onboard freezer had filled, they would come back. He said he would radio later and walked out of the kitchen.

If Carly had known that was the last time she would see her husband, she would've driven him to the dock and walked him to his boat. She would've kissed him longingly and told him how much she loved him. She had put her job in front of her husband. Just as he had put his in front of his wife, and Austin had done the same to Brooklyn.

That night, Carly and Austin had sat in Skip's fishing shack and waited for the radio to come to life. Skip was hard to hear, but they were able to make out that he was in the Strait of Georgia. As with every new place they visited, Austin marked it on the map. Austin wished his father good luck, and Carly told him she'd watch for the pink sail to come into the harbor. They signed off for the last time.

That summer the Strait of Georgia was experiencing unseasonably warm weather, often resulting in the occasional lightning storm. *Boreas*, the ship Skip Woods captained, had been hit, knocking out its entire electrical system. The crew was prepared to wait for the Coast Guard or a passing vessel. They just had to be patient. While they waited, the crew worked to repair the electricity, and Skip started Morse code. Hour after hour he flashed a light toward land, three quick flickers, followed by three longer flashes and three quick flickers.

When Carly and the other wives hadn't heard from their husbands, they came together and hired a crew to go out and look for them. With no last-known coordinates, the search took longer than expected. It was weeks before the ship returned to port, being towed by another. They radioed ahead; the *Boreas* was coming home with one lost soul on board. No one knew who had died. As the ships came in, the wives held hands, waiting for their husbands to disembark.

Carly knew, though; she felt it deep in her bones. If Skip were alive, the pink sail would've been raised and blowing in the wind. Her fears had been confirmed when the *Boreas* crew offered their condolences. It was Skip's best friend who told her that Skip had a heart attack, and there was nothing they could do for him.

Skip Woods had died on their third day stranded at sea. One of the crew had fired the flare gun and startled Skip. The incident sent his heart into tachycardia, and he couldn't recover. That was the coroner's official report.

Carly refused to believe her husband had a bad heart. He was a fit man who watched what he ate and exercised regularly. He was a social drinker and never did drugs. The coroner had to be wrong. She had his body sent to Seattle because she felt the medical staff in the big city were more knowledgeable. When the report also came back that her husband had suffered from high cholesterol and blood pressure, she was left with no other option than to believe his time had come.

"Nonnie, are you still awake?"

Carly opened her eyes at the sound of her granddaughter's voice. She smiled into the darkness and pulled the comforter back to invite Brystol to sit next to her. "Are you coming to say good night?"

"Mm-hmm," she said as she snuggled into her grandma's side. "What are you doing?"

She ran her hand through Brystol's hair. She smelled like sun and sand, two of Carly's favorite things. "I was just thinking about your grandfather."

"Skip?"

Carly sighed. She loved hearing his name. "I met him when I was about your age."

"Was it love at first sight?"

She giggled at her granddaughter's question. "Oh, heavens no. I wanted nothing to do with your grandfather, but he persisted, and when I was much older, I finally let him take me on a date."

"And the rest is history?"

"Yes, and it was a good history. I love your grandpa very much."

"Even though he's been gone for a long time?"

"You never forget your first love no matter how long they're gone. You also don't always marry your first love, but you will always remember them."

"Like my mom and dad."

"Yes, exactly."

"Mommy always says that they had a one-of-a-kind love affair."

Her words made Carly smile. "Yes. Your parents were very in love, and I had the pleasure of watching their love grow over the years."

"Do you think I would've lived here if my dad hadn't died?"

Carly hugged her granddaughter tighter. "I don't know. Your mom wanted to be a nurse, and sometimes I think she would've convinced your dad to move, but sometimes I think that they would've stayed here."

"I want to stay," Brystol said. "I don't want to move around anymore."

She leaned forward and kissed the top of her head. "I know, sweetie. We'll talk to your mom about staying. I know she's been thinking about it, but she has a very successful business, so she has to think about that and your future as well."

Brystol snuggled into her grandma's embrace. "Nonnie, can I sleep with you?"

"Of course, my sweet baby girl."

Carly closed her eyes and drifted off to sleep with her granddaughter held tightly in her arms and thoughts of Skip and Austin running through her mind.

TWENTY-THREE

Brooklyn woke to the sound of birds chirping and the sun shining, but the night before still weighed heavily on her mind. She had to find Grady and ask him what he was talking about. She needed to clear the air because his outburst had left her with a horrible feeling. She also wanted to spend more time with Bowie, but away from the inn, where people could interrupt them. They needed quality time to figure things out. When he had sat down with her and Brystol for the fireworks, she had been tempted to ask him to go back to his friends and to his wife. She had also wanted him to stay. She hated being torn in half when it came to him. Regardless of whether she stayed, she wanted Bowie and Brystol to have a relationship. He'd be able to fill in where Austin couldn't. She liked the idea of him being a part of Brystol's life, and maybe even hers, even though she knew their friendship would never be what it once was. She wasn't even sure she could go there again with him.

She thought about staying in bed all morning. Listening to the waves crash against the shore and hearing the laughter from the beachgoers soothed her. Since her return to Cape Harbor, she had found herself going to bed later, almost as if she were going to miss something important. And as much as she wanted to leave and go back to the life she'd been living, the thought of not watching the sunset over the ocean every night was weighing heavily on her mind. Despite leaving on bad terms after Austin passed away, she felt as if she could make amends and really make a home in Cape Harbor or somewhere nearby. Doing so would make Brystol happy. Being with her grandparents all the time would be a good thing for her daughter.

After making her bed, showering, and brushing her teeth, she finally made her way downstairs, shocked to find the kitchen and living room full of people. All her friends, or the ones she used to call her friends, smiled and told her good morning as she came into view. Brooklyn was looking around, trying to figure out what was going on, when Carly came into the room.

"Good morning, Brooklyn."

"Morning. What's everyone doing here, Carly?" she asked quietly.

"I invited them." Carly shrugged as if this were an everyday occurrence. She walked back into the kitchen, singing a song Brooklyn wasn't familiar with.

"I see that, but why?" she asked, following her.

"Last night I realized life's too short to not be surrounded by the people you love."

Brooklyn had a list of reasons why Carly shouldn't have these people at her house, feeding them breakfast, with the most glaring being they had all abandoned her after her son died. Brooklyn knew Carly would blame herself and say something about how she could've reached out to Austin's friends. The argument would be futile, so she left it alone.

She poured herself a cup of coffee and went into the living room. She expected awkward silence, but it was like nothing had ever changed. Monroe moved the blanket she used to keep warm, inviting Brooklyn to sit next to her on the love seat. She sat and pulled the blanket over her lap, as if she were back in time, as if they had been doing this all along.

Jason, Graham, and Bowie were lounging around the room, with their feet dangling over the sides of the sofa and overstuffed chair. Brooklyn giggled. Nothing had changed. It didn't matter that they hadn't been together for the last fifteen years; they were comfortable and back in the home where they had all grown up. Rennie, Grady, and Mila were the only ones missing. Rennie had left before the fireworks to drive back to Seattle, and it wasn't odd for Mila to skip out—she always had bigger plans—but Brooklyn felt the absence of Grady.

Carly filtered in and out of the room with trays of warm cinnamon rolls and freshly made coffee. She smiled, and for the first time Brooklyn recognized the woman she used to be. As much as she wanted to tell her to sit down and enjoy her own breakfast, she couldn't. Carly was back in her element of being the hostess. Her house was once again filled with everyone she loved.

An hour had passed when Brooklyn got up to take everyone's dishes to the sink. She didn't want Carly to have to clean up since she had made breakfast. She really didn't want Carly cooking for everyone, either, but she was going to let her have her moment. They were few and far between, and depriving her of something she wanted to do seemed mean.

Carly wasn't in the kitchen when she went in there. Brooklyn set the stack of plates down in the sink and spotted Carly through the window, sitting on the beach. She left and went to her, hoping for a few private moments with her.

Brooklyn sat down next to Carly and pulled her knees to her chest. "You're a good person for opening your doors to them. They don't deserve your hospitality. None of us do."

Carly wove her arm through Brooklyn's. "Being with everyone for Austin's memorial really opened my eyes to what I've missed over the years. I loved having everyone here."

"But to invite them over for breakfast?"

"They spent the night. Simone suggested they stay because everyone had been drinking. She didn't want them driving home."

"Where did they sleep?"

"Bowie let them into the inn. He said a few more rooms were put together, so it wouldn't be an issue."

She didn't know how long they stayed out there, but it was long enough for the rest of them to come out to say goodbye to Carly and thank her. Monroe was the first one to say goodbye. She gave Carly a hug, which Brooklyn knew Carly needed. Jason was next and then Bowie. Neither of them left, though. They lingered, almost as if they had something to say. Brooklyn wanted to talk to Bowie but wasn't sure if now was the time or later. She'd see him the next morning, and they could talk then.

Carly stood and stretched. She started walking toward the ocean. Her steps were slow and somewhat staggering. Brooklyn stood, and before she could reach her, Carly collapsed in the sand. Brooklyn and Bowie took off in a dead sprint. It seemed to take forever to get to Carly even though she hadn't walked that far. The sand was like molasses, slowing them down with every step.

"Carly, can you hear me?" Brooklyn fell to her knees and reached for her hand. Her fingers were searching for a pulse on Carly's wrist. She could feel it, but it was faint. But then again, Brooklyn wasn't sure if it was her own heart beating so rapidly that she was misconstruing the sensation.

"Jason!" Brooklyn screamed out his name. She searched the area, seeing faces she didn't know who had started to gather. Had he left? Wasn't he just with Bowie? The last few minutes of her life seemed to jumble together, and she couldn't tell if time moved slowly, or was it moving fast? How many minutes had Carly been lying on the ground? Brooklyn tried to figure out what she was supposed to do. She could see the rise and fall of Carly's chest and was sure she could feel air coming from her nostrils.

"I called for an ambulance." The voice belonged to Bowie and surprisingly reassured her. "They'll be here soon."

"What about Jason? He was just here. Where did he go?" she asked, assuming he'd be able to help Carly.

"I'm right here," he said calmly as he dropped down in the sand next to Carly and started his assessment. He hovered his ear over her nose to check her breathing, and pulled up her eyelids and flashed a penlight in her eyes.

The sound of sirens seemed a million miles away. "What's taking them so long?" Brooklyn asked. Someone put a reassuring hand on her back and told her they were on their way, but that wasn't enough. Her heart raced with panic. They hadn't been able to rouse Carly, and Brooklyn knew enough from her yearning to be a nurse that that wasn't a good sign.

She saw her daughter rushing down toward them, with Simone right by her side. "Nonnie," Brystol screamed out. "Mommy, what's wrong with Nonnie?" Brystol asked. Brooklyn glanced at Simone, who paled and shook her head slightly in warning.

"We don't know, sweetie. The ambulance is almost here," Brooklyn said to her daughter. It was meant to comfort her, but she could see the anguish in her face. She had a choice: leave Carly to be with her daughter or . . .

Bowie answered her internal plea. He went to Brystol and stood next to her, making sure Luke was with them. He set his hand on her shoulder and pulled her close to him, as if he was protecting her. Bowie was there for her daughter, just as he had been there for her in her many times of need. He was always there with the right things to say, with an encouraging hand and a shoulder to lean or cry on. He never asked for more. He never demanded Brooklyn return the favors. And now, here he was taking care of her daughter when she couldn't. He was doing what he had always done with her when it came to Austin, and now he was doing what he would've done had Brooklyn stayed. She could've given her daughter a different life, a life with a man she knew would've played a role that wasn't his. She couldn't watch them together, not now at least, and turned her attention back to Carly, saying her name over and over, praying she would wake up.

"Why isn't she responding, Jason?"

He shook his head. "I don't know. Is she sick? What medicines is she on?"

Before Brooklyn or Simone could answer, the local EMTs were on the beach and heading their way. They yelled for people to clear a path, and while one barked out questions, the other put an IV into Carly's wrist. Within a few minutes they had her on a backboard and were carrying her toward the stairs.

"Wait, where are you taking her?" Brooklyn stopped them. She knew there wasn't a hospital in town, only the office that her father used to work at. She remembered clearly that he used to be on call most of the weekends until he could hire another doctor to help fill in.

"Skagit Valley. Are you family?" Brooklyn nodded, but there was no way she could go with Carly and leave Brystol behind.

"Go," Bowie said, standing next to her. His hand softly touching her arm. "I'll bring Brystol. We'll be right behind you." Brooklyn sought confirmation from her daughter. Brystol's expression told her nothing. What spoke volumes was her daughter's white knuckles from the death grip she had on Luke's leash. This dog was giving her daughter some peace of mind and comfort, something Brooklyn wasn't capable of right now. "B." Bowie's voice was softer this time. He stepped forward, closing the gap between them. "I'd never let anything happen to her."

She knew this, deep in her heart. But it still unnerved her to see her daughter so close to a man she had spent years hating. Brooklyn took off in a dead sprint, catching up to the ambulance before they shut the doors. She expected Simone to be in the back also, but it was just her and the EMT.

"Has she been sick?" he asked.

Brooklyn shook her head. "I just got to town not too long ago. Um . . ." Brooklyn pressed her hand to her forehead, trying to think.

The truck hit a pothole, and Brooklyn slammed into the side, her arm banging hard against a protruding corner. She bit her lip to keep from crying out but couldn't stop the tears.

The EMT reached across Carly for Brooklyn's arm. He held it still with one hand while rifling through his supplies. He popped an ice pack over his knee and told her to hold it on her arm. She did as he instructed while he secured a bandage over it to hold it in place.

"Is this necessary?"

"Unfortunately, yes. Mostly precautionary, but since you were hurt in the ambulance, I have to treat you as well. Now back to my question: Has she been sick?"

Brooklyn inhaled deeply. "I don't know. I suspected something was wrong, but we're not exactly close. I've noticed tissues with blood on them in the bathroom, and yesterday she coughed up blood."

"How much?" he asked without taking his eyes off Carly.

"What do you mean?"

"Was it just a drop of blood?"

She shook her head, but he wasn't looking at her. "It was a lot. I mean for someone coughing. It was a lot of blood."

He continued to monitor Carly. She remained unconscious, lifeless. Brooklyn took her frail hand in hers and bent over. She whispered a prayer, begging Austin to spare his mother a little bit longer so his daughter wouldn't remember her grandmother this way.

Once they arrived at the hospital, everything moved quickly. Carly was rushed into the emergency room, and Brooklyn was told to stay in the waiting room. She stood there long after the doors closed, holding her arm and thinking about nothing. All her thoughts were lost, her mind blank. It was the sound of Bowie's voice that brought her back to reality. They were in the hospital, and he was standing there with her daughter glued to his side, as if they'd known each other for years and not weeks . . . as if they meant something to each other.

In that moment, she realized that was exactly what she wanted. She *wanted* Brystol and Bowie to mean something to each other. She *wanted* Bowie to mean something to her. And if she was being honest, she even wanted to mean something to Bowie. Life hit her squarely in the chest as she stared at them. She should've never left, or at least she should've come back. Instead, she had run. She had run from her life, from her mistakes, and from her future. There wasn't a doubt in her mind that she would've married Bowie if she had stayed, and that scared her now as much as it had back then. She knew that after Austin died, all she would have had to do was open the door and Bowie would've been there. He would've held her through her tears, guided her through her heartbreak, and been the hand she held while delivering her daughter. But she didn't. She couldn't. What had deterred her was her apprehension that Carly wouldn't understand, that their friends would turn their backs on them. She hadn't cared if they shunned her, but not Bowie. He would need them with Austin gone. Still, she longed for her best friend and the easy way he was able to comfort her.

He bent down and whispered into Brystol's ear. Brooklyn saw her daughter smile, and she continued to hold that smile until she reached her. "Mommy, Nonnie will be okay."

Brooklyn brought her daughter into her arms, careful not to bump the bandage, and worked hard to hold her sobs in. She didn't want to cry in front of Brystol—she wanted to remain strong and hopeful—but the truth was, Carly was sick and hiding it from everyone. Brystol tightened her hold around her mother's waist before pulling back.

"I'm going to go to the cafeteria and get a drink. Would you like something?"

She pushed the short wispy pieces of her daughter's hair away from her face and grinned. "I'm okay. I'm going to sit in the waiting room and wait for Nonnie's doctor to come out." She leaned down and kissed her daughter on the nose, not caring if the teen liked it or not.

As soon as Brystol was out of sight, Bowie moved toward Brooklyn. He reached for her arm and ran his fingers over the bandage.

"I'm okay," she said.

Bowie held her arm, letting his thumb rub over the dressing. "Okay," he said, quietly echoing the word she had said to him the night before. As soon as he looked into her eyes, all reservations were gone. She launched herself into his arms and let her tears flow. He held her tightly, and she buried her face in the crook of his neck. "It's going to be okay," he told her. She wanted to ask him how he could be so certain but couldn't bring herself to say the words.

She didn't know how long they stood there, holding each other. When others passed by, they didn't move. When another emergency came in, they continued to stand there. It wasn't until her sobs ran dry that Bowie took her hand and led her into the waiting room. He brought them to a corner, away from most of the people. Bowie rested his arm behind her, along the back of the dark-orange, two-cushioned chair, with his hand touching her shoulder and his other hand holding hers, resting on her lap. The way they were sitting was awkward; it made them look as if they were closer than they truly were, but she didn't want him to move.

Simone rushed in and looked frantically around the waiting room. Bowie called her over, and she took the open chair across from them, sighing heavily in relief. In her lap, she held a clear plastic bag full of pill bottles. She regarded the two of them, her eyes roving over them. If she had something to say about the way they were sitting, she held it in.

"What's wrong with Carly?" Brooklyn asked her pointedly.

Simone sighed. From the look in her eyes, Brooklyn could tell she had been crying. "She's sick, Brooklyn."

"How sick?" she asked, finally leaning forward. The second Bowie's hand slipped from hers, she felt the loss. She told herself it was nothing more than nostalgia playing games with her, even though deep down she knew that wasn't true. He used to be her go-to, her best friend, the guy she would dump her troubles on, and in turn he would make her laugh and tell her that everything was going to be all right. Just as he had done earlier. Bowie and she weren't friends; they were so much more, and yet, they weren't. How do you depend on someone you haven't seen or spoken to in fifteen years? How do you forget a part of your life when one moment was the catalyst for your life changing? Brooklyn wasn't sure, but she already knew that Bowie had forgiven her when he stepped up when her daughter needed someone, and he was here, being her rock like nothing had ever changed.

Simone reached for Brooklyn's hands. She tried to smile, but Brooklyn could tell it was forced. Simone cleared her throat and said, "Carly has cancer. It's stage four, and she's refused treatment. At her last checkup, she was given months to live."

Brooklyn's mouth dropped open as she leaned back slowly until her back touched the cushion of the sofa. Bowie was talking to her, but she couldn't make heads or tails of what he was saying. She couldn't even focus on Simone, as she and the people around her were nothing more than a blur. Her daughter's grandmother was dying. She was there because of this. Remodeling the inn was nothing more than a ruse to get her to return home. To have her here, along with Brystol, so that when Carly passed, what she had left for family was by her side.

It all made sense now, why Carly was so adamant that they go downtown and to the bonfire. She was preparing to say goodbye.

TWENTY-FOUR

When Brystol returned, she had a tray of snacks and drinks for everyone. That was Bowie's suggestion, to bring comfort foods. He should've gone to do it himself, but something had told him to stay and make sure Brooklyn didn't need anything. More so, he wanted an excuse to be with her alone and knew if she were vulnerable, she wouldn't push him away. But now that Brystol was back, she sat between them, and he had all but been forgotten. He used that chance to watch mother and daughter interact, and to witness how close Brystol and Simone were. Simi, as Brystol called her, seemed almost comforted each time her nickname was said. Still, it baffled and hurt Bowie that Austin's daughter had been kept a secret. He didn't know who to blame, Brooklyn or Carly, mostly himself. Deep down he thought it was Carly, but for the life of him he couldn't grasp why she would do such a thing. There was so much he wanted to ask Brooklyn, and if the time had been right, maybe he would've. As it was, they were playing the waiting game. Her, waiting to hear about Carly, and him, waiting for Brooklyn to announce that she was leaving. He hoped his plea from the other night meant something to her, enough that she would consider staying. But if Carly were to die, where would that leave them? After holding Brooklyn earlier, even though it was only meant to comfort her, he knew without a doubt he was falling back in love with her.

His phone continued to vibrate in his pocket, likely Graham or Monroe trying to find out what was going on. Shortly after he had arrived, he had seen Jason walk through the double doors of the emergency room, but he had yet to emerge. Whatever was going on with Carly was taking a lot of time. He hadn't had much experience with situations like this but felt that maybe time wasn't on their side right now. That if Carly was okay, someone would've come out to tell them already.

He excused himself to go outside to check his phone. He glanced at the display and saw a barrage of missed calls and text messages. Word traveled fast about Carly, and everyone wanted to know what was happening.

"Graham," he said into the receiver after his friend picked up.

"What's going on?"

"Carly collapsed out on the beach. She's in the ER now. I don't know much, but Simone says she's been sick."

Graham muttered a few choice words. "What can we do?"

"Can you head over to Carly's and make sure Luke's in the house? He may need to go out."

"I'm on it. Call me or Roe if you need anything."

"Oh, maybe you can call Rennie. I think Brooklyn's going to need her."

"Yeah, of course." After Bowie hung up, he inhaled deeply. Today was not going as planned. When he had awoken in the inn, he had thought he'd have a new start with Brooklyn, that they'd spend the day together. He was happy to be with her now, though, and he was going to take what time with her he could get.

He walked back into the hospital and went to the waiting room and found Brooklyn sitting by herself. "Where're Brystol and Simone?" he asked. He didn't even hesitate and sat right next to Brooklyn, putting his arm back where it had been. The only thing he couldn't bring himself to do was reach for her hand. It was almost as if the comforting moments had passed.

"They went to the nursery to look at the babies." Brooklyn sighed. She rubbed her hands down her legs and leaned forward, staring at the double doors. "What's taking so long?"

"I don't know, B. I'm sure in her fragile state they're running all sorts of tests. Did anyone tell the doctor what Simone said?"

She nodded. "She's dying, Bowie. How am I going to tell Brystol?" She covered her face and started to weep. Without hesitation he pulled her into his arms. He fought back his own wave of tears while she poured out her own. He cradled her head, feeling the smooth chocolate strands of her hair. A flood of memories came rushing back.

"What do you think?" Brooklyn asked as she pushed up the ends of her hair. Bowie smiled because it was the right thing to do, but she had cut her hair, chopping off her long locks. Gone was the ponytail he loved to tug to get her attention.

"You look so much older," he said. It was something his mother always said each time he, Austin, or the twins cut their hair.

"That's good, right? Like in my early twenties? Not thirties?"

"Definitely not." He stepped forward and rubbed a strand of hair between his thumb and index finger. It was soft and silky and had a little curl to it. He was going to love it because he was in love with her. "What did Austin say?"

"I haven't shown him yet."

"Am I the first?" Bowie wanted to be her first everything. That ship had sailed after Austin told him about their first time together. He knew Brooklyn had cried and that Austin had just sat on the edge of the bed. Bowie wasn't sure what he would've done but knew in his heart he would've held her and maybe cried with her. He liked to think that he would've cared

for her and told her how much he loved her, how he saw them having a future together. He knew he wouldn't have been like Austin and handed Brooklyn her clothes. If he had, he would've dressed her just so he could feel her skin against his flesh.

She smiled. "I figured you'd tell me the truth. Austin will tell me I look good, but he won't really see me. You, though, you always tell me when my butt looks too big in jeans."

Never, because you're perfect. *He couldn't say those words out loud, but he wanted to. He wanted to tell her that she should dump Austin because he didn't deserve someone like her. He couldn't, though. Austin was his best friend; dicks before chicks and all that stupid shit he was forced to follow. He would stay in the friend lane, being there when she needed him. He hated it, though, because he was madly in love with her and knew he'd never have the chance to show her.*

"I can be there with you, if you want. Or make sure Luke is there. She's grown very attached to my dog. I'm afraid that when you leave, he'll want to go with her." He was opening the door for her to tell him that she wasn't leaving, that they were staying. But she remained silent except for a small chuckle. Brooklyn pulled away and wiped her eyes. He wanted her back in his arms; it was where she belonged, at least in his mind.

"Brystol wants a dog."

"Sort of need a house for a dog."

She eyed him. "You pump my daughter for too much information."

He smiled. "It's the only way to find out where you've been for the last fifteen years."

Brooklyn rolled her eyes and looked away. "I don't want to talk about the past right now."

"Brooklyn Hewett?"

Both Brooklyn and Bowie stood as her name was called. Bowie honestly thought he would see Jason again or he'd at least come out with the doctor, but he was nowhere in sight.

"Hi, I'm Dr. Briggs. I wanted to talk to you about your mother." Brooklyn hadn't bothered to correct the woman. "As you know, she's battling stage four breast cancer, and the scans show it's spread. I'm sorry, but your mother doesn't have much time. We are moving her to a room now; you'll be able to see her in a little bit." The doctor put a reassuring hand on Brooklyn's arm, smiled softly, and left.

Bowie caught Brooklyn just as she was about to collapse. He helped her over to the sofa and sat them down, refusing to let go of her. "It's going to be okay," he tried to reassure her.

"It's not," she said. "None of this is going to be okay."

TWENTY-FIVE

It took over an hour, but the hospital staff finally put Carly into a private room. The first room she was assigned to had another person in there, along with their family. The room was small and crowded, and Brooklyn couldn't think with all the noise. She asked that Carly have more privacy, demanded it. Told them cost wasn't an issue. Carly was dying, and Brooklyn wanted her death to be as peaceful as possible. She wanted their small family to grieve together without others looking on. She wanted to tell Carly how much she appreciated her, loved her, and wished things could've been different. Most importantly, she wanted to tell her goodbye without strangers lingering around them. That was exceptionally important considering she never had that chance with Austin.

Once the staff had settled Carly, Brooklyn encouraged Bowie to go home and get some rest. They still had a construction project to complete, and Brooklyn still intended to open the inn, at least for the summer. After that, she had no idea what she would do and supposed her decisions would come down to whatever Carly left in her will. Brooklyn also sent Simone and Brystol home and told them to come back tomorrow with a few of Carly's things to decorate the room with. She saw the pained look in her daughter's eyes and knew she was going to have to break the news to her that her nonnie was going to heaven. Brystol was a smart girl, though, and had likely figured it out. Still, the words needed to be said so she could say goodbye; Brooklyn owed them that at least.

In the room, Brooklyn gazed out the window. Skagit Valley and Cape Harbor weren't all that different. They both had beautiful landscapes, and tulip fields that stretched on for days, but where they differed was Cape Harbor had the ocean, and right now Brooklyn missed the comforting sound of the crashing waves and the smell of sea salt. She sat on the window ledge and pulled her knees up to her chest. She closed her eyes. She needed Austin now more than ever, to give her the answers.

"Is this your house?" Brooklyn asked as Austin pulled into the circular drive-way of the inn. Brooklyn knew her parents had stayed here before, and she had seen the hotel from downtown, but being this close was awe inspiring. She was in love with it and hadn't even seen the inside yet.

"Sort of." He shut his truck off and made his way to the other side to open Brooklyn's door, then held her hand as she climbed out. Once her feet were firmly on the ground, he shut the door and pushed her up against it, kissing her. They had only been hanging out for a week, but he had already kissed her the night of the bonfire. They both had a free period together—she had wanted to study, but Austin had other ideas. He had taken her down a ramp, toward the music rooms, and into a small alcove, where he kissed her for the first time. It wasn't a peck or even two. The teens made out for an hour, grop-ing and touching each other. Still, she was curious as to what it all meant. She wanted to be his girlfriend but had a feeling Austin wouldn't appreciate the label. He hadn't seemed like the type, and she feared he had other girls waiting in the wings. Aside from Monroe and Mila, the other girls in the school gave her the cold shoulder, and she had a feeling that was because of Austin. She saw the way they stared at him, with stars in their eyes. Much like she had.

When he pulled away, his eyes were hooded, and his bottom lip was between his teeth. Seeing him like this, and knowing she was the cause of his reaction, excited her. She wanted him, and she knew he wanted her. She could feel how much when he pressed against her. He took her hand in his and led her not into the hotel but to the house attached to the side. Compared to the hotel, the house was small. As soon as she stepped inside, though, it was anything but. The cathedral ceiling made the living room look large, but it was the back wall of the house, where the kitchen was, that really took Brooklyn's breath away.

"Your mom must love to cook," she said, standing at the sink. Through the window, she could see boats coming in and out of port with sails of all different colors. Austin stood behind her with his hands on her hips.

"Do you see the one with the pink sail? That's my dad's boat. He's done fishing for the day and will sail down to the next port and sell to the market."

"He doesn't sell locally?"

"Sometimes—it depends on what he caught and who is looking for what. There's a system out on the sea."

"Why's his sail pink?"

"So my mom can always find him." Brooklyn turned to face him. He brushed her cheek with the back of his hand. "Come on—I want you to meet my mom. She's going to love you."

Again, he took her hand and led her through the main floor of the house, through a wooden door, and down a dark hallway. "It's an old passageway."

"Why aren't there any lights?"

"There's no electricity in here, and my dad doesn't want to use those oil lamps because he's afraid they'll cause a fire."

"Does your mom use this?"

"No, not usually. Normally, she walks out the front door and into the main door of the inn."

"So why are we?" Brooklyn asked, wary of where they were. She bumped into him when he stopped walking. His arms went around her instantly, and his lips found her mouth. He didn't need light or even touch; he sensed exactly where she was. His tongue sought entrance into her mouth, and she *gave him access freely. She moaned when he leaned into her, yearning for him to touch her.*

"Because I wanted to kiss you like that," he said as he pulled away. His forehead rested against hers, and his breathing was labored.

"You can kiss me anytime you want."

"Thank God, because I can't get enough of you."

His words made her heart dance. She, too, couldn't get enough of him and knew she was already falling in love with him. She knew love was dangerous, though; it led to heartbreak and turmoil.

He opened another door, and they stepped out into the lobby. There were a few people sitting by the hearth, and some were sitting in rockers by the large window overlooking the ocean. Austin led her through the lobby, where the desk clerk smiled at him; through the dining room, where staff were setting small round tables; and into the kitchen, where a dark-haired woman in a white coat barked orders.

"Mom." He said her name only once. His mother turned, and her face lit up. Seeing their connection warmed Brooklyn. It was clear that Austin was close to his mom, and she liked that. "This is Brooklyn, the one I was telling you about."

Those words meant something to Brooklyn. She felt hopeful that she and Austin were going to build a beautiful relationship. Brooklyn reached out to shake his mother's hand, but she had other ideas and pulled Brooklyn into a hug. "It's so great to meet you. Now when my son's yapping about this gorgeous, amazing girl he's met, I'll know who he's talking about."

His mother pulled away and cupped Brooklyn's cheeks between her hands. "I'm Carly. None of this Mrs. Woods crap. Got it?"

"Got it, Mrs. Woo . . . I mean, Carly."

Carly gave her another hug and told her she could raid the refrigerator whenever she wanted. At first, Brooklyn didn't understand, but as time went on and she spent more and more time at the inn, it made sense.

Brooklyn wiped the tears that had fallen. She missed Austin more than she cared to admit. She missed his laugh, how he made life seem so easy, and how he made her feel. What she didn't miss was his attitude about their future, his nonchalant way of dismissing her feelings when she saw him flirting with other girls, and the way he spoke to her the night he died. She hated that their last words were etched forever in her mind, that neither of them would ever have a chance to apologize.

She stared at the bed where Carly lay, still unconscious and with machines monitoring the last days of her life. The doctors were hopeful that she'd wake up but couldn't promise Brooklyn that she would. She needed her to, though. She needed direction, guidance, and answers. She wanted to know why Carly had kept this secret from her, and why she hadn't said anything when she and Brystol arrived. The first night would've been an opportune time, but Carly had said nothing. Not even a hint, and now it could be too late.

Carly moaned out a word. It was unintelligible but sounded like she was asking for help. Brooklyn rushed to her side and held her hand. "I'm here, Carly. What do you need?"

"Wa . . ."

"Water?"

Carly's eyes remained closed, and she tried to move her head up and down, but she was too weak. Brooklyn filled the mauve-colored cup and put the straw a nurse left earlier into the water. She held on to it tightly, bringing it to Carly's lips. "Little sips," she told her.

She drank, but it took a lot of effort. Watching her struggle was heart-breaking, and Brooklyn had to keep her emotions in check. She didn't want to upset Carly in any way. After a few swallows, Carly turned her head away. Brooklyn set the cup down and pulled the orange plastic chair over to the side of Carly's bed. She held her hand and stroked her soft skin.

"I'm gonna see Austin," Carly croaked out. Brooklyn suspected that this was why she refused treatment. She wanted to see her son again and hadn't had the opportunity after he died. With no body, there was no closure for his mother.

"I know. What do you want me to do, Carly?"

"The inn."

She couldn't help the tears that streamed down her cheeks. She was thankful Carly's eyes were closed and couldn't see the mess she had become. "What about it? Do you want me to sell it?"

She tried to shake her head. "Brystol."

Brooklyn was shooting in the dark. She didn't want to assume anything, but that was all she could do now. "Is the inn for Brystol?"

"Old . . ."

"When she's older?"

"Mm. Paper . . ."

Brooklyn sighed in relief. "Where? In your desk?"

"Mm." Carly's eyes fluttered. Brooklyn waited, but the soft snore spoke volumes. Brooklyn checked the monitors and saw no change. Her breathing held steady, as did her heart rate. She was praying that Carly would become more lucid later. They needed to finish their conversation.

Brooklyn laid her head down on the bed and watched Carly sleep. She was thankful Austin wasn't here to witness his mother dying. He wouldn't have handled it very well. She was also thankful that Carly had tracked her down after she'd left. She had found Brooklyn at her parents' house weeks after Austin's funeral. She was the only one to come looking for her. That fact had never left Brooklyn's mind. It was only Carly who came. No one else. They sat on the beach for a long time without talking, both looking out into the ocean, wondering where Austin was.

"My son loved you, and I love you. I think of you as my daughter."

"I'm pregnant, Carly. I don't know what I'm going to do." What she had thought was the flu turned out to be anything but. She had stood for an hour

in a pharmacy looking at the variety of pregnancy tests. She only needed to use one of the dozen she had bought to understand why she had been so sick.

Carly put her arm around Brooklyn and held her while they both cried. "Well, we're going to raise this baby with all the love we can muster. Between your parents and me, this child will be rather spoiled, and you won't be alone. You will never be alone. You know you can live with me, help me run the inn. I'll take care of you, Brooklyn."

"But I'm alone now, Carly. You're leaving us," she whispered. They hadn't always seen eye to eye, but Carly had never let her down, and she couldn't imagine their lives without her. When Brooklyn's career had taken off, Carly had begged her to let Brystol live in Seattle or Cape Harbor; however, like most mothers, Brooklyn hadn't wanted to be without her daughter. The compromise was that every summer, Brystol would split time between the grandparents. Brooklyn needed time to heal and grow. She wanted to find love again and felt she couldn't do that under Carly's thumb.

Sometime after the sun had risen, Brooklyn felt fingers brushing through her hair. She smiled at the sensation. She loved having her hair played with. As she opened her eyes, the day and night before came rushing back. She popped her head up and saw that Carly was awake. She looked ashen and tired. "Hi," she said.

Carly tried to smile, but her lips barely moved. "You know now?" she asked, clear as day.

"Why didn't you tell me?"

"Because you would've forced me to get treatment, and that's not what I want."

"I would've respected your wishes, but yes, I would've encouraged it." Brooklyn sat up and reached for Carly's hand. She wanted to hold it for as long as possible. "We need to talk about your wishes, and what you want to do with the inn."

Carly swallowed and spoke softly. "It's Brystol's. My will is in my desk, in my room. I'm leaving everything to her with you as the executor of my estate." She inhaled deeply, gasping slightly for air. "I want my ashes spread where the accident happened. The coordinates are in a file. You, Bowie, and Brystol will do it. Simone gets seasick, so she won't go."

"Brystol and I can manage."

Carly moved her head back and forth slowly. "I know, Brooklyn. I've known all along."

"Known what?" Brooklyn asked her, confused by her statement.

"Brystol . . . *she's Bowie's.*"

Brooklyn let out a ghastly sound, something like a laugh and choking mixed together. "I think the meds are playing with your mind, Carly—I'm going to go get the doctor." She stood, but Carly held on as tightly as she could to Brooklyn's hand. She could've easily pulled away, but something held her there.

"No. Sit."

She did as Carly requested.

"I know, and I'm telling you it's okay."

"Honestly, I don't know what you're talking about," Brooklyn told her. "You're worrying me. Please let me get the doctor."

"I'm not crazy," Carly said. "Bowie is Brystol's father. I've known it all along. But I didn't care. I know my granddaughter doesn't belong to my son."

Brooklyn shook her head as tears started to fall. Not only was Carly dying, but she was making outrageous accusations that had repercussions for everyone. "You're wrong, Carly." She ripped her hand away from hers and left the room.

TWENTY-SIX

Carly stood in the doorway of Brystol's bedroom, watching the toddler sleep. On her bedside table, a framed picture of her parents sat, watching over their daughter while she slept, played, and sat in the rocker while her grandmother read to her. As far as Carly knew, it was the last photo of Austin and Brooklyn.

Every summer, the tot returned to Washington, but this was the first year she had come to Cape Harbor for an extended visit. For the first couple of years, Carly would travel to Seattle and stay in a hotel while Brystol visited. It wasn't ideal but the only way to get to know her granddaughter. Each time she saw her, she looked for any sign her son was living in the little girl's eyes. She had yet to see anything, and still she hoped. Maybe it would take time for Austin's attributes to make their presence known, or maybe . . .

She sighed, made sure the night-light was flicked on, and checked that the baby gate was latched before she went downstairs. The last thing she wanted was for the toddler to take a tumble down the stairs if she got up in the middle of the night. So far, though, Brystol had been very good about yelling for her nonnie when she needed her. And each time Carly heard her sweet voice call for her, her heart broke.

Downstairs, Simone sat in one of the rocking chairs that faced the ocean. Carly joined her without saying a word. There were very few sailboats out on the water, and all the fishing boats had long come in. The ocean was calm, and any families that had been out had long gone back to their homes or hotels for the night.

"Took some calls today," Simone said.

"We should disconnect the phone."

"Or we should reopen the inn."

"We don't have a kitchen."

The Driftwood Inn didn't necessarily need a kitchen, but it was part of the hospitality they offered. Unfortunately, Carly was right. After Austin's passing, she had taken a sledgehammer to the appliances and cabinets, destroying the interior.

"We could call Seacoast Construction, hire them to rebuild."

"No," Carly stated. "I don't want people here anymore."

"I think that's why the kids don't come around anymore—they must feel like you don't want them."

"I don't."

"Carly—"

She held her hand up to stop Simone from speaking. She didn't want to hear what she had to say, especially about Austin's friends. She was not ready to see them and didn't know if she ever would be. They held far too many memories. Memories that hurt each time she thought of them. Her heart was better off locked away in her house than exposed to others. The only person she wanted to see was Brooklyn. At first, she had gone to her, looking for answers as to why her son would take his boat out in the middle of a storm. Deep down, Carly knew Brooklyn knew why. What had happened that night? What would possess her son to go out? It was so unlike him. He was always so cautious and aware of the weather.

Yet, when she found Brooklyn at her parents', and she told Carly she was pregnant, Carly's priorities changed. Her mission was to make sure her son's only child made it safely into the world. She had to focus on Brooklyn, which left her no choice but to close the inn. She hadn't cared, because she was in mourning; the people would understand and come back next year *or the year after or whenever she decided to finally reopen. There were more important matters to take care of.*

She had been duped, though, into thinking life was somewhat perfect and back to normal, but she knew better. She'd had suspicions since her granddaughter had arrived and was going to do the unthinkable. Even if she was wrong, it would be peace of mind.

"Brystol doesn't belong to Austin," Carly blurted out.

Simone spit her drink and wiped her mouth with the back of her hand. "Excuse me?"

"She's not my granddaughter."

"She most certainly is."

"She looks nothing like Austin, me, or Skip. Brooklyn, yes, but not my son."

"Carly, I think you're looking for another reason to shut people out. Brystol's yours, and she loves you."

Carly stood and placed her hand on the window. "I don't doubt her love for me or the love I feel for her, but when I look into her eyes, Austin isn't there."

"I think you're speaking nonsense."

"That night, something happened between Brooklyn and Austin, and only Brooklyn knows what. Maybe she told him she was in love with someone else or that she was pregnant, and the child wasn't his. Whatever happened, it led to his death. Austin knew better than to take his boat out in the storm."

Simone sighed heavily. "If that sweet, beautiful little girl upstairs isn't Austin's, then who does she belong to?"

"Bowie Holmes."

"He's Austin's best friend, Carly. He would never betray him like that."

"He was in love with Brooklyn—even I saw that."

"Are you going to ask Brooklyn?"

She turned and looked at her friend. "No. I have a friend who works at a clinic in Seattle. We're going to take Brystol there; he'll test her."

"Carly, I don't think you should do this."

"I have to know, Simone."

"And how do you plan to get Bowie's DNA?"

"Bowie used to spend nights here when he and Austin were out late together or drinking, and he had a drawer of things in the bathroom. A toothbrush, hairbrush. After Austin died, he never came back for them. It should be enough, especially with my DNA."

Simone stood and went to her friend. "Please rethink what you're about to do. I know you love that little girl, and she loves you. If you get the results you're expecting, it will change you forever. Sometimes, it's just best not to know. You could go the rest of your life feeling as if you have a piece of Austin, or you can break your own heart." Simone left her standing there with her thoughts.

TWENTY-SEVEN

Bowie yawned as he put his truck into park and turned the key to shut off the engine. He sat there in the driveway, staring at Carly's house, thinking about the events from the past couple of days. He had gone from being hopeful with Brooklyn, feeling as if they'd finally overcome the imaginary wall between them, to heartbroken and feeling desperate because Carly was sick and there wasn't anything he could do to help.

When he left the hospital last night, it was late. He stayed long past visiting hours, hoping to see Brooklyn one last time after she went to be with Carly in her room. When the nurses' station dimmed the lights, he finally drove home, surprised to find Luke waiting for him. He went to call Graham to thank him, only to find a text from his friend telling him that he had dropped his dog off and if he needed anything to call him.

As much as he wanted to see Brooklyn now, he knew she wouldn't be at work. He was going to pull double duty and make sure every part of the project was meeting deadlines. They had an inn to finish, with or without Brooklyn and Carly.

The door to the inn swung open, and a group of guys walked out, then picked up shiplap, loaded their work belts with supplies, and carried in loads of drywall. He had learned from Brooklyn that he wasn't managing his crew very well, which embarrassed him. Because of his divorce, he had slacked as a boss, and it had showed when they started on the inn. He could see now why Brooklyn shut herself off, especially while she worked. Job first, emotions later. A motto now instilled in him.

He pulled out his phone to call her to make sure she didn't need anything. He scrolled through his contacts, not once, twice, but three times looking for her number. His brow furrowed in confusion. He was certain he had added her number, but where was it? Not under the *b*'s and nothing under the *h*'s. He reached across the bench of his truck and pulled the clipboard Luke sat on. Flipping through the work orders, he scanned every inch of paper, looking. Nothing.

"Son of a bitch," he muttered. He looked at the carriage house, wondering if Simone was home. He'd have to ask her for it and couldn't even imagine how awkward that was going to be.

He finally got out of his truck, and as with every day when he arrived, Luke jumped out of his truck and ran directly to the main house, where his pooch sat at the door, waiting for Brystol. Never in his life had he seen an animal become so attached to someone and so quickly. Sure, he had pets when he was younger, but they never favored him over his father or mother. Luke was different, though. It was like he yearned to be with Brystol, or maybe he knew she was going to need the comfort that only a dog could provide.

When the door swung open, Bowie smiled at the sight of the girl. More and more, he thought she was a carbon copy of Brooklyn with a very little hint of Austin. He stood there, watching as she crouched down to greet Luke, burying her face in his scruff. His dog basked in the attention. He thought about Austin and how he would have been with a daughter. He wanted to give his friend the benefit of the doubt but wasn't sure he could. Austin was a rough-and-tumbler, "a man's man," as the saying went, and would've likely had trouble raising a girl. Although he was incredibly close to his mother, so some of their bond would surely have transferred over to his relationship with his daughter. He hated even thinking Austin wasn't around to raise his child. If he hadn't died, he and Brooklyn would've ended up married and would've probably had enough children to man a fishing vessel.

Brystol finally glanced up and waved at Bowie. He'd use this as a chance to ask about her mom; he walked over to her with his hands stuffed deep into his pockets to keep from fidgeting. Brooklyn had called him out for asking Brystol too many questions, and yet there he was again, about to do the same thing. "Your mom home?"

She shook her head. "I think she's still with Nonnie. Simi's home if you need something."

He didn't. He merely wanted to see Brooklyn, to know that she was okay. "I'll give her a call." Except he couldn't because he didn't have her number, and he wasn't about to ask Brystol for it. "Can you watch Luke for me today? I'm going to be inside a lot, and the pavers are coming to fix the driveway and parking areas. I don't want him to get in the way."

"Of course. My mom says that if I need anything after Simi leaves for the hospital, I should ask you."

On the inside, Bowie was beaming. Elated. Brooklyn trusted him with her child. "Absolutely," he told her proudly. "Do you have a cell phone?"

She rattled off her number to him. He carefully put each digit into his phone, saved the contact information, and then sent her a text.

"Call me, anytime. And if you leave the house, shoot me a text so I know where you are. Otherwise, we'll meet for lunch?"

Brystol nodded again and stood. She opened her mouth to say something but quickly closed it. There was a sadness in her eyes, one that he had seen many times with her mother. He wanted to reach out to her, give her a hug, but didn't know how Brystol would react. Instead, he offered her a soft smile and turned toward the inn, intending to use work as a distraction. When he showed up here weeks ago, he had no idea what to expect. If someone would've told him that the woman he had spent most of his life simultaneously in love with and hating was going to show up and completely rock his world, he would've easily called their bluff. Good things—and yes, he considered this a win in his book—didn't happen to Bowie. He wanted to believe his string of bad luck had run its course, but if it hadn't, he was going to do whatever he had to in order to make sure it was ending soon.

Inside, construction activity was bustling. He checked the progress in every room, jotting down notes in case Brooklyn asked. As far as he was concerned, the rooms were shaping up to match her specifications perfectly, and as much as he had initially balked at the idea of the shiplap and overdone farmhouse look, he appreciated how Carly's vision was coming together. The fine lines, attention to detail, and old-fashioned vibe were adding a lot of character. The inn was shaping up to feel like a home rather than a place people rented so they could sleep.

With Carly out of the house, Bowie did the one thing he knew he shouldn't. He ventured into the kitchen, a place he was all too familiar with while growing up. As soon as he stepped into it, a wave of emotion came over him. Memories of the sound of laughter hit him squarely in the chest. The day before Austin had died, they had stood in here, hovering over Carly as she had baked a cake. They had dipped their fingers in the batter, testing her patience. It didn't matter that they were in their twenties; every time they were here, it was like they were kids again.

Bowie ran his hand over the appliances. They were in pristine condition, and from what he could gather, recently replaced. Someone had done some work in here. The flooring was new, the walls painted, cabinets changed, and the old tile countertop was now granite. He tried not to let it bother him that he hadn't been the one who made those changes. After all, he didn't deserve to be here after the way he had treated Carly since Austin's passing.

The door to the kitchen swung open, startling Bowie. He jumped and clutched his clipboard to his chest, as if to keep his rapidly beating heart securely in place. He'd been caught with his hand in the cookie jar, and by the expression on Simone's face, she knew it.

"Bowie," she said sternly. Her tone gave everything away; she knew Carly hadn't wanted him in the kitchen.

His posture relaxed, and he tugged on his hat, adjusting the way it was sitting. "I was trying to help, to make sure everything was in working order."

Simone sighed. "Shortly after Austin died, Carly came in here with a sledgehammer. She destroyed everything. It's taken me about ten years to fix it all. The appliances arrived about two months before she called you and Brooklyn to do the renovation," she said as she ran her hand over the stove.

"You did all of this?"

Simone had a gleam in her eye. "When you spend most of your time cooped up, living with a recluse, you find yourself with a lot of time on your hands."

"How?" he asked. He shook his head and rephrased his question. "What I mean is, it looks professionally done."

"Do-it-yourself books and online videos. There isn't anything you can't learn from watching how-to videos."

He was shocked and held out his hand to give her a high five. "If you're ever looking for a job, call me."

Simone smiled. "Anyway, Carly figured your feelings would be hurt and wanted to spare you the pain. Same with Brooklyn. She's not allowed in here, either, although I suppose she's been in here at night. I haven't slept much lately and hear things."

After what he had done to her, Carly was still trying to watch out for him. The thought warmed him, humbled him, and made him want to be a better man. If she could look past how he had treated her, he could look past the pain he associated with Brooklyn.

About midafternoon, Bowie received a text from Graham saying that he needed to talk to him. He was right. The outburst from Grady during Austin's bonfire still left a bad taste in his mouth. Bowie didn't want to assume Graham had broken his trust, but all signs pointed in that direction. Nothing Grady had said that night made sense. He shouldn't be angry with Brooklyn because if he knew the real story of what went down—the truth—then Grady might not be so eager to lay blame on Brooklyn. Unless Austin had told Grady that night on the boat, but it was unlikely, judging by the way he had reacted to seeing Brooklyn on the beach. Bowie and Brooklyn had kept their secret buried, but he had a feeling it was about to open like Pandora's box.

Bowie checked in on Brystol and told her he had to cancel his lunch break due to having to run a few errands but that he would be back. He asked her if she wanted him to take her to the hospital to visit her grandmother when he got back, to which she said that would be nice and that she would ask her mom. Again, Bowie wanted to be the one to reach out to Brooklyn, but not having her number was posing a problem for him, and he was growing desperate and was close to caving and asking Brystol for it.

The Whale Spout had a few patrons inside when Bowie arrived. A couple of guys from the docks were tossing darts, and there was a couple cozied up in the corner. He took a seat at the bar, farthest away from everyone. Words were going to be said, words that could hurt people in his life, and he didn't want anyone picking up on them and spreading them like wildfire. What had happened was in the past.

"Beer?" Graham asked.

"Water." Bowie fully intended to take Brystol to the hospital later and didn't want to ruin his chances by having a beer or two at lunch.

Graham pushed the glass in front of him and set his hands on the edge of the bar. He wouldn't look at Bowie, but he could see the torment in his eyes. Graham had betrayed Bowie's trust. Bowie wished he had opted for a beer or something stronger. He was going to need booze to numb him and calm his thoughts.

"How's Carly?"

"I left the hospital late last night after they finally put her in a room. Things aren't good, man. She has stage four breast cancer. According to Simone, she's refused treatment."

Graham's face paled. "How long?"

Bowie shook his head slowly. "Not long. Brooklyn's with her now."

They sat there for a moment, not speaking until Graham pushed off the bar and sighed heavily. "That shit with Grady . . . listen, you have to know I've never said anything to him about . . . *ya know* . . ."

"So how does he know?"

"That's just it—I don't know. He's talking gibberish right now, not making much sense. Saying shit about taking the trawler out to look for Austin's body." Graham ran his hand through his hair and let out another large sigh.

"Grady needs help."

"I know. But my parents . . ." He paused when the door opened. It was one of the local fishermen coming to join his friends. "They say he's fine. They don't want to believe that their son is the town drunk."

"But he is. We've all enabled him over the years. You own the bar, so he has a safe place to drink. Your parents take care of him. I give him odd jobs when he asks for them. Maybe it's time we stop."

"You're just saying that because of his outburst the other night."

Bowie shook his head and leaned forward. "I'm saying it because it's true."

The guys from the docks hollered for another round, forcing Graham to get back to work. Bowie sat there for a few minutes thinking about how life had turned out since Austin died. Not only for him, but his friends. Graham left his fancy computer job in California to come back here to help his brother. Mila started drinking and partying too much. Jason went back to Seattle for school and stayed there. Brooklyn left and came back fifteen years later. And Bowie, he was never destined to leave and married the first girl to show him any attention after Brooklyn. There was a time when he had thought his life could've been different, and maybe it would have been if Austin hadn't died. The lives of his friends revolved so much around Austin, and he couldn't understand how or why it became that way, but he wanted to change it. It was time for them to start living in the present and not the past.

Graham returned, this time with a beer. "I have something to say, and you're going to want to drink that after I do."

"Okay," Bowie said.

He exhaled loudly, cocked his head slightly, and stared at Bowie. "Have you given any thought to the idea that Brooklyn's daughter might be yours?"

If Bowie had had a mouthful of beer or water, Graham would have been wearing it. Bowie felt his eyebrows rise as he contemplated whether Graham was messing with him. The expression on his face told Bowie that he was serious.

"Look, I'm not trying to stir the pot here, but I think the chances that she's your kid are pretty strong."

"I was with Brooklyn one time, man. She was with Austin . . ." Bowie stopped his train of thought. He didn't want to think about her with Austin. Not now, and definitely not back then. "I just . . . there's no way—besides, we used a condom."

Graham nodded. "It just takes one time, and they break. How many people do we know that have kids after a one-night stand?"

He was right, but not about Brystol being his. There was no way Brooklyn would intentionally let her daughter grow up without a father; that much Bowie knew. Brystol talked about Austin being her dad, and Carly—Carly was a devoted grandmother. He'd witnessed the two of them interact. Brooklyn wouldn't be that cruel, not to Austin's mother.

Bowie tossed a few bucks onto the bar top and slipped off the stool. "Sorry, man. But I think you're wrong." He left the Whale Spout without another glance toward Graham.

TWENTY-EIGHT

As much as Brooklyn hated deadlines, she never missed one. She liked to work at her own pace and wasn't fond of people looking over her shoulder. The impending death of Carly and everything that had to be done to prepare for it felt like the biggest deadline of all. She had to wrap her head around the fact that her daughter was about to inherit the inn. That wasn't the only thing weighing heavily on Brooklyn's mind. The bomb Carly had dropped about Bowie, the one she refused to believe, was adding so much pressure to her head she felt like a migraine was about to set in. Brooklyn wished she could blame the morphine, but she knew Carly was lucid. She had looked right into Brooklyn's eyes and said the words clearly. Lucid or not, Carly didn't know what she was talking about. There was no way Bowie was the father of her child, and she refused to even entertain the idea.

Brooklyn tried to pull into the driveway of the inn, but the enormous paving truck blocked her entrance. She considered halting the reconstruction project until after Carly passed, not knowing where her finances were, but knew doing so would only cost more in the end. The inn had to be repaired, especially with Brystol set to inherit it. As it was, Brooklyn could do the work herself. However, as she scanned the area and saw not only her men but Bowie's crew hard at work, she knew she couldn't pull the plug. Brooklyn wouldn't feel right putting all these people out of work and was pretty sure Carly would find all the strength in the world within her to leave the hospital and rehire everyone if she did.

She opened the front door a little too hard, and it banged against the wall, scaring Luke, who growled at her. She wasn't scared of the dog, but a little taken aback by his response and then relieved that he was protecting her child, and she found herself feeling consoled that Bowie was there.

Brystol shut her book and set it down on the coffee table. Within seconds, she had tears in her eyes and rushed toward her mom, and they wrapped their arms around each other's waists. They held each other, both crying. Brooklyn's heart broke for her daughter. The ache was so great she had a hard time swallowing. Brystol had never known death directly until now.

She walked her daughter over to the couch, and as soon as they sat down, Luke rested his head on Brystol's leg. Bowie was right; she would need his dog and the comfort he provided to get somewhat through this.

"Nonnie's dying, isn't she?"

Brooklyn choked on a sob and covered her mouth. "I'm so sorry, baby girl."

Her daughter's eyes were downcast, and her fingers moved back and forth on Luke's head. "What's wrong with her?"

"She's sick, Little B. It's cancer."

She looked up at her mom. "Will I get it?"

Brooklyn shook her head and pulled her child into her arms. She couldn't find the words to tell her daughter no because she wasn't sure what the science behind breast cancer was. She had heard stories of women in families from different generations having breast cancer, but she didn't want to think about this happening to her daughter.

They sat together for a while until she told Brystol that she needed to do some stuff in Nonnie's room. "Are you going to be okay for a bit?"

"I think so. I'm just sad."

"I know, sweetie. We all are. If you're feeling up to it, I'll take you to the hospital later, but I want you to know that she's hooked up to some machines and she's not very talkative. They have her on a lot of medicine, so she's not in pain."

"Okay."

They hugged, and Brooklyn kissed her daughter's forehead before heading upstairs. She paused before stepping over the threshold, hesitant to enter the "Austin sanctuary." She knew what it was like to surround herself with pictures of him, as she had been doing it from the day she met him. She could never get enough of him.

Absentmindedly, she rested her hand over her midsection, as if to keep the pain she felt after losing him tucked deep inside. Wherever she looked, Austin stared back at her, and so did Brystol, which made Carly's statement even more confusing. Brooklyn stepped into the room and slowly made her way over to the desk. She pulled the chair out and sat down. The view from the window was of the bay below and a crystal-blue sky. The colorful sails from the sailboats made the ocean look like a rainbow. She realized that Carly had arranged every room in the house and inn to look out over the water. She had wanted everyone to see what she saw. Sitting there, Brooklyn wondered if Carly had been staring out the window the night Austin's boat capsized. Had she even known her son had taken his trawler out in the storm? Brooklyn certainly hadn't known, and she often wondered if she had, would she have done what she did? That question had plagued her since his death, and still to this day, she didn't have an answer.

The white pedestal desk creaked when Brooklyn lifted the roll top. The smell of hardwood had long since dissipated. The stacked compartments and shelves were orderly and labeled, but nothing stood out as far as Carly's will or anything about the inn. The detailed ledger had enough information that Brooklyn knew all the account numbers for the utilities, and Carly had gone as far as to list which vendors delivered what for the inn. That confused Brooklyn. If Carly knew she was dying, why go to the trouble of remodeling and reopening the inn? Had she not stopped to think that Brooklyn would want to put her career first and not push everything aside to run a hotel?

No, she had thought this through, Brooklyn realized. Carly wanted Brystol to have roots, to go to school and make friends, and this was her way of making sure her granddaughter had those things. Carly was never a fan of Brooklyn traveling all over the country, dragging Brystol with her, and it seemed that what Carly couldn't do in life, she would do in death: keep Brooklyn here.

Brooklyn went right for the bottom drawer. She pulled it open to find a dozen file folders, each one meticulously marked. She reached for the one marked "Will" and set it onto the desk. The green file wasn't particularly thick, but then again, Brooklyn's will wasn't either. If anything were to happen to her, her wishes were simple: Full custody of Brystol to her parents with ample visitation for Carly, and her parents were to dissolve her business. If Brystol was of age and something happened to Brooklyn, everything was for her to do with as she wished.

Inhaling deeply and closing her eyes, Brooklyn let a calm settle over her. Someday, she would have to do this for her parents, but she had never thought she would have to be the one to do it for Carly. She had honestly expected Simone to inherit everything. However, here she was, acting as executor. She opened her eyes and flipped the file over and started reading. Carly wasn't lying: Brystol inherited everything . . . the inn, the bank accounts, Austin's trust fund. The dollar figure made Brooklyn's eyes bug out. She wouldn't have to take out a loan for college or even save at this point. The only stipulation was for Simone. She was to get a lump sum payment and to be offered a job as the full-time caretaker of the inn.

Brooklyn had a hard time understanding Carly's reasoning. If she didn't believe Brystol was her granddaughter, why would she leave everything to her? Of all men, why would she single out Bowie? Unless he went around telling people they had slept together. If he had, though, surely Carly would've said something to her years ago.

She returned the file to its location and reached for the one marked "Brystol." She wasn't sure what she would find when she opened it but steeled herself for whatever the contents were. Only a single envelope lay there. Brooklyn felt her heart drop. She glanced at the blue logo in the corner and saw that the envelope was from a lab in Seattle. Against her better judgment, she picked it up, pulled the folded sheets of paper out, and read them word for word. Then, she read the pages again for clarity. And a third time so her eyes could process what her brain was comprehending. As calmly as she could, she refolded and stuffed the letter back into the envelope, closed the folder, filed it away, and shut the drawer. She wasn't prepared to deal with its contents and didn't foresee a time she ever would be.

Downstairs, she found her daughter sitting on the floor, reading one of her required summer reading novels, with Luke resting his head on her leg. Brooklyn didn't want to disturb her and slipped out the back door. She needed to think and wanted space to do it. Miraculously, she made it all the way to the beach without one of the crew members stopping her. She was hoping that Bowie was managing the crew and could get along without her for a few days. If not, he knew where to find her.

Brooklyn ditched her shoes by the wooden staircase and proceeded to walk until the dry sand turned wet. A few more feet, where the ocean would touch her toes, was where she finally sat, looking out over the surf. She didn't care about her shorts getting wet or the fact that a sporadic wave would wash over her, drenching her. Every wave sunk her deeper into the sand, almost swallowing her. Every wave took her tears out to where Austin was.

Brooklyn stared at herself in the mirror and wiggled a bit as she pulled her dress down. She wasn't sure if this was the right dress to wear to the party, but it was going to have to do. It was too late to try and find something else. She walked out into her small living room, twirling in front of Austin as she did. When he had showed up earlier, he had been in a bad mood, and she hoped this would at least make him smile. Although it seemed lately he was always in a bad mood, even when things were going really well for him. Of course, each time she asked about moving to Seattle so she could go to school, he'd fly off the handle and tell her they'd discuss it later. The problem was, later never came.

He didn't say anything. He leaned to the side to look past her. She followed his eyes to the television and groaned when she noticed he was watching some fishing show. This show wasn't going to deter her, though; it wasn't going to ruin her night.

"Babe, are you going to get ready?"

"For what?" he asked without taking his eyes off the show.

"The housewarming party for Mr. and Mrs. Robwell. Remember? I told you they invited us because I worked on their house."

"You, what, painted a wall? Anyone can paint a freaking wall, Brooklyn."

Brooklyn bit the inside of her cheek. "It was more than just painting, Austin. I don't understand why you have to put my job down all the time."

"Because it's not a real job."

"And what, fishing is?" she asked, raising her voice.

Austin scoffed. "Fishing pays for nice shit for you. What does your job do? Put this shitty roof over your head?"

"Is that the problem? That you don't like where I live? Or is it my job? Or is it me? Which is it, Austin?"

Austin threw down the remote and stood. Even though she was in her heels, he was still taller than her. "I've told you, move into my damn house and work for my mother."

235

"I told you, I want my own career, Austin. I want to be a nurse, and until then, I'm going to work for the Holmeses and make my own money, and I won't move in, not until we're engaged."

He shook his head. "And I've told you, this is where my job is."

"You work on a boat, a boat that goes up and down the ocean all the time. There's no reason as to why you can't park that stupid boat in Seattle."

"Stupid?"

"Yeah, stupid," she said.

"You're out of your freaking mind, Brooklyn." He pointed to his head and then clenched his fist. "You've known from the second you met me that this is what I'm going to do."

"And you've known since you met me that I wanted to be a nurse. That I didn't want to stay in Cape Harbor for the rest of my life, and yet, here I am, stuck."

Austin shook his head. "Know what? Don't let me stop you."

"What happened to us, Austin? Remember when you cared about my dreams? Remember when we were going to conquer the world and be this amazing team?"

He looked down and shook his head. "I am living my dream."

"But I'm not living mine."

"Then maybe yours needs to change."

"Or yours," she threw back at him.

"Not going to happen. If I'm not the guy to make your dreams come true, maybe you should look elsewhere." He grabbed his jacket and headed toward the door.

"Where are you going?" she demanded to know.

"Leaving."

"That's all you do. You just leave."

"I'll tell you what, Brooklyn." He came toward her with his finger pointed at her. "Why don't you go cry on Bowie's shoulder about it? Go whine and cry to my best friend because that's what you're good at—you've

been doing it for years. Call him, tell him that Austin broke your heart. I don't give a flying fuck anymore."

"At least he listens to me, unlike you," she fired back, holding her ground.

"Maybe it's because you say nothing I want to hear." His words shocked her. He went to the door and put his hand on the knob.

"Austin." She said his name quietly. "If you leave—"

He glared at her sharply and shook his head. "I don't love you anymore, Brooklyn. I'm done. I'm so done with all of this. I'm not coming back, so your threat, it's falling on deaf ears." With those words, he twisted the knob and walked out. She waited for the tears to come, waited for them to ruin the hours-long makeup job she had done to look perfect for him.

She didn't know how long she stood there. It was long enough to make her feet hurt and her knees start to wobble. Still, she didn't change her clothes; instead she went to the kitchen and opened a bottle of wine, forgoing the glass and drinking it straight from the bottle. Against her better judgment, she called Austin, getting his voice mail over and over. That was when the tears came. They came hard, hot, and fierce. She hiccuped and drank more. She dialed his number and drank more, until the knock finally came. She swung the door open. "Austin."

But it wasn't Austin. It was Bowie. He stood there, leaning against the door casing, waiting for her. "He called me."

"Austin?"

Bowie stepped into the apartment. He shut the door behind him. Brooklyn stood there, looking at the guy who had been her best friend since the day she met him. The boy, turned man, who had never let her down. He was there to console her. He led her to the couch and sat down next to her. Brooklyn was pissed. Austin couldn't come himself, but he sent his friend. It was always Bowie coming to save Austin.

"You don't need to be here."

"I want to be."

"Aren't you tired of always cleaning up his mess?"

"I don't consider you a mess, Brooklyn."

Another wave of tears came, and he held her in his arms, rubbing her back to soothe her. "Austin doesn't love me anymore," she cried.

"What if there was someone else who did?"

She pulled away from him. "No one in this damn town would be foolish enough to love me."

"I'm that foolish," he said, sitting up straighter so he could look in her eyes.

"What are you talking about it?"

"I'm so in love with you, Brooklyn. I have been since we met. I've lived a life of purgatory for my feelings, always second fiddle just so I could be near you."

"Why didn't you tell me?"

He cupped her cheek. "I've tried, but I never had the courage until now. And I'm here now, telling you that I will never treat you like Austin."

"We could never be together, not here."

"I know. I know all too well. If you want to move to Seattle, Portland, or Spokane, I'll go with you. I'll give it all up, just to be with you."

She cried louder with each wave. She could scream when one hit because no one could hear her, and if anyone went by, they wouldn't know she was in pain. Her life, the perfect life she had built away from Cape Harbor, was crumbling around her, and she didn't know how to stop it. She thought about leaving. She could sell the inn, and she and Brystol could go back to living state to state, working on houses. They could act like nothing had changed and just return to their idea of normal.

Another wave was coming toward her. She closed her eyes and braced for it. Only it never hit. She screamed out as she found herself propelled into the air and carried away. She fell onto the warm sand with a thud, another body behind her. She scrambled to her knees and found Bowie doing the same.

"What are you doing?"

"I could ask you the same thing," Bowie said. He stood and helped her to feet.

"I was enjoying the waves."

"It looked to me like you were trying to become one with the ocean."

Brooklyn shivered and crossed her arms around her midsection. There was seaweed stuck to her leg, and her hair smelled like salt water. Normally, she loved the way the sea salt made her hair feel, but as she ran her hand over her hair, she hated it. She wanted to go stand under the hot water in her shower and wash everything away.

"I wasn't . . . doing what you think I was." Brooklyn sat down where she was and pulled her knees to her chest. Bowie took the spot next to her and mimicked her position.

"I don't ever want to think about you hurting yourself, B. After Austin died, I wanted to spend every waking minute with you because I thought you would do something, and when you wouldn't answer the door or return my calls, I begged Monroe to stay with you."

"She told me."

"Why did you leave after the funeral?"

She sighed. She'd been afraid this conversation was going to happen but had hoped she would be on her way out of town before it did. "I was scared. Scared of people finding out about us. Scared they'd blame us for Austin's death. Much like I was blamed the other day."

"Speaking of that. Graham knows about what happened between us. I told him right after. He swears he didn't tell anyone, and I believe him. I don't know how Grady knows or if he even does. He's a drunk, B. He spends his days and nights blitzed out of his mind. I think he was lashing out at you because you left us all that day."

Brooklyn laughed and shook her head. She knew more about the people here than he did, and he lived here. "Carly knows as well, so if Graham isn't flapping his gums . . ."

Bowie sighed. "I'm sorry, Brooklyn. I never meant for any of this to come out. I would've sung it from the top of the mountain, though, had you stayed."

"Do you want to know what I was doing down there?"

Bowie nodded.

"I was thinking about that night. The one that changed everything. For the first time in a long time, I was happy, and I was happy because of you. It took me years to realize what kind of relationship Austin and I were in, and once I did, there really wasn't anything I could do about it because to everyone else he was perfect, and I would've been the bad guy. I remember every word he said to me that night, how he told me he didn't love me anymore. Want to know what else I remember?"

"What's that?" Bowie asked.

"That you did."

TWENTY-NINE

Bowie let Brooklyn's words sink in. Truthfully, he had been pining for her for a decade and a half. Over the years, his feelings for her had teetered on the line between love and hate—he was a mixed bag of emotions after she first left, and while his relationship with Rachel had helped him heal and move on with his life, he had never truly overcome the feelings he'd had for Brooklyn.

A smile played on his lips as he inspected the sand. *She remembered.* Their night together was marred by tragedy, and he never could have fully pursued her back then, but nothing was stopping him now. Except for Graham's voice in the back of his head. As much as he didn't want to think about Brystol being his daughter, now that he was sitting next to Brooklyn, the thought weighed on his mind. What if she was his? Did Brooklyn know? Had she kept him from his daughter? The rational part of him was screaming no, Brooklyn would never do that, but he couldn't deter the nagging suspicion that as much as he didn't want it to be, it was possible. If she was afraid of how their friends and the people around town would react to them hooking up, surely she'd be scared to tell everyone that he was the father of her baby. The safe bet was to say the child belonged to Austin. Doing this also secured some financial freedom, being the only heir to Carly Woods.

No, Bowie couldn't think like that, not about Brooklyn. Besides, if there was a chance that Brystol was his daughter, wouldn't Brooklyn do everything she could to keep her away from him? Brooklyn hadn't. In fact, she encouraged them in a roundabout sort of way. She definitely hadn't intervened when Bowie would speak to Brystol, and she was appreciative of Bowie bringing her daughter to the hospital. Graham was wrong. He had to be. Bowie and Brooklyn had only been together one time. One night of passion, interrupted by a phone call that changed everything.

Bowie held Brooklyn in his arms. Every few seconds, he would kiss her bare skin and smile. He had wanted this moment for the longest time, and it had finally happened. They had finally happened. He didn't want to think about tomorrow. He didn't want to think about Austin, but he couldn't deny that he was on his mind. What the hell had his friend—probably former friend now—been thinking? Brooklyn was perfect. She put up with all of Austin's bullshit and never batted an eyelash about it. Not until Bowie started telling her to stand up for herself. She had dreams, which she had put on hold for Austin. Bowie would never think of holding her back. If she wanted to move to Seattle and follow her dreams of becoming a nurse, he was going to support her.

Brooklyn turned in his arms. She ran her fingers over his freshly shaved skin. He wanted to kiss her. He wanted to make love to her again and again, until the sun came up. What he didn't want to do was think about their future outside of her bedroom. He wasn't foolish enough to think Austin was going to walk away without a fight.

"Do you regret this?" she asked.

He shook his head. "I could never. I've been in love with you for so long."

Brooklyn ducked her head, hiding her face in his chest. Even without asking, he knew she was thinking about the ramifications of what they'd done. Their friendships were going to change, people would choose sides, and best friends would no longer be. But she was worth it to him.

"B?"

"Hmm?"

"Don't overthink things, okay? Whatever happens, I'm here. I'm not going anywhere. I haven't gone anywhere in six years. We're adults, and we made a decision."

She nodded against him and then whispered, "He doesn't love me."

Bowie moved so he could lift her chin. He wanted to see her, to look deep into her ocean-blue eyes. He saw the tears form and shook his head.

"He doesn't love me," she repeated before he could say anything. "If that's not a clear indication that we're over, I don't know what is."

He opened his mouth to tell her that he loved her, that she meant the world to him, but her phone started ringing, and then his cell phone started as well. They both scrambled to answer. All he had to do was roll over, but she had to leave the room. The scene played out in front of Bowie like he had seen many times in the movies. Brooklyn pulled the sheet from the bed and wrapped herself in it, covering her naked body. He thought about tugging on the white fabric but didn't want to embarrass her.

"Hello," he said gruffly into the receiver.

"Where are you, man?"

He looked around the room. He couldn't tell Graham where he was or what he was doing. So, he lied. "Home, why? What's up?"

"There's been an accident," Graham said hurriedly and with panic. "He's so fucking stupid. The fucker took the trawler out, and it fucking capsized. Fucking rogue wave tipped the boat over. My dad, he's heading out now, and my mom's freaking out. I can't get a flight until tomorrow."

Bowie sat up straight. When he had arrived at Brooklyn's, it was pouring and had been all day. He remembered seeing the warning lights earlier; there were two, indicating a storm. Bowie swallowed hard. "Who?"

"Austin, man. Fucking Austin, and he's gone!" Graham screamed.

"What do you mean?" Bowie had a hard time forming the words he forced out of his mouth. His throat was tightening up, and his chest started to heave. "What do you mean, Graham?" He looked up just as Brooklyn appeared in the doorway; she was white as a ghost. He pulled the phone from his ear and pressed it to his chest to muffle Graham's yelling.

"B?"

She inhaled deeply and choked on a sob. "That was Carly. Austin's boat . . . the storm . . . they can't find him." She collapsed onto the floor just as Bowie threw his phone down. He couldn't catch her in time, but he could hold her, and that's what he did until both of them were strong enough to make it down to the port to wait for news.

"You know, even in death, Austin kept us apart," he said, breaking the silence between them. He picked up a shell and tossed it toward the water. "Why did it take you fifteen years to come back?"

She shook her head. "I never found a reason to, I guess."

"Until now?"

"Carly called and asked me to come back. It was the first time she had. I really hadn't seen her after Brystol was born; I always had some excuse or some job that needed to be done. My parents saw her, though, when they would hand Brystol off for visitation."

"What are you going to do now?"

Brooklyn let out a long sigh. "Well, it seems I have two choices. Brystol inherits everything, so I can either sell the inn and go back to doing what I do, or I can run it, and let Brystol decide when she's old enough." She hugged her knees tighter to her chest.

"You weren't planning to stay, were you?" Even before he asked, he knew the answer. The other night, while it was a breakthrough for him, she still had Austin's memory to contend with.

"No, I wasn't. I came to do a job. In fact, my next one should start in October. I need to figure out a plan because I can't leave my clients hanging. With that said, Brystol wants to go to a real school. My parents want us to be close, and Carly . . ." She paused. "She wants us—and by us, she means you, Brystol, and me—to spread her ashes where Austin's boat went down. She has the coordinates written down."

"Why me?"

Brooklyn turned her head and glanced at Bowie. If she was surprised to find him looking at her, she didn't say anything. She smiled. It was soft and kind. "If I had to guess, I think she might think you're my knight in shining armor. She likes you, Bowie. And I know she regrets the way the last fifteen years turned out for her. But losing Austin, it really did a number on her."

"On all of us," he said. He turned his attention back to the water. Aside from the usual boats, a group of surfers had taken to the waves. "I told Brystol that I would take her out on the sailboat, that we'd go hiking and I'd teach her how to fish. Those are all things Austin would've taught her."

"Bowie . . ."

He held up his hand, silently asking her to let him finish. Bowie scooted in front of Brooklyn. He took her legs and placed them on either side of his hips and held her hands. "I have something to ask you, but I want you to let me say what I need to say before you reply or say anything. When I first saw you at the inn, it was like seeing a ghost. It had been years since I thought about you, and then you were standing right there, and all my feelings came rushing back. As much as I wanted to hate you, I couldn't. But I did hate you for a long time for leaving me. I couldn't understand why you left without saying anything and why you didn't ask me to go with you. And then, I see this teenage version of you, and I'm angry. I'm so damn angry that you kept Austin's daughter from us, that you didn't give us a chance to be in her life, so I'm counting the days until the project's over and I never have to see you again.

Except, I don't want you to leave because I'd rather live with the hate than not see you and not be a part of Brystol's life. I know I'm not the only one who feels this way . . . we've all missed you.

"Then you show up at Austin's bonfire memorial, and our group—the friends we grew up with—they see Brystol, and they're hurt because they didn't know about her. And then we're sharing these moments while we're working on the inn and we almost kiss—it's all confusing as hell right now, B. I haven't felt flustered by a girl since high school, but when it comes to you, my mind is a whirlwind of thoughts, and Graham isn't helping because he's talking some serious nonsense, and part of me doesn't believe him, but I still have to ask . . . is there any chance Brystol is my daughter? Because he's put this thought in my head, and I've had a chance to think about it and our night together, and I feel like there's a chance that she could be. I feel like we need to have a DNA test done, and it kills me to ask, because if it proves that Brystol isn't mine, that Austin is her father, then I'm scared that any connection we had—or have—will be gone."

Brooklyn gasped and tried to pull her hands away, but Bowie held on tightly. He wasn't letting her go. He wasn't going to allow her to run away again. He watched her expectantly, waiting for her to answer. She looked down at the sand or maybe their hands—he couldn't be sure—but she didn't say a word, and the silence was killing him.

After what seemed like an eternity, she finally met his eyes. "I told you why I left. I was ashamed, and I didn't want your friends turning on you. I didn't want the town turning on me. No one would ever believe that behind closed doors, Austin wasn't a saint. You and I know him differently, but to everyone else, he's on this pedestal. What we did that night, it wasn't going to matter what our reasoning was behind it because on the same night it happened, he died. Austin and I fought, he told me he didn't love me, and for some reason we'll never understand, he thought it was a good idea to take his boat out in the storm. It was better to let people think I was a heartbroken girlfriend instead of a woman who fell between the sheets with another man. I was weak and cared far too much about what people thought of me." Brooklyn took a deep breath and exhaled slowly.

"As far as Brystol goes, and you being involved in her life, all this time I thought you were. Brystol and I had an understanding that we didn't talk about Cape Harbor because the wounds were still so fresh for me. I would ask her how her grandmother and Simone were, and she'd answer. That was it. It was selfish of me to try and forget the life I had here, but had I known what was going on, I could've made a change. Not that it would've mattered anyway, because none of you were even visiting Carly." Brooklyn paused and took a deep breath.

"Brystol would love to do all those things with you, as long as you bring Luke along. She's infatuated with your dog, which leaves me no choice but to get her a puppy since apparently, we're staying here. But as far as a DNA test goes, we don't need one because Carly had one done already."

"What?" Bowie croaked out. It seemed he could focus only on the last part of her dissertation.

"Graham isn't the only one questioning the paternity of my daughter. Her grandmother did as well, unbeknownst to me. Earlier this morning, she told me some nonsense, as you put it, which I blew off thinking she wasn't lucid enough to know what she was saying. Turns out . . ." She paused and tilted her head toward the sky. Was she looking to Austin for guidance?

"I want you to know that never in a million years would I have ever kept Brystol from you if I had known. I have spent the last fifteen years thinking she was Austin's. Feeling deep in my heart that despite everything, we had a child. And today, I was proven wrong. Carly had a DNA test done when Brystol was about three. What made her do this, I don't think I'll ever know. *We'll* never know. But, as of today, what I *do* know is that you're her father, and I can't even begin to explain how sorry I am that you've missed her life."

Bowie sat back on his haunches, letting go of Brooklyn's hands. She had tears streaming down her face, and her eyes were sad. They weren't pleading with him for forgiveness or acceptance. She looked heartbroken and devastated. Was she devastated because Austin wasn't the father of her daughter or because Bowie was?

"Carly knew?"

"It seems so. I don't know why she never said anything to me. I think it's because in her heart, Brystol was Austin's, and now that she's dying . . ."

"A deathbed confession."

"We would've found out eventually," she said. "The test is right in her desk drawer."

"Does Brystol know?"

Her head went back and forth slowly. "No, she doesn't. When you found me trying to be washed away by the waves, I had just found out myself. I figured you'd want to know first."

Bowie pulled on his lower lip. Brooklyn reached out to calm his hand. "How will she react?"

She sighed and pulled her legs in toward her. "Brystol's a pretty amazing kid. I think she'll like the idea of having a dad around. That's if you want the job. If not, then I beg you to leave things as they are."

"Hell yeah, I want the job," he answered immediately. He wanted more than just the job of being Brystol's father. He wanted to be in Brooklyn's life as well. He had no idea where they stood, but in that moment, he didn't care. He propelled himself forward with so much force Brooklyn had no choice but to lie back in the sand. "I want to be with you too," he said before pressing his lips to hers. Without hesitation, he deepened the kiss and welcomed the warm sensation of what it felt like to kiss someone for the first time . . . all over again.

THIRTY

Kissing was something Brooklyn hadn't done in a while, and she had forgotten how much she enjoyed it. After a few dates that went nowhere and a failed relationship with one of the guys from her construction team, which turned out to be a complete and utter disaster, she had sworn off dating altogether to focus on taking her career to the next level and raising Brystol. Sure, she had missed the attention a man could bring, but the time it took to build a relationship that wasn't based on sex was more of a hassle for her than anything else.

With Bowie kissing her, she felt like a teenager all over again, like they were doing something they shouldn't, and some adult was going to tell them to knock it off . . . or stop them to preach about the proper use of a condom and explain that it was more appropriate to express themselves physically in private. Basically, the same things she would say to Brystol if she found her daughter and some boy making out in the sand. Only they *weren't* teenagers anymore, and everything between them felt different—from the way he was kissing her, to the way he angled his body, to how he was holding her like he was never going to let her go. They weren't the couple who had fumbled through anger, tears, and disappointment to find each other years ago; they were two people who had longed for each other well into adulthood, and finally had a chance to be together.

If Brooklyn left, would Bowie go with her? Deep in her heart, she knew he would. Not because of her but because of Brystol.

Brooklyn pulled away and covered her face. Her sobs were quick and painful. Hot tears streamed down her face. How could she have been so utterly stupid as to not know who the father of her baby was? How could she have robbed Brystol of her father for all these years?

She maneuvered out from under Bowie, refusing to look at him. She went toward the water, needing some space, and hoped that the rush of the waves would drown out the voices in her head. They were mocking her, telling her that she was a horrible person who had ruined innocent lives. She had kept her daughter from knowing her father, telling her for years that he had passed away. How was she going to tell her now, so many years later, that she had made a mistake? What words could be said to possibly undo the damage that she had caused? Not only was her daughter losing her grandmother, but she was also finding out that the man she had thought was her father wasn't, and she wasn't who she'd thought she was her entire life. Add to that the fact that her real father was alive—how did one come back from all of that? The knowledge that Carly had known and never said anything really boiled Brooklyn's blood. Why had she kept this a secret from her? Doing so only increased the pain and suffering her daughter was going to go through.

Brooklyn wasn't much better. She should've known there was a chance Bowie could be Brystol's father, and yet, she had refused to ever consider the possibility. Standing there, looking out over the ocean, she felt his arms wrap around her and his lips press against her collarbone from behind. She didn't deserve his affection. He should be yelling at her, calling her every name in the book, making her feel like she was nothing more than a huge mistake he had made all those years ago. But that wasn't Bowie. He was forgiving and sweet. He saw the good in everyone, even when they didn't deserve it. He was kind and gentle, and despite everything, he was still in love with her.

"Stop beating yourself up." His voice barely rose above a whisper. How did he always seem to know what she was thinking?

"You've lost all this time with Brystol. I should've known." A mother was supposed to know these things, right? She should've been able to look into her daughter's eyes and tell that she was a Holmes and not a Woods. But she hadn't, she couldn't, nor had she ever even thought of doing that, because in her heart she had thought she knew that Brystol belonged to Austin.

She felt him shake behind her. "B, let me tell you something," he stated as he turned her around in his arms to face him. He cupped her cheeks with his big calloused hands, and smiled. "From the second I saw Brystol, I thought she was Austin's. I never looked at her and wondered if she was mine, so if you're going to blame yourself for me not knowing I had a daughter, you might as well blame me too. I could've questioned you from the start. I should've known by looking at her, but I didn't. Do you know why?"

Brooklyn shook her head.

"Because I know you well enough to know that if you knew—or even *thought*—she was my daughter, you wouldn't have kept her from me. You wouldn't have raised your daughter, telling her that her father was dead, if you thought for one second I could be her dad. So, just stop. Stop with the ridiculous thoughts going through that pretty head of yours. Do you want to know if I'm mad? Hell yes, I am, but not at you. At Carly. I'm pissed because *she* kept my daughter from me. She's known for years and chose to keep that a secret, which is something I don't know that I'll ever be able to understand."

Brooklyn couldn't disagree with what Bowie was saying. Carly was in the wrong in more ways than one. When she had suspected Brystol wasn't Austin's, she should've said something to Brooklyn instead of having a DNA test done behind her back. She wasn't even sure if that was legal and would have to ask her father about that later. Not that it would make a difference in the end because Carly was dying. But to keep the results to herself, to continue acting as if Austin were Brystol's father, hurt Brystol more than anyone else involved, and that damage would have to be fixed now by Brooklyn and Bowie.

"Are you hearing me, B? Do you understand that I'm in this forever?" Forever was a long time, especially when there were so many unknowns. He pressed his lips to hers and held them there. She could taste the salt water on his lips and knew that salty kisses were something she wanted to get used to.

"Can I ask you a question?" she asked after pulling away. His hands dropped to hers, their fingers locking together.

"You can ask me anything."

"If I choose to sell the inn and go back to my job, would you come with us?"

"Does your SUV have a trailer hitch?"

"Yes, why?" She was confused by his question.

Bowie smiled. "Because we would need it in order to tow my work trailer. I mean, I'd have to buy one, but there's no way in hell you're leaving Cape Harbor without me, Brooklyn. I would've gone with you last time if you had asked."

"I've made a lot of mistakes in my life."

"I've made two," he told her. "The first one was letting Austin stake a claim over you. I should've told you from the beginning how I felt. Longing for you for six years was pure torture."

"And the second?"

"Not following you. Not chasing you. Not looking for you."

"That's like three."

He shook his head. "It's one. I should've gone after you, but I was a coward and thought you would return . . . when you didn't, I was hurt and angry. I felt like I had wasted so much time being there for you through everything with Austin. I couldn't understand why you would turn your back on me, of all people, and yet you had. I let my pride get in the way, and I let anger rule my thoughts. When I met Rachel, I tried . . . I really did . . . I went through the motions, but it just never felt right."

"Not that it matters, but why are you getting divorced?"

Bowie sighed. "Because I can't . . ." He paused, and all the color drained from his face. "Oh my God."

"What?" Brooklyn demanded, frightened by the tone in his voice. "What is it?"

"She left me because she couldn't get pregnant. She said it was me, that I was the problem. But clearly that's not the case."

Brooklyn laughed. She hadn't meant to, but it sneaked out. "Nope, there's a live wire teenager here to prove her wrong."

Bowie put his hands on the top of his head and looked to the sky. He started to laugh.

"Look, if you need time—"

"For what?" he interrupted.

"To figure shit out. To make sure this is what you want."

"The only thing I need to figure out is how to spend as much time as I can with you and Brystol. I mean, I want to be with you in every way possible, and on the other hand, I want to ditch out on work and spend days on end getting to know my daughter. I am completely in love with you, Brooklyn, and you better love me back, or we're going to have some issues," he said, smiling. "Do me a favor?"

"What's that?"

"Stay. At least until Brystol graduates, and then we'll go wherever you want. Give my parents four years to be grandparents."

"We'll stay," she said as she leaped into his arms. They kissed deeply as he held her to his body, waves lapping at his feet and drenching his shoes. As he set her down, a big wave crashed to shore, soaking them both. They briefly gasped for air before laughter took over. It had been years since she had laughed this hard.

"We have to tell Brystol," Bowie said, changing the mood.

She nodded in agreement yet offered nothing else in return. She wasn't sure how they would break the news and feared her daughter would be so hurt that she would reject them both.

"First, I think she needs to see us together like this."

"Is that so?" Brooklyn asked, raising her eyebrow.

"Unless you'd rather have some secret romance. I mean, that could be pretty exciting, sneaking away to make out." He pulled their joined hands up and kissed hers. "I've waited over twenty years for this moment, to tell you freely, without judgment. I'm too old to play games. And now with Brystol, I think we could give her the family she's never had. If that's what you want." He shrugged. "I don't know—maybe I'm reading things that aren't there."

She exhaled. "You're not. I want to be with you, Bowie. I have since long before that night. Life threw us off track a little bit, but I don't think it's too late for us."

"Neither do I. As far as telling her, I'd like to wait until after Carly passes. They're close, and I don't want Brystol upset with her grandmother during this time."

Brooklyn wiped a tear away from her cheek. "I can agree with that."

Together they started back toward the house, Brooklyn picking up her shoes before climbing the wooden staircase. Inside, the house was fairly quiet with the exception of the construction going on next door. Brooklyn felt like they should go check on the day's progress but also had faith in their crew to get the job done.

Once in the living room, they saw Brystol lying on the floor, using Luke as a pillow as usual. If the dog cared that Bowie had entered the room, he wasn't showing it. He had barely lifted his head. Brystol, on the other hand, made an effort to at least acknowledge them. She was watching a documentary on whales in the Pacific Ocean, and Brooklyn didn't want to interrupt her. She needed these moments to still be a teen and not be consumed with pain over her grandmother. Brooklyn watched Bowie as he glanced at Brystol. He was looking at her as his daughter now, and not the child his best friend had never seen grow up.

Sensing it was a good time to let their daughter in on part of their secret, Brooklyn reached for Bowie, pushing her way under his arm as he kissed her forehead, and Brystol chanted, "Mom's got a boyfriend." She smiled and leaned up to kiss Bowie on the lips . . . an action she knew her daughter would never let her live down.

"What do you know about boyfriends?" Brooklyn asked.

Brystol shrugged. "All I know is that Nonnie and Simi think you're perfect together."

"How do you know this?"

She looked at Bowie. "Sometimes, after Nonnie has had too much wine, she talks very loudly."

The three of them laughed. This was a good moment for them, even with the impending passing of their matriarch; they would be able to look back on this and say, "Remember that time Nonnie had too much wine . . ."

"Does this mean we're staying, Mom?"

Brooklyn nodded and couldn't hold back a smile as Brystol's face lit up. She went to her mom and hugged her tightly. After she let go, she crouched down, lifted Luke's snout, and said, "You're stuck with me now."

THIRTY-ONE

After Brystol stopped teasing Brooklyn about having a boyfriend, Brooklyn took Bowie upstairs to show him the paperwork she had found in Carly's desk. In a sense, he was relieved. It wasn't that he didn't trust Brooklyn, but seeing the report that there was no possible way for Austin to be Brystol's father was liberating. Still, he was plagued by the lingering voice in the back of his mind that said it was entirely possible Brooklyn could've been with someone else. As much as he refused to believe that was the case, he couldn't discount the suspicion. He glanced from the report to Brooklyn. She smiled.

"I know what you're thinking," she said.

"You do?"

She moved toward him. She lifted the sheet of paper from his hand, revealing another page. "Don't ask me how she had your DNA. Right now, I don't want to think of what went on in this house when my daughter wasn't here. I just know she did, and this report shows that you're her father."

A small smile turned into a huge grin, one that hurt his cheeks instantly. The pain was worth it, though. He was going to continue to smile like this until someone gave him a reason not to. This wasn't a victory for him . . . he had lost out on so much time with his daughter and silently vowed to do whatever he could to make up for it. However, he felt vindicated because Rachel had destroyed him when she had walked out, blaming him for their inability to have a child. And yes, maybe he couldn't anymore. Maybe something had happened to him in the last fifteen years that prevented him from getting the job done, but that didn't matter to him because he had Brystol. And whether she wanted him as a father or not didn't matter because he knew she liked him as long as Luke was around.

"Congratulations, it's a girl!" Brooklyn put her hands up in the air and tried to smile, but tears started pouring out. Bowie dropped the paperwork on the desk and pulled her into his arms. "I'm so sorry," she mumbled, pressing her face into his shirt. He held her tightly, wrapping his strong arms around her. He wanted to take away her guilt but was at a loss of how to do that. He too had the same feeling. He was sorry as well—sorry that they had missed so much time as a family—however, that wouldn't be the case moving forward.

He leaned back so he could look at her, lifting her chin so they were eye to eye. God, he loved her so much he thought his heart was going to beat right out of his chest. "No more, B. No more tears for what we can't change. Just happy thoughts."

Brooklyn choked out a bit of laughter. "You sound like Peter Pan."

"Sometimes I wish I had a little bit of magic on my side, but for right now I'm going to relish the moment, and you need to as well."

Their moment was interrupted by the shrill sound of her phone ringing.

"And if we want to make that happen, you're going to have to change that obnoxious ring tone." He laughed, stepping aside so she could answer. While she was busy talking, he carefully put the most important document of his life back in its place and returned the folder before closing the drawer.

"We have to go," Brooklyn said, staring down at her phone. He already knew from her demeanor who the call was about. "That was

Simone. She says that the doctors are telling her it's time for everyone to come say goodbye."

"Do you want . . ." Bowie paused. He wasn't sure what he wanted to ask her. Did she want him to go? Stay? Drive them and wait in the lobby?

"You're coming, right?"

"Of course." Now that she had asked, he wasn't entirely sure he wanted to be there. He was angry with Carly for the years of deceit and wondered if she weren't dying, would she have ever said anything? Deep down, there really wasn't a doubt in his mind that Carly would've held fast to the paternity of Brystol if she weren't lying on her deathbed, and that thought angered him. He wanted to lash out at Carly, berate her for keeping something so important from him. But he knew nothing good would come from doing so and would likely upset Brystol, and that was something he wasn't willing to do.

"We can go together, in my car," Brooklyn suggested.

"Is it okay if Luke comes?" he asked. "I rarely leave without him."

Brooklyn glanced at him, leery. "Does he chew on things?"

Bowie laughed. "He's better trained than some of my workers. Luke will be fine. We'll leave a window open for him, and he'll most likely sleep. Plus, he's a good comfort for Brystol, with her grandmother dying." He shrugged. Trying to sell his dog to someone else wasn't something he was used to. Everyone around town loved Luke, and Brooklyn would as well once she had a chance to get to know him.

"I think that's a good idea, especially for Brystol."

Together, they walked downstairs, and Brooklyn hollered to Brystol that they needed to head over to the hospital. She suggested that she pack a few things to keep her mind occupied. While Brystol was getting her bag ready, Brooklyn and Bowie sneaked some kisses in the kitchen. He felt like he had been with her forever, when in fact, the one night they had spent together was purely happenstance and had yet to be repeated. When he had arrived at her apartment that night, he had gone to console her, to give her a shoulder to cry on. As much as he had longed to kiss her, he had never intended to do so that night. Standing in the kitchen with her now nestled in his arms, he was thankful he had.

The drive over to the hospital was eventful, to say the least. Every window in the SUV was down, letting in a nice cool breeze. Brystol's head was resting against the door, letting the wind blow her hair around. Bowie couldn't wait to spend more time with her, to understand her mannerisms, her moods, and her facial expressions. He thought he saw worry on her face, maybe even fear or apprehension, but he wasn't sure. He thought about asking her what she was thinking about and figured the answer would be simple: her grandmother. Brooklyn eyed her daughter in the side mirror and reached for the dial on the radio, turning up the volume. Within seconds, she started belting out the tune coming through the speakers. Bowie knew what she was doing. This was her way of changing the mood. Brooklyn was trying to lift their daughter's spirits, and it was working. Brystol sat upright and sang her heart out. Bowie did his best to pay attention to the road but found himself trying to watch his girls. Brooklyn claimed she had asked him to drive because she didn't know the way, but he knew that was just an excuse. She was giving him a glimpse of what their family life was going to be like, and he fucking loved it. He didn't care that his girls were singing off-key or that his dog's slobber was getting the back of his arm wet, because he was happy. This was the life that he had been waiting for, and in a matter of hours, his whole world had changed.

"Can Luke come in?" Brystol asked as they arrived at the hospital.

"Not inside, but when you need a break, we'll come get him and take him for a walk. There's a great little place over there for Luke." Bowie pointed toward a small field that had been designated for dogs.

"He'll be okay in the car?" she asked.

Bowie caught Brystol staring at him in the rearview mirror. He winked at her and couldn't help but grin. That was his kid, and he couldn't have been happier. "We're going to leave the windows down for him. He'll be fine—I promise."

Brystol didn't look so sure as she nuzzled Luke's neck. Bowie was going to have to make sure he brought her out here to check on him often. Being in the hospital wasn't his idea of a fun time anyway, so using Luke as an excuse worked in his favor. Plus, it gave him more time with Brystol, and that was something he wouldn't pass up for anything.

The hospital was small and not equipped to handle major traumas. Broken bones, concussions, minor vehicle accidents, and the occasional nail through the hand were what they mostly saw. When news had broken of Austin's boat going down, the hospital had been flooded with people. They had come out in droves to donate blood in the event he needed it and to show support, even though he would've been airlifted to Seattle. His friends, though, had been down on the docks, loading boats for the search effort. Despite the storm, the search and rescue efforts had been well underway and had already pulled Grady from the water. When he had arrived here, his parents had obviously been relieved. Yet, all eyes had remained on the double doors, waiting for another stretcher.

Sometimes, Bowie wondered if the eyes were all still waiting. He had lost count of how many search and recovery missions had happened since that night. He, himself, had even gone diving in hopes of recovering Austin's body. Every time he heard on the news of remains being found, his hopes soared that it was Austin so they could finally lay him to rest. And if *his* hopes rose, he couldn't begin to imagine what Carly went through each time.

She lay there peacefully. Bowie had expected to see her in one of those hospital-issued gowns, but she was looking as regal as ever with her hair done and dressed in a maroon sweater. He studied her for a moment, wondering if he had been around after Austin died, if she would have told him about Brystol. Unfortunately, he just didn't think she would've. Whether Brystol was his or not, she saw the girl as an extension of Austin somehow and was going to keep that information to herself as long as possible.

Brystol stood next to Bowie and leaned into him. He wasn't sure if it was intentional or not, but he welcomed the affection. He put his arm around her shoulder and leaned down to whisper in her ear. "If you want to get out of here, just say the word and we'll go. You don't have to stay." She nodded against him and turned away. Bowie watched as she went back to her mom, who was standing at the nurses' station with Simone, getting an update.

He hesitated before crossing the threshold into the room. He pulled the hard plastic chair closer to the bed and sat down. For the life of him he couldn't grasp why hospitals insisted on using the most uncomfortable furniture. His lower back was sure to be aching by the time he was ready to go.

Carly opened her eyes, and Bowie reached for her hand. He didn't want to be nice to her. He wanted to yell, to curse her out, and tell her he wished he had never met her. He wanted to ask her why. Why would she hide something so important as a child from him? But those words would never leave his mouth. The damage had been done, and there was nothing she could say now to repair her actions.

"Love them," she muttered groggily.

"Love who?" he asked, leaning forward. He wanted to hear her say their names.

"My girls. My Bs. Love them."

He smiled, but it wasn't for her; it was for them. "I plan to, for the rest of my life." He was being completely honest with her about that. He had no intentions of ever stopping.

"Home."

Bowie wasn't sure what she was talking about, but he went ahead and talked anyway. "Your home will be fine, Carly. Construction is moving along on the inn, and it'll be open again in no time. I went into your kitchen. I know you didn't want me to, but I wanted to make sure everything was up to code. It's beautiful. Simone did a really great job." *After you destroyed it,* he thought.

A nurse came in, interrupting him.

"How is she?" Bowie asked.

"It won't be long now," she said solemnly. "She sure does like her visitors, though."

That statement confused him. Who else had come to see her? "Do you know who was here?"

She shook her head. "Not by name—they were older ladies and a few of her son's friends."

Bowie was happy that people were coming to see her, except for Austin's friends. He hadn't been the only one to disappear from Carly's life after Austin died. They all did. Death had a funny way of both breaking people apart and bringing them together, though. He guessed all that mattered was that she was loved. It didn't matter if people showed her then or now, as long as she knew.

THIRTY-TWO

Brooklyn gave Bowie some time alone with Carly, figuring he had a few things to get off his chest. Over the years, she had heard horror stories about moms who struggled as a single parent or dads finding out years later they had a child. Sure, she'd had her struggles, but they had been hers to deal with and overcome on her own. She had missed Austin. She had missed Bowie. Her heart couldn't decide which of them deserved more of her longing. Each man was there for different reasons.

When she had found out she was pregnant, she had gone through a barrage of emotions all at once—scared, happy, sad, over the moon, and confused. She and Austin hadn't been safe, and she had usually spent every month staring at the calendar, waiting for her period to start. They had been careless and had been together so long that either marriage was going to happen, or a child was bound to come at some point.

They had been fighting the last night she saw him. In fact, they had been fighting most days. Neither was happy with each other or their lives. Brooklyn wanted to move back to Seattle and had reminded Austin that his five-year plan was about to expire. He was supposed to take his fishing boat to Puget Sound while she attended nursing school. She had saved enough money to enroll, thanks to her job with Seacoast Construction. However, when she had brought it up one evening, he had told her he wasn't going. It didn't matter how much she pleaded;

he refused to budge. Business was good for him, and he didn't feel right asking Grady to move. Bowie had encouraged Brooklyn to go, to follow her dreams, but she wouldn't leave Austin. Her whole world had revolved around him since high school, and she couldn't imagine it without him, but Austin had other plans, ultimately leaving her no choice.

Brooklyn's phone rang out. She pulled it out quickly and silenced it before the staff gave her scorning looks. When she saw Rennie's name, she smiled. "Hey."

"Hey you, just letting you know that I'll be up in a couple of hours."

"What? How?" Brooklyn stammered.

"Graham, by way of Bowie."

"Oh." Despite everything going on, her heart soared. He had thought enough to find a way to reach her best friend, knowing she would need her.

"Ren, Carly's dying. She doesn't have long."

"I know, hon."

"That's not all . . ." Brooklyn paused. "Bowie is Brystol's father."

Nothing but silence.

"Say that again."

"You heard me, Rennie."

"How? I mean I know how, but how?"

"Carly suspected and had a DNA test run when Brystol was little and kept the results a secret until now."

"And now she's dying?"

Brooklyn sighed heavily. "She collapsed the morning after the bonfire and was brought to the hospital by ambulance. She has cancer. Stage four."

"And you're just now telling me!"

"Sorry, Ren, I've been sort of busy trying to piece my life back together after these two major explosions. God, I don't even know what day it is right now. I need you, though, to look over her will."

"I'll be up after work to help you out. Now tell me, what are you going to do?"

"Be with Bowie, raise our daughter, and run the inn." She said those words as Simone and Brystol came into view. Brystol would need everyone around her after her grandmother passed. Here, Brystol had everyone, including another set of grandparents, who were probably going to have heart attacks when Bowie informed them who she was. There was also Simone, who had helped raise Brystol since she was a baby. And Brooklyn's own parents weren't far from here and could come visit whenever they wanted. It made sense to stay.

"You're going to stay!"

Brooklyn smiled. She would have her best friend close again, and that made her very happy. "I am. I'm going to stay. I'm going to work to revitalize the area, maybe buy some houses and turn them into rentals. Bowie and I could do some flips. I don't know."

"I'll write your contracts for you," Rennie said.

"I expect nothing less," she said, laughing.

As for her career, she and Bowie could easily team up and start their own business. On the drive to the hospital, she had noticed numerous houses that had been abandoned. They could start flipping properties together, or she could retire and run the inn. The possibilities were endless. And the idea of finally putting down some roots, enrolling Brystol in school, where she could make some friends, outweighed everything else. She wanted to give her daughter the same experiences she'd had: homecoming, bonfires on the beach, prom, and a graduation with kids she'd known for longer than a few months. She wanted her daughter to grow into the teenager she was meant to be. She and Rennie hung up once she finally agreed that Rennie needed to be in Cape Harbor as soon as possible.

She went over to Simone and Brystol and sat across from them. "What are you ladies looking at?"

Brystol held up the newest issue of *Better Homes & Gardens*. Brooklyn blanched when she saw the cover, causing Brystol to laugh. Brooklyn had forgotten that she'd given them an interview. It was months ago when a photographer showed up and took photos of her in a kitchen she had recently finished.

"You look good, Mom."

Brooklyn smiled. "Thanks, kiddo. How are my answers?"

"They're the usual." Brystol shrugged.

"I particularly like the tips," Simone added. "I could've used these when I was repairing the kitchen."

"You did an amazing job on the kitchen, Simi," Brooklyn stated. "I've looked it over. I've checked the wiring. Everything is ready to go."

However, Simone didn't look convinced.

"Tell you what—I'll have Bowie look too. We'll make sure everything's in working order before we open." This seemed to placate Simone a bit.

Bowie came into the waiting room a few minutes later and met Brooklyn's eyes. They weren't on the same page yet but would be after spending some time together. Soon he would know exactly what she was thinking. She desperately wanted to feel his arms around her, to have him hug the both of them, but right now she had to take her daughter to say goodbye to her grandmother.

She and Brystol held hands as they walked toward Bowie. Brooklyn stopped and rested her free hand on his chest. He leaned into her, kissing her temple. "I'll be outside with Luke," he whispered.

Down the hall, mother and daughter walked toward Carly's room. Brooklyn wanted Brystol to go at her own pace; she didn't want to force her to do anything she wasn't comfortable with. Next to Carly's bed sat a chair. Bowie had left it there for the next person to come in and say their goodbyes. In the corner, a pile of folded blankets had been placed on the floor, with a pillow resting on top. Simone was preparing to stay here so that Carly wouldn't die alone.

"Can Nonnie hear me?"

"Yeah, she can. She may not be able to answer, but she can hear you."

Brystol walked into the room and sat in the chair while Brooklyn went to the windowsill. She had sat there last night, waiting and wondering how she'd ended up here. It was all Carly and some master plan of hers to change their lives. She knew that now.

"Hi, Nonnie. I know you're not feeling very well right now. Mom says you can hear me. I really hope she's right. Grandpa told me once that you should always say goodbye, no matter where you're going. I'm not the one leaving, but I guess the same applies. I don't know what I'm supposed to say, so I'm just going to tell you that you are the best grandma, and I have a lot of really fun memories. Like the time we tried to tie-dye shirts, and you spilled the color everywhere. Your backyard was a rainbow of colors until it rained. Or the time we went out during low tide to go clamming. I still don't like clams that much, but that was fun. I know we didn't get to spend a lot of time together, but coming here each summer was the most fun, with this one being the best because we got to stay home every day. You and Simi always had so many things for us to do, like flying kites or sitting in the hammock reading. There was the time we went to dinner with my grandparents at the Space Needle. We started on one side of the city and ended up on the other. Do you remember laughing all night with my grandma? What about when you snorted?" Brystol had to stop and laugh. Brooklyn glanced at her daughter and saw that her head was down, resting on Carly's leg. "I remember it so clearly."

Two people appeared in the doorway, and Brooklyn sprang to her feet. She rushed to her parents, needing to feel their arms around her. "What're you doing here?"

"Simone called us. We thought we'd come up and help with Brystol, and anything else you needed."

"I'm so happy you're here," she said, breathing them in. "I'm so sorry I didn't call. My mind is reeling right now. Rennie's on her way too. I need her to look over Carly's will."

"We understand," her mother said.

She pulled away, only to be replaced by Brystol. She yammered on about everything that had been happening since she saw them last, and filled her grandparents in about Luke, telling them that she was begging her mother for a dog now.

"Dad, you remember Bowie, right?"

"Of course, I do," David Hewett said gruffly.

"He's in the waiting room." Brooklyn gave her parents a knowing look. They knew all too well about their daughters' feelings toward Bowie, and later tonight, she would fill them in on her surprising revelation.

Brystol finally disengaged from her grandparents and brought her grandma into the room. She let her grandma sit next to Carly, and she stood by her side. Brooklyn gave her father a kiss on the cheek and asked him to please go visit Bowie, telling him she would be out in a bit. She stood at the end of the bed and watched Carly struggle in her sleep. "She's in and out of consciousness. They have her on morphine for the pain. The nurses feel it won't be long. They're not expecting her to make it through the night."

Bonnie Hewett pulled her granddaughter down on her lap and held her as she whispered to Brystol, telling her how sorry she was. As much as she wanted to remain strong, Brooklyn felt tears wet her cheeks. Her mom reached for her hand and gave it a squeeze.

"We'll get you through this, my little Bs."

Brooklyn wiped away the stream of tears with her free hand. "She has a list of things I'm supposed to do, but I still feel like I have no idea what I'm doing. I hate waiting, and I don't even know what I'm waiting for. She's just there, and in pain, and I can't do anything to help her."

"The staff here is doing everything they can for her, sweetie. Your father is very confident in their ability, and you know he's here if you have any concerns."

"I just don't like seeing her in pain."

"I know. Why don't you go out to the waiting room, round up your dad, and go get something to eat downstairs? Little B and I are going to sit here and visit with Carly. If something changes, we'll come and get you." Brooklyn went to her mom, leaned over, and hugged her from behind. Her mom kissed her cheek and told her that she loved her.

In the waiting room, Bowie and her father were arguing over football. It was something that they had done every time they saw each other. Bowie was a die-hard Seahawks fan, while her father thought they were lime-green chickens. Her father was born and raised in San Francisco and would always be a Niners fan, something that Bowie loved to give David shit about.

Watching her father kid around with the man who Brooklyn knew was her future gave her hope, and right now she needed a lot of that hope to get through everything she was facing.

She went outside, needing a break from everything the hospital represented. The smells, the background noises, the uncomfortable chairs—it all meant waiting, and in her case waiting meant dying. The double door opened as she approached. She passed a man who carried a bouquet of flowers and balloons. A quick glance and she figured his wife had just had a baby boy. Her mom and dad, Carly, and Rennie had been the only ones at the hospital when she'd had Brystol, and they too had brought her flowers. She couldn't remember if she'd had balloons in her room or not.

There was a bench not far from the double doors. She sat down on the wooden slats, leaned back, and closed her eyes. Even with the light breeze and overhead cloud cover, the sun was in perfect position to keep her warm. She let her mind drift, not to the past, but to the future. A future that finally included Bowie and them together. Before, when she had dreamed of what life could've been like if she had stayed, he had been there, but never fully. Austin's death had always kept them apart, and she knew why. Carly. Out of fear of what she would think, Brooklyn had hidden her feelings, and now knowing that she didn't have to hurt. She cried for the years they'd lost. Not only together but as a family.

Someone sat down beside her. She shifted slightly so the stranger couldn't see her red puffy eyes and ask her if she was okay. She was afraid to answer a question like that. Was she okay? In a sense, maybe. She had a healthy child and a great job, and for the most part she was happy. Deep down she knew she'd be happier with Bowie, that Brystol would thrive in Cape Harbor, and she would as well. Her parents and Rennie would be close enough they could see each other whenever they wanted, but Carly and her deathbed confession lingered like a bad aftertaste.

The person beside her cleared their throat. She glanced over her shoulder and saw Grady sitting there. She shifted and looked at his disheveled state. The Grady she remembered, the one with boyish charm, a sweet baby face, and a crooked smile was gone and replaced with despair, anger, and age. The long-term alcohol abuse had aged him at least twenty years. He no longer looked like Graham's twin but a distant relative.

"Grady." She said his name softly. He turned and glared. His menacing stare had her turning away. Her stomach twisted, and her flight sense kicked in. She set her hand down on the metal armrest and prepared to stand. His hand clamped down on her wrist, holding her in place.

"You don't get to walk away again."

"Grady . . ."

"Don't, don't say my name."

She looked at him again and saw years of sadness built up. She searched his eyes for some inkling that the Grady Chamberlain she grew up with was in there but found nothing. "I'm sorry."

"For what? For being a whore?"

"It's not—"

"Shut up!" he said loudly. "You don't get to be sorry for anything. What you did to Austin." He paused and took a deep, shuddering breath. "He fucking loved you."

She shook her head as tears fell.

"If you think the town is going to accept you and Bowie as a couple, you're mistaken. I'll tell anyone who listens what you did to Austin the night he died. I will ruin the both of you."

"You're the town drunk, Grady. No one is going to believe you." She ripped her hand from his grip. The damage was done, though; there was no way she could stay now. She stood and turned her back to him and took a few steps before turning around to say more to him, to tell him how wrong he was and what Austin had said to her. How they didn't have the picture-perfect romance they had led everyone to believe. Grady was gone. Disappeared into thin air.

The double doors opened. The people coming out were laughing, something she couldn't do. Not now. She took her phone out and sent a message to Bowie asking him to come outside. She wasn't going to prolong the inevitable, not anymore. She had wasted too much of her life avoiding conflict.

Within a minute, Bowie walked out the door. He smiled as he came toward her, but it quickly faded. "What's wrong?" He clasped his hand with hers and held on tightly as she tried to pull away. He brushed his thumb along her cheekbone, wiping away her tears. What she was going to do would break his heart, again. And shatter hers.

"Remember that job I told you about, the one that starts in October?"

He nodded.

"I'm going to take it. We can work out some custody arrangement with Brystol. I'll send her here on vacations and whatnot. She's homeschooled, and it's all online. She works well independently, so she can come for longer periods at a time."

"No," was all he said.

She worked hard to keep her emotions in check. "It's for the best. I shouldn't have come back here. Grady . . ." She trailed off.

"Was he here?"

She nodded and bit her lower lip to keep her tears at bay.

"Fucking Grady," he muttered. He said nothing else as he pulled her to her SUV. He opened the door and motioned for her to get in. "Don't worry about Brystol; she's fine. Get in."

She did, and when he slid behind the steering wheel, she asked, "Where are we going?"

"My place. Luke needs to eat."

Brooklyn glanced over her shoulder at his dog. He seemed content, with his head hanging out the window.

"I shouldn't leave Carly."

"Someone will call us if we are needed."

She didn't feel like arguing. She leaned her head back and watched the scenery go by. The almost thirty-minute trip seemed to fly by rather quickly. When they pulled into Bowie's driveway, he shut off the car and got out. She stayed and stared out the window at his house. It was small with the perfect-for-summer covered porch. Those were her favorite, especially in the houses down south. There was nothing like sipping sweet tea and watching the lightning bugs at night while swaying back and forth.

Bowie and Luke disappeared into the cornflower-blue house, leaving her to wonder what was behind the door. Curiosity got the best of her as she finally got out of the car. The cobblestone walk was done with meticulous precision. She knew Bowie had put a lot of time and effort into his home. The thought gave her pride. They were the same, wanting the same, yet she couldn't deliver on her end. Not without living with guilt.

She climbed the three steps up to the porch and walked to the door, pushing it open slightly. "Hello?" she called out foolishly.

"In here," he said, forcing her to follow his voice. She found Bowie standing in his room without his shirt on and soft music playing in the background. He'd set her up, knowing she wouldn't stay in the car.

The sight of him made her mouth water. His torso was the color of honey, just lightly kissed by the sun. He wasn't overly muscular, but he had some definition. As he stared at her, his biceps flexed. She loved that he kept his hair short but had facial hair. She longed to run her finger over the stubble, to feel his breath fan over her, to kiss him and show him that she was still in love with him. But the cost of being together weighed heavily on her mind.

"I should go."

He came toward her and placed his hand on her waist, pulling her toward him. "If you go, I go."

"It's not that easy, Bowie." She knew exactly what he was talking about.

"Being with you is the easiest thing I'll ever do."

"Grady says no one will ever accept us being together."

"Bullshit. It's been fifteen years, Brooklyn. We're allowed to move on, and once people know Brystol's mine, they'll be happy for us."

She shook her head, unable to believe him. He trailed his finger down her cheek until he reached her chin and lifted her head until he could look in her eyes. "Those demons dancing around in your pretty little head need to be exorcised."

"I can't help it."

"Maybe I can," he said moments before his lips pressed to hers. He withdrew slightly. "I am in love with you, Brooklyn Hewett. If you leave, I go with you." He kissed her deeply. "And if it means we live in hotels for the rest of our lives, so be it. You're not leaving without me."

"But—" As much as she tried to fight her attraction to Bowie, she felt it stronger, deep within her bones. The anxiety she'd felt turned to anticipation. She craved his touch, his body pressed against hers, the way he whispered her name. She wanted it all.

"There are no buts in this, B. We're in this together, no matter what. I will protect you, be your voice when yours fails you. I will not let you succumb to the guilt you feel."

"Bowie . . ." His name fell softly from her lips before she closed the small gap between them. His words, his vow, they charged her. She wrapped her arms around his neck and molded herself to him. He lifted her and carried her to his bed, then laid her down gently. Her fingers tickled his barely there beard, and he smiled.

"Your eyes are so beautiful," she told him as she gazed into his blue eyes. The same eyes their daughter had. "We made a gorgeous girl."

Bowie grinned widely. "We did. I've never forgotten that night."

"Me neither."

"Don't let Grady's words come between us, Brooklyn. We deserve a shot at happiness."

She agreed and pulled him closer. "Maybe you can make me forget what he said?"

"Are you sure I'm what you want?" he asked as he lay beside her.

"Without a doubt."

He sat back on his knees and pulled at her shirt, lifting it over her head. She lay there, letting his eyes rove over her. He came forward and kissed a trail down her chest to her stomach, where he let his lips linger. Her fingers wove through his hair as tears welled. "I'm sorry," she whispered.

"I am too," he said.

It was as if those apologies were a turning point for them. They fumbled with the rest of their clothes, almost as if they had never been together before. With each kiss and caress, the butterflies she'd had their first time came back. Her heart beat wildly with anticipation as he hovered over her. She shivered at the sensation of being with him again. She wanted this, and she wanted him.

In the early hours of the morning, as the sun rose,
turning the sky to red,
and as fishermen weighed the pros and cons of heading
out to sea for the day,
Carly Woods took her last breath.
She was surrounded by those she loved most.
Funeral services will take place at Harbor Church,
followed by a celebration of life at the Whale Spout.
In lieu of flowers, donations can be made to the Cape
Harbor Fisherman's Fund.

THIRTY-THREE

Bowie pulled his razor slowly against his skin, slicing off a couple days' worth of stubble even though he knew Brooklyn enjoyed the feel against her skin. Their lovemaking had been interrupted by their daughter asking where her mother was. After the call, they both lay there, laughing. It wasn't the first time a call had torn them apart. His free hand gripped the side of the counter as his shoulders hunched forward and he replayed yesterday in his mind. Happy, elated feelings mixed with sorrow and tears. It was hard to put into words what he felt. Hot water rushed over the razor, cleaning it off. Repeat and rinse, until very little shaving cream remained on his face. He shut the water off and stood upright, studying himself in the mirror. His eyes were puffy, the result of the tears he had shed as Carly died and from a lack of sleep. The hours prior had been hard. Sleep was nonexistent while everyone kept vigil in Carly's room. Until now, he had never witnessed someone dying, and though she had looked at peace, he had wondered if she really was. He had known the morphine kept most of the pain at bay, but as he had taken his turns staying with her, he had seen her face grimace and her eyes flutter and was curious to know if she was aware, if she was in pain, or if those were involuntary muscle spasms. She had continued to have moments of lucidity, which he would be eternally grateful for. Carly had told Brystol she loved her many times before she had taken her final breath, which to him meant everything, considering what he and Brooklyn were about to tell her. Many times, he had wanted to leave the room, but he couldn't leave Brooklyn and Brystol, so he had stayed and held on to Brooklyn when she would take a break from sitting by Carly.

Today was a day of mourning. Construction on the inn had ceased until after the funeral, and while Brooklyn and Simone needed to make final arrangements for Carly, Bowie planned to take his daughter fishing. He and Brooklyn felt that with everyone out of the house, the last thing they wanted was for Brystol to be by herself. Fishing probably wasn't ideal, but it seemed like a fitting tribute to the Woodses. Aside from the Driftwood Inn, that was what they were known for, and Bowie figured Carly would want this.

Bowie took one last look in the mirror, inhaled deeply, and squared his shoulders before he turned off the light in the bathroom. He paused in the doorway, only to turn around, flick the light back on, and look at himself again. Another inhale. "You're a dad now," he said to the man staring back at him. "You have a daughter."

"*You have a daughter.*"

"*A child.*"

"*A teenager.*"

Those were the words Bowie had said to himself, silently and aloud, since Brooklyn had told him. As much as he wanted to hate her, scream at her, tell her she was the worst person in the world for keeping his child from him, he couldn't. Even thinking those words made his stomach turn. Brooklyn might have left him, their friends, and their town behind, but she wasn't vindictive. She wasn't some evil woman who set out to hurt the people she loved.

When he had seen Brooklyn sitting in the ocean with the waves washing over her, he had thought for sure she was trying to do the unthinkable, and for the life of him he couldn't understand why. On the outside, she had an amazing life, but since her return to Cape Harbor, Bowie could tell she fought demons. There had been so many times when he wanted to lock her in one of the rooms so they could hash out their issues. Mostly, he wanted to kiss her. He wanted to bring back all the memories that had faded over time. He wanted her to feel the love they had shared but had never been able to tell anyone about. He wanted her in any way she'd allow him in her life. Mostly, he just wanted to be in her presence because when she was near, he felt alive. He saw life the way he had dreamed many years before.

Bowie smiled brightly at his reflection. Parenthood looked damn good on him—at least he thought so. He was about to face the biggest test of his life, and he was scared shitless. What if Brystol didn't like him? What if she thought he was the biggest goober and wanted nothing to do with him? *Simple,* he thought—he'd bring Luke. Brystol . . . his daughter, adored his dog, and if Bowie had to stoop to using his dog to win her over, he was going to do it.

He left the bathroom again with a newfound confidence and a bit of pep in his step. Without a doubt, he was going to make the best of his outing with Brystol. They were going to spend the day getting to know each other, hopefully bond, and not dwell on the loss of Carly. The latter was going to be a tough mountain to climb, though. He was confident he could keep Brystol's mind occupied on the task at hand, fishing.

Before he left, he picked up the teddy bear he had bought for her. He found it in the hospital gift store and knew he had to get it for her. Next to the bear, a black box sat on the counter. Years ago, his mother had given him a necklace to give to Rachel, but it had never felt right, and he had kept it hidden in his dresser drawer. The necklace had been in his family for many generations, and now that he had a daughter, he felt he'd been right in keeping it until now. He wanted Brystol to have something from his family. When he gave it to her, he wanted her to know she was loved and had a family waiting for her. Bowie wasn't usually an emotional guy, but when he had left Brooklyn the night he had found out he was a father, he'd lost it. Everything he'd held in for years since Austin's death—Brooklyn disappearing, Rachel wanting a different life, and subsequently finding out about Brystol—had hit him so hard he couldn't hold back the tears. He opened the velvet box and ran his thumb over the heart-shaped charm with a pearl in the middle of it. As far as he could remember, his great-great-grandfather had had this made after finding the pearl in an oyster. Someday soon, he would give it to Brystol, making her a Holmes.

The drive over to the inn happened in a blur. Being there every day had become second nature for him. Since the first day on the job, the one he had showed up hungover for, he'd been diligent to make sure he and his crew carried their fair share of the weight. It was almost like Brooklyn had needed to rip him a new one for him to realize he was looking a gift horse in the mouth. He had an opportunity to make a name for himself, especially by working with Brooklyn. Even if they didn't work out as a couple, he was confident she'd support his business, and her endorsement alone would keep him flush with customers.

Bowie parked along the road and held the door for Luke to jump out. He whistled for his dog to follow him through the freshly mulched flower bed, not ideal, but safer for his dog with the construction trucks clogging the driveway. Together, the pair made their way to the front door, where Bowie inhaled, gave himself a pep talk, and tapped his knuckles against the wood.

It swung open immediately. Brystol stood there wearing khaki shorts, an old Whale Spout shirt that Bowie was sure she'd gotten from her mother, and sneakers, with a sweatshirt in her hand. He opened his mouth to say something but closed it quickly. Staring back at him was his daughter, who looked so much like her mother. Brystol pushed her glasses higher up on her nose and stared back as she tilted her head. He shook the cobwebs from his mind and grinned.

"Is your mom home?"

"No, she and Simi are meeting with the funeral home director. I thought we were going to hang out?"

He nodded and felt stupid for asking about her mother. "You're right; I just . . ."

"Thought you were looking at my mom from twenty years ago?"

"Yeah."

Brystol shrugged and stepped outside. Luke whined, waiting for her to pet him. She set her hand on his head while she addressed Bowie. "Nonnie says . . ." She paused, and her lower lip quivered. "I guess I have to talk about her in the past tense now, huh?"

He placed his hand on her shoulder and gave it a squeeze. "You can talk about her any way you want. You make the rules when it comes to your grandmother."

She smiled softly, looked down at Luke and finally at Bowie again. "Nonnie always said I looked like my mom when she was younger. Sometimes, when she was tired, she called me Brooklyn. And my grandma sometimes says the same thing, which is why she calls me Little B."

Little B. He loved that nickname for her and hoped to one day use it, if she would allow it. He motioned for her to walk ahead of him, with Luke leading the way. When they approached his truck, he went around to the passenger side and held the door for her. Of course, Luke took this open invitation to leap in first, planting himself in the middle, and before he went to climb in himself, he made sure everything he needed for their outing was secured in the back.

As he drove through town, heading toward the bridge, he waved at people he saw. Some called his name or hollered a hello to Luke. "You're popular," Brystol stated as they came to a stoplight.

"That happens when you live in the same place your entire life."

"Do you know everyone?"

He thought about her question for a moment before answering. "You know, I think I do, unless they just moved here."

"Do people move here often?"

"We might get a couple new families once or twice a year. It doesn't take long for them to acclimate and get to know everyone."

Brystol looked at herself in the side mirror. "Do you think people would know me if I moved here?"

Yes, especially when I tell everyone you're my daughter. "Of course, they already do."

"Small-town tea, right?"

"Tea?" he asked, to which Brystol giggled.

"Tea is gossip."

Bowie laughed and pressed the gas pedal to move his truck along the road. "Gossip in town runs rampant. Everyone knows something, and sometimes that something is so far from the truth. You grin and move on. But, if you ever want to know the truth, you ask Peggy." He pointed at the diner as they passed by. "Peggy somehow knows everything and will set everyone straight if they're making things up."

"I sort of think it would be fun to live in a place where everyone knows you and they wave when they see you."

He nodded. Living in Cape Harbor definitely had its perks, but it also had its drawbacks. At times, he hated that everyone knew his business and was surprised Carly was able to keep Brystol's true identity a secret for as long as she had. Part of him was very resentful she had, because he could've had his daughter years ago.

Bowie drove in silence the rest of the way to their destination. When he parked, Luke let out a satisfied bark, and Brystol laughed. He could listen to her laugh all day and never tire of the sound. "Come on," he said as he opened his door. Brystol did the same, and Luke seemed torn on who to follow. When she called for him, his dog happily went to his daughter, and this made him smile. He could live with his best friend choosing Brystol over him. He took the fishing poles and bait box from the back of his truck and motioned for Brystol to follow him.

"Your father and I . . ." Calling Austin her father stung, but he had no choice at the moment. He cleared his throat and continued. "All our friends fished off this bridge. We used to have to contend with traffic, but the state closed it many years ago because it was more dangerous for the cars to drive over it with all the fishing that was going on."

"So how do cars get across now?"

He pointed to a bridge a bit farther down. "The new one added about a two-minute drive. No one really complained because most everyone in town loves using this bridge to fish." They walked to an open spot, stopping only a few times to say hello to people. Bowie introduced Brystol as Brooklyn's daughter. Soon the town would know that she was his, and honestly, he couldn't wait.

"I've never done this before," she said as she looked over the railing at the rushing water below.

"Don't worry, kiddo." The man next to her spoke. "You're with Bowie Holmes; he knows how to fish. He'll teach you." Brystol looked at Bowie and smiled. He couldn't help but return the sentiment. They shared a moment, one he would remember for the rest of his life.

Bowie explained everything to her about fishing, except how to cast. For her first time, they'd drop a line from the bridge, which would be good practice. He asked her if she wanted to bait her hook, to which she shook her head so hard the end of her ponytail smacked her glasses. They both laughed. With her hook baited, he handed her the fishing pole and walked her through how to drop her line down.

Brystol was a natural. She pulled the bail back, kept her finger under the line, and watched her worm-baited hook sail toward the water. Per Bowie's instructions, she let the fishing line unravel for a few more seconds before she wound the reel handle.

"Now what?" she asked.

"Now we wait. Every few minutes we'll bring your line up, see if it's still baited, and send it back down."

"How will I know if I have a fish?"

"You'll feel a good tug, and your pole will feel a bit heavier."

"Got it," she said as she leaned a bit over the rail. Bowie watched her for a minute before he dropped his own line.

"You know, if you want to talk about your grandmother, I've been told I'm a good listener. I've known her pretty much my whole life."

"Maybe later. Right now, talking about her makes me sad. I asked my mom, though, if I could write her eulogy. She told me that Nonnie would love if I did. I learned about those from a book I read."

"I bet it's going to be beautiful." His daughter was something else, and he was proud that she was his.

Word spread fast that Brooklyn's daughter was on the bridge, fishing for the first time. People stopped and chatted, introduced themselves and their kids. Bowie caught a few young men checking out his daughter and wanted to move her behind him but knew he couldn't, at least not yet. He would have to talk to Brooklyn about what kind of rules Brystol had so he wasn't overstepping. Most importantly, he wanted Brystol to make friends, to feel like Cape Harbor was her home.

The first few times Brystol brought her line back up, her worm was gone. Bowie's too. Everyone around them laughed and told their new friend that she'd get the hang of it, and when she hooked a small trout, she squealed so loudly that everyone on the bridge came running.

Bowie guided her as she reeled furiously. The fish was small and would have to be tossed back in the river, but not before he got a picture of her and her catch. Brystol held her pole in one hand and the line in another, while her fish flopped in the air. She smiled brightly for her photo and quickly handed her fishing pole and fish to Bowie to take care of.

They stayed for a few more hours until they were both starving and in need of the best, greasiest burger Peggy could order them up. On the way back to his truck, Brystol stopped him. "I want to thank you for today. I've always wanted to fish, and my mom . . . it's not her thing."

"I'm happy to teach you everything, Brystol."

She nodded and then surprised Bowie by launching herself into his arms. He held her tightly, wishing today was the day he could tell her he was her father.

THIRTY-FOUR

Brooklyn took her time showering, letting the hot water pound into her sore muscles. She was tired, emotionally drained, and also angry at Carly. Not only for her bombshell, but for refusing treatment and for not telling her when she found out she was sick. Brooklyn could've made sure Brystol had more time with her grandmother. Instead, they were planning her funeral and cremation.

When she came out of the bathroom, Brystol was sitting crossed-legged on her bed, flipping through a magazine. "Hey," she said as she made her way to her closet. "How was fishing?"

"So fun. I caught a fish, but Bowie said we had to put it back because he was too small to keep. How was the adult stuff today?"

Brooklyn winced. She didn't want her daughter to have to worry about anything having to do with the arrangements and instead focused on the happy part of her daughter's day. "Wow, congratulations. Where did you go?"

"To some bridge. Everyone there fished. It was crazy fun, and everyone knows Bowie."

Brooklyn thumbed through her shirts, then pulled one off the bar, looked it over, and put it back. She had no idea what to wear on her date with Bowie and was tempted to cancel. It wasn't that she didn't want to go out and spend time with him; it was that she didn't want to leave the house. She'd much rather curl up on the sofa with a blanket and turn on a good movie. Bowie wanted to take her out, wine and dine her, and she felt that she owed him at least one night.

"I used to fish there."

"You fished?" Brystol sounded shocked. "I thought you hated fishing!"

Brooklyn leaned against the doorjamb and looked at her daughter. "I never really fished, but I'd go with Austin and Bowie. Most of the time I would sit there and read, work on my tan, or visit everyone else who was there."

"Did you know everyone in town?"

"Mostly."

"Did you think that was weird?"

Brooklyn went back to looking for the right shirt for her date. Simone had insisted that Brooklyn take some time for herself, and Bowie was more than happy to help. "At first, it was crazy. Austin knew everyone, so I met a lot of people after I moved here. It didn't take long for the hype of being the new person to subside, and people weren't eager to meet me. They just knew me, from either Austin, school, or my parents. After a while, it became second nature to say hi to everyone."

"Right, but don't you think it's strange to know *everyone?*"

"I don't know," she said as she finally settled on a flowy blouse that would look good with her distressed jeans and the new flats she had ordered online a few weeks back. "Did you go out to eat?"

Brystol nodded enthusiastically. "Peggy makes the best burgers ever."

Brooklyn found herself smiling at how excited her daughter was. She remembered what it was like to go to the diner. It was one of her favorite places. She didn't have the heart to tell her that Peggy wasn't the actual cook, and the last she knew it was Peggy's husband. Brooklyn and Brystol spoke for a bit more before Brystol excused herself to go watch television. She said something about making sure the living room was ready for Luke and how they planned to watch a movie with Simone.

As soon as her daughter left her room, Brooklyn dressed quickly and decided to put her hair in a loose braid—a mermaid braid, according to Brystol. She pulled a few strands out to shape her face, added some mascara, and called it good before going downstairs to wait.

Simone was in the kitchen when Brooklyn walked in, staring out the window with a content look on her face. She went over to her and stood next to her. "You'll always have a place here, no matter what. This is your home."

"Thank you, Brooklyn."

"In fact, her will made sure of it. The job of managing the inn is yours, if you want it."

Simone smiled. "I may take the rest of the summer to think about it, if you don't mind."

"Not at all. Want to watch a movie with Brystol and me?" As much as she wanted to spend time with Bowie, she didn't want to leave Simone if she needed her.

The older woman turned and looked at her. "I thought you have a date with Bowie?"

She shrugged. "I can cancel."

"You will do no such thing, Brooklyn. You will go out with that man, tell him how you feel, and not worry about anything. Carly would want that. We can mourn tomorrow. Tonight, I plan to snuggle next to Brystol and will let my girl take all my cares away."

Brooklyn pulled Simone into her arms. "We love you. I will never be able to thank you enough for taking care of Brystol all these years."

"Hush now—it was my pleasure."

Simone and Brooklyn walked into the living room and joined Brystol on the sofa. For some reason, Brooklyn had a stomach full of butterflies. She thought it was silly to feel nervous about her date with Bowie because they already knew each other. They had been out a million times before, with and without Austin, so going out now wasn't unheard of. What was new were the feelings she had for him. For years, she had fought the demons in her heart, loving two men at the same time, and not just two men, but best friends. Back then, it wouldn't have mattered who she chose; her heart would've longed for the other. Her life was different now, changed, yet that still didn't squelch the anxiety she felt. She was about to go on a date with Bowie Holmes. A real date where he picked her up, where they would undoubtedly kiss at the end of the night because she really liked kissing that man. The date wasn't even a turning point—she already knew she wanted to be with him, to be a family, to give Brystol a mom and dad—yet she was still jumpy for no other reason than she was already in love with Bowie and wanted to tell him.

When she heard Bowie's knock, she leaped from the couch and sprinted to the door. Behind her, Brystol laughed. She thought about chiding her daughter for being childish but couldn't muster up the strength to turn away from her mission—get to Bowie. Brooklyn threw the door open, and the scent of Bowie's cologne washed over her instantly, and she barely noticed that Luke had bumped into her on his own mission to get to Brystol. She unabashedly looked him over, letting her eyes roam as slowly as possible. Bowie set his arm against the doorjamb and studied her as well. Their attraction to each other was undeniable. She wanted him. He wanted her.

Bowie tilted his head and smiled, loving the attention she was happily giving him. "Sweet baby . . ." Brooklyn couldn't finish her sentence. She was finally giving herself permission to look at the man he had become. Bowie had aged well. It wasn't one of those fine wine–type moments—he'd simply aged the way a hardworking man should. The gray shirt he wore fit him like a glove. His triceps bulged from the tight sleeves, causing her to swallow hard. Later, he would hold her with those arms, making her feel safer than she had in years.

"Are you going to stand there and stare at me all night, or are you going to come outside so we can leave for our date?"

"Yeah, Mom, you look like you've never seen Bowie before," Brystol added.

Again, Brooklyn swallowed. She was speechless at being called out by Bowie and her daughter, and the only thing she could do was stand there, looking back and forth between the two of them.

Brystol stood and walked toward her mother. "I love you," her daughter said. "Have a wonderful time tonight. You deserve it." Brystol all but shoved her mom over the threshold and slammed the door behind her.

Brooklyn stumbled. However, Bowie's hands were on her hips, holding her upright. "I got you," he whispered as one hand moved from her hip to her hair. He gently pushed her hair behind her ear and leaned in, bypassing her lips for her cheek. "I'm never letting go."

Her mind, heart, and body rejoiced. She didn't want him to ever let go. "Me neither," she managed to say. "I should've never left."

Bowie moved closer. He held her head in his hand and brushed his thumb over her lower lip. "You were right to leave, B. The only thing I wish is that I went with you. I would've followed you anywhere." He didn't wait for her to agree or tell him the many reasons why she couldn't tell him before he pulled her into a long, deep kiss. When they parted, they were breathless and smiling. "Come on," he said, reaching for her hand.

In all their years growing up, Bowie had always opened the car door for her. She was surprised when he only opened the driver's side to his truck and motioned for her to get in. "If you think you're sitting by the door, you're crazy. I want you next to me when I drive."

All in a matter of seconds, he made her feel like a teen all over again. She climbed in and scooted to the middle. He followed, and right after turning his truck on, his hand rested on her thigh. "I feel like I'm in high school all over."

He laughed and then quickly groaned.

"What's wrong?"

"Brystol—she's going to start high school in the fall. Some dude is going to want to take her on a date. He's going to want her to sit in the middle so he can touch her, like I'm touching you." Bowie looked at Brooklyn and couldn't resist kissing her. "He's going to want to kiss her." He gripped Brooklyn's thigh and started bringing her closer to him, only his truck lurched forward, causing them both to laugh, and panic a bit.

"Maybe we should make out later," Brooklyn suggested.

Bowie shook his head. "I don't want to make out, B. I want to be with you. I don't know if you want to wait or . . . shit, I don't even know what you want."

"Shh." She pressed her lips to his cheek. "We want the same thing." He nodded, smiled, and returned to driving.

There was a time when Brooklyn couldn't remember much about Cape Harbor, a time when she couldn't remember how to get to certain places when she'd tell Brystol about her former home. And when she had returned, she'd felt lost and out of place. Driving down the road with Bowie, she knew exactly where they were going. On instinct, she turned around and looked in the back of his truck. Sure enough, there was a blanket and a picnic basket. After all these years, he remembered what her favorite thing to do was.

When they stopped along the side of the road, she and Bowie rushed out of the truck. Brooklyn grabbed the blanket, Bowie the basket, and they set off down the path, stepping over exposed roots, ducking under overgrown branches, and walking through bushes that hid the trail. They came into the clearing, and she paused—it was exactly like she had remembered. A haven away from their hectic lives—even as teens, they'd come out here to destress—and he had brought her back knowing this was where she would want to be. Wildflowers of every color stood tall along the seagrass. The water of the inlet moved slowly, barely creating any waves, and the sand looked pristine. Some of her happier times had happened here, most of them with Bowie.

"Where is everyone?"

"As many times as I've been out here to think, I've never seen anyone."

"Remember when we spent days here, clearing away the dead shrubs?"

"I do. We created this place without even knowing it was here." He paused. "What are you doing?" he asked as she spread the blanket haphazardly on the ground.

She kicked off her shoes. Next, she took off her shirt and shimmied out of her jeans. Without answering him, she dove into the water, staying under until she couldn't hold her breath any longer. When she surfaced, Bowie was standing at the edge of the water, staring at her.

"Are you going to come in?"

"I'm having a little trouble here, B."

Her eyes went right to his jeans. "No one is around. I think you should join me."

"I'm going to be honest. Fifteen years is a long time to wait for the love of your life to return, to get back to where we were when things went south. It only took once, but you're burned into my soul, and from the day I saw you in your car, I've wanted you. If I come in, it's only to get you out and finish what we started at my house. I fully intend to lay you down on this blanket and make love to you. I don't know if I can wait any longer."

"What are you waiting for then, Bowie?"

Her man stripped out of his clothes, leaving him fully exposed for nature to get an eyeful. He dove into the water, much faster than she'd hoped. She wanted a minute or two to look him over, to really study him. Growing up, she had seen him change from a gangly teenager to a man, and their one time together had been rushed. They didn't have to rush anymore; however, Bowie had other ideas.

Brooklyn tried to look for him in the water but couldn't tell where he was. She circled and waited for him to pop up out of the water, and when she felt something touch her legs, her first instinct was to scream.

"People could hear you," he said after he rose out of the water. He pressed his chest to her back, making her shiver. He kissed the droplets of water from her skin, nipping along her collarbone until he got to her ear. Bowie tugged lightly on her lobe before he turned her around in his arms, picked her up, and carried her to the blanket.

Brooklyn didn't care that they were soaking wet or that they were outside, and someone could happen upon them. What she cared about was that this was where they spent most of their time growing up, this was where she saw Bowie as more than a friend, and this was where she was going to tell him she loved him. Brooklyn cupped his cheek as he hovered over her. "I love you, Bowie."

THIRTY-FIVE

Bowie stood in the sunroom and watched as the *Austin Woods* trawler left port. The crew stood starboard and waved. Its flag flew at half-mast. They would be the only ship leaving port because of the current rainstorm, and Carly's family would be on their way to church by the time the ship returned. Bowie raised his coffee cup in salute and glanced down at Carly's empty rocker. Her afghan lay folded over the armrest. It was hard to believe that little over a month ago his life had changed because of her.

He heard his girls laughing. They were upstairs, getting ready for the funeral. He smiled at the thought of them being his girls and looked to the sky, sending up a silent prayer. The weather needed to change. He needed the rain to stop because by the end of the day he wanted Brystol to know he was her father, and the plan was to tell her after they spread Carly's ashes. The past few days had been hard on him, and he was ready to tell her the truth.

The Hewett women came downstairs just as he walked into the room. He was taken aback by their beauty, even in these somber times. He reached for Brooklyn's hand and pulled her into his side, kissing her temple. Being free to love her any way he wanted had always been a dream, and now that it had come true, he couldn't get enough of her.

While everyone walked to the SUV, Bowie looked to the sky. The rain had turned to a light drizzle, the sun was working hard to penetrate through the clouds, and there, in the distance, he thought he saw the faint colors of a rainbow.

"Do you see it?" Brystol asked, pointing to the sky.

"I do."

"Nonnie never liked the rain, so I guess this is her way of making sure her day is even more special."

Bowie stared at his daughter in awe. She was something else. The entire drive to the church, he watched her in the rearview mirror as she stared out the window. He figured she was looking for the end of that rainbow.

Unlike the last time they had attended a funeral together, for Carly's, they were some of the first to arrive. There weren't any news cameras there to follow their every move, the school buses weren't being used to transport people who had to park miles away in order to attend, and there wasn't a line of mourners waiting for Austin's family to arrive so they could tell his mother how sorry they were. Carly's passing had less fanfare and would be more private.

Bowie kept his hand on Brooklyn's lower back while she held Brystol's hand and met Simone near her car. She carried the urn that contained Carly's ashes. Bowie's parents were already there, and Linda waited briefly on the steps leading to the church with the minister. She introduced everyone to Pastor Mann, having known him most of her life.

"It's a pleasure to meet you," he said. "I'm sorry it's under these circumstances. If you'll follow me, I'll show you the receiving line. Mrs. Holmes indicated that there would be only three of you in line today?"

Brooklyn spoke. "Yes, it's myself, my daughter, and Carly's best friend, Simone."

"No other family?"

"There are nieces and nephews from her husband's side, but I don't know if they'll be in attendance."

"Very well." Pastor Mann led everyone into the vestibule and showed them where to stand and then had them follow him into the church. The first two rows of pews were reserved for family, but it was unlikely they would all be filled. The pastor showed Simone where to put the urn, and the family stood there, taking in the altar. A large picture of Carly with Austin sat on an easel. The picture had been taken about twenty years ago, and it had been years since Bowie had seen a picture of Austin. But now Austin was staring back at him, with his beaming, infectious smile. Bowie checked Brooklyn to see her expression, but she was on the stage, rearranging flowers, not even paying attention to the photo. Neither was Brystol. She was off with her grandmother. Bowie took one last look and decided he needed to shut the door on the past. After today concluded, he was done worrying about Austin.

People lingered on the steps, waiting for the receiving line to open. Once it had, the Bs and Simone shook hands and hugged folks they knew as well as some complete strangers. A lot of guys from the docks showed up, some still dressed in their fishing gear, but that was to be expected, and it hadn't really shocked anyone. It also hadn't surprised Bowie to see that his friends were there—apart from Grady, who, according to Graham, hadn't been seen for a couple of days.

During the service Bowie's brave teenage daughter stood up in front of everyone in a black knee-length dress, poised and in control of her emotions, and delivered an eloquent eulogy. She told stories about her grandmother, about her summers in Cape Harbor, and about how her nonnie was her best friend. Bowie was so proud of her. What he planned to say to her played over and over in his mind. He didn't want her to stop loving Carly, or even Austin. The last thing he wanted was for her to resent him, to feel as if he were trying to take away the life she knew. That wasn't his plan. All he wanted was to be her father moving forward. He wasn't stupid—he knew he had an uphill battle—but also knew he had the support of Brooklyn, and together they would tell their daughter and both of their parents.

Before the service concluded, Brooklyn stood in front of everyone and invited them to the Whale Spout to help celebrate Carly's life. Brystol was rather excited about being able to go into a bar. She giggled every time it was brought up. No one had the heart to tell her that she could enter if she was with someone over the age of twenty-one . . . a little tidbit Bowie wanted to keep quiet for as long as possible.

They arrived at the Whale Spout, and as soon as Brooklyn stepped inside, she inhaled sharply.

"What's wrong?" Bowie asked.

She covered her mouth, shaking her head. "Your mom . . . I don't know how I'll ever thank her." Bowie took in the area in front of him. All the flowers from the church were placed strategically around the pub, and trays of food filled the bar top. Graham was behind the bar, already serving. "She did all this."

"I know she has a lot of guilt when it comes to Carly; she's only trying to help."

Brooklyn's lip was caught between her teeth, and Bowie gently tugged it free. "Hey, she loves you, and she's going to love Brystol. Everything's going to be amazing," he said, pulling her to his side. "And I love you too."

Brooklyn turned to him. "I love you," she said. He desperately wanted to kiss her but held off out of respect for Carly.

They parted ways while Brooklyn and Brystol made their rounds, thanking people for coming. The one person who was missing was Simone. She wanted time to grieve alone, which made sense. She had been with Carly, working for the inn, for a long time.

Brooklyn had yet to decide what she was going to do about her business and tossed a few ideas around. Bowie hadn't wanted to pressure her because he was simply going to follow her wherever she went.

She had a career to think about, one that would have to take a back seat if they stayed. He joked and called it an early retirement. There was something in her eyes after he said it that made him think she might agree with him.

Bowie took a seat at one of the tables and watched people mingle. These were locals he saw almost every day and yet had trouble recalling some of their names. Peggy, the waitress from the diner, sat down next to him.

"She's much better than that wife of yours." She motioned toward Brooklyn.

Bowie smiled. "Yeah, she is."

"When I heard she was back in town, I started a pool at the diner. We bet on how long it was going to take for the two of you to finally come to your senses." Bowie turned sharply toward Peggy. She shrugged and lifted her pint of beer to her lips.

"So rude," he mumbled.

"Eh," she said. "The other one was never good enough for you, but this one"—she pointed at Brooklyn—"she's the one for you."

"I know," he said to her. "I know."

"So, are you together?"

Bowie sighed. "We're not apart. We have a few things to work through, but I'm not going anywhere."

"Is she?"

He knew that for at least four years she wasn't. They were going to make a home in Cape Harbor. "If she does, I'll follow. I'm not making the same mistakes I did fifteen years ago. There's nothing standing in the way of us being together."

"Well, if it's any consolation, we'd like to see you stick around. And we want to get to know that girl of hers."

Bowie couldn't help but smile as he looked at Brystol. She was owning the room, chatting with people she was just meeting for the first time. A few people had brought their kids and were introducing them. She was making friends, and he loved it. "She's pretty amazing."

"You look at her like she's yours," Peggy stated.

Bowie glanced back at Peggy. "Someday," was all he said.

Brooklyn, Brystol, and Bowie only stayed for an hour. They had something very important to do. He hadn't taken his family's boat out in a while but wasn't going to let Carly down, especially since the rain had finally stopped. This was what she had wanted. He made sure Brystol wore a life jacket, and Brooklyn put on one as a safety precaution. He knew she could swim; however, after the recent storm, the water was choppy, and there was a sizable riptide lingering.

"Can we sleep on this boat?" Brystol asked.

"We can. Your mom can show you everything downstairs once we get out onto the water." Bowie winked at Brooklyn. He was looking forward to spending ample time with her on this boat, sailing off into the sunset.

When they drifted by Carly's, everyone waved, knowing Simone was in there, somewhere. They hoped she could see them. Once past the house, he plugged in the coordinates that Carly had left and set sail. He hadn't been out that way since the search for Austin was called off, and he was feeling a bit queasy about it now. He couldn't let this dampen his mood, though, and it wouldn't as long as he kept his eyes on his Bs. Brystol and her excitement were making everything better.

"Everything is so beautiful from out here," Brystol said, staring back at the town.

"Cape Harbor is one of the most beautiful places we've ever been," Brooklyn added. Bowie only nodded along, watching as his navigation equipment showed them growing closer to where they would spread Carly's ashes.

He shut the engine off and let the waves move them forward the last couple of yards. He dropped the anchor without saying anything, and without looking at Brooklyn. He didn't want to see her face, see the remembrance in her eyes, and he didn't want her to see it in his. Being out here, knowing this was where their lives had changed and being so close to shore, it ate him up on the inside. There were so many boats that could've easily come out to save Austin, but they hadn't. There hadn't been a Mayday call until it was too late.

Bowie motioned for his Bs to move to the stern, where the diving platform was located. It was going to be easier to access the water from here, and he didn't want Brystol leaning over the side.

"Can we swim off this boat?" she asked Bowie.

"Of course. Maybe we'll spend the night on the water."

Brystol looked excited. "Have you done that before, Mom?"

"I have. It can be fun."

Bowie unscrewed the lid of the urn and handed it to Brystol. With Brooklyn's help, they shook the contents into the ocean. Bowie hadn't planned to say anything, but the words came out of their own volition.

"You're with Austin now, Carly."

"That's all she ever wanted," Brooklyn added.

They left Brystol standing there, giving her a moment to say good-bye in private. When she climbed the ladder back to the main deck, Bowie and Brooklyn were sitting there on the semicircular white leather couch, waiting.

"Come sit with us for a second," Brooklyn said, patting the cushion between them.

"If you're going to tell me you're getting married, save it. I'm not stupid. I see you making googly eyes at Mom all the time," Brystol said.

"I do want to marry your mom someday. Right now, though, we have something really important to tell you."

Her mouth dropped open, and she gaped at her mom. "Are you pregnant? Am I going to be a big sister?"

Brooklyn pursed her lips and shook her head slowly. "Sorry, you're still going to be my baby." She leaned over and pinched her daughter's cheeks. "But what we do have to say is going to be a shock, your feelings might be hurt, and you're going to have a lot of questions. Before we say what we need to say, I want you to remember that I love you more than anything in this world. Grandma and Grandpa love you. Nonnie loved you. Simone loves you. Okay?"

Brystol seemed like she was on the verge of tears. Brooklyn inhaled deeply. Bowie wanted to be next to her, but they had agreed to put Brystol in the middle of them.

"All your life I believed with my whole heart that Austin was your father. It wasn't until I came here that I learned otherwise."

"Austin isn't my dad?" Her voice cracked.

"I'm sorry, baby girl. Austin and I hadn't been getting along for a while, and one night we had a big fight and he said some things, ending our relationship. I turned to Bowie for comfort . . ."

"Brystol, while your mom, Austin, and I were growing up, we were always together. Your mom and I were best friends, and from the first day I met her, I was in love with her. The problem was, Austin saw her first, and she fell head over heels for him. As we grew older, your mom and I started working together . . ." Bowie paused. "Man, this is hard."

"Look, baby. I'm not proud of the way I acted, but for a long time I loved two men, and when one broke my heart, the other one was there to mend it."

"You're my dad?" she asked through tears. "How do you know?"

Bowie and Brooklyn shared a look. They had agreed they would keep Carly's name out of it; they didn't want to ruin Brystol's memory of her grandma. Bowie cleared his throat. "When I first saw you, I wondered, so I had a DNA test run to be sure."

"How long have you known?"

"Not long."

"Did you know when you took me fishing?"

He nodded.

"I thought something was up when you referred to Austin . . . well, as Austin and not my dad. When we were at the party thing, you called him my dad."

"You're very perceptive. I have something for you." He dug through his pocket and pulled out the velvet box and handed it to Brystol. He had opted to leave the bear at home, for a different day.

She gasped after she opened the box. "This is beautiful."

"It was my great-grandmother's. She gave it to my grandma, who gave it to my mom. I don't have a sister, so it goes to you."

"To keep?"

"Yep, until you have a daughter, and if you don't, you give it to someone who means the world to you."

"Will you help me put it on?" Brystol asked Bowie. He checked with Brooklyn first, who had tears in her eyes. He held the delicate necklace in his hands and waited for Brystol to move her hair. He fumbled with the clasp a few times until he was finally able to secure it around her neck.

"It's been a long time since this necklace had a home."

"I love it; thank you."

"You're welcome."

"So now what?" Brystol asked.

"Now, we sail back and go have dinner with your grandparents and Bowie's parents."

"Who are my grandparents as well."

Bowie and Brooklyn nodded.

"Do your parents want a grandchild?"

"Very much so," he told her. "I haven't told them yet. We wanted to tell you first."

As the boat rocked back and forth, Brystol looked out over the water and fiddled with her necklace. "Mom, can we stay? Please?"

Brooklyn nodded again.

"We're staying?" Brystol stood, and instinctively Bowie moved closer, ready to catch her if she wobbled.

"Nonnie left everything to you, Brystol. Technically, when you turn eighteen, the inn is yours."

Her eyes went wide. "Does that mean I can paint it hot pink?"

Both Bowie and Brooklyn yelled out, "No!" and Brystol laughed. Her smile quickly diminished though, her mood changing.

"I'm going to need some time to process all of this, especially the dad part, but I think things are going to be good."

"Understood," Bowie said. "I'm still trying to process it all myself. One day, I'm just a guy, and the next day I have a teenage daughter who likes my dog more than she likes me," he said, shrugging.

Brystol laughed a bit. "Do you think we could go back? I sort of miss him."

"Me too, kiddo. Me too."

THIRTY-SIX

After they pulled into port, Brooklyn showed Brystol how to tie the boat to the dock. She was surprised she still remembered after all these years. While they waited for Bowie, she played with her daughter's necklace.

"This is beautiful."

"Thanks." Brystol looked into her mother's eyes. "Are you sad?"

"Yeah, I am. I'm sad for you and Bowie. You've lost a lot of time together. It's not fair to either of you. That's time you'll never get back."

"But we can make new memories, right?"

"I know Bowie would love that. He wants to be a part of your life, any way you want him to."

"And yours?"

Brooklyn smiled softly. "I'm going to ask Bowie to move in with us. I'm in love with him. I have been for a long time."

"Then why did it take us so long to come back here?"

She chuckled. "Oh, sweetie. I've been asking myself the same question. I don't know. I've carried a lot of guilt over your . . . Austin's death and thought people in town wouldn't want me."

"I'll always want you," Bowie said as he jumped onto the dock. "Both of you."

Brooklyn hadn't expected Brystol to answer, and she suspected that Bowie felt the same. She made sure Bowie knew exactly what she wanted, though. "I was just telling Brystol here that I'm going to ask you to move in with us. That's if you don't mind living in Carly's house."

"How do you feel?" He directed his question toward his daughter.

"I mean, Mom loves you, and Luke would be there all the time, so it's a win-win, plus you still have a lot of work to do on my inn." She brought her hands up and shrugged. Her parents started laughing, and her mother put her arm around her shoulders, and they walked toward the parking lot. "If Bowie moves in, can Luke sleep with me?"

"I have a feeling he will no matter where I tell him to sleep."

"Works for me," she said.

Bowie drove them back to the carriage house. They'd have one more day of rest before construction would pick back up on the inn. Minus the work vehicles, everything on the outside was shaping up nicely. New asphalt would be poured soon, and the landscaping had started before Carly passed away, but it was the inside that tied everything together. Between the two of them, they had taken Carly's vision and brought it to life. Everything looked pristine, and the rooms felt like the perfect tranquil getaway. They would start advertising as soon as Simone committed to running the operation. Brooklyn could do it, but she wasn't ready to give up her design company just yet.

When they arrived back at the house, both sets of parents were there, inside and waiting. No one knew why they were called over, just that they were having dinner. Brooklyn was pleased to see the table set and the many casserole dishes spread out for them.

"I'm starving," Bowie said as he entered the kitchen. Brooklyn's parents and his stared as he went by.

"I think he lost his manners at sea," Brooklyn muttered to them.

"I'm not sure the boy ever had any," Linda added.

"I heard that, Mom," he said from the other room.

"Well, you're all here, so let's eat. There's a few things we need to discuss." Brooklyn led everyone into the dining room, where they gathered around the small island, dishing various foods onto their plates.

"I can't thank you enough for all your help, Linda."

"Oh, Brooklyn, it was the least I could do. Gary and your father took the flowers over to the hospital and placed some at Austin and Skip's marker."

"Will Nonnie have a stone like Grandpa's?" Brystol asked.

"She will," Bowie spoke up. "We already made the appointment for the sculptor to come out and engrave her name." This seemed to please his daughter.

Everyone gathered around the table and engaged in small talk. It wasn't until Linda gasped that they all went silent.

"Brystol, dear, where did you get such an exquisite necklace?" Brystol picked it up and held it between her fingers with her eyes darting between her mom and dad.

Bowie cleared his throat. "Mom, Dad, Bonnie, and David, we have something to tell you."

"You're getting married?" Bonnie blurted out excitedly only to sag her shoulders when Brooklyn shook her head. Brooklyn reached for Bowie's hand and held it. There wasn't a doubt in her mind that he would ask her, and she'd say yes.

"Look, there's no easy way to say this, so I'm just going to say it because it's really my fault, I guess." Brooklyn inhaled deeply. "Brystol is Bowie's daughter. There, I said it. She knows, which is why she's wearing the necklace . . . and you're all staring at me."

"How?" Bonnie asked.

Brooklyn opened her mouth to answer but then closed it quickly. Bowie did the same.

"Honey, I think you know how babies are made." David patted his wife's hand while Brystol giggled.

"I had a suspicion, so we had a test done." Bowie spoke nonchalantly, as if having a test done was no big deal. Let alone lying about one. He should be angry, livid. Deep down, Brooklyn was. Years had been lost. A father was denied the right to know his child, grandparents too. All because of what? The unknown bothered Brooklyn greatly. Carly and her deathbed confession had left more holes than answers, and Brooklyn was fairly sure they wouldn't be hidden in her desk drawers anywhere.

Brooklyn finally studied their family members. The dads, with the exception of Bowie, didn't seem fazed, but the moms, especially Linda, looked hurt. Brooklyn set her napkin down on the table and asked Linda if they could speak outside.

Linda followed Brooklyn down the steps and into the sand. Both kicking off their shoes. After a few minutes of walking in silence, Brooklyn spoke. "Carly knew, but we're not telling Brystol. The morning after she collapsed, she told me, and I found the DNA report in her room."

They stopped and looked at each other. "When did you tell Bowie?"

"Shortly after I read the report. I came down here to think, to process the last fifteen years of mistakes I've made, and he found me. I told him. If I had known or even suspected that Brystol was his daughter, we wouldn't be having this conversation."

Linda smiled softly. "My son has missed a lot of time."

"So has Brystol, as well as you and Gary."

Linda placed her arm in the crook of Brooklyn's and turned her toward the house. "Death has a funny and odd way of bringing people closer and ripping their hearts out at the same time."

"Believe me, I know. If Carly hadn't asked me to come, I don't know if we would've ever found out."

"That thought scares me."

"Me too." They climbed up the stairs to find everyone in the backyard starting up a game of cornhole. Bowie and Brystol were on the same team, and they were about to go against the grandpas. Linda and Brooklyn sat next to Bonnie at the picnic table.

"This could get ugly," Brooklyn surmised.

"I have a feeling the old men are going down," Linda added, but Bonnie wasn't in agreement.

"Oh, I don't know. David joined a league, and he's been playing a lot. They have competitions weekly, and he's quite fond of the game."

"You know, I wish I was the person who decided to take our kindergarten beanbag-toss game and turn it into this phenomenon. I'm always missing the mark." Brooklyn sighed.

Both moms bumped their shoulders with hers, and Bonnie said, "You've hit the jackpot right there and there." She pointed at Bowie and then Brystol.

She watched them for a moment, at opposite ends of the game boards. Maybe she was imagining things, but she was certain she could see a connection between them. It was like they were already in sync, father and daughter. She knew, deep in her heart, that they were going to forge an incredible bond moving forward.

EPILOGUE

The morning sun had cast the sky in the most vibrant colors. Red, orange, pink, and a hint of yellow. Brooklyn sat in the adirondack chair, sipping her coffee and watching the boats head out for the day. The crew of the *Austin Woods* still waved every time they passed by. At first, it bothered Brooklyn; however, after meeting a couple of the crew members at the Whale Spout one night, she understood why they did it. For them, what had started out as paying homage to the boat's namesake and making sure that Carly knew they were thinking about her and Austin every time they went out had turned into superstition. Brooklyn knew she would never ask them to stop.

Sitting where Carly had sat for years had become Brooklyn's ritual, her calm before the daily storm. Since her return, life had been crazy. It had been hectic and messy, but most of all, it was perfect. Brystol started her freshman year at Cape Harbor High in September and made instant friends with everyone. The Driftwood Inn was once again filled with the laughter of teenagers, but this time they had their own space. Aside from finishing the renovations over the summer, Bowie had constructed a game room specifically for the kids. He installed a pool table, painted the walls with chalkboard paint, and added some arcade games, a flat-screen television, a reading area, and a sectional sofa. At first, Brooklyn balked at the couch, said it was inviting trouble, but finally relented after family movie night. Even though he had built the space for Brystol and her friends, the added entertainment for guests who had children was a bonus.

Most of the guests were still asleep. Only a few had checked out before dawn to beat the traffic through Seattle. Those who were awake and in no hurry to leave were being treated to a five-course breakfast. Brooklyn could smell the bacon cooking in the oven and the sweet aroma of Simone's now-famous cinnamon rolls. When Brooklyn had first tried one, she had believed she finally knew what heaven was like—the warm, gooey center with buttercream frosting made her weak in the knees.

And while she enjoyed this moment of quiet before her day fully began, she used the time to reflect on how much her life had changed over the months. She and Monroe were growing closer, and Rennie came to visit every other weekend. They spent their Saturdays shopping, either locally or in Seattle or Anacortes. Sometimes Mila would join them, but it wasn't often. She was busy, trying to become the next star in Hollywood. The gang—without Jason, who was busy saving lives in the big city—often got together on Sundays for a bonfire and barbecue. It had taken a few weekends before Grady showed up, and when he did, he sat as far away from Brooklyn as he could. Still, she treated him like he was family, making sure he always had a plate of food when he was there. By the end of the summer, he finally approached her.

"I still hate you," Grady said.

"I hate myself sometimes."

Grady rarely made eye contact with anyone, let alone Brooklyn, so when he looked at her, she saw how much pain he was in. She saw what the years of torment had done to him.

"Tell me about that night, Grady. Why did you go out?"

He watched the water and crammed his hands into the front pockets of his hoodie. "He was pissed that night. He called and said he was heading out, said he heard something on the radio about schools of fish moving because of the storm. When I got to the docks, he was throwing gear around, talking to himself. Once we got out on the water, I asked him what was up, and all he said was he had done the right thing. I figured he was talking about taking the boat out."

There was no way to know what Austin was talking about that night. Was "the right thing" telling Brooklyn that he didn't love her anymore or sending Bowie to her? Had Austin known how Bowie felt about his girl? How his girl was starting to have feelings for his best friend? That, because of Austin, Brooklyn and Bowie were so close?

Grady finally glanced at Brooklyn. "And then he dies, and I overhear you and Bowie talking outside of the limo, talking like you had sex, and then you left. I know the reason we went out that night is because he found you and Bowie together." He shook his head.

Brooklyn should've corrected him, but she suspected he wouldn't believe her. "I'm here now, Grady. And I'm hoping we can be friends."

He shrugged and stood, stalking off toward the beach.

That conversation never left Brooklyn, and she often wondered how that fateful night could've been different. What if she had refused to let Austin leave? What if Bowie hadn't shown up? What if Grady had stopped Austin from taking the boat out? Brooklyn could play the what-if game until she was blue in the face, but she eventually realized neither the questions nor the answers would ever be able to change what had happened.

As the inn came to life, Brooklyn quickly finished her coffee and sneaked back to their small house through the passageway. Bowie had decided to add electricity, making it easier for everyone. Inside, Brystol was sitting at the bar, talking to Bowie with a mouthful of cereal while he leaned against the counter with his legs crossed at his ankles. He was dressed in a flannel shirt, jeans, and the new work boots Brystol had given him for a late Father's Day gift. What sent Brooklyn's heart racing were the glasses on his face. Growing up, she'd known he wore contacts but had never seen him in his glasses, and once she had, she'd begged him to wear them more often. She loved the way he looked in them, smart and sexy. Most of all, they gave Brystol another sense of belonging . . . that she and Bowie were more than just DNA; they were the same.

"Good morning," she said, walking into the kitchen. She smiled at her daughter and went to Bowie's side to give him a kiss. She lingered there, taking in his fresh shower scent, and then went to her daughter and greeted her, rubbing her hand over her back. Brystol was well adjusted and loving school.

"Morning, Mom. May I go to Jasmine's after school? We have a project to work on for English." Brystol checked her mom, and then her dad, for approval.

"How are you getting there?" Bowie asked.

"Walking—she only lives two blocks from school."

He took the parental reins. "What time do you want me to pick you up?"

"Five would be good. It won't take us long. But I can stay later if you're not finished with work."

"I'll be there at five." He turned toward the sink, emptied his mug, and rinsed it with water. "Are you ready to go in ten?" he asked Brystol. "Do you have plans for the football game tonight?"

Brystol approached the sink with her bowl; he took it from her and rinsed it out. "I'll be ready. And yes, I thought we were going together? Although maybe you won't mind if I sit with my friends, Dad?"

"Of course not."

She smiled at him before she went to her room to finish getting ready, with Luke hot on her heels. Each time Brystol referred to Bowie as "Dad," it made Brooklyn's heart skip a beat. The first time he had heard it, he had cried in her arms for hours, thanking her for making him a father. From that point on he had started introducing Brystol as his daughter. He had hesitated, telling Brooklyn he wanted to wait until Brystol was okay with everything, and now he sought out any excuse to use the word *daughter* in a conversation. They had bonded right before Brooklyn's eyes, and she couldn't be happier.

He had been looking forward to the homecoming game for weeks and was excited that Brystol wanted him to go. He wouldn't care if she ran off to sit with her friends; he just wanted to be there with her.

"Where are you working today?" Brooklyn asked before Bowie left the room.

He walked over to her and pulled her into his arms. "I'm all over town. I'm bidding on a job downtown, and I need to check on the reno for the Goldbergs' house. Going to go to lunch with Grady." He, too, had been trying to rebuild his friendship with Grady. It was a process for all, but one that was definitely coming along.

"Do you need my help at the Goldbergs'?"

He shook his head. "The designer on the job is top notch and has laid out every detail for us to follow. I think I'm okay on this one." They both smiled. While Brooklyn was busy with the inn, she hadn't given up on her career, because Bowie had found a way for her to do both. She was a consultant for his company, helping him at night with designs. It was the best of both worlds—although she missed being knee deep in the process and watching a transformation take place, she also loved working at the inn. The place was going to be her daughter's legacy, and she wanted to make sure the business was sustainable in the future. If their calendar was any indication, Brystol wasn't going to have any issues when she took over.

"Well, you know where to find me," she said.

"That I do." He leaned down and kissed her until they heard Brystol thumping her way down the stairs.

Later that evening, while Bowie took Brystol to the football game, Simone, Monroe, Mila, and Brooklyn stood in the center of the ballroom and stared at the walls and ceiling. Brooklyn had drawn plans of what she wanted the room to look like, but bringing her ideas to life was another challenge.

"Remember when we had every school dance here?" Mila said, sipping her mocha-java-latte double shot of something that didn't make sense to anyone but her.

"The light from the lighthouse would always spotlight us when we were dancing," Monroe added.

"I think it's very special that you're hosting homecoming, Brooklyn. All of the parents dropping their children off tomorrow night will be able to reminisce," Simone said proudly. For weeks, Brooklyn had had her seek out old photos from previous homecomings. The photos were now attached to boards, categorized by years. It was Brooklyn's way of bringing the inn back to its former self.

"I think Carly would approve." Brooklyn leaned into Simone a little and gave her a smile. She was very happy that Simone had stayed on as staff. The inn ran smoothly, and Brooklyn would be lost without her. "Okay," she said, clapping her hands together. "These lights aren't going to hang themselves, and these balloons aren't going to get filled still sitting in their bags. Let's do this, ladies!"

"I'm not sure I can handle your enthusiasm," Mila retorted. Monroe gave her sister a dirty look before pushing her toward a box.

"You can and you will. I know this was where you had your first kiss, right under the chandelier." Monroe twirled her sister in a circle. "Being here was always so magical. We can be part of the team that brought that back to Cape Harbor High."

Mila rolled her eyes but smiled at her sister. They proceeded over to the mass quantity of balloons and the portable helium tank. As everyone got to work, the local DJ arrived. He brought in his equipment and tested out his new tracks as the decorations went up. While lights were strung around the room by Brooklyn, Simone put the linens on each table, and Mila and Monroe worked on the balloons. Bouquets of balloons would go on the back of every other chair, while some would be on the floor. In her mind, Brooklyn saw a fairy tale of a dance happening. She wanted to make it special, not just for the other kids but Brystol as well. This was her first homecoming of many, much to Bowie's apprehension. He was adamant that his daughter be a wall-flower because he knew all too well that male hormones were out of control at this age. Brooklyn, on the other hand, was happy to watch her daughter create lasting memories and excited to see her baby girl all dressed up.

As was tradition, the inn offered a dinner special for the teens attend-ing the dance. There weren't a lot of restaurants in the area to choose from—when Carly had started this, she had wanted to give the teens a fancier option and teach them how to make a reservation for dinner. Brooklyn was doing the same. She kept the menu simple, with roasted chicken or salmon, potatoes, and vegetables, along with rolls, butter, and a dinner salad. Dessert wasn't offered because there was a cake at the dance, but she did place dinner mints on the table to encourage those who had the fish to freshen up.

There was a valet out front to park cars and open limousine doors. Girls in pretty dresses with corsages on their wrists and young men dressed in suits entered through the double glass doors and were greeted by their principal. The string of lights gave the ballroom enough of an ambience to make the teens feel like they'd been transported anywhere but the Driftwood Inn.

Brooklyn stayed in the shadows as her daughter walked in. She was with her new friends, and the group of them had spent the day down-town getting their hair and nails done. For dinner, they had been treated to a special meal prepared by one of the girls' parents at their house, instead of coming back to the inn. Brooklyn had kept waiting for an invite from her daughter to take pictures beforehand, but it never came. She was hurt but knew Brystol was spreading her wings and discovering who she was. By the next dance, Brooklyn was confident she would be involved. Besides, she'd had a lot to do at the inn to get it ready.

Inside the ballroom, holding up the corner of the room, stood Bowie and Graham. According to Bowie, they were on hand in the event the jocks got out of control. Brooklyn knew otherwise and kept her comments to herself. The past week, Bowie had been pacing the floor, stressed about tonight. She couldn't blame him—their daughter was taking her first rite of passage into full-fledged teenage life, and for him it was too soon.

The DJ played all the hits. It didn't take Brooklyn long to figure out who were the leaders of the school. A small group, much like the one she had been in, took to the dance floor immediately. They danced together, with their hands up in the air, singing along to the songs, and when a slow one came on, they paired off.

"Bring back memories?" Monroe nudged Brooklyn and tilted her head toward the dance floor.

"So many. I was so nervous at my first dance, but you guys made me feel like I was part of your group for years instead of days. I'll never forget that."

"You just fit in with us, B. It was like we *had* known you forever."

She also knew it had a lot to do with Austin. He had a commanding presence, and people followed him everywhere. She smiled and bumped Monroe with her elbow. "You made it easy to fit in."

"I'm so happy you decided to stay."

"Me too." It was then that she caught Bowie glowering from across the room. She followed the blazing path his eyes were burning into the crowd and saw that Brystol was dancing with a boy. Brooklyn watched her baby girl, with her arms around this boy's shoulders, sway to the music. She had her hair pinned up, exposing her neck, and had taken her glasses off. She could see but wouldn't win any distance contests tonight, that was for sure. It was Brystol's strapless, form-fitting navy-blue dress that really caught Brooklyn by surprise. Her daughter was growing up right in front of her eyes, and there wasn't anything she could do to stop it.

Bowie, though, had other ideas about giving his daughter space to grow. As soon as he stepped forward, Graham reached for him and held him back. Brooklyn rushed over to him and placed her hands on his chest, pushing him out of view of the kids.

"What's wrong with you?"

"Him," he pointed to the boy their daughter was with and then quickly turned his finger toward Graham. "He's been reminding me of the things we did in high school."

Brooklyn scowled at Graham. With her attention back on Bowie, she caressed his cheek, loving the way his stubble felt against her fingertips. "Brystol is just dancing with the boy. I'm sure that if he were something serious, she would've told you. Just remember who she went to the football game with last night. I have a feeling you're going to be her number one guy for a while, so let's check our emotions at the door. And for God's sake, ignore Graham because he's up to no good and trying to goad you into being stupid. Don't think I haven't forgotten some of the really dumb shit you guys did when we were younger." Brooklyn paused and looked out over the kids, spotting Brystol immediately.

"Look at her, Bowie; she's having the best time."

"She's so beautiful, Brooklyn. Thank you."

"For what?" she asked, meeting his gaze.

"For coming back, for being here. I love you both so much."

"And we love you."

Hours later, Brooklyn moved the broom back and forth, pushing everything to the center of the floor, while Monroe and a few teachers let the helium out of the balloons and pulled the linens off the tables.

By all accounts, the dance was a success. No one got caught making out or doing anything they shouldn't have, and very few students left early. Toward the end of the night, parents came in and admired the picture boards, laughing at their hairstyles. Some even took to the dance floor, despite protests from their children. Bowie had tried to get Brooklyn to dance, but she had refused to embarrass Brystol like that, at least not at her first dance.

As much as Brooklyn wanted to leave the mess until tomorrow, she couldn't. They had back-to-back baby showers booked in the ballroom, and she would rather sleep in as long as possible. There was something about waking up in Bowie's arms that made everything feel right.

When she came to the large windows, she noticed a trail of candles outside on the beach. Not just any part of the beach, but the part the inn owned. She set the broom down and told Monroe she would be right back. It wasn't uncommon for people to set up on the beach, but they couldn't do it without her permission. She grabbed her sweater and wrapped her arms around her torso to ward off the nighttime chill.

"Excuse me," she hollered as she descended the stairs. She followed the candle path around the small shed to find Bowie there on bended knee, illuminated by the moon and soft white lights hanging from the eaves of the shed. She gasped and covered her mouth, walking slowly toward him. Resting in his palm was a black box. "What are you doing?" she whispered.

"What I would've done years ago if I had the chance. Brooklyn, I'm not perfect, but I feel pretty damn close when I'm with you, and if you wouldn't mind, I'd like to continue to feel this way forever. Will you do me the second-biggest honor of my life and become my wife?"

She nodded, but the words to follow weren't exactly what he was expecting. "Wait, what was the first?"

Bowie stood and peered over her shoulder.

"Me, of course," Brystol yelled as she came out of the shed. She hugged her dad and then turned to her mom. "I helped him pick it out," she said, pointing to the ring.

"What do you say, B? Wanna share your life with me? With us?"

"Without a doubt, yes. God, yes I do." Bowie pulled her into his arms and swung her around. When he set her down, he fumbled with the box until he could get the ring out. She held her hand out and cried as he slipped the three-gemstone ring onto her finger, one stone to represent each of them. "It's beautiful," she said, holding her hand up to catch the light of the moon.

"I love you, B."

"I love you too, Bowie."

"What about me?" Brystol asked, holding her hands up. She laughed as her parents pulled her into a hug. "Hey, what do you think about me changing my last name? I'm already using Holmes at school; might as well make it official."

Bowie leaned back so he could look at his daughter and then stared at Brooklyn. She could see it in his eyes, wondering how he . . . no, how *they* . . . got so lucky.

Deep down, they both knew. Time. It was time they had needed to grow up and accept themselves for who they were all along.

AUTHOR'S NOTE

I hope you enjoyed your visit to Cape Harbor. Some of you may recognize a few similarities to La Conner, Washington, which was the basis for the setting of this series, along with Skagit Valley and the tulips! Naturally, I took some . . . okay, a lot of creative liberties with the details since Cape Harbor is a fictionalized location. However, Washingtonians and Oregonians will find a lot of well-known and fun facts related to the Pacific Northwest, the coast, and the lovely, lush Olympic forest. Some of the shops I mention do exist, just not in La Conner. Susie's Sweet Shoppe (made-up name) was a cute little ice cream parlor that recently closed in Stowe, Vermont. O'Maddi's is a family-owned deli where I write sometimes in Northfield, Vermont. Ellie's is a roadside farm stand where I buy my flowers, vegetables, and pumpkins. The memorial wall of past fishermen you'll find in Gloucester, Massachusetts.

ACKNOWLEDGMENTS

Thank you to Lauren Plude for this opportunity and for giving me Holly Ingraham. I'm so eager about our teamwork, partnership, and this adventure. I'm excited for everything our future together holds. Thank you to Marisa Corvisiero for pounding the keyboard and networking like crazy to make this book happen.

ABOUT THE AUTHOR

Photo © 2015 Sara Eirew

Heidi McLaughlin is a *New York Times*, *Wall Street Journal*, and *USA Today* bestselling author of the Beaumont, the Boys of Summer, and the Archer Brothers series.

Originally from the Pacific Northwest, she now lives in picturesque Vermont with her husband, two daughters, and their three dogs. In 2012, McLaughlin turned her passion for reading into a full-fledged literary career and has since written over twenty novels, including the acclaimed *Forever My Girl*. When writing isn't occupying her time, you can find her sitting courtside at either of her daughters' basketball games.

McLaughlin's first novel, *Forever My Girl*, has been adapted into a motion picture with LD Entertainment and Roadside Attractions starring Alex Roe and Jessica Rothe. It opened in theaters on January 19, 2018.